Anne McCaffrey
Dragonsdawn

CORGI BOOKS

DRAGONSDAWN
A CORGI BOOK : 0 552 13098 2

Originally published in Great Britain by Bantam Press,
a division of Transworld Publishers

PRINTING HISTORY
Bantam Press edition published 1989
Corgi edition published 1989

11 13 15 17 19 20 18 16 14 12

Set in 10/11pt Linotron 202 Sabon by
Rowland Phototypesetting Ltd, Bury St Edmunds, Suffolk.

Corgi Books are published by Transworld Publishers,
61–63 Uxbridge Road, London W5 5SA,
a division of The Random House Group Ltd,
in Australia by Random House Australia (Pty) Ltd,
20 Alfred Street, Milsons Point, Sydney, NSW 2061, Australia,
in New Zealand by Random House New Zealand Ltd,
18 Poland Road, Glenfield, Auckland 10, New Zealand
and in South Africa by Random House (Pty) Ltd,
Endulini, 5a Jubilee Road, Parktown 2193, South Africa.

Printed and bound in Great Britain by
Cox & Wyman Ltd, Reading, Berkshire.

This one was always for
Judy-Lynn Benjamin Del Rey

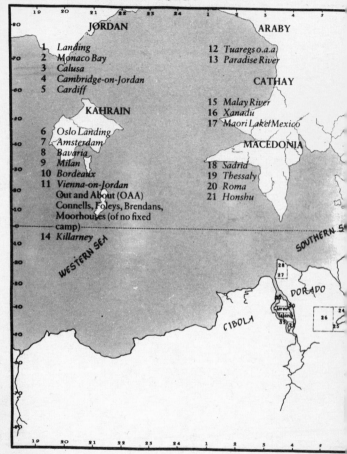

MAP COORDINATES
MAJOR PROVINCES AND STAKES

JORDAN

1 Landing
2 Monaco Bay
3 Calusa
4 Cambridge-on-Jordan
5 Cardiff

KAHRAIN

6 Oslo Landing
7 Amsterdam
8 Bavaria
9 Milan
10 Bordeaux
11 Vienna-on-Jordan
Out and About (OAA)
Connells, Foleys, Brendans,
Moorhouses (of no fixed
camp)
14 Killarney

ARABY

12 Tuaregs o.a.a
13 Paradise River

CATHAY

15 Malay River
16 Xanadu
17 Maori Lake/Mexico

MACEDONIA

18 Sadrid
19 Thessaly
20 Roma
21 Honshu

WESTERN SEA

SOUTHERN S

DORADO

CIBOLA

MAP OF FIRST PASS PERN · by Niels W. Erickson, 1987

DELTA

22 Boca River
23 Suweto
24 Drake's Lake
25 Yukon

DORADO

26 Karachi Camp
27 Seminole
28 Key Largo

IERNE ISLAND

29 Longwood
30 Uppsala
31 Orkney
32 Lochahatchee

CIBOLA
UNOCCUPIED

BIG ISLAND

33 Bitkim Camp

Northern continental has been
lightly explored and ore sites
marked for future expansion.

(YOUNG ISLAND)

Volcanic site – geological
survey on tectonic plate
activity and active volcano.

EASTERN SEA

KAHRAIN

JORDAN

MACEDONIA

CATHAY

ARABY

SEA OF AZOU

FIRST FIFTY DAYS OF THREADFALL

– 1st & 9th PASSES ON 9th PASS MAP

Calculations – Harry L. ALM, JR. ● *Research – Marilyn L. ALM*
● *Cartography Niels W. Erickson* © 1987

Benden
Weyr

Bitra

Benden
Hold

Half-
Circle

Keroon

Nerat

SEA

Cove

Cartography and calculations by HARRY ALM

PROFOUND ACKNOWLEDGMENTS

This book could not have been written without the advice, assistance, and aid of Dr Jack Cohen, DSc, lately Senior Lecturer of Reproductive Biology at Birmingham University, England, whose expertise and enthusiasm helped me *create* the dragons of Pern, and attendant botany/biology/ecology. Jack made fact out of myth, and science out of legend. I am not the only writer of his acquaintance who owes him a tremendous debt of gratitude.

I am also indebted to Harry Alm, Naval Engineer of New Orleans, Louisiana, for his configuration of the Thread Fall Patterns, based on only casual remarks in various of my books. To his wife, Marilyn, I owe the patient and correct transmission by Compuserve of this incredible technical data.

Contents

●

Anne McCaffrey
Dragonsdawn

The First Chronicle of the Colony of Pern

PART I

●

Landing

1

●

'Probe reports coming through, sir,' Sallah Telgar announced to the bridge at large without taking her eyes from the flickering lights on her terminal.

'On the screen, please, Mr Telgar,' Admiral Paul Benden replied with his punctilious courtesy. He was joint leader of the Pern Colonial Expedition on its fifteen-year voyage to the Sagittarian Sector and the strategically unimportant Rukbat star system.

Beside the Admiral, leaning against his command chair, Emily Boll, co-leader of the Pern Colonial Expedition, kept her eyes steadily on the sunlit planet, scarcely aware of the muted reports that were a constant on the bridge.

Truth be told, this was the most exciting moment of the long and boring haul as the three colony ships, the *Yokohama*, the *Bahrain* and the *Buenos Aires* rapidly approached their destination. In offices below the Bridge deck, specialists eagerly awaiting updates on the reports of that long dead Exploration and Evaluation team which had recommended Rukbat's third planet for colonization.

There had been little diversion on the long trip except the brief stimulation every five years when relief crews were awakened to serve their hitches. Of course, there'd been the flap when the Oort cloud encircling the Rukbat system had been sighted. While that phenomenon had engrossed some of the space and scientific personnel, Paul Benden had lost interest when Ezra Keroon, captain of the *Bahrain*, who was also the expedition's astronomer, had assured him that this nebulous mass of deep frozen

17

meteorites was no more than an astronomical curiosity. They'd keep an eye on it. Some comets might form and spin from its depths, Ezra had said, but he didn't consider that they were likely to be a viable threat to either the three colony ships or the planet the ships were fast approaching. After all, the Exploratory and Evaluation team had not mentioned any unusual incidence of meteor strikes on the surface of Pern. Ezra didn't think that the situation would have altered drastically in the ensuing two hundred or so years since the report had been filed.

'Screening probe reports, sir,' Sallah now confirmed, 'on two and five.' Out of the corner of her eye, she saw Admiral Benden smile slightly. Sallah suspected that he no more wished to change the image on the main screen which displayed the enthralling vision of the planet of their destination, than anyone else on the Bridge.

At the same instant the Bridge screens were activated, the reports would flash on to the screens where the specialists anxiously awaited updates to analyse, parse and discuss in the most minute detail.

'This is sort of anti-climactic, isn't it?' Paul murmured to Emily Boll.

Arms folded across her chest, she hadn't moved since the probes had been launched, except for an occasional twiddling of fingers along her upper arms. Emily Boll lifted her right eyebrow in a cynical twitch, and kept her eyes on the screen.

'Oh, I don't know. It's one more procedure which gets us nearer to the surface. Of course,' she added drily, 'we're sort of stuck with whatever's reported but I expect we can cope.'

'We'll have to, won't we?' Paul Benden murmured a trifle grimly.

This was a one-way trip, had to be, considering the cost of getting over 6000 colonists and supplies to this out-of-the-way sector of the galaxy. There would be enough fuel left in the great transport ships, once they got to Pern, to achieve and maintain a synchronous orbit above their destination while people and cargo were shuttled down to the surface. To be sure, they had homing capsules that would reach the headquarters of the Federated Sentient Planets in a mere five years, but to a retired naval tactician like Paul Benden a fragile homing capsule didn't provide much in the way of an effective back-up. Still, the Pern expedition was composed of committed and resourceful people who wished to eschew the high-tech societies of the Federated Sentient Planets. Their destination in the Rukbat system was rich enough in ores and minerals to support an agriculturally based society but poor enough not to tempt the great Technicrats this far from the centre of the galaxy.

'Only a little while longer, Paul,' Emily murmured, her voice reaching his ears alone, 'and we'll both be able to lay down the weary load.'

He grinned up at her, knowing how difficult it had been for her, too, to escape the blandishments of Technicrats who had not wished to lose two such charismatic leaders: the hero Admiral of the Cygni Space Battle and the Governor heroine of First Centauri.

'Speaking of loads,' she went on in a more audible tone, 'I'd better be there to referee my team now the reports are coming in. I suppose specialists *have* to consider their own discipline the most important one, but such contentiousness!' She stifled a groan, then grinned, her blue eyes twinkling in her rather homely face. 'Just a few more days of talking, and it'll be action stations, Admiral.'

She knew him well. He hated interminable debate over the minor points which seemed to obsess those in charge of the Landing Operation. He preferred to make quick decisions and implement them immediately, instead of talking them to death.

'You're more patient with your teams than I am,' the Admiral murmured. The last two months, as the three ships had decelerated into the Rukbat system, had been made tedious with meetings – mainly, in Paul's estimation, what seemed to be nitpicking over procedures which had been thoroughly thrashed out seventeen years before in the planning stages of the venture.

Most of the complement of 2900 colonists on the *Yokohama* had passed the entire journey in deep sleep. Personnel essential to the operation and maintenance of the three great ships had stood five-year watches. Paul Benden had elected to stand the first and last five-year periods. Emily Boll had been revived shortly before the rest of the environmental specialists. They had spent their time railing at the superficiality of the EEC report. She saw no point in reminding them of their enthusiasm for the same words when they had signed up for the Pern Expedition, either as Charter Members or specialists on Contract.

Paul continued to absorb the display information, eyes flicking from one screen to another, absently rubbing the thumb of his left hand across three fingers. Though not the sort of man Emily was attracted to, Paul Benden was undeniably handsome and Emily much preferred him with his hair grown out of the spaceman's crop that had been his trademark. Emily thought that the thick blond mass softened the strong features: the blunt nose, the forceful jaw, the wide thin-lipped mouth, now slightly pulled to the left in a little smile.

The trip had done him good: he looked fit and well able for the rigours of their next few months. Emily remembered how terribly thin he had been at the official ceremony commemorating his brilliant victory at Cygnus where he and the Purple Sector Fleet had contrived victory against astounding odds: a victory that had turned the tide of war against the Nathis. Legend said that he had remained awake and on duty for the entire seventy hours of this crucial battle. Emily believed it. She'd had to do something of the sort herself during the height of the Nathis Attack on her planet but there were many things a person could do if pushed. One paid for such physical abuses later on in life although Benden, well into his sixth decade, looked vigorously healthy. And she certainly felt no diminution of her energies. Fourteen years of deep sleep seemed to have cured the terrible fatigue that had been the inevitable result of her defence of First Centauri.

And what a world they were now approaching! Emily sighed, still unable to look away from the main screen for more than a second. She knew that everyone else on duty on the Bridge – and some of those who had stood the previous watch had not left – were totally bemused by the magnificent sight of their destination.

Who named it Pern, she did not now recall – quite probably the single letters blazoned across the published Report had stood for something else entirely, but it was Pern now, and theirs. They were on an equatorial heading, the planet's lazy rotation now hiding the northern continent and the spine of mountains up its coast while the southern land-mass exhibited its western desert. At least that's what the dusty tan terrain looked to Emily, somewhat similar to Cartagena Province on Alpha Cen A. The dominant topographical feature was the wide oceanic expanse, slightly greener than old Earth, with a ring of islands splattered across it. The atmosphere was currently decorated with the swirling cloud curl of a low-pressure area moving rapidly northeast. What a beautiful, beautiful world! She sighed again and caught Paul's quick glance. She smiled back at him without really taking her eyes from the screen.

A beautiful world! And theirs! By all the Holies, this time we won't botch it! she assured herself fervently. With all that magnificent, productive land, the old imperatives don't apply. No, she added in private cynicism, people are already discovering new ones. She thought of the friction which she had already sensed between the Charterers who had raised the staggering credits needed to finance the Pern Expedition and the Contractors, the specialists hired to round out the basic skills required for the undertaking. Each could end up with similar largeous amounts of land or mineral rights on this new world: the Charterers did get first choice, one bone of contention. At least the

Syndicates with their ruthless greed were *not* involved here on Pern, subtly distorting fact and subverting people. Emily had seen their agents at work, subtly playing on differences, often to display the power they enjoyed which could make the unsupported individual bend to their designs.

Differences! Why did there always have to be distinctions, arrogantly displayed as superiorities, or derided as inferiorities? Everyone would have the same opportunity, no matter how many 'stake acres' they could claim as Charterer or had been granted as Contractor. On Pern, it would truly be up to the individual to succeed, to prove his claim, and manage as much land as he and his cared for. That would be the catholic distinction. Once we've landed, everyone will be too bloody busy to fret over 'difference', she consoled herself and watched in fascination as a second low-pressure area began to spin down from the hidden north across the sea. If the two weather systems melded, there would be a tremendous storm over the eastern curve of the oceanic islands.

The rapid displays on Five and Two screens forced her gaze away. Meteorology and atmospherics: she saw the familiar symbols.

'Looking good,' Commander Ongola murmured in his deep, sad bass voice. He manned the science desk on this crucial watch. Emily hadn't seen him smile once in the six months she'd been awake but Paul had told her that his wife, children and entire family had been vapourized when the Nathi had attacked a service colony. Paul had specifically requested him to join the expedition. 'Atmospheric content as expected. Southern continent temperatures appear to be normal for this late winter season. Northern continent enjoying considerable precipitation due to low-pressure air masses. Analyses and temperatures consistent with EEC report.'

The first probe was doing a high-altitude circumnavigation in a pattern that would also photograph the entire planet. The second, taking a low-level course, could re-examine any portion required. The third probe was programmed for topological features.

'Probes four and six have landed, sir, five is on hold,' Sallah went on, as she interpreted the new lights that began to flash on her board. 'Scuttlebugs deployed.'

'Show them on the screens, Mr Telgar,' the Admiral said and she transferred the displays to Three, Four and Six screens.

Supremely indifferent to these incursions, Pern's image dominated the main screen, as it rotated slowly to the east, from night to day. The southern continent's coastline was daylit; some of the more prominent topological features, the spinal range of mountains and the tracks of several rivers, were visible even at this distance. The thermal scan was showing the effect of daylight on the late winter season of the southern continent.

Probe scuttlebugs had been landed at three specific points on the Southern hemisphere not yet visible on the planet, relaying updates on current conditions and terrain. The Southern continent had always been favoured as the landing site: the survey team report mentioned the more clement weather patterns on the high plateaus, a wider variety of plant life, some of it edible by humans, eminently suitable farmland and good harbours for the tough siliplex fishing vessels, now numbered pieces in the holds of the *Buenos Aires* and the *Bahrain*. The seas of Pern teemed with aquatic life, and at least a few of the species could be safely consumed by humans. The marine biologists had high hopes of populating the bays and estuaries with Terran piscine types without immediate effect on the present ecological balance and some hope of a new one. The deep-freeze tanks of the *Bahrain* contained twenty-five dolphins who had volunteered to come along. Pern's seas were eminently suitable for the support of the intelligent mammals and they enjoyed sea-shepherding as well as the opportunity to see new worlds.

Soil analyses had indicated that Terran cereals and legumes, which had already adapted well to Centauran soil, should flourish: this would be necessary as the native grasses were unsuitable for Terran animals. One of the first tasks facing the agronomists would be to plant fodder crops to sustain the variety of herbivores and ruminants, brought as fertilized ova from the Animal Reproduction Banks of Terra.

Permission to use certain of the advanced bio-genetic technics of the Eridanis to help adapt Terran animals to Pern – mainly the mentasynth, gene-paring and chromosome enhancements – had been grudgingly granted. The Federated Sentient Planets wanted no further disasters like the bio-alts which had aroused the strong Pure-Human Action Group: even if Pern were in an isolated area of the galaxy.

Emily Boll repressed a shudder. These were no thoughts to be having right now. That was the past: displayed on the screen in front of her was the future. And she'd best get down and help the specialists organize it.

'I've dallied long enough,' she murmured to Paul Benden. She gave his shoulder a farewell touch.

Paul pulled his gaze from the screen and smiled at her, giving her hand on his shoulder a friendly pat. 'Eat first!' He waggled a stern finger at her. 'You keep forgetting we're not rationed on board the *Yoko*.' She gave him a startled look.

'I will. I promise.'

'The next few weeks are going to be rough.'

'Hmm, but so stimulating!' Her blue eyes twinkled at him. Then her stomach audibly rumbled. 'Gotcha, Admiral.' She winked again and left.

He watched her walk to the nearest exit off the Bridge, a lean, almost bony woman, with grey and naturally waving hair which she wore shoulder-length. What Paul liked most about her was her wiry strength, both moral and physical, which was combined with a ruthlessness that sometimes startled him. She had tremendous personal vitality: just being in her presence gave spirits a lift. Together they'd make something of this new world. And he looked back at the main screen and the enthralling vista of Pern.

There was much debate in the large lounge which was now set up as an office for the heads of the various teams of Exobiology, Agronomy, Botany, Ecology and six representatives of the professional farmers who were still a bit groggy from their term in deep sleep. The room was ringed by multiple screens displaying a constantly altering range of micro-biology reports, statistics, comparisons, analyses. Some were hunched over desk monitors, busily collating reports and trying to ignore the tension emanating from a tight knot of the departmental heads who occupied the very centre of the room, each one with an eye out for the screens displaying reports on his/her speciality.

Mar Dook, head Agronomist and the acknowledged correlator of these final efforts, was a small man whose Earth Asiatic ancestry was evident in feature, skin tone and physiology: he was wiry, lean, slightly bowed in the shoulders but his black eyes gleamed with eager intelligence and the challenge he was reading.

'The schedule has long been decided, my dear colleagues. We're in the first wave down. The probes do not contradict any of the information we already have. The dirt and vegetation samples match. There's the same sort of red and green algae reported along the shoreline. Marine life is visible in the sea probe. One of the low probes has caught a comforting variety of insects which the EEC also found. The aerial fax came up with that flyer reported . . . what did the team call them, wherries.'

'Why wherries?' Phas Radamanth asked, scrolling through the report to that annotation. 'Ah, because they resemble airborne barges, squat, fat and full.' He allowed himself a little smile for the whimsy of that long-dead team.

'Yeah, but I don't see mention of any other predators,' Kwan Marceau said, his rather high forehead creased with a frown. This was so constant a habit that he had permanent furrows over his nosebridge and across his brow. He liked to have answers to mysteries as quickly as possible.

'There's sure to be something that eats them,' Phas replied confidently.

'Or they eat each other,' Mar Dook suggested and received a stern frown from Kwan. 'Ah, look,' and Mar Dook pointed excitedly to a new fax coming up on one screen. 'The scuttlebug got a reptiloid. Rather a large specimen, 10 centimetres thick and 7 metres long. There's your wherry eater, Kwan.'

'Another scuttle has just run through a puddle of excretal matter, semi-liquid, which contains intestinal parasites and bacteria,' Pol Nietro said, hurriedly tagging the report for later quick reference. 'There do seem to be plenty of worm-like soil livers, too. Rather a significant variety, if you ask me. Worms like nematodes, insectoids, mites that really wouldn't be out of place in a Terran compost heap. Ted, here's something for you, plants like our mycorrhizas, tree fungi. Speaking of that, I wonder where the EEC team found that luminous mycelium.'

Ted Tubberman, one of the colony botanists, gave a contemptuous snort. He was a big man, not carrying any extra flesh after nearly fifteen years in deep sleep, but he tended to be overbearing in personality as well as stature. 'Luminous organisms are usually found in deep caves, Nietro, as they use their light to attract their victims, generally insects. The mycelium reported by that team was in a cave system on that large island south of the northern continent. This planet seems to have a considerable number of cave systems. Why weren't any scuttles scheduled for subterrean investigations?' he asked in an aggrieved tone.

'There were only so many available, Ted,' Mar Dook said placatingly.

'Ah, look, now this is what I've been waiting for,' Kwan said, his usually solemn face lighting up as he bent, almost

26

nose to his small screen, 'there are reef systems. And yes, a balanced if fragile marine ecology along the Ring islands. I'm much encouraged. Possibly those polka dots they saw are from a meteorite storm.'

'No,' Ted dismissed that instantly. 'No impact and the formation of new growth does not parallel that sort of phenomenon. I intend looking into that problem the first moment I can.'

'What we have to do first,' Mar Dook said, gently reproving, 'is select the appropriate sites, plough, test and where necessary, introduce the symbiotic bacteria and fungi, even beetles, needed for pastureland.'

'But we still don't know which,' and Ted paused to stress that word, 'landing site will be chosen?' His face was now flushed with irritation.

'The three that are now being surveyed are much of a muchness,' Mar Dook replied with a tolerant smile. He found Tubberman's petulant restlessness tedious. Surely the botanist realized that all matters resolved themselves in time and all one needed was patience. 'All three give us ample scope for experimental and control fields. Our basic tasks will be the same no matter where we land. The essential point is not to miss this first vital growing season.'

'The brood animals must be revived as soon as possible,' said Pol Nietro. The head zoologist was as eager as everyone else to plunge into the practical work ahead of them. 'And reliance on the alfalfa trays for fodder is not going to adjust their digestions to a new environment. We must begin as we mean to go on, and let Pern supply our needs.'

There was a murmur of assent to his statement.

'The only new factor in these reports,' Phas Radamanth, the xeno-biologist, said encouragingly, without turning his eyes from his screens, 'is the density of vegetation. We may have to clear more than we thought in the 45S 11.75 site. See here,' and he gestured to the disparate images, 'where the EEC pic showed sparse ground cover, we now have heavy vegetation. Some of it of respectable size.'

'There should be at least that, after two hundred-odd

years,' Ted Tubberman said irritably. 'I never was happy about the barrenness. Smacked of a depauperate ecology. Hey, most of those circular features are overgrown. Felicia, run up the EEC pics that correspond,' and he doubled his big frame to peer over her shoulder at the double screen below the probe broadcast. 'Ah, see, those circles are barely discernible now. The team was right about botanical succession. And that isn't a grassoid. If that's mutant vegetation . . .' Ted began, jutting his chin out. He had loudly and frequently insisted that the success of Pern as a colony would depend on botanical health.

'I, too, am happier to see succession but according to the EEC reports, it's—' Mar Dook began.

'Shove the EEC reports. They didn't tell us the half of what we really need to know,' Ted exclaimed. 'Survey, they called it. Quick dip at the trot. No depth to it at all. The most superficial survey I've ever read.'

'I quite agree,' said the calm voice of Emily Boll who had entered while the botanist was ranting. 'The initial EEC report does seem to have been less complete now we can compare it to our new home. But the crucial, salient points were covered for us. We know what we needed to know and the FSP was quite happy to turn the planet over to us because it certainly doesn't have anything to interest them. And it's not a planet that the Syndicates would fight over. Which is why *we* were allowed to have it. I think we have to be grateful to that team, not critical,' and her smiling gaze took in everyone in the crowded room. 'The important elements – atmosphere, water, arable soil, ores, minerals, bacteria, insects, marine life – are all present and Pern is eminently suitable for human habitation. The gaps, the in-depth investigations that report did not contain, are what we shall spend a lifetime filling in. A challenge for each and every one of us, and our children!' Her voice, pitched low, nonetheless rang in the crowded room. 'Let's not worry at this very late date about what we weren't told – we'll find the answers soon enough. Let's concentrate now on the great work we have to begin in just two days' time. We're able for any surprises Pern might have for us. Now, Mar Dook, have you seen anything in the updates to suggest we must alter the schedule?'

'Nothing,' Mar Dook replied, warily glancing at Ted Tubberman who was frowning at Emily Boll. 'But those soil and vegetable matter samples would occupy us usefully.'

'I'm sure they would,' and Emily grinned broadly at him. 'We'll be busy enough . . . ah, here's the information you need. And what a bumper crop to digest.'

'We still don't know *where* we're landing,' Ted complained.

'The Admiral is discussing that right now, Ted,' Emily replied equably. 'We'll be among the first to know.'

Agronomists were to be in the first shuttleloads to reach the surface for it was vital to the colony's future to break land for crops as soon as possible. Even while the engineers were setting up the landing grids, agronomists would be ploughing fields while Ted Tubberman and his group would be setting up sheds, seeding the precious soil brought from Earth. Pat Hempenstall would set up a 'control' shed, using indigenous dirt to see if Earth or colonial variants would thrive unassisted in an alien soil. Sufficient packaged organisms had also been brought to introduce symbiotic bacteria.

'I will be very glad,' murmured Pol Nietro, the head biologist, 'if the reports confirm those insectoids, winged and subterranean, reported by the EEC team. If they should prove sufficient to do the work of dung beetles and flies on our Terran-style detritus, agronomy will be off to a good start. We've got to get nutrients back into the soil, introduce and spread the rumen bacteria and protozoans, yeasts and bacteria for our cows, sheep, goats and horses so they'll thrive.'

'If not, Pol,' Emily replied, 'Kitti,' and Emily smiled with great deference towards the tiny lady, the only one seated in the centre of the little cluster, 'will have to work a bit of her micro-magic and rearrange innards that can deal with what Pern has to offer.'

'Soil samples coming up,' Ju Adjai said into the pause. 'And here's vegetable mash for you, Ted. Get your teeth in that.'

Tubberman launched himself to the position next to Felicia, his big fingers nimble and accurate over the keyboard as he keyed in the information he required.

In moments the rattling of keys, punctuated by assorted mutters and other monosyllables of concentration, filled the room. Emily and Kitti Ping exchanged glances, tinged with amused condescension for the vagaries of their younger colleagues. Kitti Ping then turned her eyes back to the main screen and continued her contemplation of the world they were rapidly approaching.

As Emily sat down to her workspace, she wondered how under the suns the expedition had lucked out enough to number the most eminent micro-biologist in the Federated Sentient Planets: the only human who had ever been trained by the Eridanis. Emily had only seen pics of the biologically altered humans who had made the first abortive mission to Eridani. She suppressed a shudder. Pern wouldn't ever require that kind of abominable tinkering. Maybe that's why Kitti Ping was willing to come to the edge of the galaxy – to a quiet backwater to end what had already been a long and incredible life – where she, too, could practise selective amnesia. There were many on the colony's roll who had come to forget what they had seen and done.

'The grassoid on that eastern landing site is going to be hell to cut through,' Ted Tubberman said, scowling. 'High boron content. It'll dull cutting edges and foul gear.'

'It'd cushion the landing,' Pat Hempenstall said with a relieved chuckle.

'Our landing craft have landed safely on far more inhospitable terrain than that,' Emily remarked encouragingly.

'Felicia, run a comparison on the botanical succession around those crazy polka-dots,' Ted Tubberman went on, staring at his own screens. 'There's something about that configuration that still bothers me. The phenomenon is all over the planet. And I'll be happier if we could get an opinion from that geologist whiz, Tarzan . . .'

'Tarvi Andiyar,' Felicia supplied, accustomed to Ted Tubberman's memory lapses.

'Well, memo him to meet me when he's revived. Damn it, Mar, how can we function with only half the specialists awake?'

'We're doing fine, Ted. Pern is coming up roses for us. Not a joggle off the report data.'

'That's almost worrying,' Pol Nietro, the zoologist, said blandly.

Tubberman snorted, Mar Dook shrugged, and Kitti Ping smiled inscrutably.

The chrono tingled against Admiral Benden's wrist, reminding him it was time for his own meeting.

'Commander Ongola, take the conn.' Reluctantly, his eyes focusing on the main screen until the access panel of the exit closed over it, Paul Benden left the Bridge.

The corridors of the great colony ship were hourly more populated, Paul noticed as he made his way to the wardroom. Newly revived people, clutching the hand rails, were jerkily exercising stiff limbs and trying to focus eye and mind on the suddenly hazardous task of remaining upright. The old *Yoko* would be packed tighter than reserve rations while colonists waited their turn to reach the surface. With the promise of the freedom of a whole new world as the reward of patience, the crowding could be endured.

Having paid close attention to the probe reports screened on the Bridge, Paul Benden had already decided which of the three recommended landing sites he would choose. Naturally he would accord his staff and the other two captains the courtesy of a hearing, but the vast plateau below a group of strato volcanoes was the obvious choice, and one reason was the current weather. There was also a nearly level expanse, adequate to accommodate all six shuttles. The updates had only confirmed a tentative preference made seventeen years ago when he had first studied the EEC reports. He had never anticipated much difficulty with landing: it was the smooth and accident-free debarkation which caused him anxiety. There was no rescue back-up, solicitously hovering in the skies of Pern, nor disaster teams on its surface.

In organizing the debarkation, Paul had made use of a superb team, most of whom had served with him. To prepare and service the *Yoko*'s three shuttle craft and the Admiral's gig, he had the skill and experience of Fulmar Stone as Flight Officer, a man who had served with him throughout the Cygnus campaign. For the past two weeks, Fulmar's crews had been all over the shuttle vehicles which had passed the most ruthless computer checks, ensuring that there would be no malfunction after fifteen years' wrap in the cold storage of the flight deck. The *Yoko*'s twelve pilots under Kenjo Fusaiyuki had gone through rigorous simulator drills, well spiced with the most bizarre landing emergencies. Most of them had been combat fighters, fit and fully experienced at extricating themselves from tricky situations, though none had quite the record of Kenjo Fusaiyuki. There had been a few complaints about Kenjo's methods from some of the less experienced shuttle pilots which Paul Benden had courteously listened to, and ignored.

Paul had been surprised, and flattered, when Kenjo had signed up with the expedition. Somehow, he'd thought the man would have signed on to an exploratory unit where he'd continue to fly as long as his reflexes lasted. Then Paul remembered that Kenjo was cyborg, though the prosthetic left leg was probably stronger than the right. However, after a war, the Exploration and Evaluation Corps had their choice of experienced, whole personnel and cyborgs were shunted into administrative positions.

Automatically, Paul made his left hand into a fist, his thumb rubbing against the knuckles of the three replacement fingers which had always worked as well as his natural ones, even when he thought about them, as he did now. But there was still no feeling in the pseudo-flesh. Consciously, he relaxed the hand, certain once again he heard a subtle plastic squeak in the joints and the wrist.

He turned his mind to real problems, like the debarkation ahead of them, with unforeseeable delays or foul-ups which might stall the entire operation as cargo and passengers began to flow from the orbiting ships. He'd appointed good men as supercargoes, Joel Lilienkamp as Surface Co-ordinator and Desi Arthied on the *Yoko*. Ezra and Jim were equally confident in their own debarkation personnel but one minor hitch could cause endless rescheduling. The trick would be to keep everything moving, from the storage and cargo decks to the loading platforms, and the speedy alteration of the shuttles to take inert cargo or live passengers of one sort or another. Paul Benden hoped that the dolphins made it through revival. He couldn't get quite as agitated over the loss of livestock – there were plenty of sperm and egg for in vitro propagation, but the dolphins were, to him, special. The sea mammals weren't due to be revived until the third week, so there was plenty of time to work out the kinks in shuttling so many tonnes of material and people.

The Admiral turned starboard off the main corridor and reached the wardroom. Once again, Paul hoped the meeting would not drag on. As he raised his hand to brush the access panel, he could see that they had arrived with two minutes to spare before the other two captains would screen in. There would be the brief formality of Ezra Keroon, as Fleet Astrogator, confirming the exact ETA at their parking orbit and then the landing site would be chosen. Shouldn't take long.

'The betting's eleven to four now, Lili,' Paul heard Drake Bonneau saying to Joel as the access panel to his wardroom whooshed open.

'For or against?' Paul asked, grinning as he entered. Those present, led by Kenjo's example, shot to their feet, despite his dismissing gesture. He took in the two blank screens which in precisely 95 seconds should reveal the faces of Ezra Keroon and Jim Tillek, and to the centre one where Pern swam tranquilly in the black ocean of space.

'There're some civilians don't think Desi and me can make the deadline, Paul,' Joel answered the Admiral, with a smug wink at Arthied who nodded solemnly. Lilienkamp was not a tall man, but chunkily built, although his frame was spare at the moment from hibernation. He had an engaging monkey face, fringed with greying dark hair that curled tightly against his skull. His personality was ebullient, volatile and, for the lazy, caustic. His quick wits included an eidetic memory that allowed him to keep track of not only any bet he made, for how much and with whom and what odds, but every parcel, package, crate and cannister in his keeping. Desi Arthied, his second-in-command, often found his superior's levity a trial but he respected Lilienkamp's abilities. It would be Desi's job to shift the cargo Joel designated to the loading decks and on board the shuttles.

'Civilians? Who don't know you very well, do they?' asked Paul drily, taking his seat and smiling non-committally at Avril Bitra who had been in charge of the Simulation Exercises. He wished now that he hadn't been quite so involved with the sultry brunette but she was quite the most stunning creature. Still, they'd all be too busy soon for personal relationships. More and more attractive young women were appearing in the corridors: he wanted one of them to want to marry Paul Benden, not 'the Admiral'.

Just then, the two screens lit up, the right hand one showing Ezra Keroon's saturnine countenance, with his distinctive fringe of grey hair: on the left was Jim Keroon, his square face wearing his usual cheerful expression.

'G'day, Paul,' he said, just ahead of Ezra's more formal salute and acknowledgement.

'Admiral, I beg to report that we have maintained our programmed course to the minute. Estimated arrival to parking orbit is now 46 hours, 33 minutes and 20 seconds. No deviations anticipated at this point in time.'

'Very good, Captain,' and Paul returned the salute, 'any problems?'

Both captains reported that their revival programs were continuing without incident and that their shuttles were ready for launch once orbit had been achieved.

'Now that we know when, the matter of where is open for discussion,' Paul said, leaning back in his chair to signal that comment was invited.

'So, tell us, Paul,' Joel Lilienkamp said with his usual disregard for protocol, 'where we're landing?' All through the Nathi War, Joel's impertinence had amused Paul Benden — when amusement was scarce — and consistently proved himself a near miraculous scavenger. His impudence now caused Ezra Keroon to frown but Jim Tillek chuckled.

'What are the odds, Lili?' he asked, his expression sly.

'Let us discuss the matter without prejudice,' Paul suggested in a wry tone of voice. 'The three sites recommended by the EEC team have now all been probed. If you will refer to the chart, the sites are at 30S by 13.30, 45S by 11, and 47S by 4.75.'

'There's really only one, Admiral, from my point of view,' Drake Bonneau interrupted excitedly, jabbing his finger at Paul's own choice, the strato site. 'Scuttlebug scans say it's almost as level as if it had been graded for us and broad enough to accommodate all six shuttles without any danger of collision. And that's what could be a real danger. The site at 45S11 is waterlogged right now, and the western one is too far from the ocean. Temperature readings are near freezing.'

Paul saw Kenjo's perceptible nod of agreement. He glanced at the two screens, Ezra's head showing the growing bald spot as he consulted his notes. Paul smoothed his own thick hair across his pate.

'That 30S is nearer sea for me,' Jim Keroon remarked amiably. 'Good harbour about fifty klicks away. River's navigable, too.' Keroon's interest in sailing vessels was exceeded only by his love of dolphins. Accessibility to open water would be a high factor in his choice.

'Good heights for observatory and met stations all right,' Ezra replied, 'though we've no real criterion from those Reports about climatology. Don't fancy settling that close to volcanoes myself.'

'A point, Ezra, but,' and Paul screened the relevant data for a quick scan, 'no seismic readings were recorded so I don't see volcanic activity as an immediate problem. We can have Patrice de Broglie do a survey. Ah, yes, no seismic readings from the EEC, so even the one that has erupted has been dormant well over two hundred years. The weather and general conditions on the other two sites do mitigate against them.'

'Hmm, so they do. Doesn't look from a met point of view as if the conditions at either will improve in two days,' Ezra conceded.

'Hell, we don't have to *stay* where we land,' Drake exclaimed and he brought forward other arguments, talking everyone into the decision Paul had already made.

'Unless there's some freak weather brewing up,' Jim Keroon said, when Drake paused for breath, 'which I'm sure the met boys will be able to spot, let's settle on the 30S site. That's the one the EEC team favoured anyhow. Besides, the scuttlebugs say it's got a thick ground cover. That should cushion the shock when you bounce, Drake.'

'Bounce?' Drake's wide-set grey eyes protruded at the mild jibe. 'Captain Keroon, I haven't bounced a landing since my first solo.'

'Very well, then, gentlemen, we have settled on our landing site?' Paul received confirmatory nods from Ezra and Jim. 'Relevant updates and detailed charts will be in your hands by 2200 hours.'

'Well, Joel,' Jim Keroon went on, his sly grin broadening, 'didja win?'

'Me, Captain?' Joel's eyes widened with injured innocence. 'I never bet on a sure thing.'

'Any other problems to raise at this point, Captains?' Paul paused courteously, looking from one screen to the other.

'All ahead go, Paul, now I know I'll land this bucket in her parking space on time,' Jim said, 'and where to send my shuttle.' He waved a casual salute towards Ezra and then his screen blacked out.

'Good evening, Admiral,' Ezra said more formally and his image faded.

'Is that all now, Paul?' Joel asked, cradling his recorder which he was never without.

'We've got the time and the place,' Paul replied, 'but that's a tough timetable you've set, Joel. Can you keep it?'

'There's a lot of money says he will, Admiral,' Drake Bonneau quipped.

'Why do you think it took me so long to load the *Yoko*, Admiral?' Joel Lilienkamp replied with a wide grin. 'I knew I'd have to unload it all fifteen years later. You'll see.' He winked at Desi whose expression mirrored the faintest hint of scepticism.

'Then, gentlemen,' the Admiral said, standing up, 'I'll be in my cabin if any problems do arise.'

As he swung out of the wardroom, Paul heard Joel asking for bets on how soon knowledge of the landing site would circulate the *Yoko*.

'Those odds, Lili . . .' Paul heard Avril say in her throaty voice as the door panel whooshed shut behind him.

Morale was high. He hoped that Emily's meeting had been as satisfactory. Seventeen years of planning and organization were about to be put to the test.

On the deep sleep decks of all three colony ships, the medics were working double shifts to arouse the over 5500 colonists. Technicians and specialists were being revived in order of their need in the landing operation but Admiral Benden and Governor Boll had been insistent that everyone be awake by the time that the three colony ships achieved their temporarily programmed parking position in a stable lagrangian orbit, 60 degrees ahead of the larger moon, in the L-5 spot.

Once the three great colony ships had been cleared of passengers and cargo, there'd be no more chance of views of Pern from outer space. Fuel had been calculated to the last ounce: the *Yokohama*, *Buenos Aires* and *Bahrain* had enough to achieve and maintain their geo-stationary orbits above the planet during the unloading process; the fuel requirements of the six shuttle craft which would accomplish this phase of the operation had also been computed to the final drop so there would be nothing left over for extra-planetary jaunts.

With all of Pern to explore and develop, it would be centuries before the inhabitants needed to go anywhere else. By then, they could have reinstituted enough technology to make their own fuel if needed. The resources of Pern would, in good time, allow some judicious space travel – if anyone wanted it.

Sallah Telgar, coming off duty from her watch on the Bridge, decided that she'd had quite enough space travel for one lifetime.

As the only surviving dependant of serving officers, she'd spent her childhood being shunted from one Service post to another. When she'd lost both parents, she'd been eligible to sign on as a Charter Member of the Colony. War compensations had permitted her to acquire a substantial number of 'stake' acres on Pern, once the colony had become established enough for individuals to claim personal estates. Above all other considerations, Sallah Telgar yearned to set herself down in one place and stay there. She would be quite content to live out the rest of her life on the surface of beautiful Pern. She knew planets could seem innocuous and enticing from the detachment of space, but all the reports she had viewed that day only confirmed its suitability for human habitation.

As she exited Bridge territory for the main corridors, she was surprised to see so many people about. For nearly five years she'd had a cabin to herself. The cabin wasn't spacious for single occupancy and with three sharing, it offered no privacy. So Sallah made for the off-duty lounge for something to eat before she tried to get some sleep. The lounge also had a large screen so she could continue planet-gazing.

At the lounge entrance, Sallah hauled up sharp for there were very few seats available despite the size of the facility. And, in the brief moments it took her to collect food from the dispensers, her options were narrowed down to one: a wall counter seat well to the port side of the big room, with a slightly distorted view of Pern.

Sallah shrugged diffidently. Like an addict, she'd take any view she could get of Pern. However, as she slipped into the seat, she realized that her nearest neighbours were also the people she least liked on board the *Yokohama*. Avril Bitra, Bart Lemos, Nabhi Nabol and three men she didn't know. Collar tabs identified them as mason, mechanical engineer and miner. They were also about the only people in the room not avidly watching the screen. The three specialists were listening, their faces carefully expressionless, though the oldest man, the engineer, occasionally glanced around to check on the attention of the nearby people. Avril had her elbows on the table, her handsome face marred by the arrogant supercilious sneer she affected, her black eyes glinting as she leaned forward towards homely Bart Lemos who was enthusiastically punching his right fist into his left palm to emphasize his quick low words while Nabhi wore his perpetual expression of hauteur, an expression not far removed from Avril's sneer, and watched the geologist.

Enough to spoil my appetite, Sallah remarked to herself and craned her neck to see Pern.

Being astrogator for the flagship, Avril had been on duty for the entire fifteen years. Gossip had it that she had spent a good deal of that time in Admiral Paul Benden's bed during the last five years. Candidly, Sallah could see why a virile man like the Admiral would be sexually attracted by Avril's dark and flashing beauty. A mixture of ethnic ancestors had given her the best of all possible features and lineaments. She was tall, neither willowy nor overripe, with luxuriant black hair which she often wore loose in silky ripples. Her slightly sallow complexion was flawless, her movements gracefully studied but her eyes, snapping with black fire, indicated a highly intelligent and volatile personality. Not a woman to cross, in Sallah's estimation, and Sallah had carefully maintained her distance from Paul Benden, or anyone else seen more than three times in Avril's company. If the unkind said that Paul Benden was now markedly absent from Avril's side, the charitable said that he had had to be in long conferences with his staff and the time for dalliance was over. Those whom Avril's sharp tongue had hit said that she had lost her bid to be the Admiral's lady.

However, Sallah had other matters on her mind than Avril Bitra's ploys. Three minutes before her watch had ended, Commander Ongola had remarked that the choice of the landing site had been made. He didn't designate where since that was the Admiral's prerogative in a formal announcement. Bets had been surreptitiously made about how soon the rest of the ship would know. The news should percolate through the lounge real soon now, Sallah thought, all too familiar with the devious channels of unofficial reports.

'This is where,' a man suddenly exclaimed excitedly. He strode to the screen, jabbing his forefinger at a point just now visible. He wore the Agronomy plough tab on his collar. 'Right . . .' and the man paused, aware that the screen image had fractionally moved, 'here!' And he planted his forefinger just at the base of the discernible ancient volcano, a pinpoint at this distance but nevertheless recognizable as a landmark.

'How much did Lili win on that one?' some wit demanded.

'Don't care about him,' the agronomist shouted. 'I've just won an acre off Hempenstall!'

There was a ripple of applause and good-natured joking, infectious enough to make Sallah grin, until her gaze happened to spot the contemptuous smile of superiority on Avril's face. And Sallah knew that she'd known and withheld the information from her table companions. Bart Lemos and Nabhi Nabol leaned closer to make an exchange of terse sentences. Avril shrugged.

'The landing site is immaterial.' Avril's sultry voice, though low, carried to Sallah's ears. 'The gig's equipped to do the job, believe me.' She glanced away and caught Sallah's eyes. Instantly her body tensed and her eyes narrowed. With a conscious effort she relaxed, and leaned indolently back in her chair, maintaining eye contact with an insolence that Sallah found aggravating.

Sallah broke the contact, feeling slightly soiled. She drank the last gulp of coffee, grimacing at the bitter aftertaste. It wasn't very good coffee, but she would miss even this facsimile when the supply was exhausted. She hadn't much faith in the Pernese shrub bark which the survey teams had discovered and highly recommended as a substitute but coffee had failed on all the colony planets so far and there hadn't been much hope of it thriving on Pern.

After the identification of the landing site, the conversation level in the lounge had risen by many decibels to an almost intolerable pitch. Sallah looked around for some congenial company but there were so many new unfamiliar people in a place where she had known everyone by name, rank and speciality.

Sallah sighed. She ditched her rubbish in the disposer, passed her tray under the cleanser and then stacked it neatly with others. She permitted herself one last look at Pern. 'We won't spoil this planet. I personally won't let anyone spoil it.'

As she turned to leave, her glance fell on Avril's dark head. Now there was an odd one to be a colonist, Sallah thought, and not for the first time. Avril was listed as a Contractor, with a handsome 'stake' as a professional fee but scarcely the sort of personality who would be comfortable in a rural environment. She had all the sophisticated manners of the citified. The Pern Expedition had attracted some first-rate talents and people, but most of those to whom Sallah had talked had been motivated to leave behind the Technicratic society, Syndicate-ridden, with an ever-spiralling need for resources.

Sallah liked the notion of being so far from Earth and her other colonies and of living on a self-reliant planet. From the moment she had read the Pern Prospectus she had been eager to be part of it. At sixteen, with Service compulsory at that point in the bitterly fought Nathi War, she had chosen pilot training, with additional studies in probe and surveillance techniques. She had completed her training just as the War ended, and then used her skills to map devastated areas on one planet and two moons. She was not only eligible to be a Charterer, she would be a valuable addition to the professional complement.

Now, as she left the off-duty lounge to return to her quarters, she began to share the excitement palpable throughout the great ship. In two days, they would have reached their long-awaited goal. Then, life would get real interesting!

Just as Sallah turned into the main corridor, a little girl with burnished deep-red hair lurched into her, tried to regain her balance and fell heavily at Sallah's feet. Bursting into loud sobs, more frustration than hurt, the child clung to Sallah's leg in a grip astonishingly strong for one so young.

'There now, not to cry. You'll get your balance back, pet,' Sallah spoke soothingly, reaching down to stroke the child's silky hair and then to loosen her frantic grip.

'Sorka! Sorka!' The equally redheaded man holding a younger child, a boy, by one hand, and a very pretty brunette woman by the other, moved unsteadily towards Sallah.

His wife, for such Sallah identified her, had all the signs of someone only just awake: her eyes didn't quite focus

42

and while she was trying to respond to the situation, was unable to concentrate.

'I do apologize, Pilot,' the redheaded man said, grinning apologetically as his eyes flicked to Sallah's collar emblem, 'but we're really not awake yet.'

He was trying to disencumber one hand to come to Sallah's assistance but the woman refused to relinquish her grasp, and plainly he could not let go of the now tottering boy.

'You need help,' Sallah said pleasantly, wondering which medic had let this totally unstable quartet out on their own.

'Our quarters are only a few steps along,' and he nodded his head towards the splinter aisle behind Sallah. 'Or so I was told but I never appreciated how far a few steps could be.'

'What's the number? I'm off duty.'

'B-8851.'

Sallah looked at the plates on the corridor corners and nodded. 'It is just the next aisle. Here, I'll help. There now, Sorka . . . is that your name? Here, I'll just . . .'

'Excuse me,' the man said as Sallah made to lift the child into her arms, 'they kept telling us we'd be better off walking. Trying to walk, that is.'

'I can't walk,' Sorka cried in a wail of protest. 'I'm lopsided.' She clung more fiercely to Sallah's legs.

'Sorka! Behave yourself!' The redhead frowned at his daughter's response.

'Gotta idea!' Sallah said in a brisk friendly tone. 'You take both my hands,' and she peeled Sorka's off her leg, grasping each one firmly in her own, 'and walk in front of me. I'll keep you on an even keel.'

Even so, it took a few moments to persuade Sorka to attempt this for she did indeed tend to teeter to the left. Sallah provided more leverage on that side and a little pressure to the right and Sorka, encouraged by her father's no-nonsense tone of voice, began to walk forward.

Even with Sallah's help, they made slow progress,

impeded by the more agile walkers on private destinations, and the uncertainty of their own steps. The woman found that by keeping one hand on the bulkhead as well as the other in her husband's keeping, she maintained an upright posture.

'I'm Red Hanrahan,' the man said when their progress improved.

'Sallah Telgar.'

'Never thought I'd need help from a pilot before we reached Pern,' he said with a wide grin. 'This is my wife, Mairi, my son, Brian, and you've got Sorka.'

'Here we are,' Sallah said, reaching the compartment and throwing open the door. She grimaced at the size of the accommodation and then reminded herself that it would only be for a short time. Even though the bunks were strapped up against the walls in their daytime position, the remaining floor space would allow little movement for the four occupants.

'Not much larger than the quarters we just vacated,' Red remarked equably.

'How are we supposed to exercise in here?' his wife demanded, a rather shrill note in her voice as she rolled her body around the door frame and got a good look at the size of their cabin.

'One by one, I guess,' Red said. 'It's only for a few days, pet, and then we'll have a whole planet to range. In you go, Brian, Sorka. We've kept Pilot Telgar long enough. You really saved us, Telgar. Thanks.'

Sorka had propped herself against the inside wall of their cabin and her father was encouraging the rest of his family to enter. Now Sorka just slid to a sitting position on the floor, her little knees against her chest. Then she cocked her head to peer up at Sallah, sounding more self-possessed.

'Thanks from me, too. It's really silly not knowing up from down and side from side.'

'I agree, but the effect will disappear very quickly. We all had to go through it when we woke up.'

'You did?' Sorka's incredulous expression then turned into the most radiant smile Sallah had ever seen, and she found herself grinning, too.

'We did. Even Admiral Benden,' she added mendaciously and couldn't resist the temptation to ruffle the child's silky and magnificently titian hair. 'I'll see you around. Okay?'

'While you're in that position, Sorka, do those exercises we were shown. Then it'll be Brian's turn,' Red Hanrahan was saying as Sallah closed the door behind her.

She reached her own quarters without further incident though there certainly were a lot of recent sleepers lurching about, with expressions ranging from intense concentration to horrified dismay. The moment Sallah opened her door, she was aware of the sleepers and grimaced. Very carefully she slid the panel back and leaned against it, wondering what to do. She was too keyed up to sleep yet: she had to wind down somehow. Well, there was always the pilots' ready room and some stimulating simulator practice. The moment of truth about her abilities as a shuttle pilot was rapidly approaching.

Her route was impeded by those whose co-ordination suffered from prolonged disuse. The first was a man, so rake-thin that Sallah feared he would break a bone the way he lurched from side to side.

'Tarvi Andiyar, geologist,' he said, courteously introducing himself as soon as she had supported him to a vertical stance. 'Are we really orbiting Pern?' His eyes crossed as he looked at her and Sallah managed to suppress the grin his comical expression evoked. She told him their position. 'And you have seen with your own bright and pretty eyes this marvellous planet?'

'I have and it's every bit as lovely as forecast,' Sallah assured him so warmly that he smiled broadly in relief, showing her very white and even teeth. He gave a shake of his head, which seemed to correct the aberrant focus of his eyes. He also had one of the most beautiful faces she had ever seen on a man: not Benden's rugged, warrior

45

features, but a sophisticated and subtle arrangement, almost sculptured, like some of the ancient Indic and Cambodian princes from ruined stone murals. She flushed a bit, remembering what those same princes had been doing in the murals.

'Would you know if there are any updated probe reports? I am exceedingly eager to get to work.'

This time Sallah could laugh, without giving offence and easing the sensual jolt his face had given her. 'You can't even walk and you want to get to work?'

'Isn't fifteen years' holiday long enough for anyone?' His expression mildly chided her. 'Is that not Cabin C-8411?'

'It is indeed,' she said, guiding him across the corridor.

'You are as beautiful as you are kind,' he said, one hand on the panel for support as he tried to make a very courtly bow. She had to grab at his shoulders as he overbalanced. 'And quick.' With a more judicious inclination of his head and with considerable dignity under the circumstances, he opened his door.

'Sallah!' exclaimed Drake Bonneau, striding down the corridor towards her. 'Anybody told you where we're landing?' He had the eager expression of someone about to confer a favour on a friend.

'It took no more than nine minutes for the scuttlebutt to circulate,' she said coolly.

'That long?' he pretended disdain and then produced one of the smiles he assumed would charm anyone. 'Let's drink to it. Not much longer to enjoy our leisure, eh? Just you and me, huh?'

She suppressed her distrust of his flattery. He probably wasn't even conscious of his trite glib phrases. She'd heard him, trotting out the same smooth line on any reasonably attractive female. And yet, he was not a bad sort, and certainly had had courage enough to spare during the War. But right now, his casual insincerity irritated her. Then she realized that her uncharacteristic irritation was a reaction to the sudden bustle, noise and proximity of so many people after the last few years of quiet.

Would there be any place on the *Yoko* soon that would retain its calm, and lack of population? Remember, she told herself sternly, it's only for a few days and then you'll be too busy flying to worry about crowds and noise. Flying, yes, the hangar deck. That was the place to go.

'Thanks, Drake, but Kenjo has me down for simulator practice in . . .' she glanced at her wrist, '. . . five minutes. Getcha another time.'

She took the emergency tube down to the flight deck to avoid the crowded corridors, and made her way past the variety of cargo secured on the flight deck to the Captain's gig, the *Mariposa*. It was a compact little craft, with its delta wing and its perky, pointed nacelle but, as Sallah punched the hatch release, it was full of quiet and unoccupied space.

2

Pern date   18.02.01*

Sallah shared her next watch, the dog's watch, with Kenjo Fusaiyuki. There was little for either of them to do, bar reacting if a glitch halted the programmes. Sallah was hacking around, trying to find something interesting enough to keep her awake when she noticed that Kenjo had activated one of the smaller screens on his position.

'What have you got there?' she asked before she remembered that Kenjo was not generally outgoing and might resent her interruption.

'I was decoding the gen on that eccentric wanderer,' he replied, without looking up from the screen.

'Oh, the one that had the astronomers all excited?' Sallah asked. She grinned, remembering the unusual spectacle of the rather staid pedantic astronomer, Xi Chi Yuen, flushed and dancing about the bridge with excitement.

'Quite likely,' Kenjo said. 'It does seem to have an enormously eccentric orbit, more of a cometary than planetary, though its mass indicates it's a planetary size. Look,' and he tapped out a sequence which brought up the satellites of Pern solar system in relation to their primary and each other. 'It computes to come in further than the usual fourth planet position and actually intrudes on the Oort cloud at aphelion. This is supposed to be an old system, or so the EEC team leads one to believe, and that planet ought to have a more conventional orbit.'

* Eighteenth day of twenty-eight, second month of thirteen, First year of landing.

48

Sallah chuckled. 'There was talk that it could be a stray that the Rukbat sun attracted.'

Kenjo shook his head. 'That has been ruled out.' He typed out another sequence which shifted the diagram on the screen to another projection. In a few seconds, equations overlaid the system diagram. 'Look at the odds against that,' and he pointed to the blinking nine-figure probability, 'it would have to be a cometary-type orbit, right into the system. It's not.' His long, bony fingers reset the screen and reported equations. 'I can't find a harmonic with the other planets. Ah, Captain Keroon registers the opinion that it might have been captured by Rukbat about ten of its cycles ago.'

'No, I think Xi Chi Yuen ruled that out. He computed it to be just after aphelion right now,' Sallah said, recalling that rather memorable watch. 'What did he say? Ah . . .'

'His report actually reads,' and Kenjo had accessed that file, 'that the eccentric planetoid had just exited the Oort cloud, pulling some of the cloud matter with it.'

'He also said, and I remember this distinctly, that in about eight years' time, we'll have a rather spectacular meteorite show as our new world goes through the wisps of Oort material.'

Kenjo snorted. 'I'd rather we didn't. I don't repose much faith in that EEC report now it's being compared with what's there. Those polka dots may be meteor damage after all.'

'I'm not going to lose any sleep over it.'

'Nor I,' and Kenjo crossed his hands over his chest as the report continued to scroll up the screen. 'Yuen apparently believes that with such an eccentric, almost parabolic orbit, this Pluto body may exit the solar system again or fall into the sun.'

'Which wouldn't be noticed much, would it?'

Kenjo shook his head, his eyes still scanning the report. 'Frozen solid. Much too far from Rukbat to get any warmth during most of its orbit. There's a possibility of a cometary tail visible when it's close in.' He exited that programme and tapped out a new sequence. 'Pern's two moons are much more interesting.'

'Why?' Sallah wanted to know. 'Fuel consumption allows for only the one trip to the moons, to set up the relay disks.'

Kenjo shrugged. 'You *always* leave yourself an escape route.'

'To a moon?' Sallah was openly sceptical. 'C'mon, Kenjo, we're not at war with anyone or anything this far from the Hub. Give over.' She spoke kindly, knowing that Kenjo had had several very narrow escapes in the Nathi war.

'Old habits die hard,' he murmured in such a low voice that, but for the silence on the Bridge, she would have missed it.

'Yeah, they do. But we're all going to be able to start fresh.'

Kenjo merely grunted, signalling an end to his mood.

As the great colony ships slowed, there was constant activity as the immense cargo pods were opened and their contents transferred to decks, spilling into access corridors. When the shuttles had been secured for their long voyage, they had already been loaded with the grid components and other necessities to ensure the safe landing of the mass of *matériel* and people to be discharged from the colony ships. The urgency now was to have the next shipment – agricultural tools and supplies – ready to be hustled on board as soon as the shuttles returned. The agronomists had promised to break ground before the second shuttle flight could reach the planet.

There were six shuttles between the three ships: three in the *Yoko*, two in the *Buenos Aires* and one in the *Bahrain* with special fittings for transporting livestock. Once the vessels had achieved their lagrangian orbit, debarkation would commence.

Twelve hours before that event, all the sleepers had been revived though there was grumbling about the fact that many unessential people, especially young children, should have slept on until planet-side accommodations were completed.

Despite the inconvenience, Sallah agreed with the Governor's announcement that no one should be denied the chance to witness the end of the long journey and the incredible vision of their new world spinning in black space. Sallah couldn't keep her eyes off Pern on whatever screen was available, even the tiny one in her quarters. Sallah Telgar had also managed to get on the duty roster for the most important watch of the entire trip.

Afterwards, Sallah always stoutly averred that she knew the instant the *Yokohama* reached its orbital position. The great ship had been slowing for days so that the slight puff of the retros would have been infinitesimal as they reduced the forward motion to a match with the planet below. Suddenly they were turning with the planet, in position over a real point on Pern, seeming to come to a halt in relation to the geography below them. Slight though the sensation was, Sallah felt it and had actually looked up from her console just as the helmsman, with suppressed excitement, turned to salute the Commander.

'We have arrived, sir.'

At the same instant, a similar report came in from the *Bahrain* and the *Buenos Aires* and those on the Bridge erupted into cheers and undisciplined exercises of relief and exultation. Commander Ongola immediately informed the Admiral who was already on board the lead shuttle, of the completion of the manœuvre and received formal thanks. Then he ordered all screens to focus on the planet, spread out below them, curving away into night on the one side, into brilliant day on the other.

Sallah joined in the hullabaloo until she noticed a break in the chatter from the probe and checked the monitor. The probe was merely switching its site as programmed. As she looked up, she caught a very sad, oddly pensive expression on Commander Ongola's face. Aware of her scrutiny, he caught her glance, one eyebrow arching in query at her stare.

Sallah was not the sort of young woman who was intimidated by official attitudes so she smiled back in sympathy. The end of his last voyage, she thought. Who wouldn't be sad?

Both of Ongola's heavy eyebrows went up and with great dignity he turned his head away, giving the order for the shuttle bay doors to be opened. The crew and the initial landing party were already strapped into their seats aboard the shuttles, awaiting this history-making order. Under her breath, Sallah murmured a good luck to Kenjo, and Drake, and even Nabol, piloting the *Yoko*'s three shuttles.

Klaxons announced the imminent departure and immediately the main screen turned its eye to the landing site. The watch officers sat alert at their stations for there would be minute adjustments required as the shuttles left the mother ship, and more when they returned. It was imperative that the *Yoko* did not deviate more than a few metres from its orbital position. Smaller screens marked the opened shuttle bay doors from several angles so that the bridge personnel saw the shuttles begin to drift from their mother ships, dropping quickly on puffs of their jets before the main engines were ignited. They would spiral down, across the planet, entering Pern's atmosphere on the western edge of the northern continent, braking as they continued on down and around the globe until they reached their landing site on the eastern end of the southern continent. Exterior cameras picked up the other three shuttles which took their positions in the flotilla. Gracefully, they arrowed down and then out of sight over the curve of the planet.

Commander Ongola left open the audio channel until the planet covered the transmissions; then he had the code broadcast so that the progress could be watched through one medium or the other. Everyone had the right to witness this crucial phase of their momentous journey.

Sallah dutifully kept one eye on her probe console but it was functioning properly and she didn't know the code it was now broadcasting. The flight broadcast she knew very well and didn't look away from that. Not today! Not when men were hours away from landing on Pern itself.

Her watch ended before the estimated time of arrival on Pern but she made herself small against the side wall, along with everyone else from her watch, so that they would have the best view possible. Not that every screen on the ship wasn't broadcasting the same information, not that the visual of the actual landing wouldn't flash simultaneously on all three colony vessels. But it seemed more official to see it from the bridge, somehow. So she stayed, reminding herself to breathe from time to time, and shifting from one tired swollen leg to another. She'd be relieved when the spin went down in order to facilitate the moving of so much cargo but her legs were still hurting. Soon, she would be planet-side, with no convenient spin to turn off to reduce the effects of gravity.

'Got rid of your mates?' Stev Kimmer asked, stepping quickly into Avril's room, after a quick glance over his shoulder. He closed the door behind him.

Avril turned to face him, arms extended, flicking her fingers to indicate unoccupied space and smiled in smug satisfaction. 'Rank has privileges. I used mine. Lock it. Occasionally that oaf Lensdale tries to foist someone off on me but I added three names below mine and he may have given up.'

'So,' Kimmer wanted to get straight to the point as he had to be at the loading bay to take his place in one of the *Yoko*'s shuttles, 'where is this incontrovertible proof of yours?'

Still smiling, now with anticipation of her surprise, Avril opened a drawer and took out a dark wood box with no apparent seam. She handed it to him and he shook his head.

'I told you I've no time for puzzles. If this is a ploy to get a man into your bed, Avril, your timing's way off.'

She made a little grimace, annoyed by his phrasing as well as the fact that circumstances now demanded that she seek assistance from anyone. But her first plan had run aground on the reef of Paul Benden's sudden and totally unexpected indifference. She smiled away her distaste, repositioned the box on her left palm, making a pass at the side facing her, and then effortlessly lifted the top. As she had known he would, Stev Kimmer inhaled in surprise, the sparkle in his eyes fleetingly reflecting the rich glow of the ruby the box held. His hands made a movement towards it and she tilted the box, ever so slightly, so that the gem twinkled wickedly in the light.

'Magnificent, isn't it?' Avril's voice was soft with affectionate possession as she turned her hand, letting him see the brilliance in the heart of the rose-cut gem. Abruptly, she took the jewel from its bed and handed it to him. 'Feel it. Look at it through the light. Flawless.'

'How did you get it?' He shot her an accusing glance, his features set with a combination of envy, greed and admiration. The latter was all for the magnificent jewel as he held it up to the lighting strip and examined its perfection.

'Believe it or not, I inherited it.' When his expression told her that he did not believe her, she went on, leaning gracefully against the small table, arms folded across her well-formed breasts, and grinned. 'My grandmother at seven removes was a member of the EEC team that explored this mudball. Shavva bint Faroud, to give her her maiden name.'

'Fardles!' Stev Kimmer was genuinely astounded.

'Furthermore,' and Avril enjoyed his reaction, 'I have her original notes.'

'How did your family manage to keep this all those years? Why, it's priceless.'

Superciliously, Avril lifted her lovely arched eyebrows. 'Great grandmother was no fool. That bauble was not the only thing she brought back from here, or the other planets she explored.'

'But to bring this,' and it was all Kimmer could do not to clench his finger around the beautiful gem, 'with you?'

'I'm the last of my line.'

'You mean, you can claim part of this planet as the direct descendant of the EEC team?' Stev was beginning to warm to such possibilities.

She shook her head angrily at his misconstruction.

'The EEC takes bloody good care that that doesn't happen. Shavva knew that. She also knew that sooner or later the planet would be opened for colonization. The ruby and her notes,' Avril paused dramatically, 'were handed down to me. And I, and her notes, are now in orbit around Pern.'

Stev Kimmer regarded her for a long moment of appraisal. Then she reached over and took the ruby from him, negligently playing a one-handed toss with it while Kimmer nervously watched.

'Now, do you want in on my scheme? Like my beloved and far-seeing predecessor, I have no wish to remain at the end of the galaxy on a seventh-rate world.'

Stev Kimmer narrowed his eyes and shrugged. 'Have the others seen the ruby?'

'Not yet.' And she smiled slowly with sly malice. 'If you'll help me, they may never need to.'

By the time Stev Kimmer made a hurried departure to the loading dock, Avril was sure of his participation. She glanced at the chrono and was pleased to see that her timing was perfect. She smoothed her hair, dabbed on a bit more of the heavy musk scent she preferred, burnished her nails for a few moments before a discreet knock on the door.

It opened to admit Nabhi Nabol. 'Are your roommates out?'

Kenjo Fusaiyuko felt the first judder of atmosphere through the control yoke and smiled. The Admiral, seated between himself and Jiro Akamoto, his co-pilot, leaned forward eagerly, straining at his safety harness, his smile of anticipation visible to Kenjo out of the corner of his eye. He permitted himself to smile, too. And then carefully blanked his expression. Things were going far too well. There had been no problems with the countdown checklist. For all its fifteen years of inactivity, the shuttle *Eujisan* handled perfectly. They had achieved an excellent angle of entry and should make a perfect landing. The probe had disclosed the best place to make it: indeed the probe's scuttle-bug encouragingly transmitted the information that the site was as level as a natural area could be.

Kenjo preferred to worry about possible contingencies: that habit had made him one of the best transport pilots in Cygnus Sector Fleet in spite of the fact that the few emergencies he had faced had never been ones which he could have foreseen. He had survived because, in planning for foul-ups, he was ready for anything.

But this was different. No one, apart from the now dead and gone Exploration and Evaluation team, had set foot on Pern. And, in Kenjo's estimation, *they* hadn't spent enough time on it to have made a proper assessment.

Jiro, beside him, murmured reassuring readings from his instrumentation and then both pilots felt resistance as the shuttle dug deeper into the atmospheric layer. Kenjo tightened his fingers around the control yoke, setting his feet and his seat deep for steadiness. He wished the Admiral would lean back: it was unnerving to have someone breathing down your neck at a time like this. How did he get so much slack in the harness?

The exterior of the shuttle was heating up but the internal temperature remained steady. He shot a glance at the small screen. The passengers were riding well, too, and none of the cargo had shifted under its straps. Kenjo's eyes flicked from one dial to the next, noting the performance/health of his vehicle. The juddering became violent now, but that was to be expected. Hadn't he pierced the protective gases of a hundred worlds in just this same way, slipping like a penknife under the flap of an envelope, like a man into the body of his beloved?

They were on the night-side now, one moon casting a brilliant full light on the dark land-mass. They were racing towards day over the immense deserted sea of Pern. He checked altitude and found it right on target. This first landing on Pern simply could not be perfect. There would have to be something amiss, or his faith in probability would be shattered. Kenjo's eyes searched his control panel for any telltale red, or any blinking yellow malfunction light. Yet the shuttle continued its slanting plunge as the sweat of apprehension ran down Kenjo's spine, and moisture beaded his brow under his helmet.

Beside him, Jiro looked outwardly calm, but then, even as Kenjo watched, he saw Jiro bite at the corner of his lower lip and he turned his head away, careful not to let his expression betray the satisfaction he felt that his co-pilot was exhibiting tension. Between them, Admiral Benden's breath was becoming more rapid.

Will the old man expire in joy beside him? Kenjo felt a sudden stab of alarm. *Yes, that could be it. The shuttle would land safely but Admiral Benden would die on the point of arrival on his promised land. Yes, that would be the flaw in the trip. A human error, not a mechanical failure.*

Kenjo's mind played with the ramifications of this disaster and then there was less resistance on the skin of the shuttle as they dropped below the speed of sound. Skin heat was okay, shuttle responding to the helm and they were at the correct altitude, dropping as programmed in landing readiness.

Remember, Kenjo, use as little fuel in retro as possible. The more fuel saved, the more trips can be made. And then . . . Kenjo cut off that line of thinking. *There would still be the atmosphere planes to drive for many years to come. Power packs lasted for decades if carefully recharged. And if he could scrounge the right parts . . . His spirit would not be grounded for a long time yet.*

He took quick altitude readings, checked his compass, trimmed the flaps, did a quick calculation on his speed, and squinted ahead towards the shoreline, coming up in plain sight ahead of them. The screens fixed on the other shuttles told him that they were following, maintaining the prescribed safe interval. He and the shuttle *Eujisan* would be the first to touch down on Pern. Which was only suitable as both Admiral Benden and Governor Boll were *his* passengers.

The shuttle was hurtling over the eastern ocean, its shadow preceding it on the water as it overpassed the lumps of islets and larger masses in the archipelago that extended eastward from their landing site. Kenjo nearly lost his concentration as he spotted a perfect strato volcano rising above the water: its resemblance to the famed Mount Fuji of his ethnic home imprinted on his eye's mind but his duty was more compelling than that incredible vision. But surely that little volcano – for what other volcano on any world could dare to rival Fuji – was a good sign.

If only Admiral Benden would lean back! How had he managed to find so much slack in his safety harness? It was as well the man did not ask questions or babble at Governor Boll, strapped in the astrogator's chair.

Kenjo could now see surf boiling at the base of the rocky promontory that signalled they were approaching the chosen landing site.

'Retro rockets, two second blast,' he said, pleased to hear his voice steady and calm, almost bored. Jiro acknowledged and the shuttle tugged back, but evenly, as the retros broke their forward speed. Kenjo lifted the nose, slightly bleeding air speed. 'Landing gear down.'

Jiro nodded and, as Kenjo watched, hand hovering over the retros in case the landing gear failed to emerge, the green lights came on, unwinkingly, and they could feel the pull of air against the great wheels as they locked into position. A shade too much speed for landing and the vast field was coming up under them, a field that was

58

undulating like the sea itself. Kenjo fought down the panic. He had, after all, seen the grasses of fourteen different planets. The ground under those grasses was solid. He checked drag, windspeed, and, wincing at the necessity, fired the retros again briefly and pulled the nose up as he persuaded the shuttle to settle to the surface of Pern.

Once the big wheels touched, the landing became less smooth as they were jolted over the uneven ground. But there were no dangerous depressions on this immense meadow and, braking judiciously and making full use of his flaps, Kenjo swung the shuttle in a wide circle so that it faced the way it had just come and rolled to a complete stop.

Kenjo permitted himself a small smile of satisfaction, a smile he extended to Jiro.

'Fine landing, Kenjo! Jiro! My compliments,' the Admiral exclaimed and Kenjo decided that he would forgive him that enthusiastic clout on the shoulder. He was, after all, an Admiral and had every right to be elated at this moment. Then other sounds alarmed Kenjo and Jiro both: the snapping of metal clasps, and the sudden startling noise of air rapidly evacuating.

Startled, Kenjo turned just as Jiro did, and before either man could react, they saw the Admiral and the Governor disappearing down the cabin's escape hatch. Astounded by this extraordinary behaviour, Kenjo glanced frantically at his console, certain that the Admiral and Governor must be reacting to an emergency of some sort, but only the red brake light was on. A smell of burning grass and oil and rocket fuel wafted up to the two pilots through the open hatch. Simultaneously they were aware of the shouts from the passenger cabin; shouts of joy, not cries of panic.

A glance in the screens proved to Kenjo that their passengers were releasing their safety harness. A few had risen and were tentatively stretching legs and arms, talking excitedly, in great anticipation of stepping out on the surface of their new home. Why had the Admiral and the Governor left the shuttle so precipitously?

Jiro eyed him questioningly. All Kenjo could think to do was shrug. There were times when the idiosyncrasies of other ethnic groups were totally incomprehensible to him. He had always considered the Admiral a most sensible personage, unlikely to give way to panic, and certainly one of the most prestigious naval strategists since the Japanese Yamamoto or the English Nelson.

The cheering subsided while Kenjo and Jiro remained baffled by the actions of the two leaders. Then a sudden silence fell, punctuated by nervous whispers and Kenjo realized that, as pilot, it fell to him to take charge. Signalling abruptly to Jiro, he went through the landing checklist, noting the fuel expended with a grunt of pleasure at his economy. Litres under the allowance. He recalled himself to present duties, activating the cargo hold release mechanism, switching the sensors to exterior, and setting the exterior cameras to record this historic moment. Above all, he must pretend that everything was in order, although surely the Admiral and the Governor ought to have been the first off the shuttle.

But they had been! They were indeed the first persons to set foot on this new world! Kenjo unstrapped himself, motioning for Jiro to do the same. He stooped, briefly, to activate the hatch closure. Then he took the three steps to the panel between the two cabins and palmed it open.

Cheers greeted him and, modestly, he dropped his head and eyes, pleased by the acclaim but too worried about the inexplicable actions of the Admiral and Governor to respond. The cheers subsided expectantly as he reached the rear of the payload cabin and undogged the passenger hatch. With an unnecessary but satisfying force, he pushed open the door. As the aperture widened and the ramp extended, the fresh air of the new world poured in, almost visible in the recycled air of the shuttle. He was not the only one to take a deep breath of the oxygen-rich, aromatic air. Kenjo was debating with himself the protocol of such an occasion, since the logical candidates had already evacuated the vehicle, but Jiro, beside him, began to point excitedly. Kenjo peered around the slowly opening hatch and blinked in astonishment.

There, visible not only to him but to the other five shuttles which had landed in due order behind him, were two brilliant banners: one the gold and blue of the Federated Sentient Planets and the other, the brand new standard for the planet Pern, blue, white and yellow, with the design of sickle and plough in the upper-left-hand corner, signifying the pastoral nature of the colony. Occasionally hidden by the flapping of the banners in the steady breeze over the meadow were the triumphant figures of Admiral Benden and Governor Boll. The pair of them were grinning like idiots, Kenjo saw, as they enthusiastically beckoned the passengers to emerge.

'Let us welcome you, my friends, to the planet Pern,' cried the Admiral in a stentorian voice.

'Welcome to Pern,' the Governor shouted. 'Welcome! Welcome!'

They looked at each other and then began the formal words in an obviously well-rehearsed unison.

'By the power vested in us by the Federated Sentient Planets, we hereby claim this planet and name it Pern.'

3

●

The largest contingent – the Engineers led by Emthal Arthied, Boris Pahlevi's Power Resource Group, Jack Brooks' joats and every able-bodied man and woman who knew which end of a hammer to grip – were set to putting down the landing-strip grids. A second work force, headed by Joe Tobin who commandeered anyone for the Engineering group who didn't look busy enough, erected the prefabricated sections of the landing control and meteorology tower, in which Ongola and the other meteorologists would be based.

The tower was three storeys high, two square sections supported by a wider and longer rectangular base. Initially the ground level would serve as headquarters for the Admiral, the Governor and the informal Council. When the proper administrative Square had been built later on, this installation would be turned over to the meteorology and communications groups. Once the tower was erected, Ramona Galliani, Caleb Putsch and Emma Trury set up the meteorology equipment, monitors and terminals, and the main comunit.

The third and smallest group – all eight of Mar Dook's agronomists, plus a dozen able-bodied, Pol Nietro from zoology, Phas Radamanth and AC Sopers of xenobiology, Ted Tubberman and his crew – had the task of choosing the site for settlement and the experimental farm. Ramon Sifuentes, the industrial technician, with the plasticians led by Leland Estes, scouted about to find varieties of vegetation that might be efficiently converted into various plastics which the colony would need for building. On the one mini-sled brought along, Emily Boll flew between the agronomy survey and the control tower, correlating data once Ramona had told her that the tower systems were 'green for go'.

As Chief Medic Basil Tomlinson was taking a break, after the mammoth job of reviving 2500 people on the *Yoko*, and consulting with the medics on the *Bahrain* (with 1200 people) and the *Buenos Aires* (with 1500), he had sent Sue O'Hara down in his stead with sufficient staff to set up an emergency infirmary. Once that had been erected, the three male nurses joined the Agronomists, holding survey poles, patching bruises and scrapes, and peremptorily ordering rest periods for the older members who were overextending themselves in enthusiasm while the rest of the medical team unpacked.

By midday, those in orbit had a non-stop show of the disciplined but constant activities on the surface.

'It keeps people home,' Sallah remarked to Barr Hamil, her co-pilot, as they traversed nearly empty corridors on their way back from the main hangar where they'd been checking cargo manifests for their first trip down. Sallah was determined that, when Kenjo and Jiro turned the shuttle over to her command the next morning, all would be ready for her drop.

'It's fascinating, Sal. And *we'll* be there tomorrow!' Barr's eyes were shining and she wore a silly grin. 'I really can't believe we're here, and will be there!' She pointed downward. 'It's like a dream. I keep being afraid I'll wake up suddenly.'

They had reached their own quarters and both had eyes only for the vid screen in the corner.

'Good,' Barr said with a relieved sigh. 'They've got the donks assembled.'

Sallah chuckled at her companion. 'Sure. Our job is to get the shuttle down in one piece, Barr. Unloading is someone else's problem.' But she was relieved to see the sturdy load handlers, the donks, lined up at the end of the almost completed landing strip. That would facilitate unloading and speed up the shuttles' return to their mother ships for the next run. Already there were informal competitions between the various units to bring in their projects faster and more efficiently than programmed time allowed.

They watched, as everyone did, until the dark tropical moonless night rendered the broadcasts impossible to interpret. Broadcasts from the surface would be primitive until Drake Bonneau and Xi Chi Yuen, in the Admiral's Gig, had a chance to install the comsats on the two moons. Nonetheless, the last scene raised a nostalgic lump in Sallah's throat, reminding her of hunting trips which she and her parents had enjoyed in the hills around First on Centauri.

Now, on their first night on the surface of their new home, tired men and women were seated around an immense campfire, eating an evening meal that had been prepared in a huge kettle from freeze-dried Terran vegetables and meats. In the failing light, one could just see the white strips of the runway grids, and the wind sock having convulsions in the brisk breeze. The planetary flag, so proudly displayed that morning, had wrapped itself around the pole above the control tower. Someone, Joe Tobin or Kaarvan, began to play softly on a harmonica, an old old tune, so familiar – yet Sallah couldn't name it. Someone else joined in with a recorder. Softly and hesitantly at first, then with more confidence, the tired colonists began to sing or hum the words. Other voices added harmony, and Sallah remembered it was 'Home on the Range'. There certainly had been no 'discouraging words' that day. And an evening serenade did make the landing site seem a bit more like a home.

The next morning Sallah and Barr had been up long before the wakey-wake klaxon, assembling their passengers and making last-minute weight calculations. The pilots had

64

had a very serious briefing from Lt. Commander Ongola on the necessity of conserving fuel.

'We have just enough liquid fuel to get every man, woman and child, beast, parcel, package and reusable section of the ships down to the surface. Waste not, want not. Fools waste fuel! We have none to waste. Nor,' he added, shedding his sad wistful smile on his audience, 'fools among us.'

As the loading bay had its phalanx of screens, Sallah and Barr could follow the six shuttles lifting from the planet's surface. Then the scene shifted to a panoramic view of the main landing site.

'It's breathtaking, Sal, breathtaking,' Barr said. 'I've never seen so much unoccupied, unused land at one time in my life.'

'Get used to it.'

With the activities of the landing party to watch, it seemed like no time at all before the shuttles were locking on. The loading detail were trundling the first crates into the hold before Kenjo and Jiro could exit. Sallah was a little annoyed with Kenjo for his brusque dismissal of Barr's excited questions. Even Jiro looked abashed by his senior's truculence as Kenjo succinctly briefed Sallah on landing procedures, advice on handling the shuttle's idiosyncrasies, and the frequency of the now operational tower meteorological control. He wished her a safe drop, saluted and, turning on his heel, left the bay.

'Well, hail and farewell,' Barr said, recovering from the snub.

'Let's do the pre-flight even if Fussy Fusi has made such a big deal of turn-over,' Sallah said, sliding into the lock of the *Eujisan* an inch ahead of the next big crate being loaded. They had finished their check by the time loading was complete. Barr did passenger inspection, making very certain that General Cherry Duff, the oldest Charterer and the pro-tem colony magistrate, was comfortable and then they were cleared for the drop.

*

'We were barely there,' Barr complained as Sallah taxied the *Eujisan* into take-off position at the end of the runway eight hours later. 'And now we're away again.'

'Efficiency is our guide. Waste not, want not,' Sallah told her, eyes on the instrumentation as she opened the throttle on the *Eujisan* for lift-off thrust. She grimaced, eyes flicking between fuel gauge and rev counter, not wanting to use a cc more of fuel than necessary. 'Kenjo and the next eager set of colonists are chewing hunks out of the cargo hatch. We must up, up and away!'

And they were, with Barr flipping the cabin screen to a view of what they were so quickly leaving.

In the first week of unloading, the shuttles were scheduled to make three round trips a day, the pilots alternating flights which gave each team at least eight hours off. Sometimes they'd be able to spend a night on the surface. Cargo took longer to unload than passengers, even with willing hands, strong backs and the donks.

'Kenjo never made an error in his life?' Barr asked of Sallah when he made a disparaging remark about the shuttle's consumption of fuel during the trips the two women made.

'That's why he's alive today,' Sallah replied, although his comment had rankled. She had expended no more fuel than was absolutely necessary but she began keeping a private record of consumption on each of her trips. Just in case Kenjo got officious. She noticed that Kenjo generally oversaw the *Eujisan*'s refuelling and he personally supervised its fifty-hour checks. She knew she was a better than average pilot, in space or atmospheric craft but, if that was the way Kenjo wanted it, she wouldn't make waves with a hero pilot who had far more experience than she did.

Patterns were quickly established. Those on the ground began each morning by erecting the housing and work areas for those due to arrive during the day. Ramon Sifuentes, Leland Estes, Dos Muhammed and Ju Adjai kept the extruders busy night and day, worried by the high-silicate composition of much of the vegetation. The silicon-based plastics, whose ancestors on Earth had been cements and silicons, needed clear silver sand and a detail was kept busy ferrying this from a beautiful white cove on the other side of the nearby river.

Handily they cleared the marked-out 'fodder' fields with the agronomy teams. Some wit had put up street signs with estimated distances in light years for Earth, First Centauri and the home worlds of the other members of the Federated Sentient Planets.

Each morning, too, a schedule of the day's intended goals was flashed on the screen. Each evening, either Paul Benden or Emily Boll addressed ground and ships' personnel with an update. The infirmary, built on the second day while the agronomists turned the rich black soil of Pern to receive Terran seeds, had already dealt with its first clients for, despite the careful planning, accidents occurred. Fortunately, Emily went on, only minor ones. She held up hands, large, raw-looking blisters visible through their nu-skin coating.

Like everyone else waiting to drop, Sorka Hanrahan spent a lot of time watching the progress of the settlement, informally referred to as 'Landing', but only because watching passed the time. She wasn't really interested, especially after her mother kept remarking that they were seeing history made. History was something you read about in books. Sorka had always been an active child so the enforced idleness and the constriction of shipboard life quickly became frustrating. It was small comfort to *know* how important her father's profession of veterinary surgeon was *going* to be on Pern when all the kids she had met in the messhalls and corridors were getting down to Pern faster than she and her brother were.

Brian, however, was in no hurry. He had made friends with the Jepsons, two aisles away. The twins, Ben and Bob, were his age, the oldest brother, Arnold, hers but Sorka thought Arnold was a real mawk! Her mother kept telling her that there'd be girls her age on Pern whom she'd meet once she got to school.

'I need a friend now,' Sorka murmured to herself as she went on one of her long solitary walks about the ship. That was a rare privilege for a girl who had always had to be on guard against 'strangers' or 'pervs'. Even home on the farm in Clonmel, she hadn't been able to be out of sight of an adult, despite old Chip's protective canine presence. Sorka experienced an extra fillip of liberty being allowed to go where she liked on board, provided she kept out of the Engineering or Bridge territory, and didn't interfere with the crew. Which she wouldn't.

On her first long excursion, she had discovered the garden, with its great broad-leafed plants arching over the ceiling, their branches intertwining and making green caves. She liked best the marvellous aroma of moist earth and green things. Here she felt no inhibition about taking deep lungsful of air which left a clean, fresh taste at the back of her mouth. There was also a lot to see. Beneath the giant bushes were all sorts of herbs and smaller bushes with tags on them, soon to be transported and hopefully adapted to the new world. She didn't recognize most of the names, even when she could pronounce them, but she knew some of the herbs by their common names. Her mother had had a herb garden. Sorka knew which ones would leave their fragrances on her fingers and she daringly fingered the marjoram, then the tiny thyme leaves. Some plants were even in bloom, blues and pale yellows and pinks. There were hundreds of racks of shoots in little tubes of water – nutrient fluids, her dad had told her – sprouted only a few months back, to be ready for planting once they reached Pern.

She bent down to gently feel the surface of an unfamiliar hairy sort of silver-green leaf – she rather thought it had a nice smell – when she saw a pair of very blue eyes that no plant ever sprouted.

She swallowed, reminding herself that there were no pervs or strangers on the ship; she was safe. This could only be another passenger like herself, who was investigating the peaceful garden.

'Hello,' she said in a tone between surprise and cordiality.

The blue eyes blinked. 'Go 'way. You don't belong here,' a young male voice growled at her.

'Why not? This is open to anyone, so long as you don't damage the plants and you really shouldn't be crouched down in there like that.'

'Go 'way.' A grubby hand emphasized the order.

'I don't have to. Who're you?'

Her eyes now made sense of the shadows and the boy's resentful expression was clear. She hunkered down, looking in at him.

'What's your name?' she asked, for there was something oddly familiar about him.

'I doan' gotta tell nobody my name.'

'Well, excuse me, I'm sure,' she said in an affected tone and then realized. 'Hey, you're Irish. Like me.'

'I'm *not* like you.'

'Well, deny you're Irish.' When he didn't, because he couldn't, and they both knew it, she cocked her head at him, smiling agreeably. 'I can see why you'd hide in here. It's quiet and it smells so fresh. Almost like home. I don't like the ship either; I feel,' and here Sorka hugged herself, 'sort of cramped and squashed all the time.' She lengthened the words to make them express her feelings. 'I come from Clonmel. Ever been there?'

Sorka couldn't have known that she was responding to unspoken needs: the word 'empathy' was not yet a working part of her vocabulary.

'Sure.' The boy's tone was scornful but now he brushed a strand of long orangey bleached hair from his eyes and shifted his position so that he could keep his eyes on her.

'I'm Sorka Hanrahan.' She looked enquiringly at him.

'Sean Connell,' he admitted truculently after considerable delay.

'My dad's a vet. The best in Clonmel.'

Sean's expression cleared with approval. 'He works with horses?'

She nodded, 'With any sick animal. Did you have horses?'

'While we was still in Ballinasloe.' His expression clouded with resentful grief. 'We had good horses,' he added with defensive pride.

'Did you have your own pony?'

The boy's eyes blinked and he dropped his head.

'I miss my pony, too,' Sorka said compassionately. 'But I'm to get one on Pern and my dad said that they'd special ones in the Banks for you.' She wasn't at all sure of that but it seemed the proper thing to say.

'We'd better. We was promised. We can't get anywhere 'thout horses 'cause this place isn't to have hover-vans or nothing.'

'And no more *gardai*,' and Sorka grinned mischievously at him. She'd just figured out that he must be one of the travelling folk. Her father had mentioned there were some among the colonists. 'And no more farmers chasing you out of their fields, and no more move-on-in-twenty-four hours, or lousy halts, and no roads but the ones you make yourself and oh, just lots of things you really want, and none of the bad things.'

'Can't be all that good,' Sean remarked cynically.

'Say, aren't you supposed to "drop" today?'

Like a turtle, Sean drew back into the shadows.

On cue, the comunit in the garden erupted into sound. 'The boarding call has been issued for the morning drop. Passengers will assemble immediately in the loading bay on Deck 5.'

'Hey, I'll bet he means you.' She peered in, trying to see Sean's face. 'Boy, are you lucky, going so soon. Third day! We have to wait for yonks. What's the matter? Don't you *want* to go?' She got on to her hands and knees to peer in at him. Slowly she drew back for she had seen real fear often enough to recognize it. 'Gee, I'd trade places with you. I can't wait to get down. I mean, it's not that long a

70

trip. And it'll be no different from getting to the *Yoko* from Earth,' she went on, thinking to reassure him. 'That wasn't so bad, was it?'

She had been so excited, even knowing that she'd be asleep almost as soon as they got on board, that she'd been unaware of anything but the first pressure of take-off.

'We was shipped up asleep.' His words were no more than a terrified mutter.

'Gee, you missed the best part. Of course, half the adults,' she added condescendingly, 'were weeping about their last view of old Terra. I pretended that I was Spacer Yvonne Yves, and my brother, Brian, he's much younger than we are, but he made like he was Spacer Tracey Train.'

'Who're they?'

'C'mon, Sean. I know you all had vid-screens in your caravans. Didn't you ever see Space Venturers?'

'That's kid stuff.' He was openly scornful.

'Well, you're a Space Venturer right now and if it's only kid stuff, there's nothing to be afraid of, is there?'

'Who said I was afraid?' He twitched arms and legs in repudiation.

'Well, aren't you? Hiding away in the garden.'

'I just needed a decent breath of fresh air.' Suddenly he pushed himself out.

'When you've a planet full of fresh air below you, only hours away?' Sorka grinned at him: she knew silly excuses when she heard them. 'Just pretend you're an astronaut.'

The comunit came alive and she could hear the edge to the embarkation officer's voice. Desi Arthied hadn't had to remind any other passengers to assemble.

'The shuttles drop in precisely twenty minutes. Passengers scheduled for this drop who default go to the end of the list.'

'He's angry,' Sorka told Sean, and gave him a little push towards the door. 'You'd better git. Your parents'll skin you alive if you keep them from making their drop.'

71

'That's all you know,' he said in a savage tone and stomped out of the garden room.

'Scaredy cat,' she said softly, then sighed exaggeratedly. 'Well, he can't help it.'

Then she turned back to find the fragrant plant.

By the sixth day all essential personnel were on the surface. Seating was removed from all but one of the shuttles and set about the bonfire square until needed again. Now mountains of supplies were 'dropped', distributed and stored. Delicate instruments packed in shock-proof cocoons, sperm and the precious fertilized ova from Earth and First were brought down – Sallah was certain that Barr didn't take a deep breath throughout those 'drops'. By that evening, fertilized eggs had been implanted in those cows, goats and sheep which were fully recovered from their deepsleep. Small sturdy types had been brought, not themselves the best genotypes available on Earth but suitable as surrogate dams; the embryos were different again, specially adapted for the colony planets because of their special hardinesses and resistances. The resultant progeny would produce the necessary enzymes for Pern-grown materials, and would be provided with the internal bacteria needed to digest Pern-grown fodders which had much more boron than the usual Terran produce – and a good mixture of native weeds. If there were problems, Kitti Ping and her daughter, Wind Blossom, would use the Eridani techniques to alter the next generation appropriately. The projection was that at least some of the animals would be tailored to make the required enzymes in their own glands, instead of using symbiotic bacteria as their ancestors had on Earth.

Admiral Benden proudly remarked that, by the time the ships were completely evacuated, the first chicken eggs were likely to hatch on Pern. He went on to announce that the planet harboured egg-layers, too, for broken shells had been found above the high tide line on the beach where the harbour and the fish hatchery were being constructed. Zoologists were trying to figure out what sort of creature had laid the chicken-like eggs – hopefully the rather beautiful and unusual avians mentioned by the EEC team. As the analysis of the shell showed a high level of boron, the team put egg and its inhabitant on the dubious list of indigenous edibles. So far, the reptiloid creatures which were mentioned in the Survey Report had not been observed.

The shuttles made only two trips a day for the next four, since loading and unloading was time-consuming.

'I prefer a few passengers,' Barr remarked as the off-duty pilots were enjoying dinner in the now not-so-crowded messhall, 'as a leaven to crates and crates, big, little, medium. Or all those absolutely irreplaceable herbs and bushes. There's still plenty of people to go down.'

She gestured about her and Sallah noticed the redheaded family seated at the far left. Sallah waved, smiling brightly because the youngsters looked so glum.

'Gorgeous red hair, isn't it?' Sallah said wistfully.

'Too unusual,' Avril Bitra said in her derisive way.

'I dunno,' Drake remarked, staring at the party. 'Makes a nice change.'

'She's too young for you, Bonneau,' Avril said.

'I'm a patient man,' Drake countered, grinning because it wasn't often he got a rise out of the sultry beauty. 'I'll know where to find her when she grows up.' He appeared to consider the prospect. 'Of course, the boy is much too young for you, Avril. A full generation away.'

Avril gave him a long and disgusted look and, grabbing the wine carafe, stalked to the dispensers. Sallah exchanged glances with Barr for Avril was first off the next morning and the wind factors provided sufficient danger to be met without alcohol-blurred reactions. They both looked towards Nabol, her copilot, but he shrugged indifferently. Sallah hadn't hoped for much support from the man. No one had much influence on Avril these days.

'Hey, Avril, hold off more sauce,' Drake began, rising to his feet and intercepting her. 'You did promise me a re-match in gravity ball. The court'll be empty now.' His smile was challenging and, from where she sat, Sallah could see that his hand slid caressingly up Avril's arm. Avril's mouth assumed a less discontented line. 'We'd best use it while we may,' he added, smile deepening and, moving his arm up to her shoulders, he took the carafe from her hand and placed it on the nearest table as he guided Avril out of the messhall without a backward look.

'Wow! Charm has its uses,' Barr said.

'Shall we see if it's ball they're playing in the grav court?' Nabol suggested, an unsettling glitter in his eyes.

'There's ball games and ball games,' Sallah said with a diffident shrug to her shoulders. 'I've seen 'em all. Excuse me,' she added and strode over to the Hanrahans' table. She knew she'd left Barr stranded but the girl could leave, too, if Nabol made her uncomfortable. 'Hi there, when do you drop?' she asked, as she reached the Hanrahans.

'Tomorrow,' Red said with an answering grin of welcome, and pulled a chair over from the next table. 'Join us? I think we're on your ship.'

'We are?' Sorka became animated and beamed at Sallah.

'You've had a long wait,' Sallah remarked, sitting down.

'I'm vet,' Red replied, 'and Mairi's child care, so we aren't exactly essential personnel.'

'Perhaps not now,' Sallah replied with a wide grin that acknowledged the future importance of their specialities.

'Is it really as nice down there as it looks?' Sorka wanted to know.

'I can't say I've had much time to find out,' Sallah said with a rueful expression. 'We drop, unload and lift. But the air is like wine,' and she flared her nostrils in deprecation of

the recycled atmosphere of the ship. 'And a breeze, too.'
She laughed. 'Sometimes a bit stiff.' She pantomimed
fighting with the control yoke of the shuttle. Mairi looked
wistful and her husband eager. Sallah turned to the kids.
'And school's great. Outdoors! Teaching you all we know
about our new home.' The two children had groaned at
her first phrase and began to brighten considerably as she
went on. 'Sometimes the teachers are just a skip ahead of
the students.'

'They didn't have bonfires last night,' Brian said, disappointed.

'That's because they got light pylons up, but watch
tonight. You aren't the only one who missed 'em. I heard
they decided to have a bonfire square, and every night
someone new gets a chance to light it, if they've worked
very hard and earned the privilege.'

'Wow!' Brian was elated. 'Whaddya have to do to get
to light it?'

'You'll think of something, Brian,' his father assured
him.

'See you all bright and early?' Sallah rose, giving Sorka's
hair a ruffle. She was ready to turn in.

'Be there before you,' Red replied with a grin.

To Sallah's surprise, they were, for Mairi had insisted
on reassuring herself that their precious personal baggage
was safely stowed in the cargo hold. Mairi had worried
and worried about her things, precious family heirlooms,
irreplaceable items of great sentimental value, especially
the rosewood dower chest which had been in her family
for generations. It had been carefully unglued and took
up most of the weight allowed them but Mairi had insisted
that it had to accompany them to Pern. Indeed Sorka
couldn't recall her parents' bedroom without the dower
chest under the window. Sorka had had to reduce her
treasured collection of toy horses to three of the smallest
and her book tapes to ten. Brian's ship models had been
dismantled and he, too, fretted about finding the proper
glue.

That was his urgent question when Sallah and Barr greeted them.

'Glue?' Sallah blinked at the unexpectedness of the boy's query. 'They've dropped everything else; why on earth would they leave glue out?' She winked at Red who grinned. 'Otherwise our local experts are sure to be able to whomp something up. Pern seems to be well supplied. On board with you now, Clan Hanrahan, we're only a skip ahead of today's horde.'

So the family got their choice of seats and Sorka suggested that they take the last row so they'd be the first out. It was almost agonizing to have to wait until everyone else was strapped in and the drop begun. Excitement almost strangled Sorka. She was disappointed that the forward screen was malfunctioning because then she didn't know that the shuttle had actually left its bay. A display would have given her something to distract her from the shuttle's juddering and rattling. She looked anxiously at her parents, sitting beyond her, but they had their eyes closed. Brian looked as bug-eyed as she felt but she wouldn't give him the satisfaction of appearing scared. Then, suddenly, she remembered Sean Connell, hiding in the garden, and forced herself to think of Spacer Yvonne Yves. One shouldn't give advice one wouldn't follow under similar circumstances.

She was Spacer Yvonne, on her way to a mysterious shrouded planet, on a mission to discover what the cloud covered. Slowly, the more unpleasant weightfulness eased and she simply knew that they had to be almost landing. The retros pushed her back into her padded seat, nearly depriving her of breath and then the shuttle bumped lightly as its landing gear made contact.

'We've landed! We made it!' she cried.

'Don't sound so surprised, lovey!' her father said with a laugh and reached over to give her knee a pat.

'Can we eat when we get out?' Brian wanted to know in a petulant voice. Someone up front chuckled.

All sensation through the shuttle ceased and Sorka

heard the whoosh as the passenger hatch was cracked. Then the two pilots appeared at the top of the aisle, giving the order to disembark. A blast of sunlight and fresh air streamed into the spacecraft and Sorka felt her heart give an extra thump of gladness.

Laughing, her father flipped open her safety belt, urging her to move. She was both eager and anxious for her first sight of her new home. It wasn't as if she had any choice really . . .

'Go on, you little goose,' her father said, grinning as if he really did understand her hesitation, but sort of impatient with her, too, as she had the aisle seat.

'Hey, Sorka, you can leave now,' Sallah was calling.

Her legs were a bit wobbly as she stood. 'I'm heavy again,' she exclaimed, having enjoyed the half gravity of the *Yoko*. At the exit, she stopped, awed by her first glimpse of Pern, a vast panorama of the grassy plateau, with its knobs of funny bluey-looking bushes, and the greeny-blue sky.

'Don't block the exit, dear,' said a woman, standing on the ground by the ramp.

Sorka hastily obeyed, though how she made the ground with so much looking around to do, she never knew. The ground cover was so subtly different to grass on the farm. The bushes were more blue than green, with funny-shaped leaves, like put-together geometric shapes that she'd had as a pre-school toy.

'Look, daddy, clouds! Just like home!' she cried, excitedly pointing to the sky.

Her father laughed and, with an arm about her shoulders, moved her forward with him.

'Maybe they followed us, Sorka,' he said kindly, grinning broadly, and Sorka knew that he was just as excited about landing on Pern at last as she was.

Sorka threw her head back to the fresh breeze which rippled across the plateau. It smelled of marvellous things, new and exciting. She wanted to dance, free once more under a sky, without ceiling or walls to constrict her.

'Are you Hanrahan or Jepson?' the woman asked, a recorder in her hand.

'Hanrahan,' Red replied. 'Mairi, Peter, Sorka and Brian,' for they had exited and come to stand by him.

'Welcome to Pern,' she said smiling graciously before she made a tick on her sheet. Her name tag read 'Dr O. Bell'. 'You're House 14 on Asian Square,' and she waved with her right hand off to the side. 'Here's your map. All the important facilities are clearly marked. Now, if you'll just lend a hand to unload and clear the shuttle . . .' She handed him a sheet and gestured towards the float which was now backing up to the open cargo hatch and then moved on to the Jepsons who had emerged.

'We made it, Mairi love,' Red said, embracing his wife. Sorka was surprised to see tears in her parents' eyes. Brian had bounced over to talk to the twin Jepson boys but then her father called him back to help with the unloading.

There was more than just the personal luggage of the passengers. Cartons of stores still had to be checked off the supercargo's lists.

'Tell the dispatcher that more furnishings are required,' Dr Bell told Sallah once the shuttle's hold had been emptied. 'Or some people won't have beds tonight.'

'That's efficiency for you,' Sallah said, and waved a salute to the Hanrahans as she closed the hatch, preparing for the return flight. 'Soon there won't be any one above and precious little left of the ships but the hull.'

'I know,' Barr replied as they two began their take-off check. 'I half expect to find our bunks already gone. Or fall off what they humorously call cat walks.'

Sallah grinned as she made her notations. She had the glide down to perfection now, a saving of nearly 20 litres every journey. The wind was veering to stern, and she warned Barr to speed up her checklist.

'Want to take advantage of that tail wind. Saves fuel.'

'Good God, Sal, you're as bad as Fussy Fusi,' but Barr

78

completed her list with a flourish. 'What I want to know is why are we busting ass saving fuel? We can't go any place useful with what we'd be saving. And once the ships are gutted, there isn't any use for space shuttles, now is there?'

Sallah gave her a searching stare and then gave a droll chuckle. 'A very good point, my friend. A very good point. I think,' she added after a moment's thought, 'I'll check the tanks while Fussy's dropping.'

When she did, moving very carefully along single-plank walkways, she wasn't that much wiser. If they were saving so much, the level in the tanks should be higher. Fortunately Barr was enjoying a flirtation with one of the resource engineers and forgot her idle observation. Nor did Sallah call it to her mind but Sallah also took time during Kenjo's drop to do a bit of checking in the mainframe's banks.

Fuel consumption was at acceptable levels in both of *Yoko*'s remaining tanks. Sallah then computed in her average fuel consumption per trip, plus an estimate of Kenjo's, and came up with a total that should have given an extra 2000 litres of available fuel. She knocked off a percentage, based on consumption during her 'heavier' trips, when there were drift and wind factors that required a higher expenditure of fuel. Once again she came up with a deficit figure, slightly lower, but still higher than the amount available.

What good would it do anyone to hoard fuel? Avril? But Avril and Kenjo were not at all friendly. In fact, Avril had made snide remarks about Kenjo on several occasions, unacceptable ethnic-based slanders.

'Of course, if you wanted to put someone off the track . . .' Sallah murmured to herself.

Sallah did some further checking: the distance to the nearest system, interdicted a century before by the EEC team; to the nearest habitable system; the cruising range and speed of the Captain's gig; and came up with the answer that the *Mariposa* could, with the most careful management, make it to the uninhabitable system. And what good would that do anyone? Disgusted by the waste of the afternoon, Sallah went in search of Barr. They'd the evening run to make and this time they got to sleep planetside.

4

●

To Sorka's utter delight, school on Pern concentrated on adapting students to their new home. Two of the buildings set aside for school use were workshops, in which everyone was given safety instruction about common tools and those over fourteen were taught how to operate some of the less dangerous equipment in frequent use. Then all were taken out to a special plot, well fenced, and shown specimens of the plants to be avoided. Pictures of typical reactions to them were prominently displayed as additional warning. Mr Shwartz, the headmaster, got giggles of astonishment when he told the 'class' that every adult in the colony also underwent this indoctrination.

Felicia Grant, her face peeling and her hair cropped short anywhichway lectured the children on the botany so far catalogued: the varieties of fruit, leaf vegetables and tubers which were innocuous and could be eaten in moderation. One of the jobs for young colonists each afternoon would be to gather any they found to supplement transported foodstuffs. The teacher stressed moderation and went on to describe the symptoms of overindulgence in a red fruit and a delicious black berry.

Bill Duff took over the class, though he admitted that he didn't have as much to tell them as Felicia but gave the general rule of 'don't touch and call an adult'.

'They might not know either, so you can observe and learn together.'

When he started showing them slides of the variety of insectoids and herpetoids, some of the older girls acted ridiculous, until the jaundiced stares of the less squeamish stilled their affectations.

'Remember, girls,' Bill said, grinning, 'they may be more scared of you than you are of them. If that's possible.'

Bjorna Patrick and Hans Semling divided up the under 12s and took them in the main classroom while Rudi Shwartz brought the older ones outside. They would be assigned to work with adult teamleaders.

'During this settling in period,' he told the 12–16s, 'you will have a chance to work with a variety of specialists, learning what craft or profession you'd like to pursue within the context of the work force on Pern. We're going to revive an apprentice system here. It worked pretty well on old Earth, has been successful on First Centauri, and is particularly suitable to our pastoral colony. All of us will have to work hard to establish ourselves on Pern but diligence will be rewarded.'

'What with?' asked a boy at the back of the class. He sounded slightly contemptuous.

'A sense of achievement and,' Mr Shwartz raised his voice and grinned at the sceptic, 'grants of land or material when you reach your maturity and want to strike out for yourself. All of us have the same opportunities here on Pern.'

'My dad says the Charterers will still end up with all the good land,' a young male voice said from the anonymity of the group.

Surveying the group through slightly narrowed eyes, Rudolph Shwartz waited to answer until his audience began to move restlessly.

'The *Charter* permits them first choice, it is true. This is a large planet with millions of acres of arable land. Even Charterers have to prove the land they claim. There will be some left for your father, and you. Now ... how many of you already know how to manage the basic sled controls?'

Sorka had been sizing up her fellow students and reluctantly concluded that there were no girls her age. The clutch of teenaged girls had already formed a group which would exclude her, and the other girls were all much younger than she was. Resigned, Sorka then looked in vain for Sean Connell. Wasn't it just like a tinker to feck off school as fast as possible?

That initial morning session was concluded with instructions on how to apply to the Commissary for their needs, from the carefully rationed candy and treats of Earth to field boots or fresh clothing. Everyone, their headmaster insisted, had the right to certain luxury items. If they were available, they would be issued. He then gave a short lecture on moderation. They were dismissed to enjoy a lunch served from the communal kitchens set up near Bonfire Square and told to report back to the school at 1300 hours for their afternoon duties.

Sorka welcomed the fetch-and-carry tasks after nearly two weeks of inactivity on the ship. She was almost alone in her preference. The older girls particularly were appalled to be put to rough labour. Farmbred Sorka felt rather superior to these city lilies and worked so diligently in helping to clear stones from the fields that her team leader, Eba Dar, cautioned her to take it easy.

'Not that we don't appreciate your vigour, Sorka,' the woman said with a wry grin, 'but don't forget you were inactive for fifteeen years. Work those muscles in gently.'

'Well, I've got some,' Sorka replied, with a scornful glance at a team of girls who scowled sullenly as they held plastic poles in place for fencing.

'They'll get used to Pern. They're here to stay,' Eba Dar said. She gave a sort of snort. 'We all are.'

Sorka sighed with such contentment that Eba Dar reached out to ruffle her hair.

'Ever consider a career as an agronomist?' Eba asked wistfully.

'Naw, I'm going to be a vet like my dad,' Sorka replied cheerfully.

Eba Dar was the first of many adults who would have liked to have Sorka Hanrahan as an apprentice. She was only a few days on the rock-picking detail before she and five others were sent down to the harbour and the hatchery.

'You've proved you can work without supervision, Sorka,' Headmaster Shwartz told her approvingly. 'Just the attitude we need to get Pern going.'

After a morning being shown what marine specimens had already been catalogued, she and the other five young-sters were split into two groups and sent in opposite directions along the immense sweep of the natural harbour to gather any new types of seaweeds and grasses, or anything new which might have been trapped in tidal pools after the storm the previous night. Sorka was de-lighted and went off happily with Jacob Chernoff who as the oldest, was appointed leader and given a bleeper for emergencies.

'This sand ought to be different, not just the same,' complained the third member of her group as they set off.

'Chung, oceans grind stones on Pern the same way they do it on Earth and the result just has to be the same . . . sand,' Jacob said amiably. 'Where were you from?'

'Kansas,' Chung replied. 'Betcha don't know where that is,' and his mocking glance fell on Sorka.

'Bounded by the old States of Missouri and the Missis-sippi River on the east, Oklahoma on the south, Colorado in the west, and Nebraska on the north,' Sorka replied with studied diffidence even if she had taken up the dare in Chung's eyes. 'And you don't have sand out there. You got dirt!'

'Say, you know your geography,' Jacob said to Sorka with a smile of admiration. 'Where are you from?'

'Colorado?' Chung demanded sarcastically.

'Ireland.'

'Oh, one of those European islands,' Chung said dismis-sively.

'Hey, do they have this one yet?' Sorka wanted to know, pointing to a large purplish branch of weed just ahead of them.

'Don't touch,' Jacob warned as they reached it. With tongs which had been provided, he lifted the weed for a closer examination. It had thick leaves, branching irregularly from a central stem.

'Looks like it grew from the sea bottom,' Sorka remarked, pointing to a clump of tendrils at the base that looked like roots to her.

'They didn't show us anything that big,' Chung said. So they decided to wrap it in a specimen bag and bring it back.

Until they rounded an outcropping of the rough grey stone that punctuated the long crescent beach, that was almost their only find that afternoon, though they sifted through piles of already identified sea vegetation. There they found trapped in a sizeable pool a variety of marine life, things that scurried on multiple legs, and a couple of purple bladder-like objects that Sorka was certain would be poisonous, and some finger-long, transparent almost-fish.

'How can they be almost-fish?' Chung demanded when Sorka voiced her opinion. 'They're in the water, aren't they, that makes them fish.'

'Not necessarily,' Jacob replied. 'And they don't really look like fish. They look like . . . well, I don't know what they look like,' he had to admit. The life form seemed to have layers of fins along its side, some of which were in constant motion. 'Hairy they look.'

'All I know is we didn't see anything like 'em in the tanks at the hatchery,' Chung said and, taking out a specimen bottle, lowered himself at the edge of the pool to catch one.

It proved not so easy to catch, though Jacob was able to get one of the bladders into a jar, and three of the many-legged species almost leaped into captivity. The finger-fish eluded both boys and Sorka's suggestions for capture were dismissed.

Bored, she went on down the beach, around a second pile of boulders, whereupon she found the massive head.

From her angle on the beach, that's what it resembled, a man's heavy-featured head, complete with brow ridges, a nose, lips and chin, though part of the chin was buried in the sand, and lashed by the waves. Sorka was delighted and awed, and stood in rapt admiration. One of the girls in her own Asian Square had fallen down a hole, which was but one of the many entrances to a series of caves to the south and west of Landing. They'd been officially named the Catherine Caves after their inadvertent discoverer.

In her home county of Tipperary, there'd been an old Norman keep on her father's farm in which Sorka and Brian had often played ladies and knights, imagining themselves back in medieval days. Recapturing history was one thing, but to make it, to be the very first person ever to set eyes on a mountain (there was an on-going, often violent and, as yet, unresolved controversy over what to name the plateau's old volcano), a lake or a cave. That was something magical in Sorka's estimation. Poor old Ireland had been so well used by the time she'd been born.

Sorka's Head? She murmured the title under her breath. No, people might think it was her head and she didn't look like that at all. It was only then she looked above the splendidly imposing cliff and saw the creature, seemingly suspended in the air. Sorka gasped in wonder, for in that moment, the sun caught and dazzled the creature into a golden statue. Abruptly it dove and swooped out of sight, behind the pate of the stone head.

No one had shown her anything that resembled this marvellous creature and Sorka was filled with excitement. She'd have something stupendous to report when she got back to the hatchery. She ran towards the vast head which began to lose its illusory resemblance. That no longer mattered to Sorka. She had discovered something far more important – a creature of Pern.

She had to scramble up a series of boulders to reach the summit. She paused just before she reached the top and peered over, hoping to catch a closer glimpse of the winged life form. And stood up in disappointment. There was nothing visible but naked rock, pitted here and there by faults and holes. She drew back hastily when the surf, beating against the cliff face, became a fountaining plume through one of the holes, showering her with cold seawater.

Disconsolate, she completed her climb on to the pate, keeping well away from the spume holes. The height gave her a splendid view of the crescent harbour. She could see Jacob and Chung sprawled by the tidal pool, and even distinguish some activity at the hatchery and the first of the fishing ships riding at anchor. She looked to the west and saw a magnificent vista of small beaches bounded by more outcropping of the type of rock she stood on. Ahead of her was nothing but ocean, though she knew that the northern continent was somewhere over the curve of the planet. She'd almost said 'Earth'.

She turned about, looking at the thick vegetation growing to the edge of the cliff. She was thirsty suddenly, and thought she saw the distinctive leaf of the red fruit tree. One would go down a treat right now. She'd cut a few to bring to the boys. They'd need a break.

Two things happened at once: she nearly stepped into a large hollow that was occupied by a number of palely mottled eggs and something dove at her, claws just missing her head.

Sorka dropped to the stone surface, peering anxiously about to see what had attacked her. It zoomed in on her again, talons extended, and she waited, as she had once with an angry bull, and rolled away at the last moment. A wave of anger and outrage swept over her, so intense that Sorka inadvertently called out.

Confused by such feelings but quite aware of her immediate danger, Sorka scrambled to her feet and ran, half-crouched, to the cliff-edge, ducking down, and hopefully out of sight of her attacker. Screams of rage and frustration split the air and lent speed to Sorka's descent.

She ducked instinctively as she heard a whoosh of air and evaded another attack, ducking under a rocky overhang. Flattening herself against the rock face, Sorka had an all too vivid look at her assailant, dominated by eyes, rippling with red and orange fire, and an impression of goldness, gleaming in the afternoon sun. Its body was gold and its almost translucent wings were a paler shade of gold against the greeny blue sky, the dark frames showing in the diaphanous wings.

The creature screamed again, this time in confusion and surprise and soared up, out of sight. Sorka wondered if it couldn't see her in the shadow under the ledge. She heard it calling again, the sound muted by, she hoped, distance and the noise of the waves.

Abruptly a wave broke over the rocks about her, soaking her thoroughly. Anxiously, she realized that the slight Pernese tide was bringing waves higher on the shoreline and she would be well advised to move. Soon.

Cautiously she looked about her, listening, but the creature's cries were still distant. A second wave added a certain urgency and Sorka began to edge down and towards the bluff. Her descent was more of a slither as the wet rocks made footing difficult. The last metre was an uncontrollable fall. Arms thrashing for balance, she measured her length on the beach. Sorka was still young enough to cry when she was hurt and she let out an anguished wail as she scraped hands, chin and knees in the bruising fall.

From overhead came such a replica of her sounds that she forgot her bruises and stared above her where the flying creature hovered.

'Are you making fun of me?' The notion produced a wave of irritation in Sorka as profound as if one of her peer group had taunted her. 'Well, are you?' Sorka demanded of the golden creature. Abruptly it disappeared. 'Wow!'

Sorka blinked, scanned the sky for the creature, amazed by the speed with which it had disappeared from sight.

'Wow! Faster than light. Or,' she added, aware of some of the odd creatures in the galaxy, 'one of those telemapathy things.'

Rising slowly to her feet, Sorka turned a complete circle, certain that the flyer had to be visible somewhere. It had taken off at probe speed. Then another wave crashed at her feet and she hastily stepped back. Not that she wasn't thoroughly soaked already, her hands and knees stinging from the salty water, and a long walk back to the hatchery ahead of her with really nothing to show for her scrapes. She had subconsciously decided not to mention the flyer yet. She nearly jumped back into the sea when the bushes on the bluff above her parted and a blond head poked through.

'You fecking gobshite, you iggerant townie. You ske-ered her away!'

Sean Connell came slithering down the slope, his skin no longer white but red with sunburn, his blue eyes flashing. 'I've been lying doggo since dawn, hoping she'd walk into my snare and you, you blow it all on me. Fecking useless you are!'

'You'd snare her? That lovely creature? And keep her from her eggs?' Appalled, Sorka flung herself on Sean, her hands automatically flattening, fingers tight as she sliced at the boy in hard blows. 'Don't you dare! Don't you dare harm her!'

Sean ducked and managed to evade the full force of her blows.

'Not to harm! To tame!' he yelled, dodging with his hands up to deflect her jabs. 'We don't kill nuthing. I want her. For me!'

In an unexpected lunge, Sean tackled Sorka, sending her sprawling on to the sand where he fell on top of her. His longer and slightly heavier frame effectively pinned her helpless. Recovering her breath, she squirmed, trying to angle her legs to do what her hands were no longer free to.

'Don't be so stupid, girl. I wouldn't harm her. I've been

89

watching her for two days. An' I haven't told a soul about her.'

Sorka finally understood what he was saying, and lay quiescent, eyeing him suspiciously.

'You mean that?'

'Yup.'

'It'd still be wrong.' Sorka heaved against him experimentally but he pressed her harder into the sand. Stones were bruising her back. 'Taking her from her eggs.'

'I was gonna keep watch on 'em.'

'But you don't know if her hatchlings need her or not. You can't take her.'

'An' what were you going to do? There's a reward for such as her.' Sean regarded Sorka with equally angry suspicion. 'An' we need the money a lot more than you do.'

'There isn't any money on Pern! Who needs it!' Sorka regarded him with surprise and then sympathy for the dismay in his face. 'You can get anything you need at Stores. Didn't they explain that to you when you went to school?' Sean regarded her warily. 'Oh, you didn't even stay in school long enough to learn that, did you!' She gave a disgusted snort. 'Let me up. I've got stones digging holes in my back. You really are the absolute end.' She got to her feet and swatted at the worst of the sand on her clothes. But they were wet and the sand ground in. She faced Sean again. 'Did you at least wait to find out what was poisonous?' When he gave her a slow nod, she exhaled in relief. 'School isn't all bad. At least, not here.'

'No money?' Sean seemed unable to grasp this astonishing information.

'Not unless someone brought some old coins for keepsake. I doubt it: coins'd be heavy. Look,' and she caught his arm, hanging on to him when he started to twist away, 'you go to the Stores building at Landing. It's the biggest one. Tell them what you want, sign your name on a chit, and if they have it, they give it to you. That's called

90

requisitioning and everyone of us, kids included, are entitled to requisition things from Stores. Well, reasonable things.' She grinned, hoping to lighten his scowl. 'What are you doing way out here?' And Sorka felt a twinge of annoyance because if he and his family were out here, then she hadn't been the first person to see the headland and she couldn't ask to have it named after her.

'Like you told me on the spaceship,' and he grinned suddenly, a grin of amazing charm and mischief, 'once we got here, we could go where we please. Only we can't go really far yet until we got some horses.'

'Don't tell me you brought your wagons with you?' Sorka was appalled at the weight those would take up in a cargo hold.

'Wagons were brought for us,' he agreed. 'Only we've nothing to pull 'em with.' He waved towards the thick underbrush. 'But we are free again, and camping where we want until we get our animals.'

'That's going to take a couple of years, you know,' she said earnestly. Once again he nodded solemnly. 'But we've started. My dad's a vet and he said they'd woken up some horse and donkey mares, cows, goats and sheep and made 'em pregnant with our kinds of animals.'

'Woken up?' Sean's eyes protruded.

'Sure, who could muck livestock out for fifteen years? But it'll still take eleven months for the horses to be born, if that's what you're waiting for.'

'Horses, always. We were promised horses.' Sean sounded wistful as well as emphatic, and she experienced a kindliness towards him.

'You'll get them, too. My father said so,' she added mendaciously. 'He said that the ti—, the travelling folk were first on the list.'

'We'd better be.' Sean glowered darkly. 'Or there'll be trouble.'

'You see me before you make any trouble here. My da always got on well with your people in Clonmel. Believe me, you'll get your horses.' She could see that he was sceptical. 'Now, mind, I hear that you've harmed our creature and I'll see you don't, Sean Connell!' She held up a warning hand, the flat edge in an offensive position. 'Not that you could catch her. She's smart, that one. She understands what you're thinking.'

Sean eyed her, more scornful than sceptical.

'You know so much about her?'

'I'm good with animals.' She paused, grinned. 'Just like you are. See you 'round. And remember about requisitioning!'

With that parting word, she turned and started back down the beach, to catch up with Jacob and Chung. They were glad to see her, because she could help carry the samples back to the hatchery.

That evening brushwood bonfire was great fun, Sallah Telgar thought, watching children capering in and out of the shadows and the bright illumination the immense fire gave to the recently christened Bonfire Square. Half the adults had silly smiles on their faces for the antics of the kids while they sat at the trestle tables that had been erected. Tables built, Sallah noticed, out of former ship flooring. She sighed. Something in her resented this rape of the gallant colony ships. It seemed such a poor repayment for their service. And yet, silly to leave all that valuable, irreplaceable material in the refrigerator of space.

Then she'd heard the call for volunteers to make up a skeleton crew so that those who had not yet been down to the surface would have a weekend break on Pern. Sallah had hesitated until she saw the first three names of the volunteers: Avril, Bart and Nabhi. That trio did nothing that didn't further themselves. Now, why would *they* volunteer? She scrawled her name down immediately. She had more chance of finding out on the *Yoko* than fretting down here.

She was still curious about what Kenjo had been up to with his fuel economies. The *Eujisan* had drawn its quota regularly, yet her private calculations indicated a growing balance that *hadn't been burned up by the Eujisan* but was *not* in the *Yoko*'s fuel tanks. Very strange. Very soon there would be no place on the old *Yoko* to hide a thimbleful, much less the volume of this shortfall. Kenjo was not among the volunteers either. Nor was Drake Bonneau who had begun to spend spare time hanging around Sallah's quarters and she didn't think he was courting her housemate, Betty Musgrave.

All six shuttles went up to relieve the ships' crews, and bring down more bits and pieces. Sallah flew the *Eujisan* up with the skeleton crew for the *Yoko*. Avril had a smile on her face, smug enough to satisfy Sallah that the woman had personal plans for her weekend. Bart Lemos looked apprehensive and fidgeted while Nabhi continued to look supercilious and superior. They were up to something. Of the others, Sallah knew only Boris Pahlevi well, had a nodding acquaintance with Jack Brooks, Johnny Greene and Chaila Xavior.

When Sallah sprang the hatch on the *Yoko*'s landing deck, she was nearly bowled over by the jubilant men and women waiting to board the *Eujisan* for their first trip to the surface of their new home. Sallah had never seen a faster loading. Shortly all that would remain of the *Yoko* would be bare hull and the corridors leading to the Bridge. The mainframe computer banks were there and would remain intact. Not all of its vast memory had been dupli- cated for use on the surface for the bulk of the naval and military programs were protected, and irrelevant. Once passengers and crew left the three spaceships in their orbit, there'd be no need to know how to fight space battles.

The volunteers were given their orders by the crew members they were replacing and then the shore leave party merrily departed.

'Gawd, this place is eerie,' Boris Pahlevi whispered as he and Sallah made their way to the Bridge through the echoing corridors, now stripped of siding and down to the central plank of the flooring.

'Will the last man off roll the plank up behind him?'
Sallah asked facetiously.

She gave a shudder as she saw that the safety hatches
between sections had been removed. Lighting had been
reduced to three units per corridor. Sallah watched where
she put her feet.

'It's rape, though,' Boris remarked in a lugubrious tone,
gazing around him, 'gutting the old girl this way.'

'Ivan the Terrible,' Sallah said, the pilots' nickname for
the ship's Quartermaster in charge of the removal process.
'He's Alaskan, you know, and a real scrounger scrooge.'

'Tut-tut,' Boris said in his deep voice with a mock
stern expression, 'we're all Pernese now, Sal. But what's
Alaskan?'

'Fardles, you is the most iggerant bastard, Boris, even
for a second-generation Centauran. Alaska was a territory
on Earth, not far from its Arctic Circle, and cold. Alaskans
had a reputation for never throwing anything away. My
father never did. Must have been a genetic trait because
he was reared on First although my grandparents were
Alaskans.' Sallah sighed with nostalgia. 'Dad never threw
anything away. I had to chuck the whole nine yards before
we shipped out. Eighteen years of accumulated . . . well,
it wasn't junk because I got good prices on practically
everything in the mountain but it was some chore. Hercules and the Augean stables were clean in comparison.'

'Hercules?'

'Never mind,' Sallah said, wondering if Boris were
teasing her by pretending ignorance of old Earth legends
and peoples. Some people had wanted to throw everything
out, literature, legend, language, all the things that had
made people so interestingly different from each other.
But wiser, tolerant heads had prevailed and General
Cherry Duff was the official historian and colony librarian.
She had insisted that all ethnic written and visual cultures
had been recorded to be taken to Pern. What wasn't valid
in the new context would eventually fall into disuse as
new traditions were established.

'You never know,' Cherry Duff frequently admonished, 'when old information becomes new, viable, and valuable. We keep the whole *schmeer*!' The valiant lady defender of Cygnus III, now in her eleventh decade, with great-grandchildren making the trip with her on the *Buenos Aires*, affected idiomatic speech to make her points memorable. 'Takes up no space at all on the chips we've got.'

Sallah and Boris had reached Bridge territory now and found this reassuringly intact. Even the danger doors were still in place. Boris took the command chair and asked Sallah to confirm the stability of their orbit. He was an engineer who dabbled in computer programming and, as weekend Duty Officer, would probably spend all his time on the mainframe. He was certainly competent to detect and deal with any untoward deviation from orbit. He had welcomed the respite from outdoor work as he had forgotten to protect a fair skin against sunburn while he was helping to erect temporary power pylons from the hydro-electric unit. Boris was annoyed with himself for ignoring a simple precaution when everyone was shucking shirts to get planet-brown.

'Program's been left up,' she told him, sliding into the chair at the navigator's position, 'and the *Yoko*'s smack dab on orbit.'

'The duty officer really should have remained here until I officially took over,' Boris muttered and then exhaled. 'But I suppose Esther was afraid that they'd leave without her. No harm done at any rate.'

Boris began calling in the other manned stations, confirming the duty personnel from the roster he had been given. Avril Bitra and Bart Lemos were assigned to Life Support and Nabhi Nabol in Supply. While Boris was involved in rollcall, Sallah began some discreet checking of her own from the big terminal. She initiated a program to discover who else was accessing the mainframe. This sort of internal check was a function of the Bridge terminal, and not available on any of the others, except the one which had once been in the Admiral's suite. By the time Sallah left the *Yoko*, she'd know who had asked for what, if not why.

'D'you know if they've got all the library tapes down below yet?' Boris asked, relaxing in the command chair once the call had been completed and logged in.

'I think General Duff said they are but why not get your own copies while there's tape left?'

'Well, I'll just do a few for private consumption. After all, my hide has been flayed to produce power to run 'em.'

Sallah laughed, but kindly, for Boris' face was raw with sunburn and he wore the loosest possible clothing. She regarded him casually until he became absorbed in a perusal of the Library.

Avril was asking for figures on the remaining fuel in the tanks of all three colony ships. Nabol was inquiring about machine parts and replacement units. Nabol was a mechanic but the parts he was querying had already been landed. He was accessing their exact locations in Stores. So he wouldn't have to ask to get them, Sallah decided. More worrying were Avril's programs for she was the only fully qualified and experienced astrogator. Sallah did a few calculations of her own, based on the use of the captain's gig, a very frail bark to take into the Void on a long interstellar trip. The nearest inhabited star system was barely within range of the available fuel. That is, with careful piloting and no major corrections en route. And if present fuel use did not exceed the estimates. Where were the litres and litres which Kenjo had scrounged?

Both Sallah and Boris had a lot of time to kill on that twelve-hour watch. Then Avril requested the co-ordinates for the nearest planet capable of sustaining humanoids. Two had EEC reports which indicated sentient life developing. These were distant but within the range of the gig. Just. Sallah could not quite see why Avril would be at all interested in these planets, even if they were within reach of the *Mariposa*. She had never seemed, to Sallah, to be the colonial type. Granted Avril could calculate her way there, but it would be a long harrowing trip even at the maximum speed the gig could achieve. Then Sallah remembered that the gig had two deep-sleep tanks: a last resort and not one she'd undertake. She'd prefer to have someone awake and checking the dials if she were in deep sleep. The method wasn't as foolproof as all that. Only two tanks? Who was the lucky one to go with Avril? If escape from Pern was what she planned. And why escape from Pern if you'd just got here? Sallah wondered, mystified. A whole new sparkling world and Avril wasn't going to wait until she'd given it a chance? Or was she?

Sallah continued her surveillance throughout the three-day stint and took hard copy before she erased the file. By the time she boarded the shuttle to return 'home', she understood why the crews had needed shore leave. The poor old nearly gutted *Yoko* was a depressing place. The two smaller ships, *Buenos Aires* and *Bahrain*, would be claustrophobic. But the stripping was nearly complete and soon the three colony ships would be abandoned to their lonely orbit, visible at dawn and dusk as three points of light reflecting Rukbat's rays.

5

●

Despite her parents' tacit dislike of her association with
Sean Connell, Sorka found many reasons to continue
it, once he had relaxed his natural suspicions of her.
Curiously enough, Sorka also noticed that his family was
no keener on his friendship with her than her own. That
added a certain fillip.

They were bound together by their fascination with
their creature and her clutch of eggs. Sorka was watching
the nest with Sean, as much to be sure he didn't succeed
in his efforts to snare her as to be present when the eggs
hatched.

That morning – a rest day – Sorka had come prepared
for a long vigil with sandwiches in her pack. Enough to
share with Sean. They had hidden, bellies down in the
underbrush that bordered the headland rock where they
could keep the nest in sight. The little gold animal sunned
herself on the sea-side: they could see her eyes glittering
as she maintained her vigil.

'Just like a lizard,' Sean murmured in her ear, his breath
tickling it.

'Not at all,' Sorka protested, recalling illustrations in a
book of fairy tales. 'More like a little dragon. A dragonet.'
She added that almost aggressively because she didn't
think that 'lizard' was at all appropriate for such a
gorgeous being.

She carefully waved away another one of the many-
legged bugs that was urgently trundling its three-sectioned
self through the underbrush. Felicia Grant had called them

a form of millipede and was happy to see them. She had explained their reproductive cycle to the class: the 'adult' produced young which remained attached to the 'parent' until it reached the same size, whereupon it was 'dropped' off. Two maturing offspring were often in tow.

Sean watched its progress, idly building a dam of leaves to turn the bug away from him. 'Snakes eat a lot of these, and wherries eat snakes.'

'Wherries also eat wherries,' Sorka said in a disgusted tone of voice, recalling scavengers at work.

A subtle crooning alerted them as they sprawled, half-drowsing in the midday heat. The little golden 'dragonet' spread her wings.

'Protecting them,' Sorka said.

'Nope. Welcoming them.'

Sean had a habit of taking exactly the opposite line in any discussions they had. Sorka was used to it now, expected it.

'It could be both,' she suggested tolerantly.

Sean only snorted. 'I'll bet that trundle-bug was running from snakes.'

Sorka suppressed a shudder. She couldn't let Sean see how much she detested the slithery things.

'You're right. She's welcoming them.' Sorka was also willing to compromise with Sean. 'She's singing!'

Sean tilted his head and smiled, just a little, at the sound which was growing more lyrical. The little creature tilted her head so that they could see her throat vibrating.

Suddenly, the air about the rock was busy with dragonets. Sean grasped Sorka's arm, as much in surprise as to command her silence. Open-mouthed in astonishment, Sorka couldn't have uttered a sound, too delighted with the assembly to do more than stare. Blue, brown, and bronze dragonets hovered in the air, blending their voices with the little gold's.

'There must be hundreds of the dragonets, Sean.' Indeed, the way they were wheeling and darting, the air did seem overladen with them.

'Only twelve lizards,' Sean replied, impervious. 'No, sixteen.'

'Dragonets,' Sorka said firmly, defending her choice.

Sean ignored her interruption. 'I wonder why.'

'Look!' She pointed to a new flight that appeared suddenly, trailing large branches of dripping seaweeds. More arrived, each with something wiggling in its mouth, the burden deposited on the seaweeds which now made an uneven circle about the nest. 'Like a dam,' Sorka murmured wonderingly. More avians, or perhaps the same ones on a return trip, brought trundle-bugs and sandworms which flopped or hid in the weeds.

Then, as they saw the first of the eggs crack and a little wet head poked through, Sorka and Sean clung to each other in order to restrain their excitement. Pausing in their harvesting, the airborne creatures warbled an intricate pattern of sound.

'See, it is welcome!' Sean knew he'd been right all along.

'No! Protection!' Sorka pointed to the blunt snouts of two huge mottled snakes at the far side of the underbrush.

The intruders were spotted by the flyers and half a dozen dove at the protruding heads. Four of the dragonets sustained the attack right into the vegetation and there was considerable agitation of branches until the attackers emerged, chittering loudly. In that brief interval, four more eggs had cracked open. The adult avians were a living chain of supply as the first arrival shed its shell and staggered about, keening woefully. Its dam herded it, with wing motion and encouraging chirps, towards a nearby dragonet which held a flopping fishling for the hatchling to devour.

A bolder snake, emerging from the sand where it had hidden itself, attempted a rush up the rockface towards another hatchling. It braced its middle limbs as it raised its head, turtle-like mouth agape, to grab its prey. Instantly the snake was attacked by the airborne dragonets. With a good sense of preservation, the hatchling lurched over the dam-like ramparts of seaweed, towards the bush under which Sorka and Sean hid.

'Go away,' Sean muttered between clenched teeth. He waved his hand at the creeling juvenile, shooing it away from them. He had no wish to be attacked by its adult kin.

'It's starving, Sean,' Sorka said, fumbling for a packet of sandwiches. 'Can't you *feel* the hunger in it?'

'Don't you dare mother it!' he muttered, though he, too, responded to the little thing's craving. But he'd seen the flyers rend fish with their sharp talons. He'd prefer to keep them away from him.

Before he could stop her, Sorka tossed a corner of her sandwich out on to the rock. It landed right in front of the weaving, crying hatchling who pounced and seemed to inhale the bit. Its cry became urgently demanding and it hobbled more purposefully towards the source. Two more of the little creatures raised their heads and turned, with interest, in that direction, despite their dam's effort to shoo them to the adults holding out succulent marine life.

'Now you've done it,' Sean groaned.

'But it's hungry.' Sorka broke off more bits and lobbed them at the three hatchlings.

The other two scurried to secure a share of this bounty. To Sean's dismay, Sorka had crawled out of their hiding place and was offering the foremost hatchling a piece directly from her fingers. Sean made a grab for her but missed, bruising his chin on the rock.

Sorka's creature took the offered piece and then climbed into her hand, snuffling piteously.

'Oh, Sean, it's a perfect darling. And it can't be a lizard. It's warm and feels soft. Oh, do take a sandwich and feed the others. They're starving of the hunger.'

Sean spared a glance at the dam and realized with intense relief that she was far more concerned about getting the others fed than coming after the three renegades. His fascination with the creatures overcame caution. He grabbed a sandwich, and kneeling beside Sorka, coaxed the nearer brown one to him. The second brown, hearing the change in its sibling's cries, spread its wet wings and, with a screech, joined it in a frantic dive. Sorka was right, too: the critters had pliant skins and were warm to the touch. Not at all lizard-like to touch.

In short order, the sandwiches had been reduced to bulges in lizard bellies, and Sorka and Sean had unwittingly made lifelong friends. They had been so preoccupied with their three that they had failed to note the absence of the others, the disappearance of the guardians and the golden dam. Only the empty shards of discarded eggs in a hollow of the rock bore witness to the recent event.

'We can't just leave them here. Their mother's gone,' Sorka said, surprised by the abandonment of dragonet kin.

'I wasn't going to leave mine any road,' Sean said, slightly derisive of her quandary. 'I'm keeping 'em. I'll keep yours, too, if you don't want to bring it back to Landing. Your mother won't let you have a wild thing.'

'This one's not wild,' Sorka replied, taking offence. With her forefinger, she stroked the back of the tiny bronze lizard curled in the crook of her arm. It stirred and snuggled closer, exhaling on something remarkably like a purr. 'My mother's great with babies. She used to save lambs that even my father thought might die.'

Sean was pacified. He had put the browns in his shirt, one on either side, and tightened the leather belt he had dared requisition. The ease with which he had accomplished this at the Stores building had encouraged him to trust Sorka. It had also proved to his father that the 'others' were fairly distributing the wealth of *matériel* carried here in the spaceships. Two days after getting his belt, Sean began to see proper new pots replacing discarded tins over the campfire, and his mother and three sisters were wearing new shirts and shoes.

The brown dragonets felt warm against his skin, and a bit prickly where their tiny spikes pressed but he was more than pleased with his success. They only had three toes, the front one folded against the back two. Everyone in his father's camp had been trying to find lizard – well, dragonets' – nests along the coast. And snake holes. The lizards for fun, the snakes for safety. The scavenging reptiles were dangerous, for his family camped in rough shelters of woven branches and broad leaf fronds. Reptiles ate their way into the shelters, had bitten sleeping children in their blankets. Nothing was safe from their predatory habits. And they were not good eating.

His father had caught, skinned – the skin at least made fine hatbands and trims – and grilled several. He'd sampled a tiny bite of each variety and instantly had to wash his mouth out. The snake flesh had stung and caused his mouth to swell. So the order had gone to everyone in the camp: snare and kill the vermin. Of course, as soon as they had terriers or ferrets to go down the holes they could make short work of the menace. Porrig Connell had had each of his five families put in for a dog: he'd been upset because the gobshites seemed not to understand how urgent it was for his people to have dogs: they weren't pets; they were necessary adjuncts of his folk's life style. It was proving the same here as it was on Earth: the Connells were the last to get anything useful and the first to be given the back of the hand.

'Your dad'll be pleased,' Sorka said, expansive in her own pleasure, 'won't he, Sean, with two. Bet they'll be better even than dogs at going after snakes. Look at the way they attacked the mottleds.'

Sean gave a snort. 'Only because the hatchlings were being attacked.'

'I doubt it was just that,' Sorka said. 'I could almost feel the way they hated the snakes.' She wanted to believe that the flying lizards were unusual in ability and scope. Just as she had always believed that their marmalade tom, Duke, was the best hunter in the valley, and old Chip the best cattle dog in Tipperary. Doubt suddenly assailed her. 'But maybe we should leave them here for their dam?'

Sean grimaced and frowned. 'She was shooing the others off to the sea fast enough.'

Of one mind, they rose and, walking carefully so as not to disturb their sleeping burdens, reached the summit of the headland.

'Oh, look!' cried Sorka, pointing wildly just as something pulled the tattered body of a hatchling under the water. 'Oh oh oh.' Her stance, hand to mouth, and her lament were ancient attitudes. Sean watched impassively. Sorka turned away, clenching her fists. 'She's not a very good mother after all.'

'Only the best survive,' Sean said, more attuned to that age-old law. 'Our three are safe. They were smart enough to come to us!' Then he turned, peering at her through narrowed eyes, cocking his head at her. 'Will yours be *safe* at Landing? They've been after us to bring 'em specimens, you know. 'Cause my dad's special at trapping and snaring.'

Sorka hugged her sleeping charge closer to her body. 'My father wouldn't let anything happen to this lad. I know he wouldn't.'

'Yeah,' and Sean was cynical, 'but he's not head of his group, is he? He has to obey orders, doesn't he?'

'They just want to *look* at life forms. They don't want to cut 'em up or anything.'

Sean was unconvinced but, of one accord, the two children moved away from the sea and made their way through the undergrowth to the edge of the plateau.

'See ya tomorra?' Sean asked, suddenly loathe to give up these meetings now that their mutual vigil was accomplished.

'Well, tomorrow's a workday, but I'll see you in the evening?' Sorka didn't even pause a moment to think about her reply. She was no longer hampered by the stern tenets of Earth restrictions on her comings and goings. She was beginning to accept her safety on Pern as easily as she accepted her responsibility to work for her future here. Sean was also part of that sense of personal safety, despite his innate distrust of all but his own people. Even if Sean was unaware of it, a special link had been forged between Sean and herself after their momentous experience on the rock Head.

'Are you sure these creatures will hunt the snake?' was Porrig Connell's query as he examined one of Sean's sleeping acquisitions. It didn't so much as twitch as he extended one of the limp wings.

'If they're hungry,' Sean replied, holding his breath lest his father inadvertently hurt it.

Porrig snorted. 'We'll see. At least it's a creature of this place. Anything's better than being eaten alive. One of the blue mottled ones took a huge chunk out of Sinead's babee last night.'

'Sorka says the snakes can't get in their house: plastic keeps 'em out.'

Porrig gave another of his sceptical grunts, then nodded towards the sleeping hatchlings. 'Watch 'em now. They're your problem.'

At Residence 14 in Asian Square there was considerably more enthusiasm about Sorka's acquisition. Mairi despatched Brian to bring his father from the veterinary shed. Then she made a little nest in one of the baskets she had been weaving from the tough Pernese reeds, lining it with dried plant fibre, so that Sorka could have the use of her arm again.

Breathless, Mairi tenderly transferred the creature where it immediately curled itself into a ball and, with a tremendous sigh that inflated its torso to the size of its engorged belly, it fell deeper into sleep.

'It's not really a lizard, is it?' she said, softly stroking the warm skin. 'It feels like good suede. Lizards are dry and hard to the touch. And it's smiling. See?'

Obediently Sorka peered down and smiled in response. 'You should have seen it wolf down the sandwiches.'

'You mean, you've had no lunch?' Mairi was aghast and immediately bustled about to remedy that situation.

105

Though the communal kitchens catered for most of the 6000 regular inhabitants of Landing, more and more of the family units were beginning to cook for themselves for all but the evening meal. The Hanrahans' home was typical of the accommodation for families: one medium-sized bedroom, two small, a larger room for general purposes, and a sanitary unit; all the furnishings but the treasured rosewood dower chest were salvaged from the colony ships or made by Red in his infrequent spare time. At one end of the largest room was a food preparation unit, compact but adequate. Mairi prided herself on her culinary skills and was enjoying a chance to experiment with new foods.

Sorka was halfway through her third sandwich when Red Hanrahan arrived with zoologist Pol Nietro and Bay Harkenon who was the micro-biologist of Red's team.

'Don't wake the little thing,' Mairi instantly cautioned them.

Almost reverently the three peered at the sleeping lizard. Red Hanrahan let the specialists monopolize it while he gave his daughter a hug and a kiss, ruffling her hair with affectionate pride.

'Who's the clever girl!'

He sat down at the table, stretching his long legs underneath, sliding his hands into his pockets as he watched the two tut-tutting over a genuine Pernese native.

'A most amazing specimen,' Pol remarked to Bay as they straightened.

'So like a lizard,' she replied, smiling with wonder at Sorka. 'Will you please tell us exactly how you enticed the creature to you? Dr Wilcox's efforts have all been futile.'

Sorka hesitated only briefly, seeing her father's reassuring nod, before telling them all she knew about the lizards, from her first sight of the little gold beast guarding her eggs, to the point where she had coaxed the bronze one to eat from her hand. She did not, however, mention Sean Connell though she knew from the glances her parents exchanged that they surmised that he had been with her.

'Were you the only lucky one?' her father asked her in a low voice and a sly smile when the two biologists were engrossed in photographing the sleeping beast.

'Sean took two brown ones home. They have an awful time with snakes in their camp.'

'There're homes waiting for them on Canadian Square,' her father reminded her. 'And they'd have the place to themselves.'

All the ethnic nomads in the colony's complement had been duly allotted living quarters, thoughtfully set to the edge of Landing, where they might not feel so enclosed. The Tuaregs and the Romanies had remained in Canadian Square for two nights before melting into the unexplored lands beyond the settlement. Sean had never said when his family had decamped. Sorka shrugged.

Then Pol and Bay began a second round of questions, to clarify her account.

'Now, Sorka, we'd like to borrow,' and Bay Harkenon emphasized the verb, 'your new acquisition for a few hours. I assure you we won't harm a . . . well,' she added, 'a patch of its hide. There's a lot we can determine about it simply from observation and a judicious bit of hands-on examination.'

Sorka looked anxiously at her parents. She'd known that this was likely to happen the moment she brought it home but she also didn't want to relinquish it.

'Why don't we let it get used to Sorka first?' Red said easily, one hand resting lightly on his daughter's clenched fists. 'Sorka's very good with animals: they seem to trust her. And I think it's far more important right now to reassure this bitty fellow than find out what makes it tick.' Sorka remembered to breathe and let her body relax. She knew she could count on her father. 'We wouldn't want to scare it away. It only hatched this morning.'

'Zeal motivates me,' Bay Harkenon said with a rueful smile. 'But I know you're right, Red. We'll just leave it in

107

Sorka's capable care.' The woman gathered herself to rise when her associate cleared his throat.

'But if Sorka would keep track of how much it eats, how often, what it prefers . . .' Pol began.

'Besides bread and sandwich spread,' Mairi said with a laugh.

'That would improve our understanding.' Pol had a charming grin which made him appear less grey and frowsty. 'And you say that all you had to do was entice it with food?'

Sorka had a sudden mental image of the rather stooped and unathletic Pol Nietro lurking in bushes with a basket of goodies, luring lizards to him.

'I think it had something to do with its being so dreadfully hungry after it hatched,' Sorka replied thoughtfully. 'I mean, I've had sandwiches in my pockets every morning this week on the beach and the dam never came near me for food.'

'Hmmm. A good point. The newly hatched are voracious.' Pol continued to mumble to himself, mentally correlating this information.

'And the adults actually held food for the hatchlings? Fish and insects? Hmm. Interesting! Hmm. Sort of an imprinting ritual perhaps? The juveniles could fly as soon as the wings dried? Hmmm. Yes. Fascinating. The sea would be the nearest source of food,' Bay murmured. She now gathered up her notes and, after thanking Sorka and her parents, the two specialists left the house.

'I'd best go back now myself, loves,' Red said. 'Good work, Sorka. Just shows what old Irish knowhow can achieve.'

'Peter Oliver Plunkett Hanrahan,' his wife immediately chided him. 'Start thinking Pernese. Pernese. Pernese.' With each repetition she raised her voice in mock emphasis.

'Pernese, not Irish. We're Pernese,' Red obediently chanted and, grinning unrepentantly, did a dance step out of the house to the tempo of 'Pernese', 'Pernese'.

That night, to Sorka's intense and embarrassed surprise and to the total disgust of her envious brother, she was called upon to light the evening bonfire. When Pol Nietro announced why, there were cheers and vigorous applause. To Sorka's astonishment Admiral Benden and Governor Boll, who made a point of attending that little evening ceremony, were shouting and clapping like everyone else.

'It wasn't just me,' Sorka said in a loud clear voice as she was formally presented with the torch by Theo Force, acting mayor of Landing. 'Sean Connell got two brown lizards only he isn't here tonight. But you should know that he found the nest first and both of us watched it.'

She knew that Sean Connell wouldn't care if he was given due credit or not, but she did. With that thought, she plunged the burning brand into the heart of the bonfire. She jumped back quickly for the dry material had caught and flared brightly.

'Well done, Sorka,' her father said, lightly resting his hands on her shoulders, 'well done!'

Sorka, and Sean, remained the only proud owners of the pretty lizards for nearly a full week. Not for lack of trying by other hopeful residents of the new world. Indeed, there was an evening rush to the beaches and headlands. Not soon enough to prevent certain nests being plundered by natural predators. But soon enough for other nests to be staked and vigilantly guarded. Her name for the creatures – dragonets – was popular enough to be used instead of the scientific description under which Pol wanted to classify them. Guided by the routine which Sorka had accurately reported, several more of the little creatures were acquired.

The acquisition, as Sorka soon discovered, had two sides. Her little dragonet, whom she nostalgically named Duke after her old marmalade tomcat, long dust in Tipperary, was voracious. It ate anything at three-hour intervals, the first night disturbing the entire Square with its hungry creeling. Between feedings, it slept. When Sorka noticed that its skin was cracking, Persis St John, one of the pediatricians, Kwan Marceau of biology and her father prescribed a salve, prudently made of local fish oils, which solved that problem. Persis was so pleased with the result that she had Pei Pei Ting, the pharmacist, make up more as an ointment for dry skin in general. Pei Pei scented it with a drop of lavender oil intended for human use, hoping that her supply of the oil could be renewed if lavender plants adapted. Pharmacy, she believed, often depended on natural impurities.

'Duke is growing and his skin is stretching,' was the diagnosis.

The male designation was arbitrary since no one had been able to examine the creature closely enough to discover its sex, or if it had any. The golden dragonets had demonstrated a generally more feminine role in egg laying, though one of the biologists qualified that by reminding people that the males of some species on Earth were the egg tenders. Although, on Earth, females were generally larger, they could expect the alien species to differ. Kwan Marceau had quickly corrected himself to 'native', drolly reminding everyone that humans were the alien species on Pern.

The dead skin flakes were assiduously collected for analysis. The eager zoologists had not been able to X-ray Duke for he seemed to know the moment someone had designs on him. On the second day of his advent, the zoologists had attempted to place him under the Scope, Sorka waiting nervously in the next room.

'My word!' 'What?'

Sorka heard the startled exclamations from Pol and Bay at the same moment Duke reappeared above Sorka's head, considerably agitated. Dropping to her shoulder with cries of relief and anger, he wrapped his tail firmly about her neck and hooked his talons into her hair, scolding furiously, his many-faceted eyes rippling with angry reds and oranges.

The door behind Sorka slid open in a violent gesture as

110

Pol and Bay started into the room, their eyes wide with amazement.

'He just appeared,' she told the two scientists.

Recovering their composure, the two exchanged glances. Pol's broad face became wreathed in a smile and Bay looked remarkably pleased about something.

'So the Amigs do *not* have a monopoly on telekinetic abilities,' she said and her smile was smug. 'I always maintained, Pol, that they could not be unique in the galaxy. However, there's no capital to be made on knowing that here, and now.'

'How did he do that?' Sorka asked, not quite certain as she remembered other instances of perplexingly rapid departures.

'Duke must have been frightened by the Scope: he is rather small and it does look menacing,' Bay said understandingly. 'So he teleported himself away. Fortunately back to you whom he considers his protector. The Amigs use teleportation when threatened. A very useful capability.'

'I wonder if we can discover how the little creatures *do* it?' Pol mused, more to himself than to Bay or Sorka.

'We could try the Eridani equations,' Bay suggested.

Pol looked at Duke, his eyes still red with anger, but he had folded his wings to his back and clung tenaciously to Sorka.

'To try them, we need to know more about this chap and his species. Perhaps if you held him, Sorka?'

Even with Sorka's gentle reassurance, he would not permit himself to be placed under the Scope. After half an hour, Pol and Bay reluctantly allowed them to leave and Sorka took her still outraged lizard to his birthplace, reassuring him every step of the way.

Sean was there, stretched out in the shade cast by the bushes, his two browns curled up against his neck. They heard Sorka coming and were peering up at her, their eyes whirling a mild bluey-green. Duke chirped a greeting to which they replied in kind.

'I was just getting some sleep,' Sean muttered petulantly,

not so much as opening his eyes to see who had arrived. 'M'da made me bunk in with the babees to see if these fellers would scare off the snakes.'

'Well, did they?' Sorka asked when he seemed to be falling asleep again.

'Yup.' Sean yawned hugely, idly swatted at an insect which one of the browns immediately snapped out of the air and swallowed.

'They do eat anything. Omnivorous, Dr Marceau called them,' Sorka said admiringly as she sat down on the rock beside Sean. 'And they can go between places when they're scared. Dr Nietro tried to scope Duke here and made me leave the room. The next thing I knew Duke was clinging to me like he'd never let go. They said he can teleport. He uses telekinesis.' She got the words out without stumbling over them.

Sean opened one eye and cocked his head to stare up at her. 'What does that mean?'

'He can project himself out of danger instantly.'

Sean was not too impressed by this explanation and gave a huge yawn. 'Yeah? We've both seen them do their disappearing act. And they don't do it always because of danger.' He yawned again. 'You were smart to take only one. If one wasn't eating, the other was. What with that and guarding the babees, I'm fair knackered.' He closed his eye again, settled his hands across his chest and went back to sleep.

'I shall play gold then and guard you, lest a big nasty mottled blunt nose comes and takes a bite out of you!'

She didn't rouse him then when she saw a flight of the lizards in the sky, looping and diving in an aerial display that left her breathless. Duke watched with her, crooning softly to himself but despite her initial consternation that he might choose to join them, he didn't so much as ease his tailhold about her neck. Before she returned home, Sorka left Sean a jar of the ointment Pei Pei Ting had made for Duke's skin.

*

Sorka was not the only person on Pern that day watching aerial acrobatics. Half a continent to the south and west, Sallah Telgar's heart was in her mouth as she watched Drake Bonneau pull the little air-sled out of a thermal elevator above the vast inland lake which he was campaigning to call Drake's Lake. No one on their mining expedition would deny him that privilege but Drake had a tendency to beat a subject to death. Like stunning everyone with his professional skill. A foolish waste of power was not the way to Sallah Telgar's heart and esteem.

Ozzie Munson and Cobber Alhinwa emerged from the shelter where they had just stored their gear and paused to see what Sallah was staring at.

'Oh my word, he's at it again,' Ozzie said, grinning maliciously at Sallah.

'He'll crash hisself,' Cobber added, shaking his head, 'and that bleeding lake's so deep we'd never find 'im. Or the sled. And we need that.'

Svenda Olubushtu now emerged and hastily Sallah turned and made for the main shelter of the small prospecting camp. She did not need Svenda's snide remarks. It wasn't as if Sallah encouraged Drake Bonneau for, emphatically, publicly and frequently, she had made her disinterest plain enough.

Maybe I'm going about discouraging him the wrong way, she thought. *Maybe if I'd run after him, hang on his every word, and ambush him every chance I get, the way Svenda's doing, he'd leave me alone, too.*

Tarvi Andiyar was already marking the day's findings on the big screen, muttering to himself as he did so, his spidery fingers seeming to flick at the terminal keys in a typing rate so fast even the word-processor had trouble keeping up with him. No one knew what he was saying since he used his first language, an obscure Indic dialect. When asked about this eccentricity, he gave one of his melting smiles.

'For other ears to hear this beautiful liquid language, so it will be spoken even here on Pern, so that there will

113

be one person alive who still speaks it fluently, even after all these centuries,' was his response to those who asked him why. 'Is it not a lovely language, lilting, melodic, a joy to the ear?'

An intuitive, highly trained mining engineer, Tarvi had a reputation for being able to trace elusive veins through many subterranean shifts and faults. He had joined the Pern expedition because all the glorious hidden 'blood and tears of Mother Earth', as he chose to describe the products of mining, had been pried from her bosom. He'd prospected on First, too, but the alien metals had eluded his perceptions and so he'd travelled across a galaxy to ply his trade in his declining years.

As Tarvi Andiyar had only reached his sixth decade, this remark generally brought the reassurances he required from the kindly or hoots of derision from those who knew his ploys. Sallah liked him for his wry and subtle wit, generally turned on his own shortcomings, but he would not offend anyone for any reason.

Since Sallah had first encountered him after coldsleep, he hadn't put up so much as an ounce more on his long, almost emaciated frame. 'My family has had generations of gurus and mahatmas, all intent on fasting for the purification of their souls and bowels, until it has become a genetic imperative for all Andiyars to be of the thinness of a lathe. But I am strong. I do not need bulk and thews and bulging muscles. I am every bit as strong as the strongest sumi wrestler.' As he had worked all day without respite beside Ossie and Cobber, this was no idle boast.

Actually, Sallah found herself more attracted by the lanky engineer than any of the other men in the colony. If she could not impress on Drake Bonneau how little she cared for him, she was equally unable to get on more intimate relations with Tarvi. And not merely as an anodyne to Drake's importunities.

'What's the tally, Tarvi?' she asked, nodding to Valli Lieb who was already relaxing with a quikal drink.

Trust humans to make an immediate and intensive search on any new home for fermentables and devise an alcoholic beverage in the quickest possible time. Every lab at Landing, no matter what its basic function, had experimented with local fruits and had distilled or fermented potable beverages. The quikal still had been the first equipment assembled when this base camp was sited and no one had objected when Cobber and Ozzie had spent the first day producing imbibables from the fermented juices they'd brought along. Svenda had berated them fiercely while Tarvi and Sallah had merely proceeded to their surveying task. That first evening in the camp the drink was more than a tradition: it was an achievement.

Now Svenda, catching Sallah's eye, poured her a glass while Valli moved over on the bench to make room for her beside him. They looked freshly washed and in far better shape than when they had emerged from the brush that afternoon, covered with slime but bearing some very interesting samples for assay.

Then they all heard the sled landing outside the shelter.

'What was the assay, Valli?' Sallah asked, as Svenda craned her neck to watch Drake's progress up from the pad.

'Promising, promising,' the geologist said, her face glowing with achievement. 'Bauxite has so many uses! This strike alone makes this expedition profitable.'

'However, your find,' and Cobber bowed formally to Valli, 'will be far easier to work in an open pit.'

'Ha! We have enough to mine both,' Ozzie said. 'High-grade ore's always needed.'

'And there is copper and tin enough,' Tarvi said, joining them at the table though he refused the drink Svenda always offered him, 'within reasonable distance so that a mining town could profitably be established by this beautiful lake, with hydro-electric from the Falls to power refineries, and a good waterway to transport the finished products to the coast, and thence to Landing.'

'So,' and Svenda asked, 'this site is viable?' She looked about her with an air of possession that struck Sallah as slightly premature. Charterers had first choice.

'I shall certainly recommend it,' Tarvi said, smiling in the avuncular way which Sallah devoutly wished he would quit. He was not old: he was very attractive but if he kept thinking of himself as everyone's uncle, how could she get him to really look at her? 'I have recommended it. Especially as that slime into which you fell today, Valli, is high yield mineral oil.' When the cheers had subsided, he shook his head. 'Metals, yes. Petroleum, no. You all know that. To establish this as an effective colony, we must learn how to function efficiently at a lower technological level. That's where the skill comes in, and how skills are remembered.'

'Not everyone agrees with our leaders on that score,' Svenda said, scowling.

'We signed the Charter and we all agreed to honour it,' Valli said, quickly glancing at the others to see if anyone else concurred with Svenda.

'Fools,' was the blonde girl's derisive rejoinder and, slopping more quikal into her beaker, she left the shelter.

Tarvi looked after her, his mobile face anxious.

'She's all wind and piss,' Sallah said softly to him.

He raised his eyebrows, his dark eyes regarding her expressionlessly for a moment. Then his usual smile reappeared, and he patted her shoulder – unfortunately just as one would an obedient child. 'Ah, and here is Drake with our supplies and news of our comrades.'

'Hey, where was everyone?' Drake wanted to know the moment he entered, well-laden with bundles. 'There's more in the sled, too.'

Sallah dropped her head so that he wouldn't see her reaction to his chagrin at the lack of a breathless welcoming committee.

'We're celebrating, Drake,' Valli said, pouring him a glass. 'Two new finds, both of them rich and easily worked. We're in business.'

116

'So, the Drake's Lake Mining and Refinery is in business?'

Everyone laughed and, when he raised his glass in a toast, no one refuted the title.

'And I've news for you. We're all to go back to Landing three days from now.'

'What?' 'Why?' 'Is there trouble?' 'I can't go now!' were the simultaneous reactions.

Satisfied at the consternation he had wrought, Drake raised his free hand for silence, grinning with anticipating pleasure. 'For a Thanksgiving.'

'For this? How'd they know?' 'That should be in the Fall, after Harvest.' 'Why?'

'For this auspicious start to our new life. The last load from the star ships has reached Landing. We are officially landed.'

'Why make a fuss of that?' Sallah wanted to know.

'Not everyone is a workaholic like you, my lovely Sallah,' Drake said, pinching her chin affectionately. He wanted to hold her still long enough to kiss her, too. She saw that in his eyes and ducked away from him, grinning to take away the sting of her rejection. He pouted. 'Our gracious leaders have so decided and it is to be the occasion of many marvellous announcements. All the exploratory teams are being called back, and a grand time will be had by all.'

'We only got here last week!' Sallah was almost resentful.

As an escape from several unpalatable but unprovable conclusions, she had taken on the assignment of flying the geologists and miners to the immense inland lake where the EEC survey had reported ore concentrations. She hoped that distance might provide some objective answers. Two incidents had occurred to cause Sallah considerable dismay.

A week before, returning one evening to the *Eujisan* to look for a tape she had left onboard, she had seen Kenjo emerging from the small rear service hatch. He picked up

117

a brace of sacs in each hand and hurried off into the shadows. In simple curiosity, she had followed him and seen him abruptly disappear. She hid behind a bush and waited until he had re-emerged and retraced his steps. Then she tried to find out where he had put his burden.

It had taken some scrambling about, a couple of bruised shins and a scraped hand. At that she nearly stumbled into the cave. She was appalled to see the amount of fuel which he had purloined. Tonnes of it, she judged, checking a tag for the quantity, all stashed in easily handled pla-sacs. The rock fissure was well hidden at the extreme end of the landing grid behind a clump of the tough thorny bush that the farmers were clearing from the arable acres.

Two nights later, she had overheard a disturbing conversation between Avril and Stev Kimmer, the mining engineer whom Sallah had seen her with the day the landing site had been announced.

'Look, this island is stuffed with gemstones,' she was saying, and Sallah, dropping into the shadow of the delta wing of the shuttle, could hear the sound of plasfilm being unrolled. 'Here's the copy of the original survey report and I don't need to be a mining specialist to figure out what these cryptic symbols mean.' The plasfilm rippled as Avril jabbed her finger at points. 'A fortune for the taking!' There was a ring of triumph in Avril's wheedling voice. 'And I intend to take it.'

'Well, I grant you copper, gold and platinum are useful on any civilized world—'

'I'm not talking industrial, Kimmer,' Avril said sharply. 'And I don't mean little stones. That ruby was a small sample. Here, read Shavva's notes.'

Kimmer snorted in dismissal. 'Exaggerations to improve her bonus!'

'Well, I have 45 carats of exaggeration, man, and you saw it. If you're not in this with me, I'll find someone who can take a challenge.'

Avril certainly knew how to play her hook.

'That island's not on the schedule for years.'

Avril gave a low laugh. 'I can navigate more than spaceships, Stev. I'm checked out on a sled and I'm as free as everyone else on this mudball to look for the measly amount of stake acres I'm entitled to as a Contractor. But you're Charter and if we pool our allotments, we could own the entire island.'

Sallah heard Kimmer's intake of breath; knew that owning a complete island appealed to the man. As it should, if Sallah was right in guessing which island Avril was talking about. Nothing puny about Avril's aspirations.

'I thought the fishers wanted the island for the harbour!' He didn't sound too worried.

'They only want a harbour, not an island. They're fishermen, dolphineers. The land's no use to them.'

He muttered, shifting his feet uneasily.

'Who'd know anyhow?' Avril demanded silkily. 'We could go in, on the weekends, begin on the most accessible stuff, stash it in a cave. There're so many you could search for years and never find the right one. And we wouldn't have to draw attention to our activities by staking it officially, unless we're forced to.'

'But you said there was stuff in the Great Western Range.'

'And so there is,' Avril agreed, with a little chuckle, knowing that she had set the hook well and true. 'I also know where. A short hop from the island.'

'You've got it all worked out, haven't you?' Kimmer's voice had an edge of sarcasm.

'Of course,' Avril agreed easily. 'I'm not going to live out the rest of my life in this backwater. Not when I've discovered the means to live the style of life I very much prefer.' Again that rippling laugh and then a long silence, broken by the sound of moist lips parting. 'But while I'm here, and you're here, Kimmer, let's make the most of it. Here and now, under the stars.'

Sallah had slipped away, both embarrassed and disgusted by Avril's blatant sexuality. Small wonder Paul

Benden hadn't kept her in his bed: he was a sensual man, Sallah thought, but unlikely to appreciate Avril's crude abandon for long. Ju Adjai, elegant and serene, was far more suitable even if neither appeared to be rushing a noticeable alliance.

But Avril's voice had dripped of an insatiable greed. Had Stev Kimmer heard what Sallah had? Or did her enticement cloud his thinking? Sallah had always been aware of Pern's gemstone wealth. The Shavva Ruby had been as much part of the legend of Pern as the Liu Nugget even though the planet's gem deposits had never been an outstanding feature. Artur Gneiss was a trained lapidary and had already found some really fine stones which he intended to cut as personal adornments. Gold, platinum, and the rarer metals of which Pern seemed to have a modest share, were less used nowadays as the basis of wealth and more for their qualities as technologically viable metals. Earth no longer had any accessible deposits left so Avril's notion to return with a shipload would undoubtedly fund a sybaritic lifestyle. Nor would her shipload seriously deplete Pern's resources.

It was *how* Avril would contrive the fuel for such a journey that worried Sallah more acutely. Sallah knew that there was fuel left in the admiral's gig, the *Mariposa*. That wasn't common knowledge but, as a pilot, Avril would have had access to that information. Judging by the computations Avril had made during her time on the *Yokohama*, Sallah knew that she could actually make it to an uninhabited system. Then what?

Three days later, Sallah had come to no decision about reporting her suspicions to a superior. Damn Avril! She was just ruthless enough, too, to act without thought of the consequences for the rest of the colony. If, by some chance, Avril could gain access to the gig and steal the remaining fuel in the colony-ship tanks, the colony could be in serious danger. The space ships were now on automatic in their stable orbits. Not much fuel was required for the occasional adjustments but to deprive the automatics of that little would be disastrous at some future time when the uncorrected orbits decayed and the ships plunged as burning meteorites on to Pern's surface.

Three of the shuttles were already parked, forever, at the far end of the landing grid. Kenjo, Fister from the *Buenos Aires* and Logorides of the *Bahrain*, were needed to bring down the last loads from the three ships, withdrawing crew first from the *Bahrain*, then the *Buenos Aires*, and finally the last people from the great *Yoko*. Freed of space duty, Sallah had leapt at the chance to go out with an exploratory team, grimly amused that Avril had gone north, to an area where gold nuggets had been reported by the EEC team.

Sallah had liked surveying, being with Ossie and Cobber – yes, and Tarvi – and she had been kept too tired to think of her dilemma. While she had no compunction about reporting Avril, she would also have to mention Kenjo's activities. She wished she knew why Kenjo had held back fuel – unless he had some crazy notion about exploring the two moons. Or perhaps the wayward planet which, she knew by her study of its eccentric orbit, would cross Pern's orbit in roughly eight years. The initial survey had not concerned itself with Rukbat's other satellites since Pern was so obviously habitable.

It was impossible to think of Kenjo involved, in any way, with someone like Bitra. Sallah was certain that the animosity between them, on those rare occasions when they inhabited the same room, was not feigned. She suspected that flying was to Kenjo both a religion and an incurable disease. But he did have all of Pern to fly over and the packs which powered the sleds with which the colony was provided would allow that for several decades – if used circumspectly. Another reason why she deplored Drake's wasteful habits.

What worried Sallah Telgar most was that Avril Bitra might just find Kenjo Fusaiyuki's cache. The fissure was well concealed, and as Avril herself had pointed out to

Kimmer, there were hundreds of caves in which things could be hidden.

She had thought of confiding in one of the other pilots but Barr Hamil couldn't handle such a problem: Drake wouldn't take it seriously; Jiro, Kenjo's co-pilot, would never betray his superior. She didn't know the others well enough to judge their reactions to such a disclosure. Go to the top, she told herself. This sort of thing is safest there. Ongola would listen to her. Anyhow, he was her immediate superior. And he would know whether or not to burden Paul and Emil with these suspicions.

Damn! Sallah's fists clenched at her sides. Pern was supposed to be above petty schemes and intrigues. We're all working to a common goal – a secure, bountiful future, without prejudice. Why must someone like Avril touch that beautiful vision with her sour egocentricity?

Then Ossie repeated a question, touching her arm and bringing her out of her depressing thoughts.

'You'll gimme a dance, Sallah?' he repeated in his slightly nasal twang, his eyes twinkling with a challenge.

Sallah grinned and accepted his gracious invitation. As soon as they got back to Landing, she'd find Ongola and tell him. Then she'd be able to trip the light fantastic with an easy conscience.

'And then,' Ossie went on irrepressibly, 'Tarvi can dance with you and give me time to rest my sore toes.'

Tarvi gave her a look of rueful surprise, not having much choice, Sallah realized with so many witnesses and with no chance to prepare an excuse. But she was grateful to sly, old Ozzie.

By the time the mining party returned to Landing, the fire was well started in Bonfire Square and the party was gathering momentum. From her vantage point of altitude as she swung the sled to the perimeter and down to the strip, Sallah almost didn't recognize the utilitarian settlement. Lights were on in every window and, thanks to the hydro-electric plant, every lamp standard glowed.

At Bonfire Square, a dais had been set across one side, coloured spot lights strung on a frame above it: Sallah just recognized Rudi Shwartz – Drake had been full of the treats in store for them that night. Rudi was acting as stage manager for the evening's entertainment and the diminutive figure which could only be Roma Nyadezda placing sheets on what looked like music stands. Drake had said that there was a call out for anyone who could play an instrument to take a turn that evening. The white cubes of old plastic packers dotted the dais to serve as stools.

Tables and chairs had been brought from residences and set up in a freshly mowed space beyond the bonfire square. Firepits had been dug to roast huge wherries, and the last of the frozen meats brought from Earth and several smaller carcases browned on smaller spits. The aroma of roasting meats and grilling fish was mouth watering. All were dressed in their best clothes: everyone was bustling around, helping, toting, arranging, fixing the last of the delicacies brought from their starting point and saved for one last gorge on the new world. There was the look of Occasion to the settlement that was palpable in the air above it as Sallah followed Drake in to land.

Sallah parked her sled athwart the landing grid, thinking that if more were set down at random along the straight-away, the *Mariposa* parked at the other end of the field wouldn't have sufficient space for take-off. But how long would there be this many sleds at Landing?

'Hey, hurry up, Sallah,' Ozzie yelled at her as he and Cobber jumped out of the sled.

'Gotta check in at the tower,' she said, waving cheerfully at them to go on.

'Oh, leave it the once,' Cobber suggested but she waved them on again.

Ongola was just leaving the meteorology tower as she reached it. He gave her a resigned nod and opened the door again, noticing as he did so the position of her sled.

'Wise to leave it like that, Sallah?'

123

'Yes, shall we call it a precautionary measure, Commander,' she said in a tone that should warn him that she had come on a serious errand.

He did not seat himself until she was halfway through her suspicions and then he lowered himself into the chair with such a weariness about him that she hated herself for speaking out.

'Forewarned is forearmed, sir,' she said in conclusion.

'It is indeed, Mr Telgar,' and his deep sigh stressed the return of doubt. He motioned her to be seated. 'How much fuel?'

When she reluctantly gave him precise figures, he was surprised, and really concerned.

'Could Avril know of Kenjo's hoard?' Ongola sat up so quickly that she realized Ongola found her suspicions of the astrogator far more worrying than Kenjo's theft. 'No, no,' he corrected himself with a quick wave of his hand, 'their dislike of each other is genuine. I will inform the Admiral and the Governor.'

'Not tonight, sir,' Sallah said, inadvertently raising her hand to protest. 'It's only because this was the first chance I've had to approach you—'

'Forewarned is forearmed, Sallah. Have you mentioned these suspicions to anyone else?'

She shook her head vigorously. 'No, sir! It's bad enough suspecting there are maggots in the meat without offering anyone else a bite.'

'True! Eden is once again corrupted by human greed.'

'Only one human,' Sallah felt obliged to remind him.

He held up two fingers significantly. 'Two. Kimmer. And who else was she speaking to on board?'

'Kimmer, Bart Lemos and Nabhi Nabol and two other men I've never met.'

Ongola did not seem surprised about Lemos and Nabol. He took a deep breath and sighed before he put both hands on his thighs and rose to his full height.

'I am grateful and I know that the Admiral and the Governor will also be grateful.'

'Grateful?' Sallah rose, feeling none of the relief she had hoped to gain from telling her superior. She gave a snort as she rose.

'We had actually anticipated some problems as people began to realize that they are *here*,' Ongola stabbed one long finger downward, 'and cannot go anywhere else. The euphoria of the Crossing is over: tonight's celebration is planned to defuse a rebound as that realization sinks in. Well-fed, well-oiled people who have tired themselves with dancing are unlikely to plot sedition.'

Ongola opened the door, gesturing courteously for her to precede him. No one locked doors on Pern, even doors to official administrative offices. Sallah had been proud of that fact but now she worried.

'We're not that stupid, Sallah,' Ongola said, as if he'd read her mind. And tapped his forehead. 'This is still the best memory bank ever invented.'

She gave a sigh of relief and managed a more cheerful expression.

'We still have a great deal to be thankful for on Pern, you know.'

'Indeed I do!' she replied, thinking of her dance with Tarvi.

By the time Sallah had washed, changed into her own finery and reached Bonfire Square, the party was in full swing and the impromptu group playing a polka, the beaming Gus Gustavson pumping away on his accordion, ably assisted by Red Hanrahan and Ezra Keroon on fiddles, Joe Tobin and Ware Lorenzo on harmonicas, and Mairi Hanrahan beating the time on the *bodhran*. Halting in the darkness beyond all that light and sound, Sallah was astonished at the number of unexpected musicians, stomping time as they waited their turn.

Rene Mallibeau had his fingers tucked through the stops of a trumpet and was slapping his thigh in time to Mairi's beat. Bill Duff was chording on his keyboard which he had set at a low amp so the electronic didn't drown out the unamplified instruments like Sorka's penny whistle and Rudi's recorder. Pat Hempenstall had given up bowing his cello and was plucking the strings in total absorption with the music; Sabra Stein played clarinet, Mercy Doyle a small harp, Jivan Paramundi twanged on a zitar, Tim Andriades capably puffed a flute and later, to Sallah's utter astonishment, Tarvi Andiyar produced pan pipes and played an eerie little melody, quite haunting, and a quiet change after the more raucous sets.

This informal group went from dance tunes to solos, calling on the audience to sing old favourites. Gus, Red and Rudi were able to find any pitch and chord once a singer had started, just as they were able to provide background to other instrumentalists. Roma, being classically trained, was clearly dismayed by the informality but, grinning nervously, she did her best on her keyboard, with occasional questions of Gus and Bill. Emily Boll took a turn on Bill Duff's keyboard, Ezra Keroon enthusiastically fiddled a medley of hornpipes that had everyone foot tapping and several couples did hilarious imitations of the traditional seamen's dance. There were numerous guitar players, Haggie Florizel, one of Rene's fellow vintners, being the best, but Cecilia Rado, Andi Gomez and Dino Moreno had obviously been practising their party pieces and were the best trio. Basil Tomlinson did a spectacular trumpet solo and retired for the evening.

Sallah had enjoyed not one dance with Tarvi but two. In the middle of the second to an ancient tune in three-quarter time, there came a heart-stopping moment, when it seemed as if Pern had decided to dance to the new tunes it heard. Then every dish, empty or full, on the laden trestle tables rattled, dancers were thrown off-balance and those seated felt their chairs rock.

It lasted less than the time between two heartbeats and was followed by complete and utter silence.

'So Pern wants to dance, does it?' Paul Benden's amused voice rang out. He jumped to the musicians' platform, arms outspread as if he considered the quake an oblique sign of welcome.

His comment caused whispers and murmurs, but eased the tension. Even as Paul signalled the musicians to resume their music, he was scanning the audience, looking for certain faces.

Beside Sallah, Tarvi gave an almost imperceptible nod of his head and dropped his arms from Sallah.

'Come, we must go check the rhythm of this dance.'

Sallah tried to hide the intense disappointment at having her dance with Tarvi cut short. She had never felt an earth tremor before but that hadn't prevented her from instantly understanding what had just occurred. Even as she and Tarvi made their way from the dancing square, she moved warily, as if to forestall the surprise of another shock.

Jim Tillek gathered his mariners to see that the boats were moored well within the newly reinforced breakwater and hoped that the *tsunami*, when it came, would have dissipated its force against the intervening islands. The dolphineers, with the exception of Gus who was coerced into remaining behind to play his accordion, went to the harbour to speak to the marine mammals. They could signal the arrival of the *tsunami* and estimate its destructiveness.

Patrice de Broglie cornered several joats and went out to set seismic cores but in his professional opinion the shock had been a very gentle one, from a far distant epicentre.

Sallah got to finish her dance with Tarvi but only because he was told that the absence of too many specialists might cause alarm.

By morning, the epicentre had been located, east by northeast, far out in the ocean, where volcanism had been mentioned by the EEC team. As there were no further shocks penetrating to the mainland, the geologists were able to dispel the ripple of uncertainty that had marred the Thanksgiving festivities.

When Tarvi wanted to join Patrice to investigate the probable site, Sallah volunteered to pilot the big sled. She didn't even mind that the sled was crowded with curious geologists and packed with equipment. She saw to it that Tarvi occupied the right hand driving seat.

6

●

After the Thanksgiving celebration, work settled down to more routine procedures which were, considering their sites, scarcely routine. The dolphins had a high old time tracking the *tsunami* wave but it had, as Tarvi predicted, raced across the Northern Sea, spending the worst of its violence on the eastern extrusion of the northern continent, the big island and the western tip. Jim Tillek's harbour was safe although combers brought a ridge of bright red seawrack well up the beaches. This deep-sea plant was unlike anything so far deposited and samples were rushed to the lab for analysis. An edible seaweed would be valuable.

The dolphins were excited by the earthquake for they had felt its imminence in the reactions of the larger marine forms which scurried for safety and they were pleased to have this awareness from life in their new oceans. As Teresa had told Efram with indignant clicks and hisses, they had rung and rung the Seabell, put on the end of the jetty for them to summon humans, but no one had come. The marine rangers had had their work cut out to soothe and placate the blues and bottlenoses.

'What was the sense,' Teresa, the biggest blue, had demanded, 'of going through all that mentasynth infection if you humans don't come to hear what we have to tell you?'

High-quality copper, tin and vanadium ores were assayed in the north by Saki Kiffin's team, at the foot of a great range, fortuitously near a navigable river which could bring ore down to the great estuary. Andiyar, who was now Head of Mine Engineering on Pern, had inspected the site with the jubilant Saki and they had proposed to the Council that a secondary settlement there would be feasible. Ore could be processed in situ and shipped downriver, saving a lot of time, effort and trouble. Denzil Foley from Power Resources agreed that the nearby cataracts would provide ample hydro-electric power. The Council proposed to bring the matter up at the next monthly congregation. In the mean time, the geology teams were to continue their explorations on both continents.

Other explorations were going forward on land and sea. Andrew Kiersey said wheat and barley were thriving: Corazon Cervantes reported that most of the tubers were doing well but several species of squash were having trouble and nutrients were being sprayed on those crops. It also looked as if the roots of cucumbers and all but two of the gourds seemed to have been susceptible to a Pernian fungus-worm and unless they could combat it with a little cross-parasitism, they might lose the entire family Cucurbitacae. Technology was looking after the problem.

On the good side, Chuck Kimmage said his orchard stock, bar a few in each variety, had bloomed and were leafing well. Transplants of two varieties of Pern fruit plants appeared to thrive near Earth types where again Technology was hoping for some symbiosis. Two Pernian food plants showed evidence of being attacked by a human-brought virus but it was too early to tell if this would prove symbiotic or harmful. Athpathis still hadn't found suitable land for rice cultivation but Fremlich, who was colony cartographer and busy translating probe pictures to survey maps, thought the southern marsh lands might suit him.

Joel Lilienkamp, the stores-manager, reported no problems and thanked everyone, especially the kids, for doing such a grand job of bringing in edible stuffs and the mariners for their catches. Some of the indigenous 'fish' were very tasty despite their appearance. He once again warned people to be careful of the 'packtail' fins for they infected any cuts or scratches. He'd gladly supply gloves now that Andi Gomez in plastics was able to produce a tough thin film for handwear.

On the zoological front, Pol Nietro and Chuck Havers delivered a cautious report on the success of gestations. Some of each big species were progressing well but the initial turkey eggs hadn't survived. Three bitches were expecting imminently and there were seventeen kittens from four tabbies, though one mother cat had had only one. Six more bitches and the other two female cats would be in heat soon and would shortly be inseminated or receive embryos. It had regretfully been decided not to use the Eridani techniques, especially mentasynth on the dogs after considerable trouble with such adaptations on Earth. Some of the stock, and indeed many of the human beings had ancestors who had been 'enhanced' and their descend-ants still showed the extreme empathy, something that dogs apparently couldn't adapt to.

Geese, ducks and chickens had no problems, and were laying regularly. These were kept in outdoor runs, too valuable yet to be allowed to range free, and the runs much visited by adult and child. It took nearly six weeks for the omnivorous wherries to discover this source of food and for hunger to overcome their cautious, though some termed it cowardly, nature. The EEC team name for the awkward fliers had been kept, though the reason for it was already lost. Fortunately, by that time, there were thirty of the little dragonets in Landing. That thirty proved well able to chase off the bolder wherries and taught the colonists respect for both combatants.

Although smaller than their adversaries, the dragonets were more agile aerial fighters and, in some way, able to communicate with each other so that, as soon as one wherry had been driven off, one big bronze kept pace with it to be sure it left the area, while the others went to assist their fellows in fending off the attack.

Sorka noticed something else, too, in the dragonets' staunch defence: her Duke had appeared to attack one very aggressive wherry with what looked suspiciously like a little flame. Certainly there was smoke puffing up above them and the wherry broke off its attack and fled. It happened so fast that she wasn't sure what she had seen so she didn't mention the phenomenon.

There was always a cloud of smell accompanying wherries: like the sulphur of the river estuary and the mud flats. If they were upwind of you anywhere, you knew they were around. The dragonets smelled cleanly of sea and salt, and, sometimes, when Duke had curled on her pillow, a little like cinnamon and nutmeg, condiments that would soon be memories unless there was more success in the herb greenhouses.

But there was no question in the colonists' minds that the dragonets had preserved the poultry from danger.

'By all that's holy! What warriors they make,' was Admiral Benden's respectful comment. He and Emily Boll had seen the attack from their vantage point in the Met tower and hurried to help conduct the defence.

Though startled and unprepared, the settlers had rushed to the poultry run, grabbing up brooms, rakes, sticks, whatever was near to hand. There'd been no cause to unpack the few handguns or rifles for these were to be used in ceremonial displays more than protection. The firemen, however, were well drilled and had already had to control small fires. They arrived with the firehoses, which held off the few wherries that evaded the defenders. Adults and kids herded the squawking, frightened poultry back into their hutches. One of the funnier sights, Sorka told Sean afterwards, was watching the very dignified scientists trying to catch chicks. Although some people bore scratches from the raking talons of the wherries, there would have been more, and serious, casualties if the dragonets had not intervened.

'Too bad they're not bigger,' the Admiral remarked, 'they'd make good watch animals. Maybe our bio-geneticists,' and he inclined his head respectfully towards Kitti and Wind Blossom Ping, 'can create a few flying dogs for us.' Kitti Ping gave him a frosty nod. 'Not only did those dragonets use their own initiative but, by all that's holy, I swear they were communicating with each other. Did you see how they set up a perimeter watch? And how they combined their attacks? Superb tactics. Couldn't have improved on it myself.'

Pol Nietro, himself impressed by the incident, was momentarily between phases of his scheduled projects and not the sort of personality to put leisure time to leisure use. So, when order had been restored and reliable young colonists set as sentinels against a repeat of the incursion, he and Bay paid a visit to Asian Square.

Mairi Hanrahan smiled at his request. 'You're in luck, Pol, for she happens to be home. Duke's getting an extra special feed for his defence of the poultry yard.'

She ushered them into their living room which even his eye could see had been transformed from the utilitarian to homey with bright curtains at the windows, pots of flowering plants, some native and some obviously from Terran seed. Several etchings made the walls seem less bare and brightly coloured pillows improved the comfort of the plastic chairs.

'Ah, he was there, then.'

'Sorka would have it that he led the fair of dragonets,' Mairi said in a low voice, her eyes twinkling with maternal pride and tolerance.

'Fair of dragonets? Like a pride of lions? Or a gaggle of geese? Yes, a very "fair" description,' Pol Nietro said, his eyes twinkling at mother and daughter. 'Not that you're apt to have that kind of co-operation in the ordinary "fair".'

'Pol Nietro, if you're casting aspersions on Donnybrooks . . .' Mairi began with a grin.

'Cast aspersions, Mairi? Not my way at all,' and Pol winked at her. 'But that *fair* of dragonets proved very useful. They did, indeed, seem to work well together to a common goal. Paul Benden noticed this particularly and wants Kitti and myself to—'

Mairi caught him by the arm, her expression altered. 'You wouldn't—'

'Of course not, my dear.' He patted her hand reassuringly. 'But I think Sorka can help us, and Duke, if they're willing. We have already amassed quite a good deal of information about our small friends. Their potential has just taken a quantum leap. And our understanding of them! We brought no creatures with us to ward off such vicious aerial scavengers as the wherries.'

Sorka was feeding a nearly sated Duke who sat upright, tail extended on the top of the table, the tip twitching now and again with a more decisive movement that corresponded with the moment he daintily secured the morsel Sorka offered him. There was about him an odd, not completely pleasant odour which everyone was trying to ignore, out of deference to his heroism.

'Ah, the servant is worthy of his hire,' Pol said.

Sorka gave him a long look. 'I don't mean to be cheeky, sir, but I don't think of Duke as a servant of any kind. And he certainly proved he was a friend to us!' She made a wave of her hand to indicate the entire settlement.

'He and his ... cohorts ...' Pol knew when to be tactful, 'most certainly proved their friendship today.' He sat down beside Sorka, watching the little creature pinch the next piece of food in his claws. Duke regarded it from all sides, sniffed, licked and finally took a small bite. Pol watched, admiringly.

Sorka giggled. 'He's stuffed but he never turns down food.' Then she added, 'Actually, he's not eating as much as he used to. He's down to one meal a day so he may be reaching maturity. I've kept notes on his growth and really, sir, he does seem to be as big as the wild ones.'

'Interesting. Do please give me your records and I shall add them to the file.' Pol shifted his body a bit. 'Really, you know, this is a fascinating evolution, isn't it, Bay? Especially if those plankton eaters the dolphins report could represent a common ancestor for the tunnel snakes and dragonets.'

Mairi was surprised. 'Tunnel snakes *and* dragonets?'

'Hmm, yes, for life evolved from the seas here on Pern just as it did on Earth. With variations, of course,' and Pol settled happily into his lecturing mode with an attentive if incredulous audience. Bay smiled gently as he went on. 'Yes, an aquatic eel-like ancestor, in fact. With six limbs. The first pair,' and he pointed at the dragonet still clutching his morsel in his front pinchers, 'originally were nets for catching. See the action of the front claw against the stationary back pair. The dragonets dropped the net in favour of three digits. They opted for wings instead of stabilizing middle fins while the hind pair are for propulsion. The dry land adaptation, our tunnel snake, was to make the front pair diggers, the middle set remained balancers, especially when they have food in the front pair, and the rear limbs are for steering or holding on. Yes, I'm sure we'll find that the plankton eaters are like the common ancestors of our good friends here,' and Pol beamed warmly down at Duke who was deliberating taking a fresh morsel from those Sorka offered him. 'However . . .' and then he paused, looking at Bay for support.

Sorka waited politely now, knowing that the zoologist had some purpose in this visit.

'Would you happen to know of any undisturbed nests?'

'Yes, sir, but it's not a big clutch and the eggs are rather smaller than others I've seen.'

'Ah, yes, perhaps the eggs of the smaller green female,' Pol said, placatingly. 'Well, since the green is not as protective of her nest as the gold, she will suffer no great pangs if we borrow a few. But I did want to ask you one other, greater favour. I particularly remember your mentioning seeing the body of a hatchling in the water. Is this a frequent hazard?'

Sorka considered this and replied in the same objective tone of voice. 'I think so. Some of the hatchlings just don't make it. Either they can't feed themselves enough to make up for the hatching trauma,' and she didn't see the slight grin tugging at Pol Nietro's mouth, 'or they are struck down by wherries. You see, just before hatching, the older dragonets bring seaweed to form a ring about the clutch, and offer fish and crawlies and anything else they can find to the hatchlings.'

'Hmm, definitely then,' Pol murmured to Bay who nodded.

'By the time they've filled their stomachs, their wings have dried, and they can fly off with the rest of the fair. The older dragonets do a first-rate job of keeping off snakes and wherries, to give the babies a chance. One day, though, Sean spotted some eel-like thing attacking from the sea during a high tide. The hatchling didn't have a chance.'

'Sean is your elusive but oft-mentioned ally?'

'Yes, sir. He and I discovered the first nest together and kept watch on it.'

'Would he assist us in finding nests, and . . . the hatchlings?'

Sorka regarded the zoologist for a long moment. He had always kept his word to her and he'd been very good about Duke that first day. She decided that she could trust him but she was also aware of his high rank in Landing, so it wouldn't hurt to try.

'If you promise, *promise* – and I'd vouch for you, too – that his family gets one of the first horses, he'll do just about anything for you.'

'Sorka!' Mairi was embarrassed by her daughter's proposal. She spent entirely too much time with that boy and was learning some bad habits from him. To her amazement, Pol smiled cheerfully and patted Sorka's arm approvingly.

'Now, now, Mairi, your daughter has good instincts. Barter is already practised as an exchange system on Pern, you know.' He regarded Sorka with proper solemnity. 'He's one of the Connells, is he not?' And when she nodded solemnly, he went on briskly. 'In point of fact, that is the first name on the list to receive equines. Or oxen, if they prefer.'

'Horses. Horses are what they've always had,' Sorka eagerly affirmed.

'And when can I have a few words with this young man?'

'Any time you want, sir. Would this evening do? I know where Sean is likely to be.' She glanced at her mother for consent. Though Pern was safe from the dangers she had once needed to avoid, the habit was ingrained.

On consultation, Sean allowed that there were only green eggs nearby, but there being so much sandy beach along this coast, if they wanted to make their efforts worthwhile, they would do well to look a good distance from Landing's well-trampled strands. Sorka had found him on the Head, his two dragonets fishing in the shallows for the finger-fish often trapped between tides.

'May we request your services in this venture, Sean Connell?' Pol Nietro asked formally.

Casually, Sean cocked his head and gave the zoologist a long and appraising look.

'What's in it for me to go off hunting lizards?'

'Dragonets,' Sorka said firmly, but Sean ignored her.

'There aint no money here and me da needs me in the camp.'

Pol could hear Sorka moving restlessly beside him, unsure if Pol would rise to the occasion. But Pol had not been head of a prestigious zoology department in the huge university of First without learning how to deal with touchy, opinionated fellows. This young rascal who eyed him with all the ancient scepticism of his ethnic group merely presented a slightly different aspect of a well-known problem. To any other young person, the zoologist might have offered the chance to light the evening bonfire, now a much-sought-after privilege, but unlikely to be one in Sean's estimation.

'Did you have your own pony on Earth?' Pol asked,

settling himself against a rock and folding his short arms across his chest.

Sean nodded, his attention caught by such an unexpected question.

'Tell me about him.'

'What's to tell? He's long gone to meat and even them what ate him is probably worms, too.'

'Was he special in some way? Apart from being special to you?'

Sean gave him a long sideways look, glanced briefly at Sorka who kept her face expressionless. This was all between Sean and Pol Nietro. She felt the slightest twinge of guilt for having given Pol the hint of Sean's deepest desire.

'He was part Welsh mountain, part Connemara. Not many like him left.'

'How big?'

'Fourteen hands high.' Sean spoke almost sullenly.

'Colour?'

'Steel-grey.' Sean frowned, growing more suspicious. 'Why d'ya wanna know?'

'D'you know what I do on this planet?'

'Cut things up.'

'That, too, of course, but I also combine "things", among them, traits, colour, gender. That is what I and my colleagues generally do. By a judicious manipulation of gene patterns, we can produce what the client,' and Pol waved one hand towards Sean, 'wants.'

Sean stared at him, not quite understanding the terms used and not daring to hope what Pol Nietro seemed to be suggesting.

'You could have Cricket again, here on Pern,' Sorka said softly, her eyes shining. 'He can do it, too. Give you a pony just like Cricket.'

Sean caught his breath, darting glances from her to the old zoologist who regarded him with great equanimity. Then he jerked his thumb at Sorka.

'Is she right?'

'In that I could produce a grey horse – if I may venture to suggest that you're too tall now for a pony – with all the physical characteristics of your Cricket, yes, she's correct. We brought with us sperm as well as fertilized eggs from a wide variety of the Terran equine types. I know we have both Connemara and Welsh genotypes. They're both hardy, versatile breeds. It's a simple matter . . .'

'Just to find lizard eggs?' Sean's suspicious nature overcame his awe of such terms and abilities.

'Dragonet eggs.' Sorka doggedly corrected him and he scowled at her.

'We're trading eggs for eggs, young man. A fair exchange, with a riding horse from your egg in the bargain, altered to your specifications as a gratuity for your time and effort in the search.'

Sean glanced once more at Sorka who nodded reassurance and then, spitting into the palm of his right hand, extended it to Pol Nietro. Without hesitation, the zoologist sealed the bargain in the ancient way.

The speed with which Pol Nietro organized an expedition left many of his colleagues as well as the administration staff gasping for breath. By morning, Jim Tillek had agreed that they could use the *Southern Cross* if he captained the crew. He was asked to provision it for a coastal trip of up to a week's length; the Hanrahans and Porrig Connell had been asked for and given their permission for Sorka and Sean to go; and Pol had persuaded Bay Harkenon to bring along her portable microscope and a quantity of specimen cases, slides and similar paraphernalia. Xi Chi Yuen, on watch in the Meteorology Tower, assured Jim and Pol that there'd be fair winds and good weather. To Sorka's surprise and Sean's amusement, Admiral Benden, himself dressed for a sea trip, was at the jetty to wish them good luck with the venture, and helped grinning Gus and dour Limpy Obrin cast off the stern lines. With that official blessing, the *Southern Cross* glided out of the bay on a fine brisk breeze.

Landbred Sean was not all that happy about his first sea voyage but for a horse to replace his beloved Cricket and, especially in front of Sorka who showed every evidence of enjoying the adventure, he was forced to suppress both fear and nausea. He spent most of the voyage, his back against the mast, facing forward and stroking his brown dragonets who had stretched out on the sunny deck and gone to sleep. Sorka's Duke remained perched on her shoulder, one pincer holding delicately to her ear to balance himself while his tail was lightly but firmly wrapped about her neck. From time to time, she would nuzzle him reassuringly or he would croon some comment in her ear just as if he was certain of her understanding.

The 40-foot sloop, the *Southern Cross*, could be sailed with a crew of three, sleep eight and had been designed to serve as exploratory ship as well as fast courier. Jim Tillek had already sailed as far east, with a crew to set gravity meters to check the volcanism in that archipelago, as the island volcano which had erupted to mar the Thanksgiving Feast, and he'd gone as far west as the river, christened Jordan. He was hoping to get permission to make the longer crossing to the large island off the northern continent, and to explore the delta of the river proposed to carry the ore or finished metals from the projected mining site. He had, he told the enthralled Sorka, sailed all the seas and oceans of Earth during his leaves from captaining a merchantman on the Belt runs, and up as many rivers as were navigable: Nile, Thames, Amazon, Mississippi, St Lawrence, Columbia and Rhine, Volga, Yangstze and less-well-known streams.

''Course, I wasn't doing that as a professional man, and there wasn't much call on a sailor on First yet, so this expedition was my chance to ply my hobby as trade, as 'twere,' he confided in Sorka since she was a rapt audience. He wisely made no overt attempt to disturb Sean's contemplation of the shoreline. 'Damned glad I came!' He inhaled deeply. 'The air here's fabulous. What we used to have back on Earth! Used to think it was the ozone! Take a deep breath!'

Sorka did as commanded just as Bay Harkenon emerged from the cabin, looking much better than when she had hastily descended to be nauseous in private.

'Ah, the pill worked?' Jim Tillek inquired solicitously.

'I cannot thank you enough,' the microbiologist said with a tremulous but grateful smile. 'I'd no idea I was susceptible to motion sickness.'

'Had you ever sailed?'

Bay shook her head, the clusters of grey curls bobbing on her shoulders.

'Then how would you know?' he asked affably. He squinted into the distance, where the peninsula was already visible and the mouth of the Jordan River. There had been considerable fireside harangue over naming that river but so many people were already comfortably calling it the Jordan that the name became official.

Portside, the towering Mount Garben, named after the senator who had done so much to smooth the expedition's way through the intricacies of Federated Sentient Planet's bureaucracy, dominated the landscape: its cone, undamaged from this aspect, was suitably framed against the bright morning sky, its three small companions shielded by its bulk. There had been some lobbying to name them after Shavva, Liu and Turnien, the original EEC landing party. No decision had yet been made at the monthly naming sessions held around the evening campfire after the more formal official sittings of the Council.

Now Captain James Tillek dropped his gaze to the charts and with his dividers walked the distance from the jetty to the river mouth, and again, to the land beyond.

'Why do the colours stop here?' Sorka asked, noticing that the bulk of the chart was uncoloured.

Grinning approval at her, he tapped it. 'Fremlich did this for me from the probe pics, and they've been accurate to the last centimetre so far, but as we ourselves walk across the land and sail the coast, I colour it in appropriately. A good way of knowing where we've been and where we've yet to go. I've also added notations that a sailor might need, about prevalent winds and current speeds.'

It was only then that Sorka noticed these additional marks.

'It's one thing to see, and another to know, isn't it?'

He tweaked one of the braids into which she had secured her titian hair. 'Indeed, it is being there that matters.'

'And we'll really be the first people – here?' She laid the tip of her forefinger on the peninsula.

'Indeed we shall,' Tillek said with heartfelt satisfaction.

Whatever some might say about coming to Pern, he had never been so contented and happy before in a life that had already spanned six decades. A misfit in a high-tech society because of his love of seas and ships, bored by the monotonous Belt runs to which his lack of tact, or incorruptible honesty restricted him, Tillek found Pern perfect, with the added fillip of being one of the first to sail these new seas, and discover their eccentricities.

A strongly built man, though not above medium height, with pale-blue far-seeing eyes, he looked his part, complete with visored cap pulled down about his ears and an old guernsey wool sweater against the slight coolness of the fresh morning breeze. Though the *Southern Cross* could have been sailed electronically from the cockpit with the touch of buttons, he preferred to steer by the rudder and use his instinct for the wind to trim the sheets. His crew were forward, making all lines fair on the plasiplex decks and going about the routine of the little ship. The clever man always does the job with the lowest technology possible and Tillek found great joy in sailing with sheet, line and rudder.

'We'll put in at dusk, probably about here, where the chart tells me there's a deep harbour in a cove. More colour to be added. We might even find what we're looking for there, too.' He winked at Sorka and Bay Harkenon.

Which is exactly what happened. Jim Tillek anchored

the *Southern Cross* in six fathoms, and took the shore party to the beach in the little motorboat. As soon as they had landed, Sean who had had quite enough company for a while told Sorka to search to the east and he'd go west along the beach to see if they could find 'signs'. His two browns were now circling above his head, calling happily as they flew. When Jim Tillek was about to take the lad to task, Pol Nietro sent him a warning look and the Captain subsided even though it galled him to see the girl ordered about like that. Sean was already ducking into the thick vegetation bordering the strand.

'We'll have a hot meal for you when you return,' Pol called after the two youngsters. Sorka paused and waved acknowledgement.

When they returned at dusk for the promised food, both children reported success.

'I think the first two I found are only greens,' Sorka said with quiet authority, 'much too close to the water for a gold. Duke thinks so, too. He doesn't seem to like greens. But the one we found furthest away was well above high-tide marks, and the eggs are bigger. I think they're hard enough to hatch soon.'

'Two green clutches and two I'm positive are gold,' Sean said briskly and began to eat, pausing only to offer his two browns their share of his meal. 'There's a lot of 'em about, too. Are you going to take back all you can find?'

'Heavens no!' Pol Nietro exclaimed, throwing both hands up in dismay. His white hair, wiry and thick, stood out about his head like a nimbus, giving him a benign appearance which in his case was accurate. 'We won't make *that* mistake on Pern.'

'Oh, no, never,' Bay Harkenon said, leaning towards Sean as if to touch him in reassurance. 'Our investigative techniques no longer require endless specimens to confirm conclusions, you know.'

'Specimens?' Sean frowned and Sorka looked apprehensive.

'Representative would perhaps be the better word.'

'And we'd use the eggs . . . of the green, of course,' Pol added quickly, 'since the female greens do not appear to be as maternally inclined as the gold.'

'You don't want a gold's eggs at all?' Sean was confused.

'Not all of them,' Bay repeated earnestly. 'And only a dead hatchling of the other colours if one could be obtained. We've had more than enough green casualties.'

'Dead is the only way you'd get one,' Sean muttered.

'You're likely correct,' Bay said with a little sigh. She was a portly woman in her late fifth decade but fit and agile enough not to hinder the expedition. 'I've never been able to establish a rapport with animals.' She looked wistfully at Sorka's bronze, now lying in the total relaxation of sleep around the girl's neck, fore and hindlegs dangling down her chest, the limp tail extending almost to her waist.

'A dragonet's so hungry when it's born, it'll take food anywhere it can,' Sean said with marked tactlessness.

'Oh, I don't think I could deprive someone of—'

'We're all supposed to be equal here, aren't we?' Sean demanded. 'You got the same rights as anyone else, y'know.'

'Well said, young nipper,' Jim Tillek said. 'Well said!'

'If the dragonets were only a little bigger,' Pol murmured, as much to himself as to the others, and then he sighed.

'If dragonets were only a little bigger what?' Tillek asked.

'Then they'd be an equal match for the wherries.'

'They already are!' Sean said loyally, stroking one of his browns. If he had named them, he kept their names to himself. Sorka also wanted to ask him how he had trained his browns to answer his various whistled commands. Not that Duke ever disobeyed her – once he figured out what she wanted.

'Perhaps you're right,' Pol said, giving his head a little shake.

144

'Tinkering isn't something lightly undertaken. You know how many efforts abort or distort.' Bay smiled to ease her gentle chiding.

'Tinker?' Sean came alert.

'They didn't mean you, silly,' Sorka assured him in a low voice.

'Why would you want to ... ahem ... manipulate,' Jim Tillek asked, 'critters that have been doing quite well in protecting themselves for centuries. And us.'

'Out of the stew of creation, so few survive and often not the obvious, more perfectly designed or environmentally suited species,' Pol said with a long patient sigh. 'It is always amazing to me what does win the evolutionary race to become the common ancestors of a great new group. I'd never have expected anything as close to our vertebrates as wherries and dragonets on another planet. The really strange coincidence is that our storytellers so often invented a four-legged, two-winged creature in fantasy, although none ever existed on Earth. Here they are, hundreds of light years away from the people who only imagined them.' He indicated the sleeping Duke. 'Remarkable. And not as badly designed as the ancient chinese dragons ...'

'Badly designed?' asked the seaman, amused.

'Well, look at him. It's redundant to have both forelimbs and wings. Earth avian species opted for a wing instead of forelimbs, though some have vestigial claws on what had once been the forefinger before the limb became a wing. I'll grant you that a curved rear limb is useful for springing off the ground, and the dragonet's are powerful, with muscles into the back to provide that assistance, but that long back is vulnerable. I wonder how they arrange their mechanics so that they can sit up for so long without moving.' Pol peered at the sleeping Duke, touched the limp tail. 'There is one slight improvement – the excretory hole in the fork of the tail instead of under it. And there are dorsal nostrils and lungs, which are a distinct improvement. Humans are very poorly designed, you

145

know,' he went on, happy to be able to exercise his favourite complaint to a wrapt audience.

'I mean, surely you can see how ridiculous it is to have an air pipe,' he touched first his nose, 'that crosses the food pipe,' and then his rather prominent adam's apple. 'People are always choking themselves to death. And a vulnerable cranium: one good crack and the concussion can cause impairment if not fatality. Those Vegans have their brains well protected in tough internal sacs. You'd never concuss a Vegan.'

'I'd rather have bellyaches in my middle than headaches,' Tillek said in a droll tone. 'Though, from what I saw once, some of the other Vegan operating mechanisms are exceedingly unhandy, particularly the sexual and reproductive arrangements.'

Pol snorted. 'So you think having the playground between the sewers makes more sense?'

'Didn't say that, Pol,' Jim Tillek answered hurriedly with a glance at the two children, though neither were paying the adults much heed. 'It's a bit handier for us, though.'

'And more vulnerable. Oh, my, oh my, there I go again, falling into the lecture attitude. But there are endless ways in which we humans could be profitably improved . . .'

'We are doing that, though, aren't we, Pol dear?' Bay said kindly.

'Oh, yes, cybernetically we do, and *in vitro* we can correct certain gross genetic mistakes. It's true that we are allowed to use the Eridani mentasynth, though personally I don't know whether our response to it is a boon or not. It makes people too empathic with their experimental animals. But we can't do much yet, of course, with the laws which the Pure Humans forced through to prohibit drastic changes.'

'Who'd want to?' Tillek asked, and then frowned at Pol and Bay.

'Not us,' Bay assured him hastily. 'We don't have that kind of need on this world. But I sometimes feel that the

146

Pure Human Life Group was wrong to oppose alterations that would permit humans to use those water worlds in Ceti IV. Lungs exchanged for gills and webbing on hands and feet is not that great or blasphemous an adaptation. The foetus still goes through a similar stage *in utero* and there's good evidence for a more aquatic past for adults. Think how many planets would be open to Humans if we weren't so limited to land areas in our gravitational and atmospheric requirements! Even if we could provide special enzymes for some of the dangerous gases. Cyanides have kept us out of so many places. Why . . .' She threw up her hands as words failed her.

Sean was peering at the two specialists with some suspicion.

'Campfire talk,' Sorka said sagely, in a low voice to Sean. 'They don't mean it.'

Sean snorted and, carefully positioning his two brown dragonets, rose to his feet.

'I plan to be up tomorrow before dawn. Best time to catch the dragonets feeding and know who's minding the nests.'

'Me, too,' Sorka said, rising.

Tillek had rigged shelters for all well above the high-tide marks, protection against the sudden squalls which had been frequent in this early summer season. Thermal blankets had been stitched into sleeping bags and into one Sorka gratefully crawled. Duke, without apparently waking, accommodated himself to her new position. She had a little trouble falling asleep because, for a while, the beach seemed to heave beneath her.

A little warning chirp from Duke roused her. Snores drifted over from the adults but, as her eyes grew accustomed to the pre-dawn darkness, she saw Sean rise from his place. The browns' quiet murmurs had wakened Duke. She could just see Sean turn his head towards her and then westward. With an economy of movement he crept to the ashes of last night's fire, and rummaged quietly in the supply sacks, taking several items which he stuffed into his shirt.

She was suddenly sorry that she had involved him in this expedition. She'd been a right idjit, practically handing him his own horse so that he would be scotfree even before his family got their promised carthorses and crossed Jordan to lose themselves in roaming a vast new continent. Sorka didn't like to think of how terribly lonely she would be without Sean.

She waited until he was out of sight and then she rose. However, when she took a pack of rations and one of the red fruits they'd gathered before dinner, she also left a note, saying that she and Sean had gone to check nests and would be back soon after dawn to report.

As she trotted along the beach, she ate the red fruit, discarding the blemished side where a mould, perhaps a Terran one, had got at it, just as she used to eat windfall apples and throw away the brown bits back on Earth. At a little distance from each of the nests, she had piled small cairns of white ocean-smoothed stones so that she could find each clutch without stepping into them. Sometimes sand covered the nests of greens. She found the first two with no problem and hurried towards the third, the possible gold's nest. There was a faint trace of brightness on the eastern sky and she wanted to be hidden from view in the bushes before day actually broke.

It was also wonderful to be alone, and safe, in a part of a world that had never felt the tread of feet. Sorka had studied the EEC survey reports and maps often enough to know that those intrepid people had not been on this particular beach. She exulted in the special magic of being first and sighed at being so privileged, even if that knowledge was her private honour. Her earlier desire to be able to tag a special place with *her* name had altered to finding just the most beautiful spot in this new world, beautiful at least to her, a really unique place for which she, too, could be remembered. Better still would be for the colonists to wish to name a mountain, or a river, or a valley after Sorka Hanrahan because of something special that she had done which earned such an honour. On such a new world, at such an hour, are such dreams dreamed that the bright realities of day casually wither.

She was so lost in that dream that she nearly stumbled over the cairn and into the half-buried clutch. Duke saved her from the error with a warning cheep.

She stroked his little head in gratitude. If she could alter one thing about Duke, it would be to give him speech. She could interpret his various noises accurately now, and was able to understand what other dragonets said to their owners, but Duke would have been perfect if they could communicate to each other in a common language. Someone had said that forked tongues could not manage speech and she certainly didn't want any drastic changes in Duke. Especially his size. Any bigger and he wouldn't fit on her shoulder so comfortably.

Maybe she should have a chat with the marine rangers who worked with the dolphins. They communicated with each other about complex matters. It was just as likely that the dragonets did, too, judging by the way they had routed the wherries. Even Admiral Benden had commented on it.

Thinking of the hero of Cygnus, she must use strategy now, too, and hide her tracks. The gold dragonets were a lot smarter than the stupid green ones. She found a thick fronded branch from the underbrush and covered her footprints in the dry sand, retreating into the brush before making her way back to a good vantage point close to, but obscured from, the beach and the nest.

Dawn coincided with a cheerful morning chorus as a fair of dragonets swooped down to the foreshore. Only the gold approached the nest, the others, brown and bronze and blue, remained a discreet distance from it. Their bodies outlined against the white sands, Sorka could now appreciate the difference in sizes. The golden female was the largest, taller in the shoulder by the span of two fingers than the bronzes who seemed to be the next in size though one or two of the browns were nearly as big. The blues were definitely smaller, moving with quick nervous steps, examining seaweeds, discarding some and hauling others towards the nest with many smug chirps. The bronzes and browns seemed to be discussing something, murmuring and cheeping to themselves while the blues were clearly interested only in what might be edible. Or were they? For now she could see that the nest was being surrounded by a circle of weed. The browns and bronzes got busy then, depositing the scuttling sea things she had seen on the first occasion.

With an almost peremptory screech, the gold female rose from the nest, swooping down over the heads of the bronzes and browns, dipping wings at the blues as she raced towards the sea. The others followed, not as gracefully, Sorka thought, as the queen, but swiftly. She saw them climb over the gently lapping surf and then suddenly dive at the waves, creeling triumphantly as they fished. Abruptly, they all disappeared. One moment they were there, suspended above the ocean, the next the sky was completely clear of flashing dragonet bodies. Sorka blinked in astonishment.

She thought about what she had seen, about the little female's inspection and cautiously she crept from the underbrush. If the eggs were this close to hatching, and if she could get one back to Bay Harkenon in time for her to feed it, she'd finally have a creature of her own. Dr Harkenon was a nice, kind lady, not the least bit stuffy like some of the section heads were, and a dragonet would be a companion to her.

Sorka didn't think about it any further: she acted. Darting out of her hiding place, she streaked to the nest, made a grab for the nearest egg on the top of the pile and scurried as fast as she could back to the underbrush.

She was only just in time, the branches still swaying from her swift passage, when the dragonets were back again. There seemed to be more of them now. The little golden one landed right by the eggs while bronzes, browns and blues were depositing fish which flapped helplessly within the seaweed circle. Suddenly the welcoming chorus began and Sorka was torn between the desire to watch the magical moment of hatching and the need to get her purloined egg to Bay in time. To spur her to action, she felt the egg move against her skin for she had tucked it under her pullover for warmth and protection.

'Don't you dare make a sound, Duke!' she whispered harshly when she heard Duke's chest begin to rumble. She caught his little jaw between her fingers and glared him straight in his faceted eyes which had begun to whirl with happy colours. 'She'll kill me!'

He clearly understood her warning and hunched closer to her, clinging with sharp nails to her hair and hiding his face against her braid. Then she crawled backward from the beach edge until she was screened sufficiently to stand up. Dead fronds and branches underfoot conspired to tangle her feet and she encountered a disheartening variety of thorny bushes and needly plants. But her colonist garb was designed to take hard usage and it did. So did her hands and face but she plunged on.

When she could no longer hear the cries of the dragonets, she turned west and crashed back out to the beach. She pelted down the sands as fast as she could, ignoring the stitch in her side in deference to the antics of the egg beating at her ribs. Duke circled about her head, keening with an obediently muted anxiety.

Surely she must be almost back at the camp. Was that the first cairn she had passed or the second? She stumbled and Duke cried out in terrible alarm, a shrill strident shriek, like one of the peacocks that had inhabited her father's farm: a ghastly sound like someone in extreme agony. He had swooped, too, tugging valiantly at her shoulder, as if he himself could support her.

His shriek had been sufficient to rouse the sleepers. Jim Tillek was the first one to struggle to his feet, tangled in the bag for the first few steps. Pol and Bay were more laggard until they recognized Sorka.

Sorka, ignoring both Tillek's urgent queries and helping hands, staggered to the plump microbiologist, dropping

151

heavily to her knees and fumbling to get the egg into Bay's hands for she could feel its cracking running along the shell.

'Here! Here, this is yours, Bay!' she gasped, grabbing the astonished woman's hands and closing them about the egg.

Bay's reaction was to thrust it back to Sorka but the girl had thrown herself towards the supply packs, rumaging for something edible, fumbling to open a packet of protein bars and break one into newborn-dragonet size pieces. It'd be no good to have it choke to death.

'It's cracking, Sorka. Pol! What do I do with it? It's cracking all over!' Bay was exclaiming, not at all certain that she wanted to be part of this action.

'It's yours, Bay, an animal that will love only you,' Sorka said in gasps, floundering back to the woman with full hands. 'It's hatching. It'll be yours. Here, feed it these. Pol, Captain, see what you can find under the seaweed for it to eat. You be bronzes. See, watch what Duke's going after.'

For the bronze, creeling with exultation, was dragging a huge branch of seaweed up from the high-tide line.

'Just bundle the seaweed up, Pol,' Tillek was saying as he demonstrated.

'It's cracked!' Bay cried, half-afraid, half-delighted. 'There's a head! Sorka! What do I do now?'

Twenty minutes later the risen sun shone on an excited quartet as Bay, with the most beatific and incredulous expression on her face, cradled a lovely golden dragonet on her forearm. Its head was an ornament on the back of her hand, its forearms loosely encircled her wrist. Fortunately its extended belly had support from Bay's well-fleshed limb, its hindlegs dangled by her elbow and its tail was lightly twined around her upper arm. A slight noise, similar to a snore, could be discerned. Bay stroked the sleeping creature from time to time, amazed by the texture of its skin, by such details as strong but delicate claws, the translucent wings, the strength of the newborn's tail about her arm. She constantly extolled its perfections.

Once the creature had been fed, Jim Tillek regenerated the fire and served a hot drink to counteract the chilly breeze from the sea.

'I think we should go back to the nest, Pol,' Sorka said, 'to see if . . . if . . .'

'Some didn't make it?' Jim finished for her. 'You need to eat.'

'But then it'll be too late.'

'It's probably too late already, young lady,' Tillek said firmly. 'And you've acquitted yourself superbly anyhow, delivering the gold. That's the highest status of the species, isn't it?'

Pol nodded, peering detachedly at Bay's sleeping charge. 'I don't think any biologist actually has one yet. Ironic that.'

'Always the last to know, huh?' Jim asked, screwing his eyebrows sardonically but grinning. 'Ah, what have we here?' He pointed his long cooking fork at the figure plodding from the west. 'He's got something. Can you make it out better, Sorka, with your young eyes?'

'Maybe he's got more eggs and you'll have one, too, Pol and Jim.'

'I tend to doubt Sean's altruism, Sorka,' Pol remarked drily and she flushed, for, although she wished Sean to be accepted and liked as she accepted and liked him, she knew that the older members of this expedition were wary of him. 'Now, now, child. I'm not being critical. It's a difference of temperament and attitude.'

'He's carrying something and it's larger than an egg, and his two dragonets are very excited. No,' Sorka amended, 'they're upset!'

On her shoulder, Duke raised up on to his hindlegs, uttering one shrill query. She could feel him sag as he received an answer, and he gave a little moan: almost a sob, she thought and reached up to stroke him. He nuzzled her hand as if he appreciated her sympathy. She could feel

153

the tension in his small frame, in the way his feet gripped her pullover. Once again she was glad that her mother had reinforced the fabric to prevent his claws puncturing and bruising her skin. She turned her head, rubbing his side with her cheek.

Everyone watched Sean now, making his way towards them, until his bundle could be distinguished as layers of wide leaves, closely wrapped and bound with green climber vine. He was aware of their scrutiny and he looked tired. Sorka thought he also looked unhappy. He came right up to the two scientists, not really focusing on them or he would have noticed the sleeping gold dragonet, and carefully deposited his bundle by Pol.

'There you are. Two of 'em. One barely touched. And some of the green eggs. Had to search both nests to find some that snakes hadn't sucked dry.'

Pol laid one hand on Sean's offering. 'Thank you, Sean. Thank you very much. Are the two . . . from a gold's clutch or a green's.'

'Gold's of course,' Sean said with a disgusted snort. 'Greens rarely hatch. They're snake eaten. I got there just in time.' Then he looked, almost challengingly, at Sorka.

She didn't know what to say.

'So did Sorka,' Jim Tillek replied proudly, and nodded to Bay.

Only then did Sean see the sleeping dragonet. A fleeting look of surprise, admiration and annoyance crossed his face but he sat down with rather a thump.

Sorka didn't quite meet his eye. She didn't wish to detract from his accomplishment for indeed, he had returned with what the scientists had needed.

'I didn't do as well,' she heard herself saying, 'I didn't get what we were sent after. You did.'

Sean grunted, his face expressionless. Above his head, his browns exchanged news with her bronze in a rapid fire of cheeps, chirps, and murmurs. Then each gave a flip to its wings to close them back, and settled in the sun to catch the warming rays.

'Chow's up,' Jim Tillek said and began filling plates with fried fish and rings of one of the fruit nuts that was improved by cooking.

7

●

'So, Ongola, what have you to report?' Paul Benden asked.

Emily Boll, the only other member of this extraordinary meeting, poured a measure of Benden's precious brandy into three glasses and passed them around before taking her own seat. Ongola used the interval to organize his thoughts. The three had gathered, as they often did, in the meteorology tower beside the landing grid now used by the sleds and the one shuttle which had been altered for sparing use as a cargo carrier.

Both Admiral and Governor with naturally paler skin now vied with the swarthy Ongola in face colour for all had worked hard in the fields, in the mountains, on the sea, actively participating in every aspect of the colony's endeavours.

Once the colonists took up their 'stake' acres and Landing's purpose had been accomplished, the ostensible 'leaders' would turn consultants with no more authority than other stakeholders. The Council would convene regularly to discuss broad topics and redress problems which affected the entire colony. A yearly democratic meeting would vote on any issues that required the consent of all. Magistrate Cherry Duff administered justice at Landing and would have a circuit for grievances and any litigation. By the terms of the Pern Charter, Charterer and Contractors alike would be autonomous on their 'stake' acres. Idealistic, perhaps, but as Benden repeatedly insisted, there was more than enough land and resources to allow everyone a latitude of choices.

There had been no more than a few grumbles so far on Joel Lilienkamp's disposition of supplies and *matériel* brought with them. Everyone knew that once the supplies which the ships had carried had been exhausted, all would have to learn to make do with what they had, replace with their own industry or barter with the appropriate crafters. Many people prided themselves on being able to improvise and everyone took good care of irreplaceable tools and equipment.

An arbitration board had been voted on at one of the first mass meetings, comprising three ex-judges, two former governors and four non-legal people who would hold their office for two years. This board would look into grievances and settle such disputes as might occur about 'staking acres' or contractual misunderstandings. The colony had four trained legists and two attorneys though it was hoped such representations would be minimal.

'There is no dispute so bitter that it cannot be arbitrated by an impartial board or by a jury of peers,' Emily Boll had stated fervently and persuasively at one of the earliest mass meetings attended by every one, including sleeping children. 'Most of you know war firsthand.' She had paused dramatically. 'Wars of attrition over land and water, wars of terrible annihilation in space itself. Pern is now far, far from those former battle fields. You are here because you wished to avoid the contagion of territorial imperatives that has plagued humans since time began. Where there is a whole planet, with diverse and magnificent lands and wealth and prospects, there is no longer a need to covet a neighbour's possessions. Stake your own acres, build your homes, live in peace with the rest of us and help us all build a world truly a paradise.'

The power of her ringing voice, the sincerity of her fervent phrases had, on that glorious evening, motivated everyone to fulfil that dream. Emily Boll was also a realist, and knew very well that there were dissident factors among those who had listened so politely and had responded by rising to their feet with a cheering ovation for her stirring words. But she devoutly hoped that the dissident element would become so involved in their new life on Pern that they would have little time, energy or occasion to indulge in intrigue. Both leaders were constantly accessible and that often solved small discontents which were not allowed to grow into problems.

Between the weekly informal gatherings and the monthly mass meetings where most administrative matters were put to a democratic vote, the colony was running smoothly, with only technical hitches, usually sorted by a joat but occasionally needing a specialist.

Within any diverse human group, there were always a number of abrasive personalities who enjoyed making trouble, fomenting discord where there was no need, for the pleasure such manipulations gave them. Avril was the most flamboyant of these. Lemos, Nabol, Kimmer and a handful of others had been tagged as possible troublemakers. The Charter, and the contracts, had incorporated the right to discipline its signatories for 'acts against the common good'. Such acts had as yet to be defined, considering the nature of the colony, and what could be considered as an act endangering the common good.

Emily and Paul had had considerable arguments about the necessity for any sort of penal code. Paul Benden favoured the 'punishment fitting the crime' as an object lesson for miscreants and frequent breakers of the 'peace and tranquillity of the settlement'. Benden also preferred to mete out community discipline on the spot, shaming offenders in public and requiring them to do some of the more disagreeable tasks required by any large group of people. So far this rough justice had been sufficient for the need. As Paul pointed out, there were hardly the same opportunities or rewards for troublemakers here on Pern as there had been on Earth or First.

So the discreet surveillance continued on a number of folk and Paul and Emily met with Ongola from time to time to discuss the general morale of the community and those problems that were best kept discreet. Paul and Emily kept official 'office' hours six days of the established seven-day week.

'We may not be religious in the archaic meaning of the word, but it makes good sense to give worker and beast one day's rest,' Emily stated in the second of the mass meetings. 'The old Judean Bible used by some of the old religious sects on Earth contained a great many common sensible suggestions for an agricultural society and some moral and ethic traditions which are worthy of retention,' and she held up a hand, smiling benignly, 'but without any hint of fanatic adherence! We left *that* back on Earth along with war!'

While the two leaders knew that even this loose form of democratic government might be untenable when the settlers had spread out from Landing to their own acres, they did hope that the habits acquired would suffice. Early American pioneers on that western push had exhibited a keen sense of independence and mutual assistance. The later Australian and New Zealand communities had risen above tyrannical governors and isolation to build people of character, resource and incredible adaptability. The first international Moonbase had refined the art of independence, co-operation and resourcefulness. The original settlers on First had been largely the progeny of ingenious Moon and asteroid belt miner parents, and the Pern colony had many descendants of those original pioneering groups.

Paul and Emily proposed to institute yearly congregations of as many people from the isolated settlements as possible to reaffirm the basic tenets of the colony, acknowledge progress and apply the minds of many to address any general problems. Such a gathering would also be the occasion for trading and social festivities. Cabot Francis Carter, one of the legists, had proposed setting aside a certain area, mid-way on the continent, which would be the centre for these annual assemblies.

'That would be the best of all possible worlds,' Cabot had said in a mellifluous bass voice which had often stirred Supreme Courts on Earth and First. Emily had once told Paul that Cabot was the most unlikely of their Charter members, but his Legal Guild had produced the actual Charter and rammed it through the bureaucratic gunge to be ratified by the FSP Council. 'We may not achieve it on Pern. But we can damnsure try!'

Paul recalled that stirring challenge this evening as he ticked off names on his long callused fingers. 'Which is why I think we should keep tabs on people like Bitra, Tashkovich, Nabol, Lemos, Olubushtu, Kung, Usuai and Kimmer. The list is, mercifully, short, considering our numbers. I'm not adding Kenjo because he's shown absolutely no connection with any of the others.'

'That smacks too much of the subterfuges used by other governments in more parlous times,' Emily said in a grim humour when the subject of dissension and surveillance had first been raised at one of these informal evenings. 'I refuse to demean myself or my office by such tactics.'

'There's nothing demeaning in knowing who's agin you,' Paul had argued. 'An intelligence section has always proved invaluable.'

'In revolutions, wars, power struggles, yes, but not here on Pern.'

'Here as well as everywhere else in the galaxy, Em,' Paul replied forcefully, taking up the old argument, 'Mankind, not to mention Nathi, and even the Eridanites to some degree, prove in many ways that greed is universal. I don't see the bounty of Pern changing that trait.'

'Forego that futile old argument, my friends,' Ongola said with one of his wise, sad smiles. 'The necessary steps have already been taken to defunction the gig. I have, as you recommended,' Ongola said, inclining his head to

Paul, 'stripped the gig of several minor but essential parts in the ignition system which would be obvious early on, and substituted two dud chips in the guidance module which are not.' He gestured out the window. 'Sleds are allowed to park any which way, effectively but surreptitiously blocking the gig from taking off. But I don't really know why she would.'

Paul Benden winced and the other two looked away from him, knowing that he had allowed himself to be too intimate with her for an injudicious length of that outward voyage.

'Well, I'd be more worried if Avril knew about that cache of Kenjo's. Telgar's figures indicate that there's half a tank's worth for the *Mariposa*.' Paul Benden grimaced. He'd found it hard enough to believe that Kenjo Fusaiyuko had scrounged so much fuel. Paul had a grudging admiration for the sheer scope of the theft, even if he couldn't understand the motive, especially the risks that Kenjo had got away with during all those fuel-saving shuttle trips.

'Avril favours us so seldom with her company that I don't worry that she'd discover the hoard,' Emily said with a wry smile. 'I've also managed to have Lemos, Kimmer and Nabol assigned to different sections and few occasions to return here. Divide and conquer, the man said.'

'Inappropriate, Emily,' Paul replied, grinning.

'If, and I do stress that improbability, Avril should discover and use Kenjo's purloined fuel,' Ongola began, holding up a finger for each point, 'manage to find the missing pieces, and fly the gig out of here undetected, she would have a half-full tank. She would not then drain the ships' reserves to a danger point. Frankly, we would be well rid of her and whoever she deigns to take with her. I think we dwell too much on the matter. Those seismic reports from the eastern archipelago are far more worrying. Young Mountain is smoking again and twitching its feet.'

'I agree,' Paul Benden said, quite willing to turn to the more immediate problem.

'Yes, but for what purpose did Kenjo take so much fuel?' Emily wanted to know. 'You haven't answered that question. Why would he risk the safety of passengers and cargo? And he is a genuinely eager colonist. He's already chosen his stake acreage.'

'A pilot of Kenjo's ability risked nothing,' Paul replied smoothly. 'His shuttle flights were without incident. I do know that flying is his life.'

Ongola regarded Paul Benden in mild surprise. 'Hasn't he done enough flying for one lifetime?'

Paul smiled with understanding. 'Not Kenjo. What I do completely appreciate is that flying a mere power sled is a comedown, a loss of prestige, face, considering the kind of craft he's flown and where he's been. You say that he's chosen his acres, Emily? Where?'

'Down beyond what people are beginning to call the Sea of Azov, as far away from Landing as he can get but on rather a pleasant plateau to judge by the probe report,' Emily replied. She hoped that this meeting wouldn't be prolonged. Pierre had promised a special meal and she found she was enjoying those quiet dinners far more than she thought she would.

'Howinhell is Kenjo going to get those tonnes of fuel there?' Benden wanted to know.

'I suspect we'll have to wait and see,' Ongola replied with the trace of a smile on his lips. 'He's got the same right as everyone else to use power sleds to transport his goods, and he's done some close trading with work units at the Commissary. Shall I have a word with Joel about Kenjo's requisitions?'

Emily glanced quickly at Paul who was adamant in his defence of Kenjo. 'Well, I don't like unsolved riddles. I'd prefer some sort of explanation, and I think you would, too, Paul.' When Benden nodded reluctantly, Emily said that she would speak to Joel Lilienkamp.

'Which brings us back to that third tremor,' Paul Benden

said. 'How's work progressing on buttressing the Stores warehouses and the one with all the medical supplies? We can't afford to lose such irreplaceable items.'

Ongola consulted his notes. He wrote with a bold angular script that looked, from Emily's angle, like ancient manuscript ornamentations. All three of them, and most section heads, made a point of reverting to less sophisticated ways of note-taking. The power packs, whose rechargeability was good but not infinite, must be reserved for essential usages so everyone was rediscovering the art of calligraphy.

'The work will be completed by next week. The seismic net has been extended as far as the active volcano in the eastern archipelago and to Drake's Lake.'

'Are we going to let him get away with that?' Paul wanted to know, with a humorous grimace at the name.

'Why not?' Emily asked, grinning. 'No one's contending it. Drake was the first to see it. A community settling there would have ample space to grow, and plenty of industry to support it.'

'Is it scheduled for a vote?' Paul asked after an appreciative sip of his brandy.

'No,' Ongola said with another hint of a grin, 'Drake is still campaigning. He doesn't want any opposition and whatever there might have been is now worn down.'

Paul snorted and Emily cast her eyes upwards in amused exasperation with the flamboyant pilot. Then Paul pensively regarded the remainder of the brandy in his glass. As Emily went on to the next point on their informal agenda, he took another sip, rolling the liquor around in his mouth, savouring the soon to be exhausted beverage. He could and did drink the quikal but found it harsh to a palate trained to subtleties. Rene Mallibeau assured him that they would be able, in time, to produce a decent brandy on Pern. Bernard Hegelman was using the unimproved seeds of local grasses to make beer or ale without too much success; this was probably because of the high silicates and the small amount of stored carbohydrate in each seed.

'We are proceeding well in general terms,' Emily was saying briskly. 'You heard that one of the dolphins died, but Olga's death was accepted by her community with considerable equanimity. According to Ann Gabri and Efram, they had expected more fatalities. Olga was, apparently,' and now she grinned, 'older than she said she was and hadn't wished to let her last calf go into the unknown without her.'

All three chuckled and followed Paul's lead as he raised a toast to maternal love.

'Even our . . . nomads . . . have settled in,' Emily went on, after checking her note pad. 'Or rather, spread out.' She tapped it with her pencil, still unused to handwriting notes but struggling to get accustomed to archaic memory assists. The only voice-activated device still operable was the surface interface with the main computer banks on the *Yokohama* but it was rarely used now. 'The nomads've made rather a lot of inroads on clothing fabrics but when they are depleted, that's the end of it and they'll have to make their own or trade, the same as the rest of us. We have located all the campsites. Even on foot, the Tuareg contingent can travel astonishing distances but they camp for a while, in two separate sections.'

'Well, they've a whole planet to lose themselves in,' Paul said expansively. 'Have they posed any other problems, Ongola?'

The dark man shook his heavy head, lowering the lids of his deep set eyes. He was agreeably surprised by that. But, as the Admiral had said, there was a whole planet to roam in. Every week each tribe sent a representative to the veterinary sheds. The forty-two mares brought in coldsleep by the colony were all in foal and the nomads' leaders had accepted the fact that a mare's gestation period was eleven months on Pern as it had been on Earth.

'As long as the vets keep their sense of humour. But Red Hanrahan seems to understand their ways and deals with them.'

'Hanrahan? Didn't his daughter find the lizards?'

'She and a boy, one of the travellers,' Ongola replied. 'They also provided the corpses which the bios have been clucking over.'

'Could be useful creatures,' Benden said.

'They already are,' Emily added stoutly.

Ongola smiled. One day, Ongola thought, he would find a nest at the critical hatching point and he would have one of those charming, friendly, nearly intelligent creatures as a pet. He had once learned Dolphin but had never been able to overcome his fear of being constricted underwater to share their world properly. He needed space about him. Once, when Paul was sharing one of the long watches with him on the journey here, the Admiral had argued most eloquently that the dangers of outer space were even more inimical to human life than those of inner sea.

'Water is airless,' Paul had said, 'although it contains oxygen, but until the Pure Lives' hold on human adaptations is broken, no human will be able to swim without artificial help. Space has no oxygen at all.'

'But you are weightless in space. Water presses down on you. You feel it.'

'You'd better not feel space,' Paul had replied with a laugh but he had not argued the point further.

'Now, gentlemen, to more pleasant matters,' Paul said. 'How many contract marriages are to be registered tomorrow, Emily?'

Emily smiled, riffling pages of her notepad to come to the next seventh day sheet, since that had become the usual time for such celebrations. In order to widen the gene pool in the next generation, the Charter permitted unions of varying lengths, first insuring the support of a gravid woman and the early years of the resultant child. Prospective partners could choose which conditions suited their requirements but there were severe penalties, up to the loss of all stake acres, for failing to fulfil whatever contract had been agreed and signed before the requisite number of witnesses.

'Three!'

'The numbers are falling off,' Paul remarked.

'I've done my bit,' Ongola said, slyly glancing at the two staunchly single men.

Ongola had courted Sabra Stein, so adroitly that neither of his close friends had realized he had become attached until their names appeared on the marital schedule six weeks ago. In fact, Sabra was already pregnant which had led Paul to remark that that big gun wasn't firing blanks. He had let his bawdy humour disguise his relief for he knew that Ongola still grieved for the wife and family of his youth, destroyed in the holocaust of a direct Nathi hit on their colony on Ceti III. Ongola's hatred of the Nathi and his implacable desire for revenge had sustained the man throughout the War. For a long while, Paul had worried that his favourite aide and valued commander might be unable to alter that overpowering hatred now in a less frenetic era.

'Emily, has Pierre consented yet?' Ongola asked, a knowing grin lightening a sombre face that even his present felicitous state did not completely brighten.

Emily was astonished. She had thought that she and Pierre had been so discreet but she had recently noticed in herself a tendency to smile more easily, and lose the thread of conversations for no apparent reason. They were an unlikely combination of personalities but that was half the pleasure of it. It had begun quite unexpectedly about the fifth week after Landing, when Pierre had asked her opinion of a casserole, composed entirely of indigenous ingredients. He administered the mass catering of Landing, and very well, she thought, considering the wide range of tastes and dietary requirements. He had started to serve her special dishes when she ate at the big mess-hall. Then, when she would often have to work through the lunch-hour, Pierre de Courci would bring over the tray she ordered. 'If I were the possessive type, I would keep his cooking to myself,' she replied. 'Kindly remember that I am past child-bearing, an advantage you men have over me. How about it, Paul? Will you do your bit?' Emily knew her tone had a snap to it, born of envy. None of her grown children had wished to accompany her on 'a one-way journey'.

Unperturbed, Paul Benden merely smiled enigmatically and sipped at his brandy.

'Caves!' Sallah cried, nudging Tarvi's arm and pointing to the rock barrier in front of them. Sunlight outlined openings in its sheer face.

He reacted instantly and enthusiastically, with the kind of almost innocent joy of discovery that Sallah found so appealing in him. The continually unfolding beauties of Pern had not palled on Tarvi Andiyar. Each new wonder was greeted with as much interest as the last one he had extolled for its magnificence, its wealth, or its potential. She had wangled ruthlessly to get herself assigned as his expedition pilot. This was their third trip together and their first solo excursion.

Sallah was playing it cautiously, concentrating on making herself so professionally indispensable to Tarvi that an opportunity to project her femininity would not force him to retreat into his usual utterly courteous, utterly impersonal shell. She had seen other women who made a determined play for the handsome, charming geologist rebuffed by his demeanour; surprised, puzzled, and sometimes hurt, by the way in which he eluded their ploys. For a while, Sallah Telgar wondered if Tarvi liked women at all but he had shown no preference for the acknowledged male lovers in Landing. He treated everyone, man, woman, and child, with the same charming affability and understanding. Whatever his sexual preference, he was nonetheless expected to add to the next generation. Sallah was already determined to be the medium and would find the moment.

Perhaps this was it. Tarvi had a special fondness for caves: orifices of the Mother Earth, entrances to the mysteries of her creation and construction, windows into her magic and bounty. Even though this was Pern, he worshipped the same Mystery that had dominated his life so far, even the whimsical cruelty to the brash men who raped her with mines and pits, or amputated her external skin layers.

This trip was to make an aerial reconnaissance of the location of several mineral deposits noted by the metallurgy probes. Iron, vanadium, manganese and even germanium were to be found in the mountainous spine towards which Sallah was now aiming as they followed the course of a river to its source. She was also operating under the general directive that unusual sites should be recorded and photographed to offer the widest possible choice. Only a third of those with stake acreage had made their selection. There was a subtle pressure to keep everyone in the southern continent – at least in this generation – but there was no such directive in the Charter. The broad, long river valley that lay to their right as they approached the precipice was, to Sallah's mind, the most beautiful they had seen so far.

Rene Mallibeau was still looking for the proper type of slope and soil for his vineyards, though to get his project started, he had actually released some of his hoard of special soils from their sealed tanks for his experiments in viniculture. Quikal was not a universally accepted substitute for the traditional spiritous liquors. Despite being poured through a variety of filters and/or with additives, nothing could completely reduce the raw aftertaste. Rene had been promised the use of ceramic-lined metal fuel tanks which, once thoroughly cleaned, would provide him with wine vats of superior quality. Of course, once the proper oak forests had reached adequate size for use as staves, his descendants could move back to the traditional wooden barrel.

'Rather spectacular, that precipice, isn't it, Tarvi?' Sallah said, grinning rather foolishly, as if this were a surprise she herself had laid on for him.

'Indeed it is. "In Xanadu did Kubla Khan,"' he murmured in his rich deep voice.

'"Caverns measureless to man"?' Sallah capped it, careful not to sound smug that she recognized his source. Tarvi often quoted obscure Sanskrit and Pushtu texts, leaving her groping for a suitable retort.

'Precisely, o moon of my delight.'

Sallah suppressed a grimace. Sometimes Tarvi's phrases were ambiguous and she knew he didn't mean what his phrase suggested. He wouldn't be so obvious. Or would he? Had she penetrated that bland exterior after all? Infiltrated his carefully neutral façade – as perhaps they would both penetrate the palisade? She forced herself to contemplate the immense stone bulwark. Its natural fluted columns appeared carved by an inexperienced or inattentive sculptor, yet the imperfection contributed to the overall beauty of the precipice.

'This valley is six or seven klicks long,' she murmured, expressing awe for this truly impressive natural site.

From the steep right-angled fall of a spectacular *diedre*, the palisade led in a somewhat straight line for about three klicks before falling back into a less perfectly defined face that sloped down in the distance to meet the floor of the valley. She angled the sled to starboard, facing up river and they were nearly blinded by the brilliant sunlight reflecting from the water surface of the lake which had been charted by the probe.

'No, land here,' Tarvi said quickly, actually catching her arm to stress his urgency. Tarvi was not much given to personal contact and Sallah tried not to misinterpret excitement for anything else. 'I must see the caves.'

He released the safety harness and swivelled his seat around. Then he walked to the back of the sled, rummaging among the supplies.

'Lights, we'll need lights, ropes, food, water, recording devices, specimen kit,' he muttered the litany of needs as his deft movements filled two backpacks. 'Boots? Have you on proper boots . . . ah, those will do, indeed they will. Sallah, you are always well prepared.' He compounded his inadvertent injury to her feelings by one of his more ingratiating smiles.

Once again, Sallah shook her head over her whimsical fancy which had to settle on one of the most elusive males of her acquaintance. Of course, anything easily had is rarely worth having. She landed the sled at the base of the towering precipice, as near to the long narrow mouth of the cave as she could.

'Pitons, grappling hook, that first slab looks about five metres above the scree. Here you are, Sallah!'

He handed her pack over, waiting only long enough to see her grab a strap before he released the canopy, jumped down and was striding towards the towering buttress. With a resigned shrug, Sallah flipped on beacon, comunit and recorder for incoming messages, fastened her jacket, settled the rather hefty pack on her back and followed him, closing the canopy behind her.

He had scrambled up the scree and now stood with one palm flat against the slab, looking up its imposing and awesome spread, his face rapt with wonder. Gently, as a caress, he stroked the stone before he began to look right and left, assessing how best to climb to the cave. He flashed her an ingenuous smile, acknowledging her presence and assuming her willingness.

'Straight up. Not much of a climb with pitons.'

It wasn't much of a climb, but strenuous enough. Sallah could have used a breather as she crawled on to the ledge but there was the cave opening and nothing was going to deter Tarvi from immediate entrance and a leisurely inspection. Ah, well, it was just 1300 hours. They had

170

time in hand. She rolled to her feet, unlatching the hand-light from her belt just a few seconds after he had completed the same action and was at his side as he peered into the opening.

'Lords, gods and minor deities!'

His invocation was a mere whisper, solemn and awed, a susurrus of echo in the vast initial cavern. It was larger than the cargo hold of the *Yokohama*. Sallah made that instant comparison, remembering how eerily that immense barren space had struck her on her last trip, and in the next second, she wondered what this cavern would look like occupied. It would make a spectacular great hall, in the tradition of medieval times on Earth. Only more magnificent.

Tarvi held his breath, extending the hand which held the light as if reluctant to illuminate the majesty of this cavern. She heard his intake of breath, in the manner of one stealing himself to commit sacrilege and then the light came on.

Wings whirred, shadows made silent sinuous departures to the darker recesses. They both ducked as the winged denizens departed in flight lines just clearing their heads, though the cave entrance was at least four metres high. Ignoring the exodus, Tarvi moved reverently into the vast space.

'Amazing,' he murmured, 'a very thin face,' for he shined the light up and judged that the shell of the outer wall above them was barely two metres thick.

'Some bubble,' Sallah said, feeling impious and wanting to regain her equilibrium after her initial awe. 'Look, you could carve a staircase in that,' she said, her light picking out a slanting foot of rock that rose to a ledge where a large darkness indicated yet another cave.

She spoke to inattentive ears for Tarvi was prowling about with a hand gauge, determining the width of the entrance and the dimensions of the cave. She hurried after him. She was by no means afraid of anything she had yet seen flying, walking, creeping or crawling on

171

this planet but dark holes leading who-knew-where generated a critical need for companionship. When she caught up to him, it took a stern effort of her will not to grab on to his belt or the hank of rope that descended from it.

The first chamber of this cave complex measured an awesome 57 metres deep at its widest, tapering at either end to 46 metres on the left and 42 metres on the right. Along the back wall, there were innumerable, irregular openings at random levels; some on the ground level leading into apparent tunnel complexes, most of which were high enough to admit Tarvi's tall frame with considerable head space: others, like great dead eyes, peering down from higher up the inside wall. Entranced as Tarvi was by this discovery, he was the trained scientific observer as well. With Sallah's aid, he began to draft an accurate plan of the main chamber, the openings of secondary ones and the tunnel complexes leading inward. He penetrated each to a depth of 100 metres, roped to a nervous Sallah who kept glancing back at the cave's opening for the reassuring sight of the waning day.

His rough notes were refined by the light of the gasfire on which Sallah cooked their evening meal. Tarvi had elected to settle them far enough into the cave to be protected from the stiff breeze that blew down the valley, and far enough to the left not to interfere with the habits of the cave's natural residents. Later, a low flame from the protected gasfire would discourage most of Pern's wildlife from investigating the intruders.

Somehow, Sallah did feel like an intruder here, though she had not previously been bothered by that notion. The place was awe-inspiring, not an easy emotion to provoke in someone of Sallah's background and generation.

Tarvi had 'stepped' down to the sled to bring up more drafting tools and the folding table over which he now hunched. With no comment, he had eaten the stew she had carefully prepared, absently handing back his plate for a second helping.

Sallah was of two minds about Tarvi's concentration. In the first place, she was a good cook and liked to have her skill acknowledged. In the second place, she was as glad that Tarvi was distracted. Pei Pei Ting had given her a pinch of what she swore was a potent indigenous aphrodisiac with which Sallah had seasoned Tarvi's share. She didn't need it herself, not with her mind and body vibrating to his presence and their solitude. But she was beginning to wonder if the aphrodisiac was strong enough to overcome Tarvi's enchantment with this cave. Just her luck to get him to herself for a night or two and then have him be totally enthralled by Dear Old Mother Earth in Pernese costume. But she hadn't bided her time to waste this sterling opportunity. She could wait. All night. And tomorrow. She had enough of Pei's joy dust to use tomorrow night. Maybe it just took a while to act.

'It is truly magnificent in its proportions, Sallah. Here, look!' He had straightened his torso, arching his back against cramped muscles and Sallah came up behind him, knelt and considerately began to knead his taut shoulder muscles as she peered over his shoulder.

The two-dimensional sketch had been deftly drawn with bold lines: he had added back, front and side elevations, truthfully ending them where his measurements had. But that only made the cavern more imposing, and mysterious.

'What a fort it would have been in the olden days!' He looked out towards the black interior, his wide liquid eyes shining, his face alight as imagination altered the chamber before him. 'Why, it would have housed whole tribes. Kept them secure for years from invasion. There's fresh water, you understand, down the third left-hand tunnel. Of course, the valley itself would be defensible and this the protected inner hold, with that daunting slab to defeat climbers. There are no less than eighteen different exits from the main chamber.'

She had worked her hands up the column of his neck,

then across the trapezius muscles, down to the deltoids, massaging firmly but letting her fingers linger in a movement which she had found immensely effective on other occasions when she wished to relax a man.

'Ah, how kind you are, Sallah, to know where the muscles bind.' He twisted slightly, not evading her seeking, kneading fingers; more to guide them to the sorest points. He put the low table to one side so that his arms could fall naturally to his lap as he rotated his head. 'There's a point, eleventh vertebrae . . .' he suggested and she dutifully found the knot of muscle and smoothed it expertly. He sighed like a lithe dark feline, being stroked.

She said nothing, but moved ever so slightly forward so that her body touched his. As she walked her fingers back to his neck, she dared to press against him so that, he being long in the body, her breasts lightly touched his shoulder blades. She could feel her nipples harden at the contact and her respiration quickened. Her fingers ceased to knead, began to caress, moving down over his chest in long slow motions. He caught her hands then and she could feel the stillness of him, a stillness of mind and breath for his body began to tremble slightly.

'Perhaps this is the time,' he mused as if alone. 'There will never be a better. And it must be done.'

With the suppleness that was as much a trademark of Tarvi Andiyar as his ineffable charm, he had somehow gathered her in his arms, across his lap. His expression, oddly detached as if examining her for the first time, was yet not quite the tender, loving expression she had so wished to evoke. His expressive and large brown eyes were almost sad, though his perfectly shaped lips curved in an infinitely gentle smile: as if, the thought intruded on Sallah's delight in her progress, he did not wish to frighten her.

'So, Sallah,' he said in his rich low and sensual voice, 'it is you.'

She knew she should interpret that cryptic remark but

174

then he began to kiss her, his hands suddenly of an exceedingly erotic mind of their own, and she didn't wish to interpret anything.

8

Pern date   15.01.02

Four mares, three dolphins, and twelve cows produced
their young at precisely the same moment, or so the
records for that dawn hour stood. Sean had even permitted
Sorka to observe the birth of the foal designated for him
by Pol and Bay. He had maintained a pose of scepticism
over the colour and sex of the creature although, three
days previously, he had already witnessed that the first of
the draft animals produced for his father's group was
exactly as requested, a sturdy bay mare with white socks
and a face blaze who had weighed over 70 kilos at birth
and would be the image of the long dead Shire stallion
whose sperm had begot her.

Some wit, probably Grinning Gus the amiable accordi-
onist, had quipped that Landing's records right now were
the biblical begottens of Pern's chronicle. Most of them,
fortunately, were well-begotten. The new generation was
well begun and increasing daily. Human births were less
minutely reported than the successes of animalkind but at
least as well celebrated.

Sheep and the Nubian strain of goats which had somehow adapted where other tough breeds had failed, now
grazed Landing's meadows and would soon go to farm
stake acres in the temperate belts of the southern continent. These growing herds and the flocks were patrolled
by such a proliferation of dragonets that the ecologists
were becoming concerned that the creatures would lose
their natural abilities to fend for themselves. Once the
creatures reached maturity, their voracious appetites

abated and they foraged on their own. Bronzes and golds tended to remain faithful and still accepted tidbits from those who had impressed them at hatching.

There had been a bit of consternation in the biology department when Bay Harkenon had discovered a great deal more about the mating habits of the golden queens than she had previously suspected. Her little queen mated with a bronze which Pol impressed, and the sensuality in their pets surprised them with its intensity. They responded to such a stimulus in a human fashion. After the initial shock, they came to a mutual conclusion, took a larger residence together; to continue their zoological research, of course. Considering the potential of the dragonets, Bay and Pol asked for, and got, Kitti Ping's permission to try mentasynth enhancement on the fourteen eggs which Mariah conceived in her mating flight. They fussed considerably more over the little golden Mariah than was necessary but neither she nor her clutch suffered. When Mariah produced her enhanced eggs in a specially constructed facsimile of a beach, Bay and Pol were smugly pleased.

Incorporation of mentasynth, which had originally been developed by the Beltrae, a reclusive Eridani hive culture, sparked latent empathic abilities. Dragonets had already demonstrated such an ability, amounting to an almost telepathic communication with a few people. Bay and Pol felt it was worth trying to improve on nature.

The dragonets were clearly a remarkable evolutionary attempt which, like dolphins, produced an animal which understood its environment, and so controlled it. It seems to be a law of Nature that such animals also enjoy life, possibly that's what is meant by 'enjoy'. So, like the dolphins' enhancement with mentasynth, it was hoped that the dragonets would come to a closer empathy with people.

Initially, humans from Beltrae who had been 'touched' were regarded with great suspicion, of course, but as soon as their remarkable empathetical powers with animals and other people were realized, the technique became widespread: luckily, well before the Pure Human Group became powerful. Many, even of the nomadic races, had a few valued 'healers' whose abilities had been amplified in this way.

From their studies of the tunnel snakes and wherries, Bay and Pol had come to an appreciation of the potential of the charming and useful dragonets. They were the 'chimps' among monkeys, dolphins among porpoises. It had taken many experiments with dragonet tissues, and with several generations of the little tunnel snakes, to incorporate the mentasynth system successfully but the accumulated expertise with such originally alien species as dolphins – and of course man – paid off.

Everyone in Landing now had a working knowledge of the habits of the dragonets, biological as well as psychological, for there was good cause to be grateful to the creatures and tolerate their few natural excesses. Theoretically, Bay had known that some of the owners seemed to feel the 'primitive urges' of the creatures: hunger, fear, anger, and an intense mating imperative. She had simply never thought that she would be as vulnerable as her younger colleagues. It had been an exceedingly delightful surprise. Just as long as it didn't happen too often. Which she took pains to inhibit.

Red and Mairi Hanrahan had been relieved that Sorka had impressed – the word had crept into the language about dragonets – a bronze, and Sean had browns. Occasionally Duke was absent from his usual position on Sorka's shoulder but not for a length of time that would worry the girl. She appreciated the difference between domesticated animals of long association with Mankind, and wild ones who chose to make friends with aliens.

On this eventful morning, nearly twelve months after Landing, as the mare Sean had chosen to produce his promised foal laboured to give birth, there was no doubt that Sorka, now thirteen years of age, and Sean, two years older, were in rapport with their eagerly anticipating dragonets. The three had perched on the top rail of the stable partition, their eyes whirling with growing excitement as they crooned their birth song. The little chestnut mare dropped to the straw to deliver the forelegs and head of her foal.

Above, the rafters of the barn seemed to ripple with its temporary adornment of the dragonet population of Landing, crooning and chirping continual encouragement to the labouring animals, and bugling in high-pitched tenor voices at each new arrival. Dragonets were sentimental about births and missed none in Landing, though they discreetly remained outside human habitations.

The colony's obstetricians, Basil Tomlinson, Sue O'Hara, Jivan Paramundi and Angelo Cervantes had lately been working non-stop and had drafted the nurses, and taken on apprentices. An array of dragonets on a roof became an irrefutable sign of impending birth: the dragonets were never wrong. The obstetricians could gauge the labour's progress – a little too accurately Louise Auster said – by the growing intensity of the dragonets' welcoming song. This chorus might deprive neighbours of sleep but most of the community took it in good part. Even the most jaundiced had seen the dragonets protecting the flocks and herds, and had to appreciate their value.

The chestnut mare heaved again, extruding the foal further. Since its legs, head and forequarters were wet with birth fluids, Sean could not distinguish exactly what colour the animal was. Then the rest of the body emerged and, with a final push, the hindquarters. There was no doubt that he was not only darkly dappled but male. Sean gave a crow of incredulous joy and dropped to the little fellow's head to mop it dry, even before the mare could form her bond. Tears streaming down a dusty face, Sorka hugged herself for the joy of the event. Dimly she heard the excited comments of the other animal midwives sharing this large barn.

'He's the only colt,' her father said, returning to Sean and Sorka. 'As ordered.' Though the colony actually needed as many female animals as it could breed, Sean's preference for a colt had been duly considered. And one local stallion would be a safeguard, though there were more than enough varied sperms in reserve. 'Grand fellow though,' Red remarked, nodding his head approvingly. 'Make a good sixteen hands if I'm any judge. A sturdy nine stone, I'd say. Fine good fellow and she bore him like a trooper.' He stroked the neck of the little mare who was now licking the colt as he suckled her with vigour and enjoyment. 'Come now, Sorka,' he went on, seeing her tear-streaked face. 'I'll keep my promise that you'll have a horse, too.' He gave her a reassuring hug.

'I know you will, Da,' she said, burrowing into his chest. 'I'm crying because I'm so happy for Sean. He didn't believe Pol, you know. Not for one moment.'

Red Hanrahan laughed softly, for it wouldn't do for Sean to hear. Not that the boy was likely to be aware of anything but the colt, twisting its stump of a tail as if that would speed its suckling. For once, Sean's customary wary, often cynical expression had softened with amazed tenderness as he devoured the colt with his eyes. The miracle, the wonder of what he beheld, was the knowledge that he owned this animal, this embodiment of his dream.

Now, after Sorka gave her father a hug for his assurances, she stepped away from him and her bronze glided down to her shoulder, chattering in a happy social tone as he wrapped his tail possessively about her neck. Then Duke leaned down Sorka's chest, his eyes sparkling blue and green as he, too, examined the new arrival closely. Encouraged, Sean's brown pair dropped to the lower rail of the foaling box, exchanging cheeps and chirps with him.

'You approve?' Sean asked them, grinning despite the challenge in his tone.

Bobbing their heads up and down vigorously, they extended wings, complained that the other's wing was in the way, and flicking their wings to their backs, assured

180

Sean volubly that they approved. He grinned back at them.

'He's a real beauty, Sean, just what you wanted,' Sorka said.

Unaccountably Sean shook his head, looking dubious. 'Too young to tell if he'll match Cricket.'

'Oh, you are the utter limit!' Sorka's vivid eyes flashed angrily. She left the box, nearly jamming the door rail as she closed it with considerable vehemence.

'What'd I say?' Sean demanded of Red Hanrahan, startled by her unexpected departure.

'I think you'll have to figure that one out yourself, boyo!' Red clapped him on the shoulder, torn between amusement and a certain concern for his daughter.

As Red Hanrahan walked down the aisle, checking on the other new arrivals, he considered Sorka's behaviour. She was thirteen but a well-developed girl, had been menstruating for nearly a year (her arrival on Pern had also heralded that evidence of maturity). That she 'doted' – Mairi's word for the girl's attachment – on Sean was patent to everyone but Sean. He tolerated her. As did Sean's family. Mairi and Red had talked it over, wary of Sean's background though both Hanrahans acknowledged that this was the time to discard old attitudes and opinions.

Sean, too, had made several notable concessions: whether it was competition with Sorka or male arrogance, he had improved his reading and writing skills and now frequently used a viewer to scan veterinary texts in Red's office. Red had carefully cultivated the boy's interest and encouraged him to help with the breeding stock. The boy unquestionably had a way with animals, not just horses, though he ignored sheep altogether.

'Sean says sheep are for stealing, trading and eating,' Sorka told her father when he had remarked on this exception.

The older Hanrahans had been sensible enough not to prohibit the association. She always told them where the two would be going, and had obeyed the night-time curfew which applied to all Landing's young people.

Mairi did worry occasionally that Sorka was inevitably partnered with Sean when they were assigned together to the zoological expeditions. But, as Sorka blithely explained, she got along with Sean and they were both more used to handling animals and wild life than urban-bred young people. So long as they did their obligatory share of work for the colony, and enjoyed it, they were ahead of the game. Sean was also making more of a contribution to Landing's efforts than most of his people. It was just that Sean and Sorka were becoming linked together in the collective Landing mind, as Mairi wistfully remarked one evening to Red. To his surprise, Red found himself in the position of Devil's advocate. But then, like Sorka, he had grown accustomed to Sean's ways and knew what to ignore.

Sorka's exhibition of female exasperation this morning was the first of its kind, to Red's knowledge, and he wondered ruefully if her patience with Sean's obtuseness was exhausted, or their relationship was merely entering a new phase. Sorka had had an appropriate theoretical education in sexual relationships but, until today, had shown only a patient acceptance of Sean's behaviour and eccentricities. He would have to talk with Mairi. When he got the chance.

'Red! Reeeeddd!' At such an urgent summons by another veterinarian, he ran to see what alarmed Cesar Galliani. It wasn't until much later that night that he remembered Sorka and Sean, but Mairi was already long asleep and, as well as being in the second trimester of a pregnancy, she was working hard enough in the crèche to deserve her rest.

The westward jutting finger of the northern continent pointed directly at the big island which loomed lavender above the grey of the morning sea. Avril had lifted off from the desert camp well before dawn, leaving a message

182

that she was taking a day off. Saki Kiffin wouldn't mind, and she was as tired of Ozzie Munson and Cobber Alhinwa as they were of her.

Yesterday, the two miners had found some really good turquoise and refused to tell her where, tantalizing her with brief glimpses of the very fine sky-blue banded rock. She'd known when they came in to camp the previous evening that they were excited about the hunk that they were tossing back and forth. She'd merely asked to see it and had allowed herself to become irritated when the two miners had acted mincey over the stone. She'd have to be very cautious with those two: they thought themselves so clever. Anyhow, turquoise, though valued for its rarity on Earth, was not really worth the trouble of ingratiating herself to those two nards.

Then, at supper, when they were still whispering between themselves and glancing at her with sly smiles, she began to wonder if they had heard something that had made them react as they had to her polite and diffident query.

She tried to remember if they'd ever teamed up with Bart Lemos. But he was at Andiyar's ore mountain. He must, for once, have kept quiet about the gold nuggets which he'd been panning out of a mountain stream above the camp. Obedient to the pact they'd made last year on the *Yoko*, he'd given them to her to hide in her cache at Landing. She had not confided much of her scheme to him for, given a few mugs of quikal, Bart Lemos would give you his life history with chapter and verse of how he had been mistreated and neglected at every step of his three decades.

Maybe Stev Kimmer was not as good a choice of ally as she'd initially thought, hearing his sly and witty complaints during the last year of that interminable journey to this godforsaken planet. He was more attractive than the others, in fact extremely attractive, and more important, lusty, with a willingness to experiment which the much-vaunted Admiral Benden had never displayed. A bit of a bore in bed, our dear Admiral. Damn Paul Benden. Why had he turned so cool towards her? After all those protestations of admiration and devotion. She'd been so certain that she had felt the marriage contract in her hand. Then, a scant year away from their destination, when Rukbat grew from a spark to a gleam in the blackness of space, Benden had altered. Had had no time for her at all. Well, if he'd kept the astrogator sweet only while he needed to be sure of her loyalty, he'd find out what Avril Bitra was capable of. And then it'd be too late.

Fortunately, Avril had sensed the onset of Benden's disenchantment: he was actually applying to her the tricks she had herself used to cool a no-longer-glowing liaison. She'd been stunned, bitterly disappointed, but Avril Bitra was no fool, whatever the Great Admiral of the Cygnus Fleet thought. She was a handsome woman, a true voluptuary, and she looked about her for someone else who might further Avril Bitra's revised Plan.

If she had failed to capture Paul Benden who would be Pern's first leader – in her estimation, the less colourful Emily Boll would soon be overshadowed by the more flamboyant Admiral once they landed on Pern – she decided that living the rest of her life in obscurity at the end of the Milky Way was insupportable. She was, after all, a competent astrogator and, given a ship, charts, and a deepsleep tank, she could make her way to some other civilized and sophisticated planet that catered for the lifestyle she wished to enjoy.

She had begun with Stev Kimmer, to ease the pain of losing Paul Benden and really, Stev had some rather stimulating notions about pleasing an uninhibited woman. When she'd noticed that Bart Lemos managed to attach himself to her whenever Stev was on duty, she encouraged him, too. Nabhi Nabol joined the group one evening, and several others. Bart and Nabhi were pilots with secondary skills, Bart in mining, Nabhi in computers. Stev was a mechanical engineer with an uncanny ability to diagnose computer failures and rearrange chips to do twice the work they'd been designed to handle.

For the Plan taking shape in her mind, she assembled useful cronies. Most were Contractors like herself, or small stake Charterers beginning to feel that they had been short-changed on the deal. In the back of Avril's mind was the notion that it would be fun to see if she could foment sufficient discord to overthrow their benevolent Leaders and rule Pern on her own instead of as Paul Benden's consort. But that would have to wait for a propitious moment once the colony had been settled in and troubles began.

So far, except for minor hitches, there hadn't been any 'trouble' which she could use for her purposes. Everyone was too busy scurrying around, settling in, raising livestock and zipping here and there looking at real estate. She despised the colonists for being so enthusiastic about this ghastly empty wasteland of a world, with its noisy wild-life and the thousands of things that crawled, wriggled or flew. Not a decent useful 'animal' on the entire planet and she was getting very tired of eating fish or wherry, which sometimes tasted more like fish than what came out of the sea. Even tank-beef would have been an acceptable substitute.

More and more her determination to leave this wretched backwater world was reinforced. But she'd leave it in style and the hell with the rest of them.

Stev Kimmer was essential to that escape. He was constructing the emergency beacon from parts he had 'found' on the *Yokohama* and she had to be sure of that essential piece of equipment or her scheme would have to be aborted. Kimmer had to be kept on the mark, too, when she wanted to appropriate the captain's gig.

More important was his willingness to participate in her plan to 'stake' the right sections of the island to prospect for the gemstones that she knew were there. Grandmama Shavva had left her single remaining descendant a legacy that had to be grasped.

Kimmer was to requisition a sled for a sevenday in a quite legitimate search for a stake. He was supposed to imply that he was looking about the southern continent. As a veteran of the Nathi War, he had twice her allotment, a fact which had never sat well with Avril: that the Charterers had more than any Contractor, especially she, the astrogator, who had delivered them safely to this wretched place.

Colonizing had seemed like a good idea back on Earth when the excitement of the Nathi War had died down. Over the years, she'd had enough experience with psycho profiles to know how to control her pulse and what answers to give to the asinine questions that were supposed to separate truth from fiction. Any alternative, save First Centauri which everyone knew was controlled by the First Families and Founding Companies, was better than Earth or mouldering at grade on a lumbering merchantman. She had even toyed with the challenge of navigating mining ships within the Belts until the Roosevelt Dome had exploded for no apparent reason, killing all but a handful of the 10,000 inhabitants.

Damn Munson and Alhinwa. They could have told her where they'd unearthed the turquoise. This was a virgin world, with metal and mineral aplenty, untouched as yet by careless prospectors and greedy merchants. There was plenty for everyone. Back on sophisticated worlds, any large well-coloured hunks of that sky-blue stone would be snatched up by ardent collectors: the higher the asking price the more collectable!

And why hadn't she heard from Nabhi? She suspected he might be trying to run a program of his own, instead of the one she had set. She'd have to watch that one: he was a devious sort. Much as she was. In the long run, she had the upper hand: she was the astrogator and Nabhi did not have the skills required to get home by himself. He had to have her but she did not have to have him. Unless it suited her. Nabol was not as good overall for her purposes as Kimmer was but he'd do in a pinch.

186

She had almost bridged the distance between continent and island now, and could see waves lashing the granite rock. She veered to port, looking for the mouth of the natural harbour where the long-dead survey team had made camp. She'd told Kimmer to meet her there. She felt better about being some place that had already been occupied. She couldn't stand listening to the nardy damned colonists going on and on about being 'first' to see that or 'first' to step here, or the naming arguments that continually dominated conversation night after night around the bonfire. Shit in Drake's Lake! Fatuous ass! Lousy gravity-ball-player!

She corrected her course as she spotted the two natural spurs of rock which formed a breakwater to the roughly oval natural harbour. Kimmer would have hid the sled anyhow just in case . . . She caught herself and snorted in sour amusement. As if anyone on this goody-good world was checking up on anyone else? 'We are all equal here.' Our brave and noble leaders have so ordained it. With equal rights to share in Pern's wealth. You just bet. Only I'll get my equal share before anyone else and shake this planet's dirt off my boots!

Just as she passed over the breakwater, she saw the glint of metal under the lush foliage to starboard on a ledge above the sandy shoreline. And the smoke of a small fire. Kimmer had made it. She landed her sled neatly beside his.

'You were right about this place, baby,' he greeted her, a closed fist upraised and shaken in victory. 'I got here yesterday afternoon, good tail wind all the way, so I did a decco. And see what I found first thing!'

'Let me see,' she said, displaying a bright breathless eagerness, though she did not at all like his presumptive solo explorations.

He smiled broadly as he slowly opened his fingers and let his hand drop so that she could see the large grey rock in his hand. Her eagerness drained with discouragement until he turned the stone just slightly and she caught the unmistakable glint of green, half buried in one end.

'Fardles!' She snatched the stone from his hand and whirled to the sun, now risen over the ocean. She wet her finger and rubbed at the green glint.

'I also found this,' Kimmer was saying and she caught the note in his voice. Looking up, she saw him holding a squarish green stone the size of a spoon bowl, rough-edged where it had been prized from the limestone cavity.

She almost threw away the rock with its still-hidden treasure in her eagerness to take the rough emerald from him. She held it up to the sun, saw the flaw but had no complaint about the clear deep green. She weighed it in her hand: why it must be 30 or 40 carats. A clever lapidary to cut beyond the flaw and there'd be 15 carats of gemstone. Old Artur was good, but was he discreet? Rod Messurier was too besotted with that silly wife of his to trust. And if this was just a sample . . . The idea of using this magnificent jewel in her apprenticeship as a gemstone cutter amused her.

'Where?' she demanded, her breath constricted with the need to know instantly where he found the two.

'Over there,' and he half-turned, pointing up into the thick vegetation. 'There's a whole cave of them embedded in the rock.'

'You just walked in and it winked at you?' She forced herself to speak lightly, amusedly, smiling up approvingly at his beaming face. He looked so bloody pleased with himself: she continued to smile but ground her teeth.

'I've *klah* for you,' he said, gesturing to the fire where he'd rigged a spit and a protecting rock for his kettle.

'That abominable stuff,' she exclaimed. She had a fleet-incurred preference for strong coffee and the last had been served at that pathetic Thanksgiving shindig. And spilled when the tremor had shaken the urns from their stand. The last coffee from Earth had seeped, undrunk, into the dirt of Pern. What she wouldn't give for a cup, half a cup, a spoonful of it now.

'Oh, if you use enough sweetening, it's not all that bad.' He poured her a cup even though she hadn't said she

188

wanted one. 'They say it's got as much caffeine in it as coffee or tea. The secret's in drying the bark thoroughly before grinding and steeping it.'

He had lashed sweetener into the cup and handed it to her, expecting her to be grateful for his thoughtfulness. She couldn't afford to alienate Kimmer even if he sounded revoltingly like a good little colonist and approving of good colonial substitutes.

'Sorry, Stev,' she said, smiling apologetically at him as she took the cup, 'early morning nerves. I really do miss coffee.'

He gave a shrug. 'We won't for long, now, will we?'

She kept her smile in place, wondering if he knew how inane he sounded. Then, she cautioned herself severely, if she'd only been more careful with Paul, she might have been first lady here. What *had* she done wrong? She could have sworn she'd be able to maintain his interest in her. All had gone perfectly right up until they entered the Rukbat system. Then it was as if she hadn't existed. And she'd got them here!

'Avril . . .?' She came back to the present at the impatience in Stev Kimmer's voice.

'Sorry!'

'I said,' and he emphasized the verb, 'that I've already got food for the day so as soon as you finish that we can go.'

She tipped her cup, watching the dark liquid momentarily stain the white sand. She jiggled the cup to scatter the last drops, put it upside-down by the fire like a good little colonist, and rose to her feet, smiling brightly at Kimmer. 'Well, let's go!'

Part II

●

Thread

9

Perhaps it was because people were so accustomed to
dragonet behaviour after nearly eight years of close association. Those who noticed their unusual antics thought the
dragonets were merely playing some sort of a new game,
for the creatures were inventively amusing. Later people
would remember that the dragonets attempted to herd the
flocks and herds back to the barns. Later marine rangers
Jan Regan and her apprentice Corte Poel would remember
that the bottlenoses Bessie, Lottie and Maximilian had
urgently tried to explain to their human friends why the
indigenous marine life was rushing eastward to a food
source.

At her home in Europe Square, Sabra Ongola-Stein
actually thought that Fancy, the family dragonet, was
attacking her three-year-old son at play in the yard. The
little gold was grabbing at Shuvin's shirt, attempting to
haul him from his sandpile and his favourite toy truck. As
soon as Sabra had rescued the boy, batting at Fancy,
the dragonet had hovered, cheeping with relief. Puzzling
behaviour to be sure, but, though the fabric of the shirt
was torn, Sabra could see no marks on Shuvin's flesh from
the dragonet talons. Nor was Shuvin crying. He merely
wanted to go back to his truck while Sabra wanted to
change his shirt.

To her utter surprise, Fancy tried to duck in the house
with them but Sabra'd got the door closed in time. As she
leaned against it, catching her breath, she noticed through
the rear window that other dragonets were acting in the

most peculiar fashion. She was somewhat reassured by the fact that there had never been reports of dragonets *hurting* people, even in the ardour of mating . . . But that didn't seem to be what was agitating them, because greens were wheeling as frantically as the other colours. Greens got out of the way when a gold was mating. And it was certainly the wrong time for Fancy to be in season.

As Sabra changed Shuvin's shirt, handling the little boy's squirms deftly, she realized that the cries that penetrated the thick plastic walls of the house sounded frightened. Sabra knew the usual dragonet sounds as well as anyone in Landing. Frightened of what?

Over eight years on the planet and the only large predators were the new arrivals, the humans. The large flying creature – perhaps a very big wherry – which had been occasionally spotted soaring near the Western Barrier Range would be unlikely to range this far east. What other danger could there be on a fine early spring morning? That smudge of grey cloud far off on the horizon suggested rain later on in the day but that would be good for the crops already sprouting in the grain fields. Maybe she should get the clothes in off the line. Sometimes she missed the push-button conveniences that had eliminated the drudgery of monotonous household tasks back on old Earth. Too bad that the Council never considered requiring miscreants to do *domestic* duties as punishment for disorderly conduct: a fit penalty for women offenders. She pulled Shuvin's shirt down over his trousers and he gave her a moist, loving kiss.

'Truck, mommie, truck? Now?'

His wistful question made her aware, suddenly, of silence. Of the absence of the usual cheerful cacophony of dragonet choruses which was the background to daily life in Landing, and in nearly every settlement across the southern continent. Such a complete silence was frightening. Startled, and restraining Shuvin who wanted urgently to get back out and play in the sand, Sabra peered out the back window, then through the plasglas behind her,

194

and saw not a dragonet in sight. Not even on Betty Musgrave-Blake's house where there had been the usual natal congregation. Betty was expecting her second child; and Sabra had seen Basil, the o.b., arriving with Greta, his very capable apprentice midwife.

Where were the dragonets now? They never missed a birth.

One was supposed to report anything unusual on Pern, well-established as Landing was. She tried Ongola's number on the comunit but it was engaged. While she was using the handset, Shuvin reached his grubby hand up to the door-pull and slid it open, with a mischievous grin over his shoulder at his mother as he performed that new skill. She smiled her acquiescence as she tapped out Bay's number. The zoologist might know what was amiss with her favourite critters.

Well east and slightly south of Landing, Sean and Sorka had been hunting wherry for Restday meals. Nowadays foragers had to go further afield for game, even with dragonets to scout out their natural enemies.

'They're not even trying to hunt, Sorka,' Sean said, scowling. 'They've spent half the morning arguing. Fardling fools.' He lifted one brown muscled bare arm in an angry gesture to his eight dragonets. 'Shape up, you winged wimps. We're here to hunt!'

He was ignored as his veteran browns seemed to be arguing with the mentasynths: and arguing most aggressively with Sean's queen, Blazer. That was extraordinary in itself for though Blazer had been biogenetically improved by Bay Harkenon's tinkering, she was usually accorded the obedience any of the lesser colours rendered the fertile gold females.

'Mine, too,' Sorka said, nodding as her own five joined Sean's. 'Oh, jays, they're coming for *us*!' Slackening her reins, she began to tighten her legs to her bay mare but saw Sean wheel Cricket to face the oncoming dragonets, holding up an imperious hand.

She was even more startled to see the dragonets assume an attack formation, their cries were clamours of unspeakable fright and danger. Danger for herself and Sean, and the horses. Horse and dragonet had a good interspecies relationship that vied with human and dolphin.

'Danger? Where?' Sean spun Cricket around on his haunches, a trick that Sorka had never been able to teach Doove despite Sean's assistance and her own endless patience. He searched the skies and stayed Cricket as the dragonets solidly turned their heads to the east.

Blazer landed on his shoulder, swirling her tail about his neck and left bicep, shrieking to the others now to reinforce her orders. A queen taking orders from browns? Sean noticed that fleetingly because then her thoughts became vividly apprehensive.

'Landing in danger? Shelter?'

Once Sean had spoken, Sorka realized that that was what her bronzes were trying to convey to her. Sean was quicker to read the images from his enhanced dragonets than Sorka, especially Blazer who was the most coherent. She had often wished for a golden female but loved her bronzes and the brown too much to voice a complaint.

'That's what they all give me, too,' Sorka said, as her five then began to tug various parts of her clothing. Sean could hunt bare to the waist but she bobbled too much to ride topless comfortably. Her sleeveless leather vest provided support as well as protection from the claw-holds of the dragonets. Bronze Emmett settled on Doove's poll long enough to secure a grip on one ear and the mare's forelock, trying to pull the mare's head around.

'Something big, something dangerous and shelter!' Sean said, shaking his head. 'It's only a thunderstorm, fellas. Look, just a cloud!'

Sorka frowned as she looked eastward. They were high enough on the plateau to have just a glimpse of the sea.

'That's a funny-looking cloud formation, Sean. I've never seen anything like it. More like the snowclouds we'd

196

have now and again in Ireland.' Sorka had as good a weather sense as Sean.

Sean scowled and tightened his legs. Cricket was being affected by the dragonets' urgent fears. He pranced in place in the piaffe he'd been taught but it would turn into a mad gallop the minute Sean gave him his head. The gelding's eyes were rolling white in distress as he snorted. Doove was fretting with Emmett's peculiar urgency.

'Doesn't snow here, Sorka, but you're right about the colour and shape. By jays, whatever it's raining, it's damned near visible. Rain here doesn't fall like that.'

Duke and Sean's original two browns saw it and shrieked in utter frustration and terror. Blazer trumpeted a fierce command. The next thing Sean and Sorka knew, both horses had been spurred by well-placed dragonet stabs across their rumps into a headlong stampede which the massed fair of dragonets aimed north and west. Rein, leg, seat or voice had no effect on the two pain-crazed horses for whenever they tried to obey their riders, they got another slash from the vigilant dragonets.

'Whatinhell's got into them?' Sean cried, hauling on the hackamore which he used in place of a bit in Cricket's soft mouth. 'I'll break his bloody nose for him, I will.'

'No, Sean,' Sorka cried, leaning into her mare's forward plunge. 'Duke's terrified of that cloud. All of mine are. They'd never hurt the horses! We'd be fools to ignore them.'

'As if we could!'

The horses were diving headlong down a ravine now and Sean needed all his skill to stay on Cricket but he also sensed Blazer's relief that she had succeeded in moving them towards safety.

'Safety from what?' he muttered in a savage growl, hating the sense of impotence on an animal that had never disobeyed him in its seven years; of an inexplicable fear and insane behaviour from creatures whom he thought he understood better than anyone on the whole bleeding planet.

The headlong pace did not falter, even when Sean felt the grey gelding, fit as he was, begin to tire. The dragonets drove both horses onwards. Onwards and straight towards one of the small lakes that dotted this part of the continent.

'Why water, Sean?' Sorka cried, sitting back and hauling on Doove's mouth. When the mare willingly slowed, Duke and the other two bronzes screamed a protest and once again gouged her bleeding rump.

Neighing and white-eyed with fear, the mare catleapt into the water, nearly unseating her rider. The stallion plunged beside her, galled by the spurred talons of Sean's group.

There was little beach to the lake, a deep basin collecting the water shed of the nearby hills, and the horses were soon swimming, determinedly herded by the dragonets towards the rocky overhang on the far side. It was a ledge where Sean and Sorka had often sunbathed, had often dived from the height, knowing the water below was deep enough for such acrobatics.

'The ledge? They want us *under* the ledge? The water's fardling deep there.'

'Why?' Sorka still asked. 'It's only rain coming.' She was swimming beside Doove, now, one hand on the pommel of her saddle, the reins in the other, letting the mare's efforts drag her forward. 'Where'd they all go?'

Sean, swimming alongside Cricket, turned on his side, to look back the way they had been herded. His eyes widened.

'That's not *rain*. Swim for it, Sorka! Swim for the ledge!'

She cast a glance over her shoulder and saw the phenomenon that had startled the previously imperturbable young man. Terror lent strength to her arms so that she gained on the mare, urging Doove to greater efforts and tugging at the reins. They were nearly to the ledge, nearly to what little safety that offered from the hissing silver fall that splatted so ominously across the woods they had only just left.

'Where are the dragonets?' Sorka wailed just as she got under the ledge, and tugged at Doove to get the mare's head sheltered, too.

'Safer where they are, no doubt!' Sean sounded bitterly angry as he forced Cricket under the ledge. There was just room enough for the longer horse heads to remain above the level of the water, but no purchase for their flailing legs.

Suddenly both horses ceased resisting their riders, and indeed began to press Sean and Sorka against the inner wall, whinnying in abject terror.

'Jack your legs up, Sorka, balance against the inside wall!' Sean shouted, doing exactly that.

Then they heard the hiss on the water. Peering around frightened horses' heads, on a level with the surface of the lake, they could actually see the long thin threads plunging into the water which was suddenly roiling and cut every which way with fins of the minnows that had been seeded in the streams.

'Jays! Look at that!' Sean pointed excitedly to a jet of flame at the water surface, charring a large tangle of the stuff before it landed on the lake.

'Over there, too!' Sorka said, and then they heard the agitated but exultant chatter of dragonets. Crowded back under the ledge, they caught only fleeting glimpses of dragonets and the unexpected flame.

Now she remembered that long ago day when the dragonets had helped the humans defend the poultry flocks. She'd been certain then that Duke had flamed at a wherry. 'Somehow they breathe fire. Maybe that's what the second stomach is for.'

'Well, I'm as glad they weren't cowards,' Sean muttered, cautiously propelling himself to the opening. 'No,' he said in a relieved voice, expelling a big sigh, 'they're by no means cowards. C'mere, Sorka.'

She glanced anxiously at Doove but the mare was too busy pumping her legs to keep above water, and too frightened of what was outside to leave. Sorka joined Sean and cried out with surprised elation.

Their fair of dragonets had been augmented by a mass of others. They seemed to take turns diving at the evil rainfall, their spouts of flame reducing the terror to char which fell as ashes to the surface of the lake, there to be gobbled by quick fish mouths.

'See, Sorka, the dragonets are protecting this ledge.'

Sorka could indeed appreciate the truth of that for they now had a clear view of a broader panorama. The menacing rain fell unimpeded to the lake on either side of the dragonet fire zone.

'Jays, Sean, look what it does to the bushes!' She pointed to the shore line, where only moments before they had sent their horses plunging through thick clumps of tough bushes. These were no longer visible, covered by a writhing mass of 'things' that seemed to enlarge as they watched. Sorka felt sick to her stomach and only intense concentration prevented her heaving breakfast up. Sean had gone white about the mouth and his eyes seemed to burn in their sockets. His hands, moving rhythmically to keep him in position in the water, clenched into fists.

'No bleeding wonder the dragonets were scared.' He smashed impotent fists into the water, sending ripples out. A dragonet instantly hovered, peering in. Duke waited just long enough to squeak a reassurance and then literally disappeared in front of their eyes. One moment he was there, the next gone. 'Well, now, if I were Pol Nietro, I'd call that instantaneous flit of theirs the best defence mechanism a species could develop.' A long thread slithered from the ledge, hanging a moment in front of their horrified eyes before a flame charred it.

Revolted, Sean splashed water on the remains, whisking the floating motes away from Sorka and himself. Behind them the horses' breathing showed signs of real distress.

'How long?' Sean said, gliding over to Cricket's head and soothing the horse with his hands. 'How long?'

*

It is *not* mating activity,' Bay told Sabra when she called, 'and it is a totally irrational pattern of behaviour.' With her mind riffling through all she knew and had observed about the dragonets, Bay continued to peer out her window and observed a sled, lifting from a parking spot near the met tower. It headed at full speed towards the storm. 'Let me check my behavioural files and have a word with Pol. I'll call you back. It really is most unusual.'

Pol was working on their vegetable patch behind their home. He saw her coming and waved cheerfully, tipping back his visored cap and mopping his brow. The garden soil had been carefully enriched and enhanced by a variety of terran beetles and worms that were as happy to aerate the soil of Pern as of Earth and augmented the local, lazier kinds. Bay saw Pol's hand stop, mid wipe, and stare about him, as if only then discovering the absence of the dragonets.

'Where've they all gone?' He glanced towards other residential squares, and Betty's empty roof. 'That was sudden, wasn't it?'

'Sabra's just been on to me. She said their Fancy appeared to attack little Shuvin. For no reason, although her claws did not pierce the skin. Fancy then attempted to enter the house with them. Sabra said she sounded frightened.'

Pol raised his eyebrows in surprise and continued to wipe his brow and then the hat band before replacing it. Leaning on his hoe, he glanced all around, finally noticing the grey clouds.

'Don't like the look of that, m'luv,' he said. 'I'll take a bit of a break until it blows over.' He smiled at her. 'While we access your notes on the menta-breed. Fancy's a menta, not a native.'

Suddenly the air was full of shrieking, screaming, bugling and very frightened dragonets.

'Where have they been, the little pests?' Pol demanded, snatching off his cap to wave it furiously in front of his face. 'Faugh! They stink!'

Bay pinched her nostrils, hurrying her steps towards the refuge of the house. 'They do, indeed, positively sulphurous.'

Six dragonets detached themselves from the swirling hundreds and dove for Bay and Pol, screeching and battering their backs to hurry them forward.

'I do believe they're driving us into the house, Pol,' Bay said. When she stopped to survey this totally eccentric behaviour, her queen grabbed a lock of her hair, the two bronzes secured holds on the front of her tunic, pulling her forward. Their cries grew more frantic.

'I believe you're correct. And they're doing it to others, too.'

'I've never seen so many dragonets. We don't normally have such a concentration here,' Bay went on, co-operating to the point of a lumbering jog trot. 'Most of them are wilds! Look how much smaller some queens are. A preponderance of greens as well. Fascinating.'

'Extremely,' Pol remarked, mildly amused that the dragonets who were their particular friends had entered the house and were co-operating in a joint effort to close the door behind the humans. 'Most remarkable.'

Bay was already sitting down at the terminal. 'Patently, it's something harmful to them as well as to us.'

'I'd prefer them to settle,' Pol said, for their particular little friends were flitting about the lounge, into the bedroom, the bathroom, and even into the addition to the house that constituted a small but well-equipped home laboratory for the two scientists. 'This is a bit much. Bay, tell your queen to settle and the others will follow suit.'

'Tell her yourself, Pol, while I access the behavioural program. She'll obey you as well as me.'

Pol did attempt to coax Mariah to land on his arm. She'd touch down and then be off again, the others after her. A tidbit of her favourite fish was ignored. Pol no longer thought this conduct amusing. Maybe ignoring these antics . . . He looked out of the window, to see if

202

others were experiencing the same mass hysteria and noticed that the squares had been cleared of humans. He could see clouds of dust over by the veterinary barns and the dark dashes of dragonets attempting to herd the animals. He could also hear the distant discord of frightened beasts.

'There had better be an explanation for this,' he murmured, pausing behind Bay to read the screen. 'My word, look at Betty's house!' He pointed over the screen, out the window, towards a structure fully clothed in dragonets. 'My God, should I call them to see if they need help?'

When he put his hand out to reach for the door pull, Mariah, screaming with anger, dove at his hand and pushed it away, scratching him.

'Don't go, Pol. Don't go out, Pol! Look!'

Bay had half-risen from her chair and remained frozen in the semi-crouch, a look of utter horror on her face. Throwing a protective arm about her shoulders, Pol saw what she did. They both heard the hiss of the terrible rain that fell on Landing. They could see the individual elongated 'rain drops' strike the surface, sometimes meeting only dust, other times writhing about the shrubs and grasses which disappeared, leaving behind engorged slug-like forms which rapidly attacked anything green in their way. Pol's nicely sprouting garden was a waste of squirming greyish 'things', bloating larger within seconds on each new feast.

Mariah let out a raucous call and disappeared from the house, the other five dragonets following instantly.

'I don't believe what I saw,' Pol said in an amazed whisper. 'They're teleporting in droves: almost formations. So the telekinesis was developed as a survival technique first. Hmm.'

The hideous rain had advanced, spreading its mindless burden behind and inexorably falling across Pol's neat-patterned stonework patio towards the house.

'They can't devour stone,' Pol remarked with clinical

detachment. 'I trust our silicon plastic roof provides a similar deterrent.'

'The dragonets have more than one unexplored skill, Pol my dear,' Bay said proudly and pointed.

Outside their dragonets were swooping and soaring, breathing flame to incinerate the attacking life form before it could reach the house.

'I would be happier if I knew the things could not penetrate plastic,' Pol repeated, with a slight tremor in his voice, looking up at the opaque roof.

He winced and hunched in self-protection as he heard a slithering impact, then another, then saw the brief spurt of flame in gouts across the dark roof material.

'Well, that's a relief,' he said, straightening his shoulders.

'They did strike the roof, however, until the dragonets, bless their little hearts, set them ablaze.' Bay peered out the window facing Betty Musgrave-Blake's. 'My word! Look at that!'

The house seemed ringed by fiery whirls and gouts, an umbrella of dragonets frantically making certain that not a single piece of this grotesque rain reached the home of a labouring woman.

Pol had the presence of mind now to collect his binoculars from the clutter on a shelf. These he turned towards the fields and the veterinary sheds.

'I wonder if they'll protect our livestock. There're too many animals to get all under shelter. But dragonets do seem to be massing in that area.'

Keenly interested in the safety of herds and flocks they had helped create, Pol and Bay took turns watching. Training the glasses on two strays, Bay suddenly dropped the glasses, shuddering as she passed them wordlessly to Pol. Though in her work she dealt constantly with the habits of microscopic organisms, she had been shocked by the sight of a full-grown cow reduced in a few moments to a seared corpse covered by masses of writhing strings. Pol altered the focus and then groaned in helpless dismay, dropping the binoculars.

'Deadly, they are. Voracious, insatiable. It would appear they consume anything organic,' he murmured and, taking a deep resolute breath, raised the binoculars again. 'And, unfortunately, to judge by the marks on the roofs of some of those shelters we put up first, carbon-based plastics, too.'

'Oh dear. That could be terrible. Could this be a regional phenomenon?' Bay wanted to know, her voice still trembling. 'There were those odd circles on the vegetated areas, the ones in the original survey fax . . .'

Turning from the disaster going on about her, Bay sat down at the keyboard and, clearing the screen, called up different files.

'I hope no one is foolish enough to go out after those last few cows and sheep,' Pol said, an edge to his otherwise even voice. 'I hope they got all the horses in safely. The new equine strain is too promising to lose to a ravening disaster.'

Almost as an afterthought the alarm klaxon on the meteorology tower began to bleat.

'Now that's a bit after the fact, old fellow,' Pol said, turning to focus the binoculars on the tower. He could see Ongola in the tower, holding a rag against his cheek. He could also see that the sled which had gone to investigate the storm was now parked so close to the tower entrance that Ongola had probably dived from sled to the tower door.

'No, the sound carries and sets off the relays,' Bay said absently as her fingers flew over the keys.

'Ah, yes, I'd forgot that. Quite a few went out on hunting parties this morning, you know.'

Bay's quick fingers stilled and she turned slowly in the swivel chair to stare at Pol, her face ashen.

'There now, old dear, so many people have dragonets on Pern now, and at least one of the smarter mentas you developed.' He crossed to her and gave her a reassuring pat on the head. 'They've done a first-class job of warning, and protecting us. Ah! Listen!'

There was no mistaking the exultant warble of the dragonets that always heralded a birth. Whatever was occurring on Pern at that bizarre moment, a new life had entered it. The welcome did not, however, interfere for as much as a moment with the protective net of flame about the house.

'The poor baby! To be born now!' Bay said, her plump cheeks drawn and her eyes sunken in her face.

Heedless of the stinging pain on the left side of his face, Ongola kept one finger on the klaxon even as he began calling out to the other stations on the network.

'Mayday! Mayday! Mayday at Landing! Take shelter! Get livestock under cover! Extreme Danger. Shelter all living things,' and he shuddered as Bay had for the horrific memory of two wayward sheep consumed in an eye blink by the descending vileness. 'Shelter under rock, metal, in water! An unnatural rain heading westward in uneven fall. Deadly! Deadly! Shelter. Mayday from Landing. Mayday from Landing. Mayday from Landing!' Drops of blood from his head and neck dripped in punctuation to his terse phrases. 'Cloud unnatural. Rainfall deadly. Mayday from Landing! Take shelter! Mayday. Mayday.'

He could not keep himself from watching his own home, barely visible through the sheeting fall but he did see the gouts of flame above those houses in Landing still occupied by humans. He accepted the sheer thousands of dragonets massing to assist their human friends, the living flaming shield over Betty Musgrave-Blake's, the multitude swirling above the veterinary sheds and the pastures. Now he remembered that Fancy had tried to fly into the window where he was sitting out his watch. When he suddenly realized that none of the meteorological devices was registering the cloud-mass approaching steadily from the east, he had phoned Emily at her home.

'Go have a look, Ongola. Could be just a good stiff equinoctial squall but, if the water-vapour instruments are not registering, you'd better check the wind speed and see if there's hail or sleet in the clouds. There're hunters and fishers out today as well as farmers.'

Ongola had got close enough to the cloud to register its unusual composition and quite close enough to see the damage it did. He tried to raise Emily on the sled's com-unit. He tried to reach Jim Tillek at Harbour Control. But he'd taken the nearest sled, a small fast one, which did not have the sophisticated equipment the bigger ones did. He tried every number he could think of and only reached Kitti who generally stayed in her home, frail now in her 10th decade despite prostheses that gave her mobility if not the energy to use the aids.

'Thank you for the warning, Ongola. A prudent person is well advised. I will contact the Veterinary sheds for them to get the livestock under cover. A hungry rain?'

Ongola had thrown the little sled to its maximum speed, hoping that there was enough power in the packs to withstand such a drain. The sled responded but he only just made it back to the tower, the engine dying as he touched ground.

The stuff pelted down on the sled canopy. He had not managed to outrun the leading edge. He grabbed the flightplan board, an inadequate shield from this deadly rain but better than nothing after what he'd seen it do. Taking a deep breath, he punched auto-close and was under the canopy when it had lifted enough to let him duck out. He took three long strides, more jump than run and made it to the tower door just as a tangle descended. The tilted edge of the board deflected it right on to the unprotected left side of his head. Screaming with the pain of the searing assault, Ongola batted the stuff from his ear, just as a dragonet came flaming up to his assistance. Whether the fiery breath burned him or not, Ongola didn't pause to discover though he shouted 'Thanks' for the dragonet's aid as he slammed the door. Automatically, he threw the bolt and, snorting at useless instinct, he took the steps to the tower in twos and threes.

The stinging pain continued and he felt something oozing

down his neck. Blood! He blotted at the injury with his handkerchief, noticing that the blood was mixed with black fragments and he was now aware of the stench of burned wool. The dragonet's breath had scorched his sweater.

The warning delivered, he was flipping on the recording when a second stinging pain on his left shoulder made him glance down. He saw the front end of a waving strand that did not look at all like wool, and where the strand was, was the pain. He never undressed as fast as he did then. And just fast enough, for the strand had become thicker, moved with more rapidity and purpose and, even as he watched in horror at his close escape, the wool was ingested and the grotesque, quivering segment left in its place filled him with revulsion.

Water! He reached for both the water pitcher and klah thermos and dumped them over the . . . the thing. It writhed and bubbled but slowly subsided into a soggy inert mass. He stamped on it with as much satisfaction as he'd felt destroying Nathi surface positions.

Then he looked at his shoulder and saw the thin bloodied line scored in his flesh by his close encounter with that deadly piece of thread. A convulsive shudder took hold of his body and he had to grab the nearer chair to keep from falling to his knees from shock.

The comunit began to bleat at him and, taking several deep breaths, he got to his feet and back on duty.

'Thanks for the klaxon, Ongola. We had just time enough to batten down the hatches. Knew the critters were telling us something but howinhell could we guess *that*?' Jim Tillek reported from the bridge of the *Southern Star*. 'Thank the powers that be, our ships are all siliplex.'

Monaco Bay Harbour office reported overturned small craft and was instigating rescues.

The Infirmary reported that human casualties in and about Landing had been minimal: mainly dragonet scratches. They had the dragonets to thank for saving lives.

Red Hanrahan at Vet said they'd lost fifty to sixty assorted livestock of the breeding herds pastured about Landing, thanking the good fortune of having just shipped out three hundred calves, lambs, kids and piglets to new homes the previous month. There were, however, large numbers at nearby stakes which did not have stabling facilities and were in the path of this abominable rain. Red added that all of the animals left loose to graze could be considered lost.

Two of the larger fishing vessels reported severe burn injuries for those who hadn't made it under cover in time. One of the Hegelman boys had jumped overboard and drowned when the things landed in a clump on his face. Maximilian, escorting the *Perseus*, had been unable to save him. The dolphin had added that native marine life was swarming to the surface, fighting over the drowning wrigglers. He didn't much like them: no substance.

Ongola's board now had messages stacking up: he rang Emily to send her some assistance. Jacob Chernoff came with the oldest Logorides girl and two of the Shwartz boys.

Per Ragnesjo, fishing to the north on *Maid of the Sea*, wanted to know what was happening. The skies about him were clear to the southern horizon. Patrice de Broglie stationed out at Young Mountain with the seismic team asked whether he should send his crew back. There'd been only a few rumbles, though there were some interesting changes in the gravity metre graphs in the past weeks. Ongola told him to send as many back as he could, not wanting to think what might have happened to home-steads in the path of this malevolent threadfall.

Bonneau at Drake's Lake phoned in but it was still night and very clear. Should he send a contingent?

Sallah Telgar-Andiyar got through from Karachi Camp and said assistance was already on its way. How wide-spread was this rain?

Ongola shunted all those calls when the first of the nearby settlements reported.

'If it hadn't been for those dragonets,' said Aisling Hempenstall of Bordeaux, 'we'd all be ... have been eaten alive.' Her swallow was audible. 'Not a green thing to be seen and all the livestock gone. Except the cow the dragonets drove into the river, and she's a mess.'

'Any casualties?'

'None we can't take care of myself, but we've little fresh food. Oh, and Kwan wants to know do you need him at Landing?'

'I'd say yes indeed we do,' Ongola replied fervently. Then he tried again to raise the Du Vieux, the Radelins, the Grant-van Toorns, the Ciottis and Holstroms. 'Keep trying these, Jacob.' He passed the list over. 'Kurt, Heinrich, try the River numbers, Calusa, Cambridge and Vienna. Joel,' Ongola got through to Lilienkamp at Stores, 'how many checked out for hunting today?'

'Too many, Ongola, too many.' The tough Joel was weeping.

'Including your boys?'

'Yes,' and Joel's response was the barest whisper.

'I am sorry to hear that, Joel. We've organized searches. And the boys have dragonets.'

'Sure, but look how many it took to protect Landing!' His voice rose shrilly.

'Sir,' and Kurt tugged urgently at Ongola's bare elbow, 'one of the sleds—'

'Back to you, Joel. Yes?'

'Whaddya do to kill this stuff, Ongola?' The anguished cry from Ziv Marchane sent a stab of pure terror and fury to Ongola's guts.

'Cautery, Ziv. Who is it?'

'What's left of young Joel Lilienkamp.'

'Bad?'

'Very.'

Ongola paused, closed his eyes tightly for a moment, remembering the two sheep, and said, 'Then give him mercy!'

Ziv broke the connection and Ongola stared at the

console, paralysed. He had given mercy several times, too many times, during the Nathi war when seamen were blown apart after Nathi hits on his destroyer. The practice was standard procedure in surface engagements. You didn't leave your wounded to Nathi mercy. Mercy, yes, it was mercy to do so. Ongola had never thought that necessity would ever arise again.

'Whatinhell's happening, Ongola?' Paul Benden's vibrant voice broke through his pained trance.

'Wish the hell I knew, Admiral.' Ongola shook his head and then gave him a precise report and a list of casualties known or suspected.

'I'm coming in.' Paul had staked his claim on the heights above the delta on the Boca River. It would soon be dawn there. 'I'll check other stakes on the way in.'

'Pol and Kitti want samples if they can be safely got. Of the stuff in the air. It scores holes through thin materials so be sure to use heavy gauge metal or siliplex. We've got enough of what ate our fields bare. I've sent all our big sleds out, Bruce Olivine, Rudi Shwartz, Arkady Sturt and AC Sopers, to track the frigging fall. Kenjo's flying in from Honshu in that augmented speeder of his. The stuff just came out of nowhere, Paul, nowhere!'

'Didn't register on anything? No? Well, we'll check it all out.'

The absolute confidence in Paul Benden's voice was a tonic for Ongola. He'd heard that same note all through the Cygnus Battle and he took heart.

He needed it. Before Paul Benden arrived late that afternoon, the casualties had mounted to a frightening total. Only three of the twenty who had gone hunting that morning returned: Sorka Hanrahan, Sean Connell and David Catarel who had seen his companion, Lucy Tubberman, dissolve on the river bank under the rain despite the efforts of their dragonets while Dave watched helpless in the water. He had deep scores on his scalp, left cheek, arms, and shoulders, and he was suffering from shock and grief.

Two babies, thrust in a small metal cabinet, were the only survivors of the main Tuareg camp on the plains west of the big bend in the Paradise River. Sean and Sorka had gone to find the Connells who had last been reported on the eastern spur of Kahrain Province. No one answered from the northern stakes on the Jordan river. It looked bad.

Porrig Connell had, for once, listened to the warnings of the dragonets and had taken shelter in a cave. It had not been large enough to accommodate all his horses and four of the mares had died. When they screamed outside, the stallion had gone berserk in the confines of the cave and Porrig had had to cut his throat. There was no fodder for the remaining mares so Sean and Sorka returned with hay and food rations. Porrig knew where the Moorhouses had last camped and the Foleys, but he had no idea where the Brennans might be. So Sean and Sorka went off to search for survivors.

The Du Vieux and Holstroms at Amsterdam Stake, the Radelins and Duquesnes at Bavaria, the Ciottis at Milan Stake were dead, with no trace of them or their livestock. The metals and heavy gauge silicon-based plastic roofing, though it was heavily pocked, remained to give evidence of their once thriving settlement. They had used the new pressed vegetable fibre slabs for their homes. No one on Pern ever would use such building material again.

The swathe of destruction cut by the falling thread-like rain was obvious from the air, the fringes seething with bloated worm-like excrescences which squadrons of dragonets attacked with flaming breath. The path ended seventy-five clicks beyond the narrow Paradise River where it had annihilated the Tuareg camps.

By evening, the exhausted settlers fed their dragonets first, and left out mounds of cooked grain for the wild ones that would not approach near enough to be handfed.

'Nothing was said about this sort of thing in the EEC report,' Mar Dook muttered in a bitter tone.

'Those wretched polka-dots no one ever explained,'

Aisling Hempenstall said, her voice just loud enough to be heard.

'We've been investigating that possibility,' Pol Nietro said, nodding to a weary Bay who was resting her head against his shoulder.

'Nevertheless, I think we should arrive at some preliminary conclusions before tomorrow,' Kitti said, her low voice audible despite low private conversations. 'People will need facts to be reassured.'

'Bill and I looked up the reports we did,' Carol Duff-Vassaloe said, 'on the polka-dots,' she gave a grim smile, 'during Landing Year. We didn't investigate every site, but the ones we examined where tree development could be measured suggests a time lapse of at least 167 years. I think it's rather obvious that it was this terrible life form which caused the patterning, turning all organic material it meets into more of itself. Thank heavens most of our building plastics are silicon-based. If they were carbon-based, we'd all have been killed, without a doubt. This infestation . . .'

'Infestation?' Chuck Havers' voice broke in incredulous anger.

'What else to call it?' Phas Radamanth remarked in his dogmatic fashion. 'What we need to know is how often it occurs? Every 150 years? That patterning was planet-wide, wasn't it, Carol?' When she nodded, 'And how long it lasts once it starts?'

'Lasts?' Chuck demanded, appalled.

'We'll get the answers,' Paul Benden said, firmly but with utter confidence in the abilities of the experts.

10

•

Both psychologists, Tom Patrick of Longwood, Ierne Island and Cos Melvinah from Seminole in Dorado Province, flew in late that evening when the Infirmary was still crowded with the injured and shocked. They set to work immediately to help reduce traumas. Cherry Duff had suffered a stroke at the news, but was recovering splendidly. Joel and his wife were both prostrated by the loss of their sons. Bernard Hegelman had submerged his own grief to comfort his shattered wife and the other families bereft by loss.

Sean and Sorka had tirelessly sledded in the wounded Brennans, Foleys and Moorhouses. Even those uninjured were dazed, some weeping uncontrollably until sedated, others pathetically quiet. Porrig Connell had sent his eldest daughter, Sinead, and his wife to help cope with the survivors while he stayed with his extended family in the cave.

'The first time Porrig Connell ever did anything for anyone else,' his son remarked under his breath to Sorka who berated him for such cynicism. 'He wants to use Cricket to service the rest of his mares when they foal. He expects me to give up *my* stallion because he hadn't trained his!'

Sorka wisely said nothing.

With one exception, the distant holdings had contacted Landing, offering either assistance or sympathy. The one exception was the Big Island mining camp, comprising Avril Bitra, Stev Kimmer, Nabhi Nabol, Dasha Chernoff,

214

Purdee Mott, Tony Gale and Becky Nielson. Ongola, scanning over the log, noticed the absence.

Kenjo, appearing like magic from his distant Honshu plateau, headed the aerial survey. By nightfall, he and his team produced accurate maps and pics of the extent of this terrible 'threadfall', as it soon came to be called. The original complement of biologists reconvened at Landing to ascertain the nature of the beast. Kitti Ping and Wind Blossom lent their special skills to analyse the life forms as soon as samples were brought in.

Unfortunately too many, acquired at considerable danger to the volunteers, were found apparently moribund in the metal or heavy-plastic containers in which they had been contained. Seemingly, after about twenty minutes, all the frenetic activity, the replication of the original strand several thousand times into big wriggling 'sausages', ceased. The form unravelled, blackened and turned into a sticky tarry mess, utterly lifeless, within a tougher 'shell'.

Captain Bernard Shattuck inadvertently discovered a segment of thread in a pail of fishbait. He and his crew on the *Mayflower* had been trawling at the ragged northern edge of the Fall. He saw the squirming object and slapped on a tight lid, reporting his find to Landing. He was told to keep it alive, if he could, by judicious feeding until it could be flown from his ship to Landing.

By then, the 'thread' had to be housed in the biggest heavy gauge plastic barrel on board the *Mayflower*. Ongola transported the tightly sealed barrel, using a long steel cable attached to the big engineering sled. No way was he getting close to that monstrosity. Only when Bernard's crew saw the sled disappearing in the distance would they come on deck. Bernard, a clever, imperturbable young captain, was later astonished to learn that his act was considered one of extreme bravery.

By the time the pulsing life form reached Landing, it coiled, a gross metre long and perhaps 10 cm in circumference, resembling heavy hawser. Ivan Chernoff, who had come from Karachi Camp with Tarvi and others, rigged double thick slabs of transparent silicon-based building plastic, tightly banded with metal strips, into a cage, its base quikplased to the floor. Several thin slits with locking flaps were created. A hole the size of the barrel opening was incised in the top, the barrel lid readied and, with the help of grimly anxious volunteers, the terrible creature was transferred from barrel to cage. The top opening was sealed as soon as the life form, now crushed against the sides of its prison, was dropped into the plastic cube.

One of the men scrambled for a corner to be sick in, and even Ivan Chernoff, nicknamed the Terrible, went white. Red Hanrahan, Sean Connell, Pat Hempenstall, Jim Tillek and Paul Benden averted their faces. Only Tarvi and Mar Dook seemed unmoved by the creature's writhing as it engulfed the food that had been placed in the cube.

It rippled in its urgency to ingest: waves of grey greasy colours, tinged with sickly greens and dull pink tones, and an occasional streak of yellow, flowed across its surface, sickeningly distorted by the thick clear plastic. The outer covering of the beast seemed to thicken and its growth was apparently double-ended. The thick shell probably formed at its demise, for these had been found in rocky places where the organism had starved. The interior of the beast evidently deteriorated as rapidly as its initial expansion. Was it really alive? Or some malevolent chemical entity feeding on life? Certainly its appetite was voracious, although the very act seemed to destroy whatever organization the beast had had, as if what it ate hastened its destruction.

From the wide window into the containment area Kitti, too, was able to watch with dispassionate interest.

'Its rate of growth is remarkable,' Bay said in a very calm voice, for which Pol later praised her, saying it had provided an example to the others, stunned by the sight of this gross menace. 'One expects such expansion under the microscope but not in the macrocosm. Where can it have come from? Outer space?'

Blank silence met this astonishing query and those in the room exchanged glances, partly of surprise, partly of embarrassment at Bay's suggestion.

'Do we have any data on the periodicity of comets in this system?' Mar Dook asked hopefully. 'That eccentric body? Something brought in from our Oort cloud? Then there's the Hoyle-Wickramansingh theory which has never been totally discredited, citing the possibility of viruses.'

'That's one helluva virus, Mar,' Bill Duff said sceptically, 'and didn't someone on Ceti III confound that old theory?'

'Considering it drops from the skies,' Jim Tillek said, 'why couldn't it have a space origin? I'm not the only one who's noticed that "red" morning-star in the east getting brighter these past weeks. A bit of a coincidence, isn't it, that that planet with the crazy orbit is coming right in to the inner planets, at the same time this stuff hits us? Could that be the source? Is there any data in the library on that planet? On this sort of thing?'

'I'll ask Cherry. No,' and Bill Duff corrected himself before anyone could remind him that the redoubtable Magistrate was indisposed, 'I'll access the information myself and bring back hardcopy to study.' He hurried from the room as if glad to have a valid excuse to leave.

'I'll get a sample from that section pressing against the lower slot,' Kwan Marceau said, gathering up the necessary implements in the rush of someone who dares not overlong consider what he's about to do.

'A record's being kept of the . . . intake?' Bay asked. She couldn't quite say 'food', remembering what the creatures had already eaten since they'd fallen on Pern.

'Now, to judge the frequency of . . . intake,' Pol seized gratefully on that euphemism, 'sufficient to keep the . . . organism alive.'

'And to see how it dies,' Kitti added in a voice so bland that it rang with satisfaction.

'And why all its ilk died in this first infestation,' Phas

217

Radamanth added, pulling the EEC pics out of the welter of hardcopy in front of him.

'*Did* all die?' Kitti asked.

By morning, with no report from scientists who had worked through the night, the muttering began. A still-shocked whisper over morning klah; a rumour that began to seep into every office and the hastily re-opened living quarters on the abandoned residential Squares. A huge blaze had been started the previous evening and continued to burn at Bonfire Square. Torches, pitched and ready to be lit, had been piled at each corner, and more were added to the piles throughout the day.

Many of the lighter sleds that had been on the ground at Landing needed new canopies. Sweeping out the detritus of putrid thread shells was undertaken with masks and the heaviest work-gloves Andi Gomez could fashion.

There was a new and respectful title for the winged friends – fire-dragons – the diminutive ending was dropped. Even those who had previously scorned the creatures carried tidbits for them in their pockets. Landing was dotted with fat-bellied dragonets sleeping in the sun.

By lunchtime, a meal was served from the old communal kitchens, and rumour was rife. By midafternoon, Ted Tubberman and George Milan, their faces streaked and drawn by grief, led bereaved relatives to the door of the containment unit. As spokesman, Ted demanded answers.

Paul and Emily came out, with Phas Radamanth and Mar Dook.

'Well? Have you discovered what that *thing* is?'

'It is a complex but understandable network of fila-ments, analogous to a Terran mycorrhiza,' Mar Dook began, resenting Tubberman's manner but respecting his grief.

'That explains very little, Mar,' Ted replied, belliger-ently sticking out his chin. 'In all my years as a botanist, I never saw a plant symbiont dangerous to humans. What do we get next? A death moss?'

Emily reached out to touch Tubberman's arm in sympathy but Ted jerked away.

'We have little to go on,' Phas said in a sharp tone because he was tired and working all night near the monstrosity had been a terrible strain, 'because nothing like this has ever been recorded, on any of the planets humans have explored: the nearest that has been even imagined were some of the fictional inventions during the Age of Religions. We're still refining our understanding of it.'

'It's still alive? You're *keeping* it alive!' Ted was livid with irrational outrage. Beside him, George Milan nodded agreement as fresh tears streamed down his face. The delegation, murmuring angrily among themselves, crowded closer to the entrance, every one of them seeking an outlet for their frustration and impotent grief.

'Of course, we have to study it, man,' Mar Dook said, keeping his voice steady although the mere thought of thousands of those voracious things crawling about this beautiful land made his stomach heave. 'And find out exactly what it is and to do that it must be fed to ... continue. We've got to ascertain if this is only the beginning of its life-cycle.'

'Only the beginning . . .' Tubberman began. Paul and Emily leaped forward to restrain the grief-mad botanist. Lucy had been his apprentice as well as his daughter and they had shared a deep and affectionate bond. 'By all that's holy, I'll end it now!'

'Ted, be rational. You're a scientist!'

'I'm a father first and my daughter was ... devoured by one of those creatures! So was Joe Milan, and Patsy Swann, Eric Hegelman, Bob Jorgensen and . . .' Ted Tubberman's face was livid, his fists clenched at his sides, his whole body strained with rage and frustration. He glared accusingly at Emily and Paul Benden. 'We trusted you two. How could you bring us to a place that devours our children and all we've achieved the past eight years!' The murmurs of the delegation supported his accusation.

219

'We—' and his wide gesture took in the packed numbers behind him, 'want that thing dead. You've had long enough to study it. C'mon, George. We know what we have to do!' With a final bitter searing look at the biologists, he turned, roughly pushing aside those in his path. 'Fire kills it!'

He stomped off, raging. George Milan, a pleading look on his tear-streaked face, followed and the rest of the delegation left with him.

'It won't matter what they do, Paul,' Mar Dook said, restraining Paul Benden from following Ted. 'The beast is moribund now. Give them the corpse to vent their feelings on. We've about finished what examinations we can make anyhow.' Kwan shrugged wearily. 'For all the good it does us.'

'And that is?' Paul inquired, encouragingly. Mar Dook and Phas gestured him and Emily to re-enter the containment unit where Pol, Bay and two geneticists were still writing up their notes.

Wearily, Mar Dook scrubbed at his face, his sallow skin nearly grey as he slumped on to a table that was littered with tapes and slide containers. 'We now know that it is carbon-based, has complex, very large proteins which flick from state to state and produce movement, and others which attack and digest an incredible range of organic substances. It is almost as if the creature was designed to be inimical to our kind of life.'

'I'm glad you kept that to yourself,' Emily said wryly, looking over her shoulder at the door swinging shut on a view of the angry group heading away. 'I'm going to get Tom Patrick over here. We'll need him when they get back.'

'Mar Dook, you can't mean what you just said,' Paul began, resting both hands on the shoulders of the weary biologist. 'It may be dangerous, yes – but designed to kill *us*?'

'That *is* just a thought,' Mar Dook replied, looking a bit sheepish. 'Phas here has a more bizarre suggestion.'

220

Phas cleared his throat nervously. 'Well, it's come out of the blue so unexpectedly, I wondered if it could possibly be a weapon, preparing the ground for an invasion?' Dumbfounded, Paul Benden and Emily Boll stared at him, aware of Bay's sniff of disagreement and the amused expression on Kitti Ping's face. 'That is not an illogical interpretation, you know. I like it better than Bay's suggestion: that this might be only the beginning of a life-cycle. I dread what could follow.'

Paul and Emily glanced around them, stunned by such a dreadful possibility. But Pol Nietro rose from his chair, clearing his throat, a tolerant expression on his round face despite his deep fatigue.

'That is also a suggestion from the fiction of the Age of Religions, Mar,' Pol Nietro said with a wry smile. He glanced apologetically at his wife and then noticed, and was heartened by Kitti Ping's reassuring smile. 'And, in my opinion, highly improbable. If the life-cycle produced inimical forms, where are the descendants of subsequent metamorphoses? The EEC team may have erred in considering the polka-dots non-dangerous but they also discovered no other incongruous life forms.

'As for an invasion from outer space, every other planet in this sector of space was found to be inimical to carbon-based life forms,' Pol began to warm to his own theory and saw Emily recovering from the shock of the other revelations. 'And we have determined that that,' and he jerked his thumb at the now discoloured cube, 'is carbon-based. So that would seem to more or less limit it to this system. And we will find out how.' Pol's burst of explanation seemed to have drained the last energy from him and he leaned wearily against the high laboratory stand. 'I believe I'm right though, airing the worst possible interpretations of the data we have gleaned has cleared the air, so to speak.' He gave a little, almost apologetic shrug and smiled hopefully at Phas and Bay.

'I still feel we have missed something in our investigations,' Phas said, shaking his head. 'Something obvious, and important.'

'No one thinks straight after forty hours on the trot,' Paul said, clasping Phas by the shoulder to give him a reassuring shake. 'Let's look at your notes again when you've had some rest and something to eat away from the stench in here. Jim, Emily and I will wait and deal with Ted's delegation. They're over-reacting,' and he sighed, 'not that I blame them. Sudden grief is always a shock. However, I personally would rather plan for the worst that can happen. As you've suggested several dire options, we won't be surprised by anything that happens. And we should plan to reduce its effects on the settlements.'

Although Paul and Red both thought the exercise macabre, they had a quiet word with Tom Patrick. His opinion was that the thwarted tensions of the bereaved might be eased by what he termed 'a ritual incineration'. So they stepped aside when Ted Tubberman and his adherents demanded the cube and destroyed it in a blazing fire. The combination of the unknown decomposing creature and hot plastic produced a stench that gagged many. It also sped the dispersal of onlookers with the exception of Ted, George and Simone Jorgenson who remained to watch the embers cool.

As Paul and Emily left the scene with Tom Patrick, the psychologist shook his head slowly. 'I think I'll keep an eye on Ted Tubberman for a while. That was apparently not enough to assuage his grief.'

Telescopes were trained on the eccentric planet early the next morning. It appeared to many as reddish in cast, due, Ezra Keroon suggested, to the aggregated dust swirls it had brought in from the edge of the system. Despite the fact that most of its observers had some scientific qualifications and training, the sighting reinforced the suggestion that the planet was somehow responsible for the disaster.

During the day, Kenjo's group discovered traces of an earlier fall on Ierne Island which Tom remembered as more of a rainstorm littered with black motes than a fall of thread. He sent one scout to the northern continent who reported traces of recent destruction across the eastern peninsula. That discovery dispersed the vain hope that the fall was unique or confined to a specific area. A review of the probe pics from the EEC did nothing to alleviate tension for the fax incontrovertibly showed the fall to have been widespread two hundred years before. They figured that the event must have happened just prior to the team's arrival. The demand to know the extent and frequency of the falls increased ominously.

To assuage mounting fears and tension, Betty Musgrave-Blake and Bill Duff undertook to review the Survey's original botanical data. With the demise of Arvi Du Vieux and Felicia Grant-von Toorn, Ted Tubberman was the only trained botanist but he spent his days tracking down every thread 'shell' and burning the piles every evening, an aberrant behaviour which Tom Patrick continued to monitor.

Based on the original data, Betty and Bill Duff deduced a two-hundred-year gap since the last incursion, allowing a span of ten to fifteen years for the vegetation to regenerate on the damaged circles after taking into account the age of some of the largest 'trees' in and near the previous occurrence. Betty delivered this conclusion as a positive statement, meant to engender optimism but she could provide no answer to the vital question of how long the deadly rain continued to fall.

In an attempt to disprove Mar's theory of an invasion or Phas' equally disturbing suggestion, Ezra Keroon spent that day on the link with the *Yokohama*'s main frame. His calculations checked beyond question that the eccentric planet had an orbit of 250 years. But it only stayed in the inner system for a little while, like Halley's Comet around Sol. It was too much to suppose there was no connection and, after consulting Paul and Emily, Ezra programmed one of the *Yokohama*'s few remaining probes to circumnavigate the planet and discover its composition: especially the components of its apparently gaseous envelope.

Though these reports were honestly and fully presented to the community as soon as available, by evening speculation produced alarming interpretations. Grimly the more responsible members tried to dissuade those who gave way to panic.

Then a perplexed Kenjo sought Betty out with a disturbing observation. Betty immediately informed Paul and Emily and a quiet meeting was arranged with those who were able to discuss the situation with some detachment.

'You all know that I've overflown to map the damage,' Kenjo began. 'I didn't know what I'd seen until I'd seen it often enough to realize what was *not* there.' He paused, as if steeling himself for rebuke or disbelief. 'I don't think all thread starved to death. And crazy Tubberman hasn't gotten as far as I have. In most places, there are shells! But in nine circles that I have seen – and landed to be sure I make no mistake – there were no shells.' He made a cutting gesture with both hands. 'None. And these circles were by themselves, not in a group, and the area – demolished – was not as big as usual.' He glanced at each of the serious faces about him. 'I see. I observe. I have pics, too.'

'Well,' Pol said, heaving a weary sigh and absently patting the folded hands of his wife beside him at the table, 'it is biologically consistent that to perpetuate a species many are sent and few are chosen. Perhaps the journey through space vitiates most of the organisms. I'm almost relieved that a few can survive and flourish. It makes more sense. I prefer your theory to some of the others that have been bruited about.'

'Yes, but what do they become in the next metamorphosis?' Bay wondered, her face reflecting depression. Sometimes being right was another sort of failure.

'We'd better find out,' Paul said, glancing around for support. 'Is there one nearby, Kenjo?' When Kenjo pointed to its position on the map, Paul nodded. 'Good, then, Phas, Pol, Bill, Ezra, Bay and Emily, just slip out of Landing in small sleds. Let's see if we can prevent a new batch of wild notions. Report back here as soon as you can.'

Paul sent Betty back to her home and her baby, and told her to rest while he and Ongola tackled other problems as they waited for the biologists to return.

Pol, Bay and Phas were the first back, with little good news.

'All the insects, slug-forms, and grubs we found on those sites,' Phas reported, 'appear harmless enough. Some of them have already been catalogued but,' he added with a shrug, 'we've barely begun to identify creatures and their roles in the ecology of this planet. Kenjo was right to alert us. Clearly some of the thread survives to propagate itself so Bay's theory is the most viable to date.' Phas seemed relieved. 'But I won't rest easy until we have discovered the entire cycle.'

Late in the afternoon of the third day after that first Fall, an almost hysterical Wade Lorenzo reported from Sadrid in Macedonia Province. Jacob Chernoff took the call and immediately contacted Ongola and Paul at the Administration building.

'He says it's coming straight across the sea, right at him, sir. His stake is due west on the 20 degree line. I'm holding him on Channel 37.'

Even as Paul picked up the handset and punched for the channel, he located the coastal stake of Sadrid on the big map of the Continent.

'Wade, get everyone in under silicon plastic, use fire to ignite the stuff where it hits the surface. Use torches if necessary. D'you have any dragonets?'

Wade's deep breath was audible as he fought for self-control. 'We have some dragonets, sir, and we've two flame-throwers, used 'em to cut down bush. Egend thought it was just a very bad rain squall until he saw the fish eating. Can't you come?'

'We'll get there as soon as possible!'

When Wade had rung off, Paul told Jacob to say nothing of this to anyone else.

'I don't want to cause more panic than there already is, sir.'

The boy's fervent assurance brought a brief smile to Paul's face as he then dialled Jim Tillek at the Monaco Bay Harbourmaster's office. He inquired if there were any trawlers southwest near Sadrid.

'Not today. Any trouble?'

So much for trying to sound casual, Paul thought. 'Can you get here to Admin without appearing to rush?'

Ongola was looking grimly at the map, his eyes flicking from Macedonia to Delta. 'Your Boca River Stake is not that far from Sadrid.'

'I noticed.' He dialled the channel link to his Stake and in terse sentences told his wife the grim news and told her what precautions to take. 'Ju, it may not reach us but . . .'

'It's best to be on the safe side with something like this, isn't it?'

Paul was proud of her calm response. 'I'll give you an update as soon as we've got one. With any luck, you've got at least an hour's leeway if it's just now at Sadrid. I'll be there as soon as I can. Quite possibly, Boca's far enough north. This stuff seems to fall in a southwesterly drift.'

'Ask her if her dragonets are acting normally?' Ongola suggested.

'Sunning themselves at this time of day,' Ju replied. 'I'll watch them. They really do anticipate this stuff?'

'Ongola thinks so. I'll check with you later, Ju.'

'I've just got through to the Logorides at Thessaly,' Ongola said. 'They might be in the path. Had we better

226

warn Caesar at Roma Stake? He's got all that live-stock.'

'He was also smart enough to put up stone buildings, but call him and then find out if Boris and Dieter have run their new program. I wish the hell we knew when it started, how far it'll travel,' Paul muttered anxiously. 'I'll organize transport.' He dialled the main engineering shed and asked for Kenjo.

'There's more Thread? How far away?' Kenjo asked. 'Sadrid? On the 20th? I've got something that could make it in just over an hour.' There was a ripple of excitement in Kenjo's usually even tone. 'Fulmar worked out jet-assist units on one of the medium sleds. Fulmar thinks we could get 700 kph out of it, at least, even fully loaded. More if we run light.'

'We're going to have to pack as many of the flame-throwers as possible plus emergency supplies. Pol and Bay don't weigh much and they'll be invaluable as observers. We need at least one medic, a couple of joats, Tarvi, Jim and me. Eight. All right, then, we'll be with you directly.' Paul turned to Ongola. 'Any luck?'

'Since we can't tell them when it started, they want to know when it ends,' Ongola said. 'The more data we can give them, the more accurate they will be . . . next time. Am I among the eight?'

Paul shook his head with regret. 'I need you here to deal with any panic. Blast it, but we've got to get organized for this.'

Ongola snorted to himself: Paul Benden was already a legend in organizing and operating at high efficiency in emergency situations. Observers, crew and supplies boarded the augmented sled within twenty minutes of the initial call and it was airborne and out of sight before Ongola heard the muted roar of its improved drive.

Kenjo drove the sled at its maximum speed, passengers and supplies securely strapped in safely harnesses. They sped across the verdant tip of the untouched peninsula past the Jordan River, and then out to sea where the turbulence of sporadic but heavy squalls added more discomfort to an already rough ride in a vehicle not designed for such velocities.

'No sign of the leading edge of fall. Half of that cloud to the south of us is more squalls,' Paul said, looking up from the scope and rubbing his eyes. 'Maybe, just maybe,' he added softly, 'those squalls also saved Wade and Egend.'

Despite the excessive speed, the journey, mainly over water, seemed to continue endlessly. Suddenly Kenjo reduced speed. The sea became less of a blur to starboard, and on the portside the vast approaching land was just visible through the mist of squall. Sunlight broke through cloud to shine impartially on tossing vegetation and denuded alleys.

'It's an ill wind,' Jim Tillek remarked, pointing to the sea which was disturbed more by underwater activity than wind. 'By the way, before I left Monaco Bay, I sent our finny friends to see what they could find out.'

'Good heavens,' Bay exclaimed, pressing her face against the thick plastic canopy, 'they can't have made it here so fast.'

'Not likely,' Jim replied, chuckling 'but the locals are feeding very well indeed.'

'Stay seated!' Kenjo cried, fighting the yoke of the sled.

'If the dolphins can find out where it started . . . Data, that's what Dieter and Boris need.' Paul resumed manning the forward scope. 'Sadrid wasn't entirely lucky,' he added, frowning. 'Just as if someone had shaved the vegetation off the ground with a hot knife,' he muttered under his breath and turned away. 'Get us down as fast as possible, Kenjo!'

'It was the wind,' Wade Lorenzo told the rescue team. 'The wind saved us, and the squall. Came down in sheets but it was water, not thread. No, we're mostly okay,' he assured them, pointing to the dragonets, grooming

228

themselves on the rooftrees. 'They saved us, just like I heard they did at Landing.' The younger children were just being shepherded out of one of the larger buildings, wide-eyed with apprehension as they looked about them. 'But we don't know if Jiva and Bahka are all right. They were trawling.' He gestured hopelessly to the west.

'If they went west and north, they'd've had a good chance,' Jim told him.

'But we are ruined,' Athpathis added, his face a picture of defeat as he indicated the ravaged fields and orchards.

'There're still plenty of seedlings at Landing,' Pol assured him, patting his back with clumsy sympathy, 'and one can grow several crops a year in this climate.'

'We'll be back to you later,' Paul said, helping to unload flamethrowers. 'Jim, will you organize the mop-up here? You know what to do. We've got to track the main fall to its end. There you are, Wade. Go char the bastards!'

'But, Admiral,' Athpathis began, the whites of his large fearful eyes accentuated in his sun-darkened face.

'There're two other stakes in the way of this menace,' Paul said and climbed back into the sled, fastening the hatch.

'Straight to your place, Paul?' Kenjo asked, lifting the sled.

'No, I want you to go north first. See if we can find Jiva and Bahka. And until we find the edge of the fall.'

As soon as Kenjo had hoisted the sled, he slapped on the jet assist, slamming his passengers back into their seats. But almost immediately, he eased back on the power. 'Sir, I think it's missed your place.'

Instantly Paul pressed his eyes to the scope and, with incredible relief, could see where vegetation along the beach tossed in the wake of squall winds. Now he could concentrate without divided priorities.

'Why, it just cuts off,' Bay said surprised.

'Rain, I think,' Pol remarked as he, too, craned his neck

to see out the siliplex canopy. 'And look, isn't that an orange sail?'

Paul looked up from the 'scope with a weary smile. 'Indeed it is, and intact. Mark your position, Mister Fusaiyuki, and let's get to Caesar's with all available speed.' He took a more comfortable position in his seat and gripped the arm rests.

'Aye, aye, sir.'

The six passengers once again endured the effects of speed. And once again, Kenjo's abrupt braking. This time he added such a turn to port that the sled seemed to spin on its tail.

'I've marked my position, Admiral. Your orders, sir?'

Paul Benden's spine gave an involuntary shudder which he hoped was due more to the unexpected manoeuvre than to Kenjo's naval address.

'Let's follow the path and see how wide a corridor it punches. I'll contact the other stakes to stand down from the alert.'

He permitted himself to contact his wife first and gave her a brief report, as much to lock the details in his own mind as to relieve hers.

'Shall I send a crew to help?' she asked. 'Landing's report says the stuff often has to be burnt to be killed.'

'Send Johnny Greene and Greg Keating in the faster sled. We've spare flamethrowers with us.'

Gyorgy Logorides volunteered to send his son, Alexi, and Stepan Wladyka who both were clamouring to see this menace firsthand. Paul accepted that offer as he did Caesar Galliani's, though the vet wanted his sons back before it was time to milk the big Roma herd.

'I was right, wasn't I,' Caesar added with a chuckle, 'to spend so much energy on stone buildings?'

'You were indeed, Caesar.'

'There's nothing like stone walls to make you feel secure. The boys'll be on their way as soon as you give me a position. You'll keep us posted, won't you, Admiral?'

Paul winced at this second unconscious use of his former rank. He had no wish to resume responsibilities. He'd been happily settled as a civilian agronomist for the past seven years. Then his eyes were caught by the circles of destruction, so hideously apparent from the air, interspersed with untouched swathes where squally rain had drowned thread before it could reach the surface. Rain and dragonets! Fragile allies against such devastation. If he had his way . . . Paul halted this train of thought. He was not in command here, he did not wish to be obliged to take command. There were younger men to assume such burdens.

'I make the corridor fifty klicks wide, Admiral,' Kenjo announced.

Paul realized that the others had been quietly conferring on details.

'You can watch vegetation disintegrating by the yard,' Bay said anxiously. She caught Paul's eyes. 'Rain isn't enough.'

'It helped,' Tarvi answered her but he, too, looked at Paul.

'We've got reinforcements coming from Thessaly and Roma. We'll scorch where we have to on our way back to Sadrid. Set down where you can, Kenjo. Landing will need to know the details we've gotten today. Data they want, data they'll have.'

By the time all the available HNO-3 cylinders were exhausted so were the crews. Pol and Bay had followed diligently after the flamethrower teams, taking notes on the pattern of the stuff, grateful that squall activity had somewhat limited its destruction. When Paul had thanked the men from Thessaly and Roma, he told Kenjo to make reasonable speed to Sadrid to collect Jim Tillek.

'And so we must arm ourselves with tongues of flame against this menace to our kind and generous planet,' Tarvi said softly to Paul as they finally headed eastward towards a fast-approaching night. 'Will Sadrid be safe now?'

'On the premise that lightning doesn't strike twice in the same place?' Paul's tone was droll. 'No promises can be made on that score, Tarvi. I am hoping, however, that Boris and Dieter will soon come up with a few answers.' Then, his expression anxious, he turned to Pol. 'This couldn't fall at random, could it?'

'You prefer the theory that it's planned? No, Paul, we've established that we're dealing with an unreasoning, voraciously hungry organism. There isn't a discernible intelligence,' Pol replied, clenching and releasing his fist, surprised at his own vehemence, 'much less a trace of sentience. I continue to favour Bay's theory of a two- or three-stage life-cycle. Even so, it is only remotely possible that intelligence develops at a later stage.'

'The wherries?' Tarvi asked facetiously.

'No, no, don't be ridiculous. We've traced them back to a sea eel, a common ancestor for them, and the dragonets.'

'The ones at Sadrid – and Alexi's three – were more of a help than I expected,' Tarvi said in mild surprise. 'Sallah insists they've a high level of intelligence.'

'Pol, have you or Bay attempted to measure that intelligence when you used mentasynth enhancement?' Paul Benden asked.

Pol blinked in surprise. 'No, not really. There's been no need to, once we demonstrated that an enhanced empathy made them more biddable. There have been other priorities.'

'The main priority as of now is establishing the parameters of this menace,' Paul muttered. 'We'd all better get some rest.'

Once the rescue team had returned to Landing, it was impossible to deny the new incursion. Despite a conn silence on their trip, rumours were inevitable.

'The only good thing about it,' Paul told Emily as he consumed a hastily prepared meal, 'was that it was sufficiently far away from here.'

'We still don't have enough data to establish either frequency or probable "corridors" of the stuff,' Dieter

Clissmann announced. 'Theo Force said that the dolphins could not find out where or when it started. Marine life doesn't keep time. Boris is adding in random factors of temperature variations, high- and low-pressure areas, frequency of rain and wind velocity to the data.' He gave a long sigh, combing thick hair back from his forehead. 'Drowns in the rain, huh? Fire and water kill it! That's some consolation.'

11

•

Few were as easily consoled. There were even some at
Landing who were relieved that other sections of the
continent suffered the same disaster. Tom Patrick said
that was a normal enough human reaction, even if he
couldn't condone it.

This second incident – or Threadfall – had a positive
benefit: emergency measures were no longer resisted. Some
had felt that precautions emanating from Landing violated
their Charter autonomy. The more outspoken revised their
objections when pictures of the devastation on the Sadrid
corridor – as Pol termed it – were distributed. After that,
Ongola and his communications team were kept busy
briefing distant stake holders.

Tarvi drafted a crew of joats and apprentices to work
round the clock, adapting empty cylinders into flamethrowers and filling them with HNO-3. This was the most
easily made oxidant and very effective, combining the
thread-destructive effects of fire *and* water: it could be
synthesized cheaply from air and water, using only hydro-
electricity and was not a pollutant. Most important, dragonet hide and human skin were usually not severely
damaged from any spillage. A wet cloth, applied within
about twenty seconds, prevented a bad burn. Kenjo, Fulmar Stone, Francesco Vassaloe, Bruce Olivine and three
technicians began to rig holders for flamethrowers on the
heavier sleds. Kenjo was adamant that the best defence
was not only offence but aerial. He had many willing

supporters among those at Landing who had lived through the First Fall.

As one wit said, since no one had ever figured out how to make rain on demand, fire was the only reliable defence. Even the most ardent supporters of the dragonets didn't wish to rely totally on their continued assistance.

There were not hands enough to do all the jobs required. Twice Paul and Emily were called in to arbitrate labour-pirating. The agronomists and veterinarians hastily reinforced livestock shelters and checked nearby caves for possible alternative accommodations. Empty warehouses at Landing were made into shelters for any stake holders who wished to house stock for safety's sake. Joel Lilienkamp insisted that the holders themselves would have to reinforce any buildings they pre-empted for there was a worker shortage. Stake holders felt that that was Landing's job, some being unwilling to leave their stakes unless, and until, assured of safe quarters. In eight years, the population of the settlers had increased far beyond the point where the original site could house even half the current numbers.

Porrig Connell remained in his cave, having discovered that there were sufficient interlinking chambers to accommodate his entire extended family and their livestock. In addition to stabling for his mares and foals, he had also constructed a stallion box in which Cricket was made very comfortable. Magnanimously, he allowed the remaining Brennans and Foleys to remain in his cavesite until they found their own.

Because they had been the Colony's leaders, Paul Benden and Emily Boll, as well as Jim Tillek, Ezra Keroon and Ongola found that many decisions were being referred to them, despite the fact that they had stepped down from their previous administrative duties.

'I'd far rather they came to me,' Paul remarked wearily to Ongola when the communications officer brought him the latest urgent queries from outlying stakes, 'than Ted Tubberman.' He turned to the psychologist who was also

reporting on the latest round of gripes and rumours.
'Tom?'

'I don't think you can stall a show-down much longer,'
Tom Patrick said, 'or you and Emily will lose all credibility. That would be a big error. You two may not want
to take command, but someone will have to. Tubberman's
constantly undermining community effort and spirit. He's
so totally negative that you ought to be thankful that most
of the time he's out trying singlehandedly to clear the
continent of rotting threadshell. Grief has totally distorted
his perceptions and judgement.'

'Surely no one believes his ranting?' Emily asked.

'There're just enough long buried gripes and resentments, and good honest gut-fear, right now so that some
people do listen to him. Especially in the absence of
authorized versions,' Tom replied. 'Tubberman's complaints have a certain factual basis. Warped, to be sure.'
Tom Patrick shrugged, raising both hands, palms up. 'In
time, he'll work against himself – I hope. Meanwhile he's
roused a substantial undercurrent of resentment which
had better be countered soon. Preferably by you gentlemen, and Emily and the other captains. They still trust
you, you know, in spite of Tubberman's accusations.'

'So the Rubicon must be crossed again,' Paul said
whimsically and exhaled. He caught himself rubbing his
left thumb against the insensitive skin of the replacement
fingers and stopped. Leaning wearily back in his chair, he
put both hands behind his head as if supporting an extra
weight.

'I can lead a meeting, Paul,' Cabot told him when Paul
contacted him on a secured com channel, 'but they subconsciously consider you and Emily their leaders. Force of
habit.'

'Any decision to reinstate us must be spontaneous,' Paul
replied after a long and thoughtful pause. Slowly Emily
nodded. The last days had aged both Admiral and
Governor. 'The matter must be handled strictly on the

Charter protocol, though by all that's holy, I never anticipated having to invoke those contingency clauses.'

'Thank all the powers that be, they're there,' Cabot said
fervently. 'It'll take an hour or two to organize things
here. Oh, by the way, we also had a few messages across
the river early yesterday morning. Didn't notice until
about noon today. Hit the southern edge of Bordeaux.
We gave Pat and his crew a hand. All's safe here.'

With that, he rang off, leaving Paul dumbfounded.

'After our little brush with the stuff,' Cabot said when
he arrived from Cambridge Stake, 'I'm beginning to appreciate the gravity of the colony's situation.' A hopeful
smile, not echoed by the expression in his keen grey eyes,
curved the strong mouth in his handsome face. 'Is it as
bad as rumour has it?'

'Probably. Depends on the source of the rumour,' Paul
answered with an honest grimace.

'Depends on whether you're an optimist or pessimist,'
Jim Tillek added. 'I've been in worse fixes on the Asteroid
runs, and come out with life and lung. I prefer to have a
planet to manoeuvre in, on, over. And the seas.'

Cabot's smile faded as he regarded the five people
gathered discreetly in the Met Tower.

'Most of what we *know*,' Paul said, 'is negative. But
the threads are unlikely to be the forerunner of an alien
invasion,' he refuted the prevalent rumours by ticking
them off on his strong, work-stained fingers, 'it was not
unique to this area. It did strike the planet in much the
same way, to judge by the EEC records, almost exactly
200 years ago. It may or may not emanate from the
eccentric planet which also has a 250-year orbit. And
although we do not know what its life-cycle is, or even if
it does have one – that is the most viable theory – but
thread is not the initial stage of tunnel snakes, for example,
who have a much more respectable lineage. Nor of
any of the other kinds of life we've had a look at so
far.'

'I see,' and Cabot nodded his handsome leonine head

237

slowly as he fingered his lips in thought. 'No reassuring forecast available?'

'Not yet. As Tom here recommends, we need a forum in which to air grievances and correct misconceptions,' Paul went on. 'It didn't miss Boca Stake because Paul Benden owns it, or drop on Sadrid because they're the newest, or stop short of Thessaly because Gyorgy was one of the first Charterers to claim his stake. We can, and will, survive this hazard, but we cannot have the indiscriminate conscription of technicians and able-bodied workers. It is apparent to anyone pausing to think that we also cannot survive if everyone hares off in opposite directions. Or if some of the wilder notions, including Tubberman's, are not dismissed and morale restored.'

'In short, what you want is a suspension of autonomy?'

'Not what I want,' Paul replied clearly and with emphasis, 'but a centralized administration . . .' Cabot grinned at his choice of words, '. . . will be able to efficiently organize available workers, distribute *matériel* and supplies, and make sure that the majority survive. Joel Lilienkamp locked up Stores today, claiming inventory to prevent panic requisitions. People must realize that this *is* a survival situation.'

'Together we stand, divided we fall?' Cabot used the old saying with respect.

'That's it.'

'The trick will be in getting all our independent spirits to see the wisdom,' Tom Patrick said and Cabot nodded agreement.

'I must emphasize,' Paul went on, looking quickly at Emily who nodded approval, 'that it doesn't matter *who* administers during the emergency so long as some authority is recognized, and obeyed, that will ensure survival.'

After a pause, Cabot added thoughtfully, 'We're years from help. Did we burn all our bridges?'

Considerable surprise and relief permeated Landing the next morning when Cabot Francis Carter, the colony's senior legist, broadcast the announcement that a mass meeting was scheduled for the following evening. Representatives of every major Stake, Charter or Contract, would be expected to attend.

By the night of the meeting, the electricians had managed to restore power to one end of Bonfire Square by means of underground conduits. Where lamps were still dark, torches had been secured to the standards. The lighted area was filled with benches and chairs. The platform, originally constructed for musicians for the nightly Bonfires, contained a long table, set with six chairs along one side. There was light enough to see those who took places.

A murmur of surprise rippled around those assembled as neither Paul Benden nor Emily Boll appeared. Cabot Francis Carter led Mar Dook, Pol and Bay Harkenon-Nietro, Ezra Keroon and Jim Tillek on to the stage.

'We have had time to mourn our losses,' Cabot began, his sonorous voice easily reaching to the very last bench. Even the children listened in silence. 'And they have been heavy. They could have been worse and there can't be one among us who doesn't give thanks to our small fire-breathing, dragon-like allies.

'I don't have all bad news for you tonight. I wish I had better. We can give a name to the stuff that killed some of our loved ones and wiped out five Stakes: it's a very primitive mycorrhizoid life form. Mar Dook here tells me that on other planets, including our own Earth, very simple fungi can be generally found in a symbiotic association with trees, the mycelium of the fungus with the roots of a seed plant. We've all seen it attack vegetation—'

'And just about anything else,' Ted Tubberman shouted from the lefthand side of the audience.

'Yes, that is tragically true.' Cabot did not look at the man or attempt to lighten the tone of the meeting but he intended to control it. He raised his voice slightly. 'What we are only just beginning to realize is that the phenomenon is planet-wide and the last occurrence was approximately two hundred years ago.' He paused to allow the listeners to absorb that fact, then stolidly held up his hands to silence the murmurs. 'Soon we will be able to predict exactly when and where this Threadfall is likely to strike again because, unfortunately, it will. But this is our planet,' and his expression altered to fierce determination, 'and no damned mindless thread is going to make us leave.'

'You stupid bastard, we *can't* leave!' Ted Tubberman jumped to his feet, wildly waving clenched fists in the air in his impotent rage. 'You fixed it so we'll rot here, sucked up by those effing things. We can't leave! We'll all die here.'

His outburst started a sullen, murmurous roll. Sean, sitting with Sorka to edge of the crowd, was indignant.

'Damfool loud-mouth Charterer,' Sean murmured to Sorka. 'He knew this was a one-way trip, only now everything's not running smooth enough for him, it has to be *someone's* fault?' Sean snorted his contempt.

Sorka shushed him to hear Cabot's rebuttal.

'I don't look at our situation,' Cabot began, his trained voice drowning the murmurs in a firm, confident and determined tone, 'as hopeless, Tubberman. Far from it! I prefer to think positively. I see this as a challenge to our ingenuity, to our adaptability. Mankind has survived more dangerous environments than Pern. We've got a problem and we must cope with it. We must solve it to survive. And survive we will!' When Cabot saw the big botanist gathering breath, he raised his voice. 'When we signed the Charter, we all knew there'd be no turning back. Even if we could, I, for one, wouldn't consider running home,' his voice became rich with contempt for the faint of heart, the coward, the quitter, 'for there's more on this planet for me than First or Earth ever held! I'm not going to let this phenomenon do me out of the home I've built, the stock I plan to raise, the quality of life I enjoy!' With a contemptuous sweep of his hand, he dismissed the menace as a minor inconvenience. 'I'll fight it every time it strikes my Stake or my neighbours, with every ounce of strength and every resource I possess.

'Now,' he went on in a less fervent tone, 'this meeting has been called, in the democratic manner outlined by our Charter, to make plans on how best to sustain our colony during this emergency. We are, in effect, under siege by this mycorrhizoid. So we must initiate measures and develop the necessary strategy by which to minimize its effect on our lives and property.'

'Are you suggesting martial law, Cabot?' Rudi Shwartz demanded, rising to his feet, his expression carefully guarded.

Cabot gave a wry chuckle. 'As there is no army on Pern, Rudi, martial law is impossible. However, circumstances force us to consider suspending our present autonomy in order to reduce the damage which this thread apparently can,' Cabot paused significantly, 'and will do to both the ecology of the planet and the economy of this colony. I'm suggesting that a reversion to the centralized government of our first year on Pern be considered at this point in time.' His next words rose to a near bellow to drown out the protests. '*And* whatever measures are required to ensure the survival of the colony, unpalatable though they may be to us as individuals, who have enjoyed our autonomy.'

'And these measures have already been decided?' Sue O'Hara asked.

'By no means,' Cabot assured her. 'We don't even yet know that much about our – "adversary" – but plans must be made now, for every possible contingency. We know that Thread falls on a world-wide scale so sooner or later it will affect every Stake. We have to minimize that danger. That will mean centralization of existing food supplies and *matériel*, a return to hydroponics. It definitely means that some of you technicians will be asked to return to Landing since your particular skills can be best exercised here. It means we're all going to have to work together again instead of going our separate ways.'

241

'What option do we have?' a woman asked in the slight pause that followed. She sounded resigned.

'Some of you have fairly large common stakes,' Cabot answered in the most reasonable of tones. 'You could probably do quite well on your own. Any central organization here at Landing would have to consider the needs of its population first but it wouldn't be the case of never darken our doorstep again.' He gave a brief reassuring smile in her general direction. 'That's why we meet here tonight. To discuss all the options as thoroughly as the Charter's conditions and the colony's prospects were initially discussed.'

'Wait just a minute,' Ted Tubberman cried, jumping to his feet again, spreading out his arms and looking around, his chin jutting forward aggressively. 'We've got a sure-fire option, a realistic one. We can send a homing capsule to Earth and ask for assistance. This is a state of emergency. We need help!'

'I told ya,' Sean murmured to Sorka, 'squealing like a stuck pig. Earth lands here, girl, and we make for the Barrier Range and stay lost!'

'I wouldn't bet on Earth sending any,' Joel Lilienkamp said from the front of the audience, his words drowned by the cries from all sides to send a capsule back.

'We don't need Earth mucking about Pern,' Sean cried, jumping to his feet and flourishing his arm. 'This is *our* planet!'

Cabot called for order but very little of the commotion subsided. Ezra Keroon got to his feet, trying to help. Finally, making a megaphone of his hands, he bellowed his message.

'Hold it down, now, friends. I have to remind you all . . . *Listen to me* . . . it'd be over ten years before we got a reply. Of any kind.'

'Well, I for one don't want old Terra,' Jim Tillek said in the murmurous reaction to that, 'or even First, poking their noses in *our* business. That is, if they'd bother to respond. For sure, if they condescended to help, they'd mortgage all of us to the hilt for aid. And end up owning all the mineral rights and most of the arable land. Or have you all forgotten Ceti III? I also don't see why a central administration during this emergency is such a big deal. Makes sense to me. Share and share alike!'

A low murmur of agreement could be clearly heard, although many faces wore discouraged or sullen expressions.

'He's right, Sorka,' Sean said in a loud enough voice for others around him to hear.

'Dad and mother think so too,' and Sorka pointed out her parents, sitting several rows in front of them.

'We've got to send a message,' Ted Tubberman shouted, shaking off the attempts of his immediate neighbours to make him sit down. 'We've got to tell them we're in trouble. We've a right to help! What's wrong in sending a message?'

'What's wrong?' Wade Lorenzo shouted from the back of the audience. 'We need help right now, Tubberman, not ten to thirty years from now. Why, by then, we'd probably have the thing licked. A fall's not all that bad,' he added with the confidence of experience.

He sat down amid hoots and shouts of dissent, mainly from those who had been at Landing.

'And don't forget that it took half a century before Earth went to Ceti III's assistance,' said Betty Musgrave-Blake, jumping to her feet.

Other comments were voiced. 'Yeah, Captain Tillek's right. We've got to solve our own problems. We can't wait for Earth.' 'Forget it, Tubberman.' 'Sit down and shut up, Tubberman.' 'Cabot, call him to order. Let's get on with this meeting.'

Similar sentiments rose from all sides, Sean and Sorka on their feet, adding their encouragement. His neighbours forced the botanist down and, dismayed by the lack of support, Ted shook off the compelling hands and crossed his arms defiantly on his chest. Tarvi and Fulmar had moved to his side of the audience. Sean saw them and nudged Sorka.

'They'll shut him up and then we can get to the meat of all this talking,' Sean said to Sorka as they sat down again. 'I hate meetings like this, people sounding off just to make a noise and act big when they don't know what they're talking about.'

Raising a hand to be recognized, Rudi Shwartz again got to his feet. 'If, as you've suggested, Cabot, the larger stakes could remain self-governing, how would a central government be organized? Would the large stakes be at all responsible to it?'

'It's more a matter of the fair allocation of food, materials, and shelter, Rudi,' Joel Lilienkamp said, rising to his feet, 'rather than—'

'You mean, we don't have enough food?' an anxious voice broke in.

'For now, yes, but if this threadstuff is planet-wide – we all see what it did to Landing's fields,' Joel went on, motioning to the dark, ravaged area, 'and if it keeps coming back, well—' a woman made a protest of dismay that was clearly audible, 'well,' he went on, hitching up his trousers, 'everyone deserves a fair share of what we've got. I see nothing wrong with going back to hydroponics for a while. We did just fine for fifteen years on shipboard, didn't we? I'll take any odds we can do it again.'

His jovial challenge met with mixed reactions, some cheering him, others clearly apprehensive.

'Remember, too, folks, that Thread doesn't affect the sea,' Jim Tillek said, his cheerfulness unforced. 'We can live, and live well, from the sea alone.'

'Most early civilizations lived almost entirely from the sea,' Mairi Hanrahan cried in a ringing, challenging tone. 'Joel's right – we can use alternative methods of growing. And, as long as we can harvest the sea for fresh protein, we'll be just fine. I think we all ought to buck up, instead of collapsing under the first little snag.' She stared significantly at Ted Tubberman.

'Little snag?' He roared his protest and would have

shoved through the crowd to get to Mairi if he hadn't been restrained. Tarvi and Fulmar moved again.

'Hardly a *little* snag,' Mar Dook said quickly, raising his voice over the ripple of mixed remonstrance and support. 'And certainly tragic for many of us. But let's not fight among ourselves. It's equally useless for us to bitch that the EEC team did not do a thorough inspection of this planet, and grossly misled us. But this world has already proved that it can survive such an incursion and regenerate. Are we humans any less resilient with the resources we have at hand?' He tapped his forehead significantly.

'I don't want just to survive, hand to mouth,' Ted Tubberman shouted, his chin jerking out belligerently, 'cooped up in a building, wondering if those things are going to eat their way through me!'

'Ted, that's the biggest bunch of bilgewash I've ever heard from a grown man,' Jim Tillek said. 'We got a bit of a problem with our new world that I sure as hell am going to help solve. So quit your bitching and let's figure out just how to cope. We're here, man, and we're going to survive!'

'I want us to send home for help,' Persis St John said calm but firm. 'I feel that we're going to need the defences a sophisticated society can supply, especially as we brought so little technology with us. And most especially if this stuff returns so often.'

'Once we've sent for help, we have to take what is sent,' Cabot said quickly.

'Lili, what odds are you taking that Earth would send us help?'

Ted Tubberman jumped to his feet again. 'Don't bet on it. Vote on it! If this meeting's really democratic that is, let's vote to send a Mayday to Federated Sentient Planets.'

'I second the motion,' Sue O'Hara said before anyone else could.

'Rudi,' Cabot said, 'appoint two other stewards and let's take a hand vote.'

'Not everyone's here tonight,' Wade Lorenzo pointed out.

'If they don't wish to attend a scheduled meeting, they will have to abide by the decision of those who did,' Cabot replied sternly and was met with shouts of agreement. 'Let the vote be taken on the motion before us. Those in favour of sending a homing capsule to the Federated Sentient Planets for assistance, raise their hands.'

Hands were duly raised and counted by the stewards, Rudi Shwartz taking due note of the count. When Cabot called for those opposed to sending for help, the majority was marked. As soon as Cabot announced the results, Ted Tubberman was vituperative.

'You're damned fools. We can't lick this stuff by ourselves. There's no place safe from it on this planet. Don't you remember the EEC reports? The entire planet was eaten up. It took more than two hundred years to recover. What chance have we?'

'That is enough, Ted Tubberman,' Cabot roared at him. 'You asked for a vote. It was taken in sight of all and the *majority*, have voted against sending for help. Even if the decision had been in favour, our situation is serious enough so that certain measures must be initiated immediately.

'One priority is the manufacture of metal sheeting to protect existing buildings, no matter where they are. The second is to manufacture HNO-3 cylinders and flame-thrower components. A third is to conserve all materials and supplies. Another problem is keeping a good eastern watch at every Stake until a pattern can be established for Threadfall.

'I'm asking that we temporarily reinstate Emily Boll and Paul Benden as leaders. Governor Boll's had a lot of experience in keeping a planet functioning through a space-embargo. Admiral Benden is by far the best man to organize an effective defense strategy.

'I'm calling for a show of hands now, and we'll publish a proper referendum when we know exactly how long the state of emergency will last.' A ripple of assent greeted his crisp decisive statements. 'Rudi, prepare for another count.' He waited a moment as the crowd shifted restlessly. 'Let's have a show of hands on implementing those priorities tonight with Admiral Benden and Governor Boll in charge.'

Many hands were immediately thrust in the air, others came up more slowly as the undecided took heart from their neighbours' resolution. Even before Rudi gave him the count, Cabot could see that the vote was heavily in favour of the emergency measures.

'Governor Boll, Admiral Benden, will you accept this mandate?'

'It was rigged,' Ted Tubberman began to shout, 'I tell you, rigged. They just want to get back into power again.' His accusations broke off suddenly as Tarvi and Fulmar pushed him inexorably down on the bench.

'Governor? Admiral?' Cabot ignored the interruption. 'You two still have the best qualifications for the jobs to be done, but if you decline, I will accept nominations from the floor.' He waited expectantly, giving no hint to those watching him of his personal preference in the matter, paying no attention to the restless audience and a rising murmur of anxious whispers.

Slowly Emily Boll rose to her feet. 'I accept.'

'As I do,' Paul Benden said, standing beside the Governor. 'But only for the duration of this emergency.'

'You believe that?' Tubberman roared, breaking loose from his restrainers.

'That is quite enough, Ted Tubberman,' Cabot shouted, appearing to lose his professional detachment. 'The majority support this temporary measure even if you won't.' Slowly the audience quietened in the silence he allowed to fall. 'Now, I've saved the worst news until I was certain we were all resolved to work together. Thanks to Kenjo and his survey teams, Boris and Dieter believe that there is a pattern emerging. If they're right, we have to expect this Thread to fall again tomorrow afternoon at Malay

247

River and proceed across Cathay Province to Mexico on Maori Lake.'

'On Malay?' Chuck Kimmage jumped to his feet, Chaila clutching his arm, both of them horrified. Phas had managed to find and warn all the other Stakers at Malay and Mexico but Chuck and Chaila had arrived just before the meeting, too late to be privately informed.

'And all of us will help preserve your stakes,' Emily Boll said in a loud firm voice.

Paul jumped up on the platform, raising his hands and glancing at Cabot for permission to speak.

'I'm asking for volunteers to man sleds and flamethrowers. Kenjo and Fulmar have worked out a way of mounting them. Some are already in place on what sleds they could commandeer. Those of you with medium and large sleds just volunteered them. The best way to get the Thread is while it's still airborne, before it has a chance to land. We will also need people on the ground, mopping up what does slip through . . .'

'What about the fire lizards, or whatever you call 'em. Won't they help?'

'They helped us that day at Landing,' a woman added, a note of fearful apprehension making her voice break.

'They helped at Sadrid Stake two days ago,' Wade said.

'The rain helped a lot, too,' Kenjo added, not at all convinced of assistance from a non-mechanical quarter.

'Any of you with dragonets would be very welcome in ground crews,' Paul went on, willing to entertain any reinforcements though he, too, was sceptical. He had been too busy to attach a dragonet though his wife and older son had two each. 'I particularly need those of you who've had any combat or flight experience. Our enemy isn't the Nathi this time but it's our world that is being invaded. Let's stop it, tomorrow and whenever it's necessary!'

A spontaneous cheer went up in response to Paul Benden's rousing words and was repeated, growing in volume as people got to their feet, waving clenched fists. Those on the platform watched the demonstration, relieved and reassured. Perhaps only Ongola took note of those who remained seated or silent.

12

●

If Dieter and Boris were correct, this fall would give the Kahrain Peninsula a near miss, beginning at approximately 1630 hours, roughly 120 klicks northwest of the mouth of the Paradise River, 25° South. Dieter and Boris were not sure if the fall would extend as far southwestward as Mexico on Lake Maori but precautions were being taken there as well.

Acting Commander Kenjo Fusaiyuki assembled his squadrons at the required point. Though Thread drowned in the sea, his teams would at least have some practice throwing flame at the 'real thing'.

'Practice' was not the appropriate term for the chaos that resulted. Kenjo was reduced to snarling peremptory orders over the comunit as the inept but eager sled pilots plummeted through the skies after Thread, frequently favouring each other with a glancing touch of thrown HNO-3.

Fighting Thread required entirely different techniques from hunting wherry or scoring a hit on a large flying machine driven by a reasonably intelligent enemy. Thread was mindless. It just fell – in a slanting southwesterly direction, occasionally buffeted into tangles by gusting winds. It was the inexorability of that insensate fall that infuriated, defeated, depressed, frustrated. No matter how much was seared to ash in the sky, more followed relentlessly. Nervous pilots swooped, veered and dove. Unskilled gunners fired at anything that moved into range, rather more often than not another sled chasing down a tangle of Thread. Nine domesticated dragonets fell victim to this inexpertise and there was suddenly a marked decrease in the wild ones who had joined the fray.

In the first half hour of the fall, seven sleds were involved in mid-air collisions – three badly damaged and two with cracked siliplex canopies which made them unairworthy. Even Kenjo's sled bore scorch marks. Four broken arms, six broken or sprained hands, three cracked collarbones and a broken leg put fourteen gunners out of action: many others struggled on with lacerations and bruises. No one had thought about rigging any safety harness for the flame-gunners.

A hasty conference was called on a secured channel between the Squadron leaders at the beginning of the second hour while the fall was still over water. The squadron leaders – Kenjo, Sabra Stein-Ongola, Theo Force, Drake Bonneau – and Paul Benden as leader of the ground-support crews decided to assign each squadron their own altitude level of 100 metre intervals. The squadron would fly in a stacked wedge formation back and forth across the 50 klick width of the Thread corridor. The important factor was for each wedge of seven sleds to stick to its designated altitude.

Once the sleds began to maintain these distances, always following the leading edge of Threadfall, mid-air collisions and scorchings were immediately reduced. Kenjo led the most capable fliers at ground level to catch as much missed Thread as possible and to inform the surface crews where tangles got through. As Wade Lorenzo, the Logorides and Galliani boys had already had some experience with mopping up, Paul coordinated the movements of their fast ground-skimmers which carried teams with small portable flamers. Evvie Duff and Martha Chernoff kept channels open to air, ground and Landing. Joel Lilienkamp organized replacement of empty HNO-3 cylinders and power packs while Basil Tomlinson headed a medical team.

By mid-fall, Paul knew that his ground support teams were too thinly spread to be truly effective. Towards the end, when weary pilots were running low on energy and the sled power packs were nearly depleted, more Thread got through. It was all part of the bad luck that this was over thick vegetation and the home farm of the Mexico Stake.

The abrupt end of the Fall, on the verge of Maori Lake and the main buildings of Mexico, came as a distinct shock to those who had been concentrating so hard on destroying Thread. Squadron leaders ordered their fighters to land on the lakeside while they had a chance to confer with the ground crew marshalls. Those at Mexico who had not been in ground defence provided hot soup and klah, fresh bread and fruit and had prepared an infirmary in one of the houses. Tarvi and the Karachi team had managed to complete metal roofing just before the Fall reached the area. Then Joel Lilienkamp's supply barge arrived with fresh power packs and HNO-3 cylinders, 'just off the assembly line'.

The day wasn't over yet. Pilots were to cruise slowly back over the Fall corridor, checking for any 'live' Thread. Paul drove himself and his sweat-smeared, soot-covered weary teams back towards Malay Stake and the coast, a thin line indeed to try to spot signs of a secondary infestation where no shell or dissolving matter was visible. Only two such points were discovered and, on Paul's order, the ground was saturated with sustained blasts of HNO-3. Bernard Shattuck, working as ground crew on that detail, told the Admiral that he thought that was a waste of fuel.

'The dragonets weren't at all concerned, Admiral,' he reported. 'They are when there's Thread.'

'We take no chances at this stage, Captain,' Paul replied, a slight smile removing any hint of rebuke. He didn't look upon the fiery bath as an over-kill. The dragonets were palpably alerted by Thread, but obviously unaware of the presence of the second, and possibly more fearful stage of its life-cycle.

However, Paul Benden's respect for the dragonets was

increased by their diligent searching out of newly fallen Thread. Several times during the Fall, he spotted the 'fair' of dragonets fighting alongside Sean Connell and the red-headed Hanrahan girl. The creatures seemed to be obeying orders. Their movements had a discipline, while other groups flitted about in a kind of chaotic frenzy.

On almost too many occasions, Paul saw the little creatures suddenly disappearing just when one seemed certain to be seared by the fiery breath of another. He could wish sleds had that sort of ability, or even more agility. Sleds were not the most efficient fighter craft. He recalled his admiration of the dragonets during the wherry attack. From accounts of their now legendary 'umbrella' defence of Landing from the First Fall, he knew that hundreds of wild ones had assisted their domesticated kin. They could be splendid reinforcements. Paul wondered what the chances were to mobilize *all* the dragonets, and to be trained by Connell and Hanrahan.

This Fall had left denuded patches on the surface but, despite all initial bungling and inexperience of sled and ground crews, the devastation was not as widespread as in the first horrific Fall.

Most of the exhausted fighters chose to remain the night at Malay Stake. Pierre de Courci took it upon himself to act as Chef and his team had prepared baked fish and tubers in great pits on the beach. Weary men, women and youngsters sat around the reassuring bonfires, too spent to talk, glad enough to have survived the rigours of the day.

Sean and Sorka opened an emergency clinic on Malay beach to tend to the wounded fire-dragonets, slathering numbweed on Threadscored wings and seared hide did comfort the poor creeling creatures, and much eased the discomfort of their owners.

'D'you think that once Sira stops crying, my bronze and brown will come back?' Tarrie Chernoff asked. She was dirty with black grease and vegetation green stains, her wherry-hide jerkin showing numerous char spots, new and old, but like all devoted fire-dragonet owners, she was caring for her creature before seeing to her own relief.

Sean shrugged non-committally but Sorka laid a re-assuring hand on Tarrie's arm. 'They usually do. They get pretty upset when one of their own fair's hurt, especially a queen. You get a good night's sleep and see what the morning brings.'

'Why'd you give her false comfort like that, Sorka?' Sean murmured when Tarrie had trudged back to the bonfires, her comforted queen cradled in the crook of her arm. 'You know bloody well by now that if they're hurt badly enough, a fire-lizard doesn't come back.'

'She needs a good night's sleep without worrying herself sick. And a lot do come back.'

Sorka gave a weary sigh as she closed the medicine case. She arched her back against tired back muscles.

'Give me a rub, would you, Sean? My right shoulder.' She turned her back to him and sighed in relief as his strong fingers kneaded the strain away.

Sean's hands were marvellous and he knew just how to ease away the tension. Then his hands moved caressingly, up the nape of her neck, and lovingly into her hair. Tired as she was, she responded to the silent question. She stepped away from him, smiling as she looked quickly about to see where their fair had taken themselves.

'They've all found quiet nests to curl up in.' Sean's low voice was suggestive.

'Then let's find us one of our own,' and she caught his hand and led him off the beach and into the thick grove of arrow-leaf plants which they had helped save from Threadscore.

Revived by the hot meal and a generous beaker of a very smooth quikal fermented by Chaika Xavior-Kimmage from local fruits, Paul and Emily quietly organized a discreet council which they held in one of the unscathed

Malay outbuildings. Besides the Admiral and the Governor, Ongola, Drake, Kenjo, Jim Tillek, Ezra Keroon, and Joel Lilienkamp attended.

'We'll do better next time, Admiral,' Drake Bonneau assured him with a cocky salute. Kenjo, entering behind him, regarded the tall war ace with amused condescension. 'Today taught us that this Thread requires entirely different flight and strike techniques. We'll refine that wedge manoeuvre so nothing gets through. Sled pilots must drill to maintain altitude patterns. Gunners must learn to control their blasts. It's more than just holding the button down. We had some mighty close encounters. We lost some of the little dragonets, too. We can't risk so many lives much less the sleds.'

'We can repair the sleds, Drake,' Joel Lilienkamp remarked drily before Paul spoke, 'but power packs won't last forever. We can't afford to expend them uselessly on drills. Despite our resupply system, which I bet I can improve, nine pilots had to glide-land at Maori. That's clumsy management. That wedge formation, by the way, Drake, is economical on the packs. But . . . it still takes days to recharge exhausted ones. How long will this stuff keep falling, Paul?' Joel looked up from his calculating pad.

'We haven't established that yet,' Paul said, his left thumb rubbing his knuckles. 'Boris and Dieter are collating information from the pilot debriefing.'

'Hellfire, that's not going to tell us what we need to know, Paul,' Drake said, his weary tone a complaint. 'Where does this stuff come *from*?'

'Probe's gone off,' said Ezra Keroon. 'It'll be a couple more days before any reports come back.'

Drake continued almost as if he hadn't heard. 'I want to find out if the stuff mightn't be more vulnerable in the stratosphere. Even if we only have ten pressurized sleds, would a high-altitude strike be more effective? Does this junk hit the atmosphere in clumps and then disperse? Can we develop a defence less clumsy than flamethrowers? We need to know more about this enemy.'

'It doesn't fight back,' Ongola remarked, rubbing his temples to ease the pounding sort of headache battle had always given him.

'True,' Paul Benden replied with a grim smile as he turned to Kenjo. 'I wonder if we would gain any useful data from an orbital reconnaissance flight? How much fuel in the *Mariposa's* tanks?'

'If I pilot it, enough for three, maybe four flights,' Kenjo replied, deliberately avoiding Drake's eyes, 'depending on how much manoeuvring is required and how many orbits.'

'You're the man for it, Kenjo,' Drake said with a flourish of his hand and a rueful expression. 'You can land on a breath of fuel.' Kenjo gave a short quick bow from the waist and a slight smile. 'Do we know when, or where, the stuff hits us again?'

'We do,' Paul assured them in a flat tone. 'If the data is correct, and it was today, Stakeholders are lucky. It strikes in two places – 1930 hours across Araby to the Sea of Azov—' his expression reflected his continued regret at the loss of Araby's original Stakeowners—' and 0330 from the sea across the tip of Delta. Both those areas are unoccupied.'

'We can't let that stuff go unchecked anywhere, Paul,' Ezra said in alarm.

'I know, but if we're going to have to mount crews every three days, we'll all soon be exhausted.'

'Not everything needs to be protected,' Drake said, unfolding his flight map. 'Lots of marsh, scrubland.'

'The fall will still be attended,' Paul said in an inarguable tone of voice. 'Look on it as a chance to refine manoeuvres and train teams, Drake. It is undeniably best to get the stuff while it's airborne. Thread didn't eat through as much land today but we can't afford to lose wide corridors every time it hits us.'

'Draft some more of those dragonets,' Joel suggested facetiously. 'They're as good on the ground as in the air.'

Emily regarded him sadly as the others grinned. 'Unfortunately they just aren't big enough.'

Paul turned round in his chair to give the Governor a searching look. 'That's the best idea today, Emily.'

Drake and Kenjo looked at each other, puzzled, but Ongola, Joel and Ezra Keroon sat up, their expressions expectant. Jim Tillek grinned.

There were five main islands off the southern coast of Big Island and several small prominences, the remains of volcanoes poking above the brilliant green-blue sea. The one Avril and Stev now approached so eagerly was no more than the crater of a sunken volcano. Its sides sloped into the sea, providing a narrow shore, except to the south where the lip of the crater was lowest. There was enough space for Stev to land the sled on the north shore. Avril had hopped out even before he had shut down the power.

'Hurry up, Stev. All this can't possibly be black diamond,' she added as she made her way up the shifting, sliding stony beach, glancing this way and that.

'You'd glut the market with this, old dear,' Stev remarked, amused.

'Here!' She bent and thrust at him the large stone she had selected. 'Is this diamond, too?'

It took Stev a moment to examine it and he could hear her impatiently tapping her booted foot, incongruously utilitarian at the end of her tanned and shapely legs, her toes scattering what were probably other black diamonds. He looked long enough to be sure, and then held the rock up with a flourish.

'It is indeed diamond. Around 400 carats and relatively unflawed. Congratulations, my dear, you've struck it rich.'

She grimaced, her eyes flashing at his mocking tone, as she snatched the diamond from him, clasping it against her, almost protectively.

'It can't all be black diamond?' she muttered.

'Why not? There's nothing to keep diamonds from being hatched from a volcano, if you have the right ingredients and sufficient pressure at some point in time. I grant you, this might be the only beach composed of black

257

diamond, or any diamond, in the universe, but that's what . . .' and Stev's grin was pure malice now, '. . . you have here.' He emphasized the pronoun lightly but she glanced at him, her eyes wary though she managed an easy smile.

'What *we* have, Stev.' She leaned into him, her skin warm against his, for no one in such a tropical climate wore many clothes. 'This is the most exciting moment of my life.' She wound her free hand about his neck and kissed him passionately, her body pressing against him until he felt the diamond gouging his ribs.

'Not even diamonds must come between us, my love,' he murmured, taking it from her resisting fingers and dropping it behind him into the open sled.

Stev was not unduly surprised the next morning when he found that both Avril and the fastest sled were gone. He made a second check, in the rock hollow where he knew Avril secreted the more spectacular gemstones that had been found. It was empty.

Stev grinned maliciously. She might have ignored the Mayday from Landing but he had not. He had kept track of what was happening on the southern continent as well as an eye to the east whenever cloud appeared. He had made contingency plans. He doubted that Avril had. He would have liked to see her expression when she found out that Landing was swarming with industrious people, and the take-off grid crammed with sleds and technicians. So he roared with amusement when Becky anxiously reported that she couldn't find Avril anywhere.

Nabhi Nabol was not at all pleased.

Kenjo achieved orbit with a minimum of fuel expenditure. He kept his mind on the task at hand, the upward thrust of the versatile craft, the glorious elation of release from gravity. He could wish that all his cares would fall away as easily. But he had not lost his touch with space craft. He slid appreciative fingers down the edge of the console. The last three days had been frantic, servicing the

258

Mariposa's dormant systems, checking any possible fatigue or perishing of essential parts. He had even allowed Theo Force to command his squadron when Thread fell over the mountain southeast of Karachi and brushed Longwood on Ierne Island. It was more important to recommission the *Mariposa*. Ongola had spared some time to tune the comunit circuits and help with the terminal checks. The little ship had been designed for inactivity in the vacuum of space and although the more important circuits had been stored in vacuum containers, there was always the fear that some minor but critical connection had *not* been properly scrutinized. All systems had proved go-green and a trial blast of her engines had been reassuringly loud and steady. Kenjo had objected, though, when he was forced to rest the last twelve hours before take-off.

'You may be a bloody good jockey, Kenjo, but there are better mechanics on Pern than you,' Paul Benden had told him in no uncertain terms. 'You need rest *now* to keep you alert in space where we can't help you.'

Xi Chi had calculated the flight plan in the dawn window, to allow Kenjo to be in the orbit where Boris and Dieter had calculated the next batch of Thread would enter Pern's atmosphere. Their program indicated that Thread fell in approximately 72 hour bursts, give or take an hour or two. Kenjo's mission was to measure the accuracy of their program, the composition of Thread prior to entry, if possible trace its trajectory backward. And, last was scarcely least, destroy it before it entered the atmosphere. The next Fall was due to hit Kahrain Province, just above the deserted Oslo Landing, fall on Paradise River Stake, ending in the Araby Plains.

Kenjo was a hundred miles below the empty space ships and they were too far away to register on his scope. Nevertheless he strained to see them, magnifying the viewscope to its limit. Then he shrugged. The ships were past history: he was going to make a new contribution, an unparalleled one. Kenjo Fusaiyuko would discover the source of Thread, he would eradicate it at source and be a planetary hero. Then no one would condemn him for 'conserving' so much fuel for his private use. He could relieve his sense of honour and his scouring bouts of conscience.

Building the extra light aircraft had been most rewarding. He'd found the design on tape in the *Yokohama*'s history of airflight section. It wasn't the most fuel-efficient even when he had redesigned the engine. What he had saved from each shuttle drop had made that saucy plane possible. Flying it over his isolated Honshu Stake in the Western Barrier Range had given him satisfaction far beyond his imagining, even if it had given rise to rumours of a large, and hitherto unknown flying creature. His wife, patient and calm Ika, had ventured no opinion on his avocation, aiding him in its construction. A mechanical engineer, she managed a small hydro-electric plant which served their plateau home and three small stakes in the next valley. She was a good mother to his four children, three of them sons, and even managed to help him cultivate the fruit trees which he raised as a credit crop.

Ika was safe from Thread for they had cut their home right into the mountain, and had used wood only on the interior. She had been quite willing to help him carve a hangar for his aircraft with the stone-cutters he had borrowed from Drake Bonneau. But she did not know that he had a second, well-concealed cave in which to store his hoard of liquid fuel. He had not yet managed to transfer all of it to Honshu from the cave at Landing.

Yes, no one would object to what Kenjo did when he brought them the information they sought. And he would see to it that it took three or four missions to do so. He had missed the tranquillity, and the challenge, of deep space. How pitiful his little atmospheric craft was in comparison to the beautiful, powerful *Mariposa*. How clumsy the sled he had flown as a squadron leader.

This was his true medium – space!

The ship's alarms went off and moments later the pinging began. He was in the midst of a shower: a shower of small ovoids. With a cry once uttered by warriors of his ethnic past, Kenjo fired his starboard repulsors, grinning when the screen blossomed with tiny stars of destruction.

Avril Bitra was livid. She could not believe the change in Landing especially as she had counted on it being nearly deserted. When Stev had talked her into taking apprentices so that no one would question exactly what it was they were doing on Big Island, Landing's population was down to a mere two hundred.

This evening, there were lights everywhere, and people bustling about despite the late hour. Worst of all, the *Mariposa* was not on the landing strip which was crowded with sleds, large, small, medium, and technicians swarmed about. What under the suns had happened?

She had settled her sled to one edge of the strip, near where she had last seen the little space gig. She fumed impotently again over that disappointment. She had a fortune with which to depart this wretched mudball. She had even managed to shake off any companions. She had no qualms about leaving Stev Kimmer. He had been useful as well as amusing – until just lately. Until he had assessed those black diamonds. Yes, she'd been right to leave immediately, before he thought to dismantle the sleds or do something drastic so that she had to take him with her. Where in all the hells of seventeen worlds was the *Mariposa*? Who was using up the fuel she needed to get her to the colony ships? She struggled to control her rage. She had to think!

Belatedly she remembered the Mayday. She wished now that she'd listened in. Well, it couldn't have been that serious, not with Landing a hive of industry. Still, that could work in her favour. With so many people about, no one would notice another 'busy' person.

She shivered, only now aware of the chill in the night air of the plateau. Cursing inventively under her breath, she rooted through the sled's storage compartments and found a reasonably clean coverall. Living on Big Island in a tropical climate, she had dressed lightly. Now she was grateful for a garment she had once despised. She also girded on the mechanic's belt she found beneath the coverall; probably Stev's. He was always well equipped. She smirked. Not always prepared, however.

Before she left to hunt for the *Mariposa*, she would have to hide her sled.

In the darkness, she tried to locate at least one of the dense shrubs that grew at this edge of the strip but she couldn't find any. Instead she stumbled into a small hole and, with a handbeam, saw that it was large enough to conceal her sacks of treasure. She piled loose stone and dirt over them and then shone the handbeam to see if they were well hidden. A few minor adjustments and she was satisfied.

With brazen strides she walked down the grid to the lights and activity.

Glancing out of the ground-floor window of the Met Tower where Drake Bonneau was conducting a training session, Sallah Telgar-Andiyar thought she had to be mistaken: the woman only *looked* like Avril Bitra. She was wearing a tool-belt and strode purposefully towards a stripped-down sled. Yet no one else Sallah knew had that same arrogant walk, the provocative swing of the hip. Then the woman stopped and began to work on the sled. Sallah shook her head. Avril was at Big Island, had not responded to the Mayday, or the more recent recall to Landing for pilot duty. No one had seen her, or really cared to, but Stev Kimmer's genius with circuits would have been invaluable. Ongola was trying to get Paul Benden to *order* the return of Big Island miners.

'Don't keep your finger on the release button.' Drake's voice penetrated her moment of inattention.

He was trying, poor fellow, Sallah thought, to teach all the eager youngsters how to fight this Thread. If half of what Tarvi had told her on their return was true, it was devilish to combat.

'Always sweep from bow to stern. Thread falls in a sou'westerly direction so if you come in under the leading edge, you char a larger portion.' Drake was running out of space on the operational board with his diagrams and flight patterns. Sallah had yet to fight the stuff so she had paid attention, until she thought she'd recognized Avril.

The day had had the quality of a reunion for the shuttle pilots. All the old crowd with the exception of Nabhi Nabol and Kenjo had answered the summons. She knew where Kenjo was, and was a trifle envious of him, and was as glad of Nabol's absence. He would certainly have sneered to be in the company of all the young ones who had earned their flying tickets since Landing. Why, she'd known some of them as adolescents.

Settling in at Karachi had eaten more time than she realized. And brought so many changes: such as the dragonets perched on young shoulders or curled up on hide-trousered legs. Her three – a gold and two bronzes – had picked up some basic manners, just as her older children had. They were perched on the top shelves of the big ready room. Two were menthas and she wondered if they understood what was going on under their watchful rainbow eyes.

'Don't,' and Drake's imperative warning interrupted her musing, 'deviate from your assigned altitude. We're trying to rig cruising devices that will warn you hair-trigger pilots when you're out of line. We've got to maintain flight levels to avoid collisions. We've got more people to fly than sleds to fly in. *You*,' and he jabbed his finger at his audience, 'can be replaced. The sled cannot and we're going to need every one we can keep in the air.'

'Now, a sweep from bow to stern, in a one-second blast chars as much Thread for the range of these throwers. Catch the end of the stuff and fire runs back up most of it. Don't waste the HNO_3—' his rapid-fire use of the chemical designation made it sound more like 'agen-othree', thought Sallah, losing concentration once again. Damn, she must pay attention, but she was so used to

263

listening for sounds, not words. And silences. The silence children make when they're being naughty or trying forbidden things. And hers were inventive. She felt her lips widen in a proudly maternal smile and disciplined her expression as Drake's eyes fastened on her face.

She already missed her children dreadfully. Bessie Sifuentes had remained at Karachi to program the diggerdonks and she had promised to spend as much time as possible with the three children. Ram Da, Sallah's sturdy, reliable seven-year-old son, had promised to look out for Dena and Ben. Sallah had brought three-month-old Cara with her and the baby was safely installed with Mairi Hanrahan's lot so she wasn't totally deprived. But Tarvi was back at Karachi, extruding metal sheets on a round-the-clock basis, slaving as hard as the people he drove to their limits. She hoped that Jivan Paramundi would remember to feed them properly. She had left as much prepared food as she had had time to cook and freeze.

'. . . and make each cylinder last as long as possible. Conserve agenothree and power, and you'll last longer in the flight line. Which is where you're needed. Now, most of you have had experience with turbulence. *Don't* shuck your safety harness until you're on the ground. The lighter sleds can be flipped on landing if the wind suddenly gusts because they're nose heavy with the flame-thrower mounts.'

With Tarvi on such a schedule, it was just as well she had work of her own to do. He had little enough time for her and she wouldn't even have the comfort of sleeping beside him. Or be able to rouse him to a dawn lusting when he was too drowsy to resist her caresses.

What was wrong with her? she wondered for the millionth time. She hadn't trapped Tarvi: there had been a mutual need and passion that day in the cave that couldn't have been faked. When the chance union had resulted in pregnancy, he had immediately offered to make a formal arrangement. She hadn't insisted but she had been much relieved that the initiative had been his. He had been considerate, tender and solicitous throughout the gestation and sincerely overjoyed when his firstborn was a strong healthy boy. He adored all his children, rejoiced at their birth and in their development. It was his wife he avoided, dismissed, ignored.

Sallah sighed and Barr shot her a quizzical glance. She smiled and gave a shrug, intimating that Drake caused her reaction. What would her life have been like with Drake Bonneau, happily ensconced on his Lake? Svenda looked complacent, boasting about limiting her childbearing to two. Drake might act the confident fly-boy in public but, last night, he had been noticeably dancing attendance on his imperious wife. Sallah had always thought Drake was more 'show' than 'do'. Yet, for all Tarvi's eccentricities, Sallah preferred the geologist and treasured those ever more rare occasions when she could rouse him to passion. Perhaps that was the problem: Tarvi should be allowed the initiative. No, she had tried that tack, and had had a miserable year before she thought of her 'dawn attacks'.

Jivan had taught her some Pushtu phrases, and artlessly, she had inquired about feminine names. Whoever Tarvi called for at the height of passion, it wasn't another woman. Or another man, from all she could discover.

'So,' Drake was saying, 'here is the roster for the next Fall. Remember, it's a double hit, at Jordan and at Dorado. We're going to send you Dorado squadrons on ahead so you can be well rested by the time you have to fight.' Again Drake's eagle gaze swept his adoring students. Sallah found it easy to use such adjectives for the flamboyant ace. 'Now, back to your sleds to lend the technicians what assistance you can. House lights'll go out at midnight. We all need our rest,' he added cheerfully as he waved their dismissal.

Svenda quickly moved to his side, her scowl a deterrent to those who approached Drake with private questions.

'When did you get in, Sallah?' Barr asked, turning with her usual friendly grin. 'I only arrived in from our stake around noon. No one of the old group knew when you'd make it. I didn't realize this thing was so serious until I saw what it had done on my way up.'

Sallah laughed, Barr's bubbling personality hadn't changed a micro, though her figure had rounded.

'How many kids do you have now, Barr?' Sallah asked. 'We've sort of lost track of each other with you the other side of the continent.'

'Five!' and Barr managed a girlish giggle, glancing slyly at Sallah. 'The last was a set of twins which I'd never have expected. Then Jess told me that he was a twin and twin births were common in his family. I could have strangled him.'

'You didn't, though.'

'Naw! He's a good man, a loving father, and a hard worker.' Barr gave a sharp nod of her head at each virtue, grinning at Sallah again. Then her mobile face changed to one of concern. 'Are you all right, Sallah?'

'Me, certainly. I've four kids. Brought Cara with me. She's only three months old.'

'Is she at Mairi's or Chris MacArdle-Cooney's?'

'At Mairi's. We'd better check that roster and see when we're on duty. Where's Sorka these days?' Sallah added for she had also lost track of the redheaded Hanrahan girl. 'I saw all the others.'

'Oh, she's living with another vet. Over on Irish Square.'

'How appropriate!' Suddenly Sallah felt a surge of resentment, something to do with the freedom young people had, her frustration with Tarvi's diffidence, the sudden realization that she had relatively few responsibilities at that moment, and that her professional skills were once again in demand. 'C'mon, let's go find a drink and catch up on our lives!'

Sorka and Sean arrived at their quarters from different directions; Sean from an unexpected meeting with Admiral Benden, Sorka from the barn. She knew by his jarring stride that Sean was barely containing a fine fit of rage. He held it back until they were inside the house.

'Damn fool, hell'n'damned fool,' he said, slamming the door behind him. 'That pompous, pig-headed, butt-stupid git.'

'Admiral Benden?' she inquired surprised. Sean had never had reason to criticize the Admiral and he'd been chuffed to be called to a special interview.

'That stupid Admiral wants a cavalry unit!'

'Cavalry?' Sorka paused as she picked their evening meal out of the freezer compartment.

'To charge about the countryside with flame throwers, no less . . .'

'Doesn't he realize horses hate fire?'

'He does now.' Sean went past her to the small cabinet, hauled out a bottle of quikal, holding it up suggestively.

'Yes, please. If I don't unwind too, my food won't do me any good at all.' She curtailed her anxiety. The need for a drink indicated how tense he was for Sean wasn't a drinking man.

'We don't have to eat up above, do we?' he asked, jerking his head over his shoulder in the direction of the re-established community kitchen.

'No, I raided Mother's freezer.' She set the container in the warming unit and dialled to the appropriate time.

Sean handed over her glass and raised his in a toast.

'To idiot Admirals who are very good in space and real dumb washout stupid about animals. As if we had enough horses to waste in such an asinine caper. He also envisions me training squadrons of fire-lizards' (Sean had persisted in using his own name for them) 'swooping down on Thread at command. He even feels that he should have one, too. He doesn't effing know they won't be hatching till summer! That is, if those fly boys don't flame 'em all down.'

Sorka had never seen Sean so infuriated. He paced about, throwing out his left arm in extravagant gestures, sipping at his drink between phrases as he vented his anger. His blue eyes flashed, making him handsomer than ever in her opinion, but she was concerned to see his face

267

flushed with the intensity of his emotions. He flicked his head, to flip the sun-lightened hair out of his eyes. A grimace made him appear inscrutable, almost frightening in his anger. On one level she listened to his words, agreeing with his anxieties and opinions: on another, she revelled that, beneath the contained, almost coldly detached impression he gave most people, was this passionate, intelligent, critical, rational and dedicated personality.

Sorka didn't quite know when she realized she loved him – it seemed that she always had – but she remembered the day she realized that he loved her: the first time he had exploded in her presence over a minor incident. Sean would not have permitted himself that luxury if he hadn't felt totally secure in her presence, if he hadn't unconsciously sought her soothing affection and reassurance. Watching him work off his aggravation tonight, Sorka permitted herself a small smile which she tactfully hid behind her glass.

'Now, Sean, the Admiral paid you a compliment, too,' she remarked and caught his surprised glance. She smiled. 'By consulting *you*. I noticed, even if you didn't, that he watched us out there on the Malay corridor: saw how well our fair behaved. And I'm sure that he knows that you're more likely to discover where the queens are hiding their eggs than anyone else.'

'Humph. Yes, I guess that's true enough,' and Sean was somewhat mollified. He continued to pace but with less agitation.

Sorka loved Sean in every mood but his infrequent explosive ones fascinated her. His anger had never been directed at her: they were so alike that he rarely criticized and then only in a crisp impersonal tone. Some of her girl friends had wondered how she should stand his taciturn, almost sullen moodiness. Sorka had never found him sullen in her company: thoughtful, unwilling to offend even in a complete disagreement, and certainly a man who kept his own counsel. Unless horses were at risk. His lithe figure was graceful even as he thudded back and forth, his heels pounding and leaving dents in the thick wool carpet she had woven for their home. She let his tirade continue, amused by the language in which he described the probable antecedents of the Admiral whom he usually respected, the idiocy of the entire biological team who tampered with creatures whose natures they hadn't the wit to understand.

'Well, did you offer to find the Admiral a dragonet egg when the time's right?' she asked when he paused for breath after another elaboration of the stupidity of brass asses.

'Ha! I will if I can.' He spun on his heel and sprawled beside her on the couch, his face suddenly still, rage and frustration dissipated, his eyes on the amber liquid in his glass. From that look, she knew something else worried him deeply. 'You know as well as I do that we haven't caught a glimmer of any of the wild ones around here. They've made themselves scarce since the Sadrid Fall. Jays, if there were anywhere safe on this planet, they'd find it!'

'There were a lot helping us at the Malay corridor.'

'Up until some ijiits started flaming them, too!' Sean finished the last of his drink to drown his disgust over that.

'We won't get the wild ones to help if that gets about.' He poured himself another drink. 'Say, where're yours?' He suddenly realized that the usual perches were vacant.

'Same place yours are, out and about,' she answered in a mild tone. He had shed his rage.

Then Sean began to laugh, as much at himself as the fact that he had only just realized that his fire-lizards had made themselves scarce the moment he left the Admin building.

'Not surprising, is it?' she teased, grinning back at him. He shoved one arm behind her shoulders and pulled her, unresisting, closer to him. 'When Emmett told me Blazer was in a tizzy over your righteous wrath, I told mine they'd have to find their own food tonight. They don't like cheesy things anyway.'

'It's not often we get a night alone,' Sean said softly, his voice a seductive whisper in her ear. 'Finish your drink, redheaded gal,' he ruffled her fringe, then his hand travelled in a caress down her cheek to her chin, 'and turn off the cooker,' he added just before he kissed her.

Sorka did as she was told, well-pleased. It was awkward having to invent excuses to send the dragonets off on specious errands. But the creatures delighted in strong emotions, even if they weren't in season, and with thirteen in a chorus of encouragement, the entire neighbourhood knew what was happening in the Hanrahan–Connell quarters.

Later that night, when the sounds of Landing's industry were muted, Sorka wondered if this time she had conceived. Sean slept neatly and quietly beside her, his fingers lightly encircling her upper arm. She had never mentioned a formal arrangement to Sean or the common assumption of Landing's population that they were a tempered team. She and Sean were of one mind in nearly everything they did, utilizing their veterinary apprenticeship to breed strong horses, finding the very best cross among the genetic stock available from either the banks or the live stallions. They were soon to sit their final exams in veterinary medicine and they had located a valley, halfway down the Eastern Barrier Range, the perfect spot – with very few additions. Sean had taken Red to see the proposed Killarney Stake and her father had approved emphatically. Sorka took that as a tacit approval of their still-informal union.

Although her parents had acquiesced, Porrig Connell still treated her formally as a guest he wished to see less often. His wife, Bridey, had never ceased in her efforts to bring her son back to his proper hearth. Bridey had chosen another daughter-in-law for Sean and sometimes embarrassed all concerned by pushing Lally Moorhouse at Sean on every opportunity.

'I won't breed so close, Mam,' Sean had informed her when she had nagged him once too often. 'It's bad for the blood. Lally Moorhouse's father was your first cousin. We need to spread the gene pool, not enclose it.'

Sorka had overheard but she knew Sean well enough by then not to be hurt that he had said no more about choosing. Perhaps he hadn't known then that he loved fifteen-year-old Sorka Hanrahan who was already certain where her heart had been given.

She'd been seventeen before he'd touched her with any kind of passion and that had been a night to remember. Their roles became reversed, she the wanton, he the hesitant, tender lover. Her ardent response to his gentle overtures had surprised and pleased them both but they hadn't moved to separate quarters until she had passed her eighteenth birthday. It had become a custom in their generation to have a trial period prior to a formal declaration before the Magistrate.

Now Sorka wanted Sean's child badly. Ever since that hideous half hour, treading water under a stone ledge, she had been aware of their mortality. She wanted something of Sean – just in case. Not that he was wild or incautious, but the Lilienkamp boys hadn't been reckless, and certainly poor Lucy Tubberman had not. So many people had been wiped out in that First Fall.

Sorka didn't want to be left with nothing of Sean. She hadn't tried before to get pregnant: it would have interfered with their plans for Killarney Stake. They needed the work credits for every acre they could purchase. Now she desperately wondered if there was something wrong with her that she hadn't got pregnant before, with all the fooling she and Sean had done. Tonight hadn't been fooling though. Tonight she had meant business.

Wind Blossom opened the door to Paul Benden, Emily Boll, Zi Ongola, Pol and Bay Harkenon-Nietro. She gracefully inclined her head in her welcome and held the door wide for them to enter.

Kitti Ping was seated on a padded chair which, Paul decided, was raised off the ground under its cover, giving it the semblance of an archaic throne. Kitti looked imposing, a feat for someone half his height. A beautiful soft woven rug had been tucked about a frail body and a long-sleeved tunic with elaborate embroideries also increased her general look of substance. And authority.

She raised one delicate hand, no larger than his oldest daughter's, and indicated they were to be seated on the stools, set in an irregular circle in front of her.

As Paul doubled his long legs to sit, he realized that she had achieved a subtle advantage over her visitors. Amused by the tactic, he smiled up at her and thought he could detect the merest hint of an acknowledgement.

Only a few strong ethnic traditions survived the Age of Religions but the Chinese, Japanese, Maori and Amazon-Kapayan were four that had retained some of their ancient ways. In this Pernese house, exquisitely furnished with heirlooms from her family, Paul knew better than to disrupt a hospitality ritual. Wind Blossom served the visitors fragrant tea in delicate little porcelain cups. The little plantation of tea bushes, grown to sustain this lovely ceremony, had been a casualty in the First Fall. Paul was poignantly aware that this might be the last cup of tea he'd ever taste.

'Has Mar Dook had a chance to inform you, Kitti Ping, that he had several tea bushes in reserve in the conservatory?' Paul asked when everyone had had time to savour the beverage.

Kitti Ping inclined her head in a deep bow of gratitude and smiled.

'It is a great reassurance.'

Such a bland reply gave him no opening wedge. Paul moved restlessly, trying to find a comfortable position on the stool and he knew that Pol and Bay were bursting to discuss the reason for the interview.

'All of us would be more reassured, Kitti Ping,' he said. Abruptly he modulated his voice which sounded so much

272

louder after her delicate response, 'If we had ... some form of reliable assistance in combating this menace.'

'Ah?' Her pencil-thin eyebrows raised and then her tiny hands made a vague gesture above the armrests.

'Yes,' and Paul cleared his throat, annoyed at himself for being so gauche, and more annoyed that he could be so disconcerted by a trivial seating arrangement. She must know why he had arranged this private conference. 'The truth is we are very badly positioned to defend ourselves against Thread. Bluntly, we will run out of resources in five years. We do not have the equipment to manufacture either sleds or power packs when those we brought are worn out. Kenjo's attempt to destroy Thread in space was only partially successful and there isn't much fuel left for the *Mariposa*.

'As you know, none of the colony ships carried any defensive or destructive weaponry. Even if we could construct laser sweep beams, there isn't fuel enough to move even one ship into an effective position to annihilate the pods. Nevertheless the best way to protect the surface is to destroy this menace in the air.

'Boris and Dieter have confirmed our worst fears: Thread will sweep across Pern in a pattern that will denude the planet unless we can stop it. We cannot entertain much hope that Ezra Keroon's probe will bring us any useful information ...' Paul spread his hands with the hopelessness that threatened to overwhelm him.

Kitti raised her delicate eyebrows in unfeigned surprise. 'The morning star is the source?'

Paul sighed heavily. 'That is the currently viable theory. We'll know more when the probe returns its survey.'

Kitti Ping nodded thoughtfully, her willow-slender fingers tightening on the armrests.

'We are, Kitti Ping,' Emily said, sitting even more erect on her stool, 'in a desperate situation.'

Paul Benden was heartened in an obscure way to see the Governor as much like a nervous schoolchild as himself. Pol and Bay nodded encouragement. Kitti Ping and

Wind Blossom, now standing slightly behind her mother's left side, waited patiently.

'If the dragonets were only larger, Kitti,' Bay broke in, her manner unusually brusque, 'intelligent enough to obey commands, they'd be an immense help to us. I was able to use mentasynth to enhance their own latent empathies, but that's a relatively simple matter. To breed large enough dragonets – dragons—' and Bay stretched her arms full length, 'we need them *big*,' and she flicked her fingers to indicate room size, 'intelligent, obedient, strong enough to do the job needed – flame Thread out of the sky.' She ran out of words then, knowing very well how Kitti Ping felt about bio-engineering beyond simple adjustments to adapt creatures to new ecological parameters.

Kitti Ping nodded again while her daughter blinked and regarded her mother with surprise.

'Yes, size, strength, and considerable intelligence would be required,' she said in her softly audible voice. Now she hid her hands in the cuffs of her long sleeves and folded them across her stomach. She bent her head and was silent for so long her audience wondered if she had nodded off in the easy sleep of the aged. 'And dedication which is easy to instil in some creatures: impossible in others. The dragonets already possess the traits you wish to enhance and magnify.' Then she smiled, a gentle, faintly apologetic smile of great sadness and compassion. 'I was the merest student, though a very willing and eager one in the Great Beltrae Halls on Eridani. I was taught what would happen if I did this, or that; enlarged or reduced; severed that synapse or modified this gene pattern. Most of the time what I was taught to do worked, but, alas,' and she raised one hand warningly, 'I never knew why sometimes the modification failed and the organism died. Or should have. The Beltrae would teach us the how but never the why.'

Paul sighed deeply, despair threatening to overwhelm him.

'But I can try. And I will. For though my years are

274

nearly accomplished, there are others to be considered.'

She had turned to smile gently upon Wind Blossom who ducked her head with humility.

Paul shook his head, not quite believing what she had just said.

'You will?' Bay said, jumping to her feet and stopped just short of rushing to Kitti's raised chair.

'Of course I will *try*!' She raised one tiny hand in warning. 'But I must caution you that success cannot be assumed. What we undertake is dangerous to the species, could be dangerous for us, and cannot be guaranteed. It is good fortune of the highest degree that the little dragonets already possess so many of the qualities required in the bio-genetically altered animal that suits the urgent need. Even so, we may not be able to achieve the exact creature, or even be sure of a genetic progression. We have no sophisticated laboratory equipment, nor methods of analysis which could lighten our burden. We must let repetition, the work of many hands and eyes, replace precision and delicacy. The task is appropriate, but the means are barbaric.'

'But we have to try!' Paul Benden said, rising to his feet with clenched fists.

13

●

All medical staff not on duty or on ground crew duty, the veterinarians and the apprentices, Sean and Sorka included, worked shifts as Kitti Ping's project was given top priority. Anyone with training in biology, chemistry, laboratory procedures – sometimes even those with nimble fingers to prepare slides or those convalescing from Threadfall injuries who could watch monitors – were put to service. Kitti, Wind Blossom, Bay, and Pol extracted a genetic code from the chromosomes of the fire-dragonets. The hereditary arrangements were not like those of Earth, but they were not too dissimilar to work with.

'We succeeded with the chiropteroids on Centauri,' Pol said, 'and they had chains of silicons as their genetic material.'

A great deal of schedule juggling was required to muster enough people to fight Fall over populated areas. The detailed sequence of Threadfall, established by the exhausted team of Boris Pahlevi and Dieter Clissmann, gave a structure to which even Kitti's project had to bow. A four-shift rota was established that attempted to provide everyone with some time for themselves and care of their own Stakes though some of the specialists ignored such considerations and had to be ordered to sleep.

Everyone over the age of twelve was brought in when Thread fell. The hope that Kenjo in the *Mariposa* could deflect Thread pods in the upper reaches of the atmosphere turned out to be ineffective. The predicted Double Fall – over Cardiff in mid-Jordan and Bordeaux in Kahrain; and

Seminole and Ierne Island – was patchy but the gaps perversely did not include occupied sites.

More double falls could be anticipated: on the 31st day after First Fall, Thread would sweep across Karachi camp and the tip of the Kahrain peninsula: three days later a single land corridor would range from Kahrain across Paradise River Stake: a second fall would pass harmlessly at sea well above the tip of Cibola Province. Three days later, a dangerous double would hit Boca Stake and the thick forests of lower Kahrain and Araby, stocks of the one real 'wood' vitally needed to shore up mine pits at busy Karachi Camp and Drake's Lake.

Ezra spent hours in the booth which housed the link with the *Yokohama*'s mainframe, scanning the naval and military histories to find some means of combating this menace. Or, less optimistically, discover obscure equations or devices that could alter the orbit of the planet. Then the next Fall could perhaps be avoided, but the present pass had seeded Pern's orbit with spirals of the encapsulated Thread. He also did mainframe comparisons with data from Kitti's program, delving into bio-genetic files, using his security ID to access secret or 'need to know' information. He was waiting, too, for the probe's findings to be relayed back to him. Because everyone knew where to find Ezra, he often intercepted complaints and minor problems that would have added unnecessary burdens to the Admiral and the Governor.

Kenjo was sent on three more missions, each time trying to find a more efficient way of destroying enough Thread in space to justify the expenditure of precious fuel. The gauges on the *Mariposa* dropped only slightly with each trip and Kenjo was commended on his economy. Drake was openly envious of the space pilot's skill.

'Jays, man,' Drake would say, 'you're driving it on the fumes!'

Kenjo would nod modestly and say nothing. He was however rather relieved that he had not managed to transfer all the fuel sacks to their hiding place at Honshu.

All too soon, he would have to broach that supply to ensure continued trips into space. Only there did he feel
totally aware and alive in every sense and nerve of his
body.

But each time he had brought back useful information:
that Thread travelled in a pod which burned away when
it hit the atmosphere of Pern, leaving an inner capsule.
About 15,000 feet above the surface, the inner capsule
opened into ribbons, some of which were not thick enough
to survive in the upper reaches. Enough fell to the surface
as it was.

Most of the sleds were unpressurized so they had an
effective ceiling of 10,000 feet. There was still only one
way to clear Thread from the skies – by flamethrowers.

With Thread due to fall on the Big Island Stake on Day
40, Paul Benden ordered Avril Bitra and Stev Kimmer to
return to Landing. When Stev asked what Landing needed
in the way of the ores mined at Big Island, Joel Lilienkamp
was more than happy to supply a list. So, when they
arrived at Landing with four sleds crammed canopy-high
with metal ingots, no one mentioned their long delin-
quency.

'I don't see Avril,' Ongola asked as the sleds were being
unloaded at the metals supply sheds.

Stev looked at him, slightly surprised. 'She flew back
weeks ago.' He peered back at the Landing Grid and saw
the sun glint off the *Mariposa's* hull. 'Hasn't she reported
in?' Ongola shook his head slowly. 'Well, now, fancy
that!' Stev's gaze lingered thoughtfully on the *Mariposa*
just long enough for Ongola to notice. 'Maybe Thread
got her!'

'Maybe her but not the sled,' Ongola replied, knowing
that Avril Bitra was too adept at preserving her skin to be
scored. 'We'll keep an eye out for her.'

Threadfall charts were displayed everywhere and constantly updated; previous Falls deleted and future ones
limited to the next three so that people could plan a week
ahead. Avril couldn't have stopped ten minutes in Landing

without *knowing* the dangers of Thread. Ongola reminded himself to move that guidance chip from the *Mariposa* as soon as Kenjo landed. He knew exactly how the space pilot extended the fuel: he didn't want anyone else, especially Avril Bitra, to discover how. Admiral Benden had been right about Kenjo. Ongola didn't want to be right about Bitra!

'Where do you want me to work now I'm back, Ongola?' Stev asked with a wry grin.

'Find out where Fulmar Stone needs you most, Kimmer. Glad to see you in one piece.'

Avril had stayed around Landing just long enough that night to know that she didn't wish to be conscripted into any of the several teams who could use her special skills. The only one she preferred to employ – space navigation – was thwarted by a variety of factors. So, before dawn broke on Landing and before anyone noticed a spare sled, she lifted it again, loaded with useful supplies, both food and *matériel*. They were so idiotically honest down here that she had walked right into Stores and picked up what she wanted.

She touched down on the rocky height above the ravaged Milan Stake that gave her a clear view of Landing and more importantly, a good view of the busy illuminated Grid where the *Mariposa* would touch down. She spent the early morning hours arranging an umbrella over the sled's siliplex canopy of the metal sheets she had filched. She preferred to take every precaution against this airborne stuff. By mid-morning she had camouflaged her eyrie and tuned the sled's scope on her objective. She was rewarded by a provocative view of Kenjo's return.

By listening carefully to all the channels available on the sled's comunit, she managed to discover the facts of his mission and its limited success.

Over the next several days, she began to feel secure in her hide-out. Because of the old volcanoes, most air traffic took corridors well to either side of her. During the morning the shadow of the biggest peak lurked over the retreat, like a broad digit pointing directly at her. Enough to make her flesh creep. She had no real appreciation of views, although the fact that she could look up the Jordan to the Bay, or down towards Bordeaux, meant that she was unlikely to be surprised. She began to relax and wait. Considering the reward, she had trouble practising patience.

'Have you *any* progress to report, Kitti?' Paul Benden asked the tiny bio-geneticist.

He had never found that close surveillance improved performance but he needed some morsel of encouragement to light the depression of his people. Tom Patrick and Cos Melvinah reported a lowering of morale as the second month of Threadfall ground on. The initial enthusiasm and resolution was being eroded by fierce work schedules and few distractions. Landing's facilities, once generous, were crowded with technicians drafted into the laboratories and stakeholders' families returned to the dubious safety of the first settlement.

No one was idle. Mairi Hanrahan had made a game for the five- and six-year-olds with good motor controls to assemble control panels by the colour of the chips. Even the most awkward ones could help gather fruits and edible vegetables from the undamaged lands, or compete with each other in collecting the unusual-coloured seaweeds from the beaches after high tides or storms. The seven- and eight-year-olds were permitted to help fish with handlines under the watchful eyes of Captains Shattuck and Ragnesjo. But even the youngest toddlers were reacting to mounting tensions.

There was considerable talk about allowing more holders to return to their Stakes and fly out to meet Thread from their homes. But that would mean splitting up the supply depots, disarranging work schedules of the more valuable technicians. Paul and Emily had to remain adamant on the centralization.

Tonight Kitti regarded Paul and Emily with a wise and compassionate smile. As she sat erect on the stool by the massive micro-biological unit, its minute laser units pushed back from the manipulation 'chamber', she did not appear to look fatigued, except for her eyes which showed the bloodshot strain of her labours. A program was running with whispering clicks, flashing incomprehensible displays on its several monitors. Kitti paused briefly, regarding the graph on one screen, the equations on another before she returned her gaze to the anxious pair.

'There is no way, Admiral, to accelerate gestation, not if you wish a healthy, viable specimen. Not even the Beltrae managed to hasten that process. As I mentioned in my last reports, we pinpointed the cause of our original failures and made the necessary corrections. Time consuming, I realize, but well worth the effort. The twenty-two bio-engineered prototypes we now have are proceeding well into the first semester. We all,' and her delicate hand made the most graceful sweeping gesture that included all the technicians working in the huge laboratory block, 'are immensely cheered by such a high rate of success.' She turned her head slightly to watch the flicker of a reading. 'We constantly monitor the specimens. They show the same responses as the little tunnel-snakes whose development we understand well. Let us earnestly hope that all proceeds without incident. We have been infinitely fortunate so far. Patience is required of you now.'

'Patience,' Paul echoed ruefully. 'Patience is in very short supply.'

Kitti raised her hands in a gesture of impotence.

'Day by day, the embryos grow. Wind Blossom and Bay continue to refine the program. In two days we shall start a second group. We shall continue to refine the manipulations. Always seeking to improve. We do not stand still. We move forward.

'Our task is great and full of responsibility. One does not irresponsibly change the nature and purpose of any creature. As it was said, the person of intellect is careful in the differentiation of things, so that each finds its place. Before completion, deliberation and caution are the prerequisites of success.'

Kitti then smiled a courtly dismissal of the two and turned her complete attention to the rapidly shifting monitors. Paul and Emily executed an equally courteous bow to her slender back and left the room.

'Well,' Paul began, shrugging off his frustration, 'that's that.'

'What city wasn't built in a day, Paul?' Emily asked whimsically.

'Roma,' Paul grinned at Emily's astonishment for such a prompt reply. 'Old Earth, first-century, I think. Good land-fighters and road-builders.'

'Militarists.'

'Yes,' and Paul's voice slowed. 'They also had a way of keeping people content. They called it circus. I wonder . . .'

On the 42nd day after First Fall, with Thread crossing uninhabited parts of Araby and Cathay, and falling harmlessly in the Northern Sea above Delta, missing Dorado's western prong, Admiral Benden and Governor Boll decreed a day of rest and leisure for all. Governor Boll asked department heads to schedule work loads to allow everyone to participate in the afternoon feast and evening dancing. The most distant Stakeholders were invited to come for whatever time they could spare. Admiral Boll asked for two squadrons of volunteers to fly Thread at 9.30 over the eastern Corridor, and another two to be ready in the early evening to check the western one.

The platform on Bonfire Square was gay with multicoloured bunting and a new planetary flag was hoisted on the pole to flap in the breeze. Tables, benches and chairs were placed around the square, leaving its centre clear for dancers. Vats of quikal were to be broached, and

Hegelman would produce ale – no one wished to think that it might be the last made for a long while. Joel Lilienkamp released generous supplies without grudge: 'Thank the kids that gathered them! Child labour can be efficient.' The Monaco Bay fishermen brought in shining loads of fish and the more succulent seaweeds to be baked in the big, long-unused pits; twenty steers were donated by as many farm Stakes to turn on spits: 'Better to fatten humans than Thread!' Pierre de Courci had worked all the previous night, baking cakes and making extravagant sweets. He was always happiest when overseeing a large effort.

'It's good to hear music and singing and laughter,' Paul murmured to Ongola as they wandered from one group to another.

'I think it would be a good custom to establish,' Ongola replied. 'Something to look forward to. Reunites old friends, improves bonds, gives everyone a chance to air and compare.' He nodded to the group which included his wife, Sabra, Sallah Telgar-Andiyar and Barr Hamil-Jessup, each with a sleepy child on her lap, chatting and laughing together. 'We need to gather together more often.'

Paul nodded, then glanced at his wrist chrono and, swearing softly under his breath, went off to lead the volunteers against the western Fall.

Ongola was not feeling exactly top of the mark the next morning when he arrived for his watch at the Met tower. In fact, he'd called in first at the Infirmary where an unsolicitous Pei Pei Ting had given him a hangover tablet and assured him that he was one of many. But her comments about disturbing casualties during that Threadfall had only made his headache worse.

The report that awaited him at the Met tower was a shock and a surprise. One sled had been totalled and its crew of three killed; the second sled had been badly crumpled and the starboard gunner killed, pilot and port gunner badly injured in the midair head-on collision. Someone had not been obeying the altitude restrictions. A groan came involuntarily from Ongola as he read the casualty list: Becky Nielson, just fresh back from Big Island – she'd been safer after all with Avril; Bart Nilwan, a very promising young mechanic, and Ben Jepson. Ongola cleared his blurred eyes. And Bob Jepson was the other dead pilot. Two in the same family. Those twins! Farting around in break-ass fashion instead of following orders! Stinkin' air! What could he say to their parents? A minor Fall with a party to come back to and they died!

Ongola put his hand on the comunit, about to dial Administration. And heard someone tapping hesitantly at the door.

'Come!'

Catherine Radelin-Doyle stood there, her eyes round, her face pale.

'Yes, Cathy?'

'Sir, Mr Ongola . . .'

'Either will do.' He mustered an encouraging smile. Considering the amount of trouble Cathy could get into, from stumbling into caves at an early age, to marrying the most feckless joat on the planet, he wondered at her shy demeanour. She was, poor child, just one of those people to whom events occur with no connivance from themselves at all. What was the matter now?

'Sir, I've found a cave.'

'Yes . . .' he encouraged when she hesitated. She was constantly finding caves.

'It wasn't empty.'

Ongola sat straight. 'It had a lot of fuel sacks in it?' he asked. If Catherine had, would Avril? No, Avril did not have the same sort of luck Catherine had.

'However did you know, Mr Ongola?' She looked faint with relief.

'Possibly because I know they're there.'

'You do? They are? I mean, they weren't put there by "them".'

284

'No, by us,' he wanted to make as little fuss about Kenjo's hoard as possible. He'd been counting the dwindling numbers and wondering why Kenjo seemed so complacent after each trip. Ongola flicked a glance at the corner of the shadowed shelving where the guidance chips were hidden in their dark-foam case.

Catherine suddenly sank to the nearest chair. 'Oh, sir, you don't know what a fright it gave me. Thinking that someone else was here, because everyone *knows* there's so little fuel left. And then to see—'

'But you saw nothing, Catherine,' Ongola told her crisply. 'Nothing whatever. There's no cave worth noticing down that particular crevasse and you won't say a thing about it to anyone else. I will personally tell the Admiral. But you will tell no one.'

'Oh no, sir.'

'This information cannot – I repeat, can *not* be divulged to any other person.'

'That's right, Mr Ongola,' and she nodded solemnly several times. Then, with a very winsome smile, she added, 'Shall I keep on looking?'

'Yes, I think you'd better. And find something!'

'Oh, but I have, Mr Ongola and Joel Lilienkamp says they're going to be excellent storage space . . .' Her face clouded briefly, 'but he didn't say for what?'

'Go, Cathy, and find something . . . else.'

She left and Ongola had no sooner started to brood over the first serious losses to their defence than Tarvi came storming up the stairs.

'It's been staring us in the face, Zi,' he said, swinging his arms in one of his expansive gestures: his face was alight with enthusiasm although his skin looked a bit grey from the excesses of the night before.

'What?' Ongola was in no mood for puzzles.

'Them! There!' Tarvi gestured extravagantly out the northern windows. 'All the time.'

It was probably the headache, Ongola thought, but he had no idea what Tarvi was talking about.

'What do you mean?'

'All this time we have been slavering away at mining ore, refining, moulding it, adding weeks to our labours, when all the time we've had what we need in front of us.'

'No puzzles, Tarvi.'

Tarvi's expressive eyes widened in surprise and consternation. 'I give you no puzzles, Zi, my friend, but the source of much valuable metals and *matériels*. The shuttles, Zi, the shuttles can be dismantled and their components used for our specific purposes here and now. Theirs is done. Why let them slowly decay on the meadow?' Tarvi emphasized each new sentence with a flick of long fingers out the window and then, exasperated with Ongola's incomprehension, hauled the man to his feet and pointed a very long, slightly dirty forefinger directly at the tail fins of the old shuttles. 'There. We'll use them. Hundreds of relays, miles of the proper flex and tubing, six small mountains of re-cyclable material. Have you any idea of how much is in them?' In an instant, all the exuberance drained from the volatile engineer. He put both hands on Ongola's shoulders. 'We can replace the sled we lost today even if we cannot replace those marvellous young lives or comfort their stricken families. The parts make a new whole.'

Work dulled the edge of the sorrow that hung over Landing at the loss of four young people. The two survivors reluctantly admitted that the Jepson twins, towards the end of that Fall, had indulged in some fatal foolery. Ben's sled had been scheduled for servicing after the Fall because its previous pilot had reported a sluggish reaction on portside turns. The sled had been considered safe enough for what should have been a monitoring flight.

Rather than prevent other such collisions, the next few Falls saw a rash of them even as Tarvi's crew began to strip the first shuttle and Fulmar's teams began to service and replace from the bonanza of salvage.

The longest hours were still put in at Kitti Ping's labora-

286

tory, monitoring the developing specimens for any signs of difference from the hoped-for results – (though they were, in truth, a result of controlled aberration of the original genetic material).

'Patience' was Kitti's response to all queries. 'All proceeds vigorously.'

Three days after the mid-air collision, Wind Blossom discovered her, still at the electronic microscope, apparently peering at yet another slide. But when Wind Blossom touched her mother's arm, the movement produced an unexpected result. The dainty fingers slipped from their relaxed position on the keyboard, and the body slumped forward, only kept upright by the brace that held her to the stool for her long sessions at the microscope. Wind Blossom let out a moan and dropped to her knees, holding one tiny cold hand to her forehead.

Bay heard her disconsolate weeping and came to see what had happened. Instantly she called to Pol and Kwan, then phoned for Basil Tomlinson. Once Wind Blossom had followed the gurney with her mother's body out of the room, Bay straightened her plump shoulders and stood at the console. She asked the computer if it had finished its program.

'PROGRAM COMPLETED' flashed the screen, almost indignantly, Bay thought in the portion of her mind that wasn't sorrowing.

She tapped out an information query. The screen displayed a dazzling series of computations and ended with 'REMOVE UNIT! DANGER IF UNIT IS NOT IMMEDIATELY REMOVED!'

Astonished, Bay now recognized the paraphernalia on the workspace beside the electronic microscope. Kitti Ping had been manipulating gene patterns again, a complicated process which Bay found as daunting as Wind Blossom despite Kitti Ping's encouragements. So Kitti had made those infinitesimal alterations in the chromosomes. Bay felt the chill of a terrible apprehension sweep through her plump body. She pressed her lips together. Now was not the time to panic. They must not lose what Kitti Ping had been making of the raw material of Pern.

With hands that were not quite steady, she unlocked the micro-cylinder, removed the tiny gel-encapsulated unit and placed it in the culture dish which Kitti had readied. An agony as severe as a knife stab almost doubled Bay up but she fought the grief and the knowledge that Kitti Ping Yung had died to produce this altered egg cell. The label was even prepared:

TRIAL 2684/16/M: NUCLEUS #22A, MENTASYNTH GENERATION B2, BORON/SILICON SYSTEM 4, SIZE 2H; 16.204.8

Walking as fast as her shaky legs would permit and gradually recovering her composure, Bay took the final legacy of the brilliant technician to the gestation chamber and put it carefully beside the forty-one similar units that held the hopes of Pern.

'*That* was the second probe to malfunction,' Ezra told Paul and Emily, his quiet voice ragged with disappointment. 'When the first one blew up, or whatever, I thought it a mischance. Even vacuum isn't perfect insulation against decay. Probe motors could misfire, their recording device clog somehow or other. So I refined the program for the second one. It got exactly as far as the first one and then every light went red. Either that atmosphere is so corrosive even our probe enamels melt, or the garage on the *Yokohama* has somehow been damaged and the probes too. I dunno, guys.'

Ezra was not much given to agitated gestures but he paced up and down Paul's office, strutting and waving his arms about him like a scarecrow in a high wind. The last few days had wearied and aged him. Paul and Emily exchanged concerned glances. Kitti Ping's death had been such a shock, following so closely on the sled collision disaster. The bio-geneticist had seemed so indestructible, despite the fact that everyone knew of her physical frailty. She had exuded a quality of immortality, however false that proved.

'Whose theory was it that we were being bombarded from outer space to reduce us to submission?' Ezra said, stopping suddenly in his tracks and staring in a wild gaze at the two leaders.

'Ah, c'mon now, Ezra!' Paul was bluntly derisive. 'Think a minute, man. We're all under a strain but not one that makes us lose our wits. We all know that there are atmospheres that can and have melted probes. Furthermore—' he halted, not certain what would suffice to reassure Ezra, and himself.

'Furthermore, the organism attacking us,' Emily went on with superb composure, 'is hydro-carbon based and, if it comes from that planet, then its atmosphere is not corrosive. I favour malfunction.'

'My opinion, too,' Paul said, nodding his head vigorously. 'Fardles, Ezra, let's not talk ourselves into more problems than we've got.'

'We've *got* . . .' and Ezra brought both fists down on the desk, 'to probe that planet or we won't know enough to combat the stuff. Half the settlers want to know the source and destroy it so we can get back to our lives. Rake up the debris and forget all this.'

'What aren't you telling us, Ezra?' Emily asked, cocking her head slightly and regarding the Captain with an unflinching gaze.

Paul could see that her question was valid. Ezra stared back at her for a very long moment, then straightened from his half-crouch over the desk and began to smile wryly.

'You've been sitting in the interface booth long hours, Ezra, and you weren't playing tiddlywinks while the programs were running,' Emily went on.

'My calculations are frightening,' he said in a low voice, glancing over each shoulder, not wishing his words to penetrate further than the other side of the desk. 'If the program is in any way accurate, and I've run it five times now from start to finish, we have to put up with Thread for long after that red planet crosses out of the inner system.'

'How long will that be?' Paul felt his fingers gripping the arm- rests and made a conscious effort to relax them while he tried to recall some reassuring facet of planetary orbits.

'I get between forty and fifty years!'

Emily grimaced, her mouth forming an 'O' of surprise before she slowly exhaled. 'Forty or fifty years, you say.'

'If,' Ezra added grimly, 'the menace originated from that planet.'

Paul caught his eyes and saw the ineffably weary and discouraged look in them. 'If? There is another alternative?'

'I have discerned a haze about the planet, irrespective of its atmospheric envelope. A haze that spreads backwards in this system and swirls along the eccentric's path. I cannot refine that telescope enough to tell more. It could be space debris, a nebulosity, the remnants of a cometary tail, a whole bunch of things that are harmless.'

'But if it should be harmful?' Emily asked since Paul did not.

'That tail would take nearly fifty years to diffuse out of Pern's orbit, some into Rukbat, the rest, who knows?'

There was a long moment of silence. The three regarded each other almost passively.

'Any suggestions?'

'Yes,' Ezra said, straightening his shoulders with a wrench. He held up two fingers. 'Take a trip to the *Yokohama* and find out what's bugging the probes and send two of 'em down to the planet to gather as much information as we can. Send the other two along the line of that cometary dust and use the *Yoko*'s more powerful space 'scope with no planetary interference to see if we can identify its source and components.' Ezra then locked his fingers together and cracked his knuckles, a habit which made Emily shudder. 'Sorry, Em.'

'At least you can recommend some positive action.'

'The big question is, Paul, is there enough fuel to get someone to the *Yoko* and back? Kenjo's already made more trips than I thought possible . . .'

'Good pilot,' Paul said discreetly. 'There's enough for what we need now. Kenjo will pilot and did you wish to go with him?'

Ezra shook his head slowly. 'Avril Bitra has the training for the job.'

'Avril?' Paul gave a harsh bark and then shook his head, grinning sourly. 'Avril's the last person I'd put on the *Mariposa* for any reason. Even if we knew where she is.'

'Really?' Ezra looked at Emily for an explanation but she shrugged. 'Well, then, Kenjo can double. No,' he corrected himself. 'If something's wrong with the probes, we'd need a good technician. Stev Kimmer. He's back, isn't he?'

'Who else?' Paul jotted down names rather than worry Ezra with more suspicions.

'Kenjo is a very capable technician,' Emily insisted.

'There should be two on the mission, for safety sake,' Ezra said, furrowing his brow. 'This mission has got to give us the results we need.'

'Zi Ongola,' Paul suggested.

'Yes, the very one.' Ezra was comfortable with that choice. 'If he runs into any trouble, I can have Stev at the interface for expert advice.'

'Forty years, huh?' Emily said, watching Paul underline the two final choices on the pad. 'Rather longer than we'd bargained for, my friend. Let's start training replacements.'

Inevitably their thoughts went to Wind Blossom, so obviously now a frail vessel to continue the work her mother had begun.

*

Avril's suspicious nature was aroused not by anything she heard, although what she didn't hear was as significant, but by what she saw in the weary hours she manned the sled's scope. It was usually trained on the *Mariposa*, sitting at the far end of the landing grid. The night before every one of Kenjo's jaunts he had done exterior and internal checks of the craft. Fussy Fusi! The nickname was not quite derisive because Avril could not figure out how he had managed to stretch the small reserve of fuel on the *Mariposa* as far as he already had. She had seen some activity about it last night but no sign of Kenjo. In fact, with neither moon about, she had just barely seen the shifting of shadow that indicated activity about the craft. She had been quite agitated. The only thing that reassured her was that several figures were involved. But no one entered the gig. That perplexed her.

At first light, so early that no one was yet working the donks at the skeleton of the shuttle that had been the center of considerable activity all week, she was surprised to see Fulmar Stone and Zi Ongola approaching the vessel. Her apprehension, honed by weeks of waiting, spurred her to remove the protective cover from her sled in preparation for a quick departure. She could reach the landing grid in less than fifteen minutes at full speed. Early morning traffic into Landing would be sufficient to give her cover.

She was surprised then to see Fulmar Stone and Zi Ongola approaching the vessel at first light, so early that no one was yet working the donks at the skeleton of the shuttle that had been the centre of considerable activity all week.

She had a moment's apprehension, thinking that perhaps the *Mariposa* had developed a problem and they were scavenging replacement parts from the shuttle. Kenjo had flown a mission three days before with his usual economical take-off and landing.

She had to hand it to him, gliding in with no power at all. Only where was he getting the fuel to lift. The three men who were moving with almost stealthy speed slipped inside the little spaceship and closed the airlock. Well, the access to the engines was through exterior panels so she began to relax. They remained inside the ship for three hours. Long enough for a full interior systems check. But that did not presage a usual flight. Maybe the *Mariposa* was bollixed. Scorch Kenjo for ineptitude. The *Mariposa* had to be space-worthy.

Avril swore. Or had something happened to Kenjo and Ongola was taking the ship up. And how? There couldn't be much fuel left. So why were they checking internal systems? Why were they making yet another jaunt? Displeased, Avril finished her preparations to fly.

Sallah Telgar-Andiyar was feeding her daughter breakfast in the shady covered porch of Mairi Hanrahan's Asian Square house when she caught sight of a familiar figure, striding down the path. Overalls again, and a peaked cap pulled well down over the face. But the walk was undeniably Avril's, especially from the rear. Never mind the greasy hands, the exhaust pipe carried so ostentatiously in one hand, a clipboard in the other. That was Avril who only sullied her hands for a good cause. No one had seen her since she'd left Big Island. Sallah continued to watch until Avril mingled in with the crowd at the main Depot as technicians jostled each other for parts and *matériel*.

Ever since Sallah had overheard Avril's conversation with Kimmer, she had known the woman would attempt to leave Pern. Did Avril know of Kenjo's fuel dump? Irritably Sallah shook her head. Cara blinked her huge brown eyes and stared apprehensively at her mother.

'Sorry, love, your mother's mind is klicks away.' Sallah gathered more purée on the spoon and deposited it into Cara's obediently open mouth. No, Sallah told herself fiercely, because she wanted to believe it so badly, Avril could not have discovered that fuel: she'd been too busy mining gemstones on Big Island. At least, up until three weeks ago. And where had Avril been since then, Sallah asked herself. Watching while Kenjo flew the *Mariposa*? That would certainly set Avril Bitra to thinking hard.

Well, Sallah was due on her shift soon anyway, and as luck would have it, the sled she was servicing was on the grid. She would have a clear view of the *Mariposa* and those who approached it. If Avril did, then Sallah would set up an alarm.

There had been no talk of Kenjo's making another attempt to clear Thread in the atmosphere. Then, too, Kenjo's flights were usually plotted for the dawn window, and it was well past that time now.

It all happened rather quickly. Sallah was walking towards the sled she was servicing as Ongola and Kenjo, suited for space travel, left the tower with Ezra Keroon, Dieter Clissmann and two other overalled figures whom Sallah was astonished to recognize by their postures as Paul and Emily. Ongola and Kenjo had the appearance of men listening to last-minute instructions. Then they continued on, almost at a stroll, towards the *Mariposa* while the others turned back into the Met Tower. Suddenly another suited figure began to walk across the grid on a path that would intercept Ongola and Kenjo. Even in the baggy space-gear the figure walked as only Avril did!

Sallah grabbed the nearest big spanner and started at a jog-trot across the grid. Ongola and Kenjo disappeared behind the pile of discarded sled parts at the edge of the field. Avril was running now and Sallah increased her pace. She lost sight of Ongola and Kenjo. And then saw Avril pick up a short strut from the pile and disappear out of sight.

Rounding the pile, Sallah saw both Kenjo and Ongola flat on the ground, but only one helmet. The back of Kenjo's head was bloody and Ongola's shoulder and neck. Sallah ran flat out now, ducking down to keep scrap heaps

294

between her and the *Mariposa*. As it was, she just made it as the airlock was closing. She threw herself inside, felt something scrape her left foot, there was an immense hissing and then she blacked out.

14

●

Mairi Hanrahan thought it odd that Sallah had not rung at lunchtime to tell her she was delayed. With so many small ones to feed, every mother tried to be there at mealtimes. Mairi got one of her older children to feed Cara instead, thinking that something important occupied Sallah Telgar-Andiyar.

None of the people at the Met Tower or Admin Building expected any contact from Ongola or Kenjo while the shuttle was moving through the ionized atmosphere. Ezra, seated at the desk of the voice-activated interface, could follow its course via the activated monitor screens on board the *Yokohama*. The *Mariposa* was closing fast and soon reached the docking port.

'Safely there,' he said when he rang through to both Tower and Administration building.

Half an hour later, children playing at the edge of the grid came screaming back to their teacher about the dead men. Ongola was not quite dead. Paul met the medic team at the Infirmary.

'He'll live, but he's lost more blood than I like,' Basil Tomlinson told the Admiral. 'What'n'hell happened to him and Kenjo?'

'How was Kenjo killed?'

'The old blunt instrument. The paras found a bloodied strut nearby. Probably that. Kenjo never knew what hit him.'

Paul wasn't sure he did either for his legs suddenly would not support him. Basil beckoned fiercely for one of the paras to help the Admiral to a seat and poured a glass of quikal.

'You've known Kenjo a long time, haven't you, Admiral?' Basil said, gesturing for someone to bring Paul Benden a stimulant.

Paul tried to dismiss the eager hands. The implications of the two deaths greatly disturbed him. There was no antidote for Kenjo's loss, though the wretched quikal eased the intense shock that had rocked him. Through the back of his mind as he knocked back the drink, he wondered where Kenjo had cached the rest of the fuel. Why, Paul seethed at himself, hadn't he asked the man before? He could have done so adroitly any time before or after the last few flights Kenjo had taken in the *Mariposa*. As Admiral he knew exactly how much fuel there'd been left in the gig on its last drop. Now it was too late! Unless Ongola knew. He had mentioned that there wasn't much left at the original site but Kenjo had been supplying the *Mariposa*. The figures Sallah had initially reported to Ongola indicated a lot more than Paul had seen in that cave the other night. Well, the misappropriation – yes, that was the right term – had had a final appropriate usage. Maybe Ika knew where Kenjo had stored the remainder.

Yes, Paul consoled himself with that knowledge. Kenjo's wife would know if there were more fuel sacks at the Honshu Stake. Odds favoured that conclusion. Paul forced himself to deal with present issues: a man had been murdered and another lay close to death on a planet which had, until that moment, suffered no capital crime.

'Ongola will survive,' Basil was saying, pouring Paul a second shot. 'He's got a splendid constitution and we'll work any miracle required. We could probably have saved Kenjo if we'd got there earlier. Brain dead. Drink this, your colour's lousy.'

Paul finished the quikal and put the glass down with a decisive movement. He took a deep breath and rose to his feet.

'I'm fine, Basil, get on with saving Ongola. We'll need to know what happened when he recovers consciousness. Keep the rumours down, people!' he added, addressing the others in the room.

He strode out of the emergency facility, turning immediately for the building which housed the interface chamber, and Ezra. As he strode, he reviewed the puzzle that rattled his orderly mind: he had seen the *Mariposa* take off. Who had flown her? He collected Emily from her office on the way, briefing her on the calamity. Ezra was surprised by the arrival of both Admiral and Governor – this flight of the *Mariposa* was being treated as routine.

'Kenjo's dead and Ongola seriously injured, Ezra. So, who's flying the *Mariposa*?' Paul said as soon as he'd closed and locked the door behind them.

'Gods in the heavens!' Ezra leapt to his feet and pointed to the monitor which clearly showed the safely docked *Mariposa*. 'The flight was precalculated to hit the right window but the docking process was left to the pilot and very smoothly done. Not everyone can do that.'

'I'll run a check on the whereabouts of pilots, Paul,' Emily said, picking up a handset.

Paul glared at the monitor and its incontrovertible evidence. 'I don't think we need to do that. Call . . .' Paul had started to say 'Ongola' and washed his hand across his face, 'who's at the Met Tower?'

'Jake Chernoff and Dieter Clissmann . . .' Emily reported.

'Then ask Jake if there're any unmodified sleds on the grid. Find out exactly where Stev Kimmer, Nabol Nahbi and Bart Lemos are. And,' Paul held up a warning hand, 'if anyone's seen Avril Bitra anywhere.'

'Avril?' Ezra echoed and then clamped his mouth firmly shut.

Suddenly Paul swore in a violent torrent of abusive language that made even Ezra regard him with amazement and slammed out of the room. Emily concentrated on finding the pilots and locating them all, before Paul

298

returned. He leaned back against the closed door, catching his breath.

'Stev, Nabhi and Lemos are accounted for. Where did you go?' Emily asked.

'To check Ongola's space suit. Basil says he'll recover from his injuries. The strut just missed severing the shoulder muscle and leaving him a cripple. But,' Paul held up a crystal packet between forefinger and thumb, 'no one is going to get very far in the *Mariposa*.' He nodded grimly as Ezra realized what he held. 'One of the more essential parts of the guidance system! Ongola had not yet put it in place.'

'Then how did ... Avril?' Emily asked, pausing for confirmation. Paul nodded slowly. 'Yes, it has to be Avril, doesn't it? But why would she want to get to the *Yoko*?'

'First step to leaving the system, Emily. We've been stupidly lax. Yes, I know we have this,' he nodded when Emily pointed to the chip panel, 'but we shouldn't have allowed her to get that far in the first place. And we all knew what she was like. Sallah warned us and the years—'

'And recent unusual events ...' Ezra put in, mildly hinting that Paul need not excoriate himself.

'We should have guarded the *Mariposa* as long as she'd an ounce of fuel in her.'

'We also ought to have had the sense to ask Kenjo where he was getting all the fuel,' Ezra added.

'We knew that,' Emily said with a wry grin.

'You did?' Ezra was amazed.

'At least Ongola took no chances,' Paul went on, wincing as he remembered the sight of the man's battered shoulder and neck. 'This ...' he put the guidance chip very carefully down on the shelf above the worktop, 'was Ongola's special precaution with Kenjo's complete concurrence.'

Emily sat down heavily in the nearest chair. 'So where does that leave us now?'

'The next move would appear to be Avril's.' Ezra shook

his head sadly. 'She's got more than enough fuel to get back down.'

'That is not her intention,' Paul said.

'Unfortunately, she has a hostage,' Emily said, 'whether she knows it or not. Sallah Telgar-Andiyar is also missing.'

Sallah returned to consciousness aware of severe discomfort and a throbbing pain in her left foot. She was bound tightly and efficiently in an uncomfortable position. She was lying on her side just brushing the floor of the spacecraft: the lack of gravity told her that she was no longer on Pern. There was a rhythmic but unpleasant background noise of things clattering and slipping about.

Then she recognized the monotonous and vicious sounds to be the curses of Avril Bitra.

'Whatinhell did you *do* to the guidance systems, Telgar?' she asked, kicking at the bound woman's ribs.

The kick lifted Sallah from the floor and she floated within inches of the enraged face of Avril Bitra. Probably the only reason Sallah was still breathing was because the cabin of the *Mariposa* had its own oxygen supply. Kenjo would have charged the tanks up to full, wouldn't he? Sallah asked herself in a moment of panic as she continued to float beyond Avril. She was suited, the helmet on the rack above the pilot's seat, ready for use. The woman reached up and grabbed her arm.

'What do you know about this? Tell me, and be quick about it or I'll evacuate you and save the air for me to breathe!'

Sallah had no doubts the woman was capable of doing that.

'I know nothing about anything, Avril. I saw you stalking Ongola and Kenjo and knew you were up to something. So I followed you and got in the airlock just as you took off.'

'You followed me?' Avril lashed out with a fist. The impact caused both women to bounce apart. Avril steadied herself on a handhold. 'How dare you?'

300

'Well, as I hadn't seen you in months and longed to know how you were faring, it seemed a good idea at the time.' Hang for the fleece, hang for the sheep, Sallah thought but couldn't shrug her shoulders. What had she done to her foot? It was an aching mess.

'Bloody hell. You've flown this frigging crate. How do I override the preflight instructions? You must know that.'

'I might if you'd let me see the console.' She saw hope, and then manic doubt in Avril's eyes. Sallah wasn't lying. 'How could I possibly tell from over here? I don't know where we are. I've been just another Thread sledder.' Even to a woman slightly paranoid the truth would be obvious. Sallah warned herself to be very careful. 'Just let me look.'

She didn't ask to be untied although that was what she desperately wanted – needed. Her right shoulder must have been bruised by her fall into the cabin and all the muscles were spasming.

'Don't think I'll untie you,' Avril warned and contemptuously she pushed Sallah across the cabin to the console. Grabbing a handhold, then Avril corrected Sallah's spin to a painful halt against the command console. 'Look!'

The *Mariposa* though a small ship, was designed to traverse interplanetary distances, dock with all kinds of stations or other craft and had the sophisticated controls to perform a considerable variety of manoeuvres in space and on a planetary surface. Much of its instrumentation would be unfamiliar to Avril.

'To find out what this ship just did, hit the rerun button on the bottom tier of the greens. No, the portside.'

Avril jerked at Sallah, tweaking strained arm and back muscles and jamming Sallah's head against the view scope. Sallah's long hair was freed completely from the pins and flowed over her face.

'Don't get cute!' Avril snapped, her finger hovering on the appropriate button. 'This one?'

Sallah nodded, floating away again. Avril punched the button with one hand and hauled her back into position with the other. Then caught the handhold to keep herself in place.

Every action has a reaction, Sallah thought, trying to clear her head of pain and confusion.

The monitor came up with a pre-flight instruction plan.

'The *Mariposa* was programmed to dock here on the *Yoko*.' It was nice to know where she was, Sallah thought. 'Once you hit the power, you couldn't alter its course.'

'Well,' and Avril's tone altered considerably. 'I wanted to come here first anyhow. I just wanted to come on my own.' Sallah, hair falling over her face, felt a lessening of the tension emanating from the woman. Some of her beauty returned to a face no longer contorted with frustration. 'I don't need you hanging about then.' Avril reached up and gave Sallah's body a calculated shove that sent her to the opposite end of the cabin, to bump harmlessly against the other wall and then hang, suspended a few centimetres away. 'Well, I'll just get to work.'

How long Sallah was suspended in that fashion she didn't know. She managed to tilt her head and get her hair to float away from her eyes but she didn't dare move much . . . action produced reaction and she did not wish to draw attention to herself. She also couldn't do anything about releasing herself without causing movement. She ached all over but her foot ached worse than anything else.

A tirade of malevolent and resentful oaths spun from Avril's lips.

'None of the programs run, of all the frigging luck. Nothing runs!'

Sallah had just enough time to duck her head to avoid Avril's projectile's arrival against her. As it was, she went head over heels in a spin that Avril then, laughing gleefully, assisted until the rotation made Sallah retch.

'You bitch woman!' Avril stopped Sallah who no more wanted to fly about in her own vomit than Avril. 'Okay! If that's the way of it, you know what I need to know. And you're going to tell me or I'll kill you by inches.' A spaceman's knife, with its many handle-packed implements, sliced across the tip of Sallah's nose.

Then she felt the blade none too gently cutting the bindings on her hands and feet. Blood rushed through starved arteries and her strained muscles reacted painfully. If Sallah hadn't been in free-fall, she would have fallen. As it was, the agony of release made her sob and shake.

'Clean up your spew first,' Avril said, shoving the appropriate slop jar at her.

Sallah did as she was told, grateful for the lack of gravity, grateful for the release and wondering what she could do now to gain an upper hand. She had little opportunity to enjoy her freedom for Avril had other ways of securing her prisoner's co-operation.

Before Sallah realized what she was about, Avril had secured a tether to the injured foot and tweaked the line. Pain shot through Sallah's leg, like a shard of glass, through blood and muscle to her groin. There was little left in her stomach to retch up. Avril jerked Sallah over to the console, pushed her into the pilot's chair and tied her down, twitching her 'lead line' to remind Sallah of her helplessness.

'Now, check the fuel on board, check the quantity in the *Yoko*'s tanks – I've done that, I know the answers, so don't try anything clever—' a jerk against Sallah's injured foot reinforced her threat '—and then enter a program that gets me out of this wretched ass-hole of a midden system.'

Sallah did as she was told, though her head ached and her eyes blurred repeatedly. She could not suppress the surprise she felt at the amount of fuel in the *Mariposa*'s tanks.

'Yes, someone was holding back on it. You?' A jerk on the line.

'Kenjo, I suspect,' Sallah replied coolly, managing to suppress a cry. She mustn't give Avril any satisfaction. Well, not yet.

'Fussy Fusi? Yes, that computes. I thought he'd given

up all too tamely! Where did he hide it?' The line tightened. Sallah had to bite hard on her lip against a cry.

'Probably at his stake. It's back of beyond. No one goes there. He could hide anything there.'

Avril snorted and remained silent. Sallah made herself breathe deeply, forcing more adrenaline into her system to combat pain, fatigue and fear.

'All right, compute me a course to . . .' and Avril consulted a notebook. 'Here.'

Only because Sallah already knew the co-ordinates did she recognize the numbers. Avril wished to go to the uninhabited system nearest them, but a system which was closer to the populated sectors of space. The course would stretch the *Mariposa* to the end of available fuel, even if Avril also drained the *Yoko*'s tanks. It gave Sallah no consolation to think that the little ship might drift for centuries with Avril safe and composed in coldsleep. Or just maybe, Ongola had tampered with the sleep tanks, too. She liked that idea. But she knew Ongola too well to presume that kind of foresight.

Unfortunately the Avrils of the galaxy could make themselves at home in any time and culture. So if Avril went into deepsleep, eventually someone, or something, would rescue her and the *Mariposa*. Sallah didn't need to see them to know that Avril had several fortunes' worth of gemstones and precious metals aboard the *Mariposa*. There had never been any doubt in anyone's mind why Avril had chosen Big Island as her stake. But then, no one else would have been mad enough to leave Pern, even now, with Threadfall threatening the planet.

Sallah wondered why Avril had not been able to complete laying such a simple course. *She* was the astrogator. But Sallah did as she was ordered: she had more experience with the *Mariposa*'s drive board. But the program was not accepted. 'ERROR 259 AT LINE 57465534511' was the message.

Avril jerked hard on her foot and Sallah hissed against the burning, crippling pain of it.

304

'Try again. There's more than one way of entering a course.'

Sallah obeyed. 'I'll have to go around the existing parameters.'

'Reset the entire effing thing but plot that course,' Avril told her.

As Sallah began the more laborious deviation into the command centre of the gig's course computer, she was aware that Avril had picked up a long narrow cylinder from the rack by her helmet. She fiddled with it, humming tunelessly under her breath, thoroughly delighted with herself.

When Sallah finally tapped the 'return' tab, she became aware of Avril's intense interest in the flickering console. She chanced a look at what the woman had been fondling. A home-made capsule. Not a homer – they were thicker and longer. This was more like the standard beacon shape.

Suddenly, she clearly saw Avril's plan. Avril would take the *Mariposa* as far away from the Rukbat System as possible and then direct the distress beacon towards shipping lanes. Every planetary system involved with the Federated Sentient Planets, and some life forms who were not, traced distress beacons to origin. The devices were automatically released if a ship was destroyed. And were traced by those who wished to turn whatever profit they could on the flotsam.

Avril's plan was not as insane as it seemed. Sallah felt certain that Stev Kimmer had intended to take the trip with her, to be rescued by the distress beacon he had made for her.

'NO ACCESS WITHOUR STANDARD FCP/120/GM.'

'Fuckit! That's all I could get out of it. Try again, Telgar,' and Avril pressed Sallah's foot against the base of the console module, increasing the pain to the point Sallah felt herself losing consciousness. Avril viciously pinched her left breast. 'You don't pass out on me, Telgar!'

'Look,' Sallah said, her voice rather more shaken than she liked, 'I've tried twice, you've tried. I've tried the fail-safe I was taught. Someone anticipated you, Bitra. Open up this panel and I'll tell you if we've been wasting effort.'

She was not only trembling now with pain but with the effort not to relieve her bladder. But she dare not ask even that favour.

Swearing, her face livid with frustration and rage, Avril deftly enough removed the panel; kicking the console in her frenzy. Sallah leaned as far away from her as her bonds permitted, hoping to escape any stray blows.

'How did they do it? What did they take, Telgar, or I'll start carving you up?' Avril had flattened Sallah's left hand over the exposed chips and her knife blade had already cut through to the bone of the little finger. 'You don't need this one at all!'

'Blood hangs in the air just like vomit and urine, Bitra. And if you don't stop, you'll have both in free fall!'

They locked eyes in this contest of wills and though it took every nerve in Sallah's body to do so, she did not drop hers from the fierce and mordant black eyes.

'What . . . did . . . they . . . remove?' with each word Avril sawed against the little finger, showing her complete disregard for the consequences. Sallah screamed. It felt good to scream and it would complete the picture of her in Avril's mind. Soft. Sallah had never felt harder in her life.

'Guidance. They removed the guidance chip. You can't go anywhere.'

The blade left her finger and Sallah stared in fascination at the drops of blood that formed and floated. The contemplation took her mind off Avril's ranting until the woman snagged her shoulder.

'Are all the spare parts down there? Did they strip everything from the *Yoko*?'

Sallah forced herself away from the blood and the pain, clamping down on all but the important consideration: how to thwart Avril without seeming to.

'I'd say that there would be guidance chips left in the main board that could be substituted.'

'There'd better be.' Avril slipped the knife through the flex that bound Sallah to the pilot's seat. 'Okay. We suit up and head for the Bridge.'

'Not before I go to the head, Avril,' Sallah replied and, nodding at her hand, 'and attend to this. You don't want blood on the chips, you know.' She let herself scream with the pain of the jerk to her foot. She felt she had handled her submission well. Avril would have suspected a more immediate capitulation. 'And another boot.'

Sallah could now spare a dispassionate look at her foot: half her heel was missing and a puddle of blood rocked slowly back and forth, moved by the agitation of Avril's kicks.

'Wait!'

Avril had also noticed the blood. She spun away to the lockers by the hatch and came back with a space suit and a dirty cloth. 'There! Strip!'

Sallah tied up her finger with the least soiled strip of cloth, and used the rest to bind her foot. It hurt badly and she could feel that fragments of her work boot had been jammed into the flesh. She was allowed the use of the head, while Avril watched and made snide and denigrating comments about maternal changes in a woman's body. Sallah pretended to be more humiliated than she actually was. It made Avril feel so superior. The higher the summit, the harder the fall, thought Sallah grimly.

'She's left the gig, Admiral,' Ezra said suddenly in the tense silence in the crowded interface chamber. Tarvi had been called in. Silent tears streamed down his face. 'She's passed the sensors at the docking area. No,' he corrected himself, 'two bodies have passed the sensors.' Tarvi let out a ragged sob but said nothing.

Bit by bit, the pieces had been put together to solve the puzzle of Sallah's disappearance and Avril Bitra's reappearance.

Taffy Pugh, working on a remount job on the sled nearest Sallah's, remembered seeing her leave her task and wander towards the scrap pile at the edge of the grid. He had also noticed Kenjo and Ongola walking to the *Mariposa*. He had not seen anyone else in that vicinity. Shortly afterwards he had seen the *Mariposa* lift off.

The sled Avril had used was easily spotted, when someone thought to look for it. It carried none of the modifications that all Pernese sleds now bore, had been left at the edge of the grid, among others that had been called in for servicing. Stev Kimmer was called to identify it. She had removed every trace of her occupancy although Stev pointed to scrape marks that were new to him. He also kept his personal comments about his erstwhile partner to himself though his expression had been sufficiently grim for Paul and Emily to suspect he'd been doublecrossed. Then, with a shrug, he answered every question they asked him.

'She won't . . . get . . . anywhere,' Emily said striving for optimism.

'No, she won't.' Paul looked at the guidance cartridge, not daring to glance in Tarvi's direction.

'Couldn't she replace it from similar chips on the Bridge?' Tarvi asked, his face an odd shade, his lips dry and his liquid eyes tormented.

'Not the right size,' Ezra said, his expression infinitely sad. 'The *Mariposa* was more modern, used smaller, more sophisticated crystals.'

'Besides,' Paul added heavily, 'the chip she really needs is the one Ongola replaced with a blank. Oh, she can probably set a course and it will appear to be accepted. The ship will reverse out of the dock but the moment she touches the firing pin, it'll just go straight ahead.'

'But Sallah? Would Sallah . . . ?' Tarvi demanded in an anguished voice. 'What will happen to my wife?'

Sallah waited until Avril had reversed the *Mariposa* from the dock, let it drift away from the *Yokohama*'s bulk, until the *Mariposa*'s tailflame ignited before she operated the comunit. Avril had done as much damage to the circuitry in the Bridge console as she could but she had forgotten the override at the Admiral's position. As soon as she had left the Bridge, Sallah accessed it.

'*Yokohama* to Landing. Come in, Ezra. You must be there!'

'Keroon here, Telgar! What's your position?'

'Sitting,' Sallah said.

'Goddamn it, Telgar, don't be facetious at a time like this,' Ezra Keroon cried.

'Sorry, sir,' Sallah said. 'I don't have visuals.' That was a lie but she didn't wish anyone to see her condition. Avril had taken her frustrations out on her. There was also the possibility that Tarvi might be in the interface chamber and Sallah still had a certain amount of vanity. 'I'm accessing the probe garage. There is no damage report for that area. You've three probes left. How shall I program them?'

'Hellfire, girl, don't talk about probes now! How're we going to get you down?'

'I don't think you are, sir,' she said cheerfully. 'Tarvi?'

'Sal-lah!' Two syllables said in a tone that brought her heart to her mouth and tears to her eyes. Why had he never spoken her name that way before? Did it mean the long-awaited avowal of his love? The anguish in his voice: the intensity of the last 'ah' evoked a spirit tortured and distressed.

'Tarvi, my love,' she kept her voice level though her throat kept closing. 'Tarvi, who's with you there?'

'Paul, Emily, Ezra,' he replied in broken tones. 'Sallah! You must return!'

'On the wings of a prayer? No. Go to Cara! Get out of the room. I've got some business to do, Pern business. Paul, make him leave. I can't think if I know he's listening.'

'Sallah!' Her name echoed and re-echoed in her ears.

'Okay, Ezra, tell me where you want them?'

There was a choking, throat-clearing noise. 'I want two

309

to go, one to the body of the cometary, the second to circumnavigate.' Ezra kept having to clear his throat. 'I want the last to follow the spiral curve of that nebulosity. If the big scope is operable, I'd like Bridge readings all along that damned thing. We can't track it with the telescope we have here: not powerful enough for the definition we need. Never thought we'd need the big one so we didn't dismantle it.' He was maundering, Sallah thought affectionately, to get himself under control. Did she hear someone crying through that conversation? Surely Governor Boll or the Admiral would have been kind enough to get Tarvi out of the room.

Then she needed to concentrate on the information Ezra was giving her to encode the duties and destinations of the individual probes.

'Probes away, sir,' she said, remembering the last time she had given that response. Looking up, she saw Pern on the big screen, only this time she was looking down at the place she had known as her home. 'Now I'm sending some data for Dieter to decipher. Avril said she'd killed both Ongola and Kenjo. Has she?'

'Kenjo, yes, Ongola will pull through.'

'Old soldiers don't die easy. Look, Ezra, what I'm sending for Dieter are some notations I made on available fuel. Ongola will know what I mean. And I've sent down Avril's course. She went off in the right direction but I saw a very odd looking crystal in that guidance system, one I never saw on the *Mariposa* when I was driving her. Am I right? She won't go anywhere?'

'Once Bitra hits the engine button, she goes in a straight line.'

'Very good,' Sallah said with a feeling of immense satisfaction. 'The straight and narrow for our dear departed friend. Now, I'm activating the big scope. I'll program it to report through the interface to you. All right?'

'Give me the readings yourself, Mr Telgar,' Ezra ordered gruffly.

'I don't think so, Captain,' she said, glad to rely on the impersonal address. She visualized Captain Ezra Keroon's thin frame hunched over the interface. 'I don't have that much time. Only the oxygen in my tanks. They were full when Avril let me put them on but she told me she was switching off the Bridge's independent system. I have no reason to doubt her. That's another reason why I'm switching the scope's readings to you. Space gloves are good but they don't allow for fine tunings. I just about managed some repairs to the mess Avril made of the console. Jury rig at least so . . . when . . . someone gets a chance to get up here, most everything will work.'

'How much time do you have, Sallah?'

'I don't know.' She could feel the blood reaching to her calf in the big boot and her left glove was full. How much blood did a person have? She felt weak, too, and she was aware that it was getting harder to breathe. It was all of a piece. She would miss knowing Cara better.

'Sallah?' Ezra's voice was very kind. 'Sallah, talk to Tarvi. We can't keep him out of here. He's like a madman. He just wants to talk to you.'

'Oh, sure, fine. I want to talk to him,' she said, her voice sounding funny even to herself.

'Sallah!' Tarvi had his voice under control now. 'Get out of here, all of you! She's mine now. Sallah, jewel in my night, my golden girl, my emerald-eyed ranee, why did I never tell you before how much you mean to me? I was too proud. I was too vain. But you taught me to love: taught me by your sacrifice when I was too engrossed in my other love – my worklove – to see the inestimable gift of your affection and kindness. How could I have been so stupid? How could I have failed to see that you were more than just a body to receive my seed, more than an ear to hear my ambitions, more than hands to . . . Sallah? Sallah! Answer me, Sallah!'

'You – loved – me?'

'I do love you, Sallah. I do! Sallah? Sallah! *Salllllaaaaah!*'

*

311

'What do you think, Dieter?' Paul asked the programmer as he consulted the figures Ezra had given them.

'Well, this first lot of figures gives us over 2000 litres of fuel. The second is a guesstimate of how much Kenjo used on the four missions he flew and what was used by the *Mariposa* today. There's a substantial quantity unused somewhere down here on the surface. The third set is evidently what was left in the *Yoko*'s tanks and is now in the *Mariposa*'s. But, I do point out, as Sallah does, that there's enough in the *Yoko*'s sumptank for centuries of corrections.'

Paul nodded brusquely. 'Go on.'

'Now this section is the course Bitra tried to set. The first course correction should have been initiated about now,' Dieter said, frowning at the equations on his monitor. 'In fact, she should be plunging straight towards our eccentric planet. Maybe we'll find out sooner than we knew what the surface is like.'

'Not that Avril is likely to stand by and give us any useful information as . . . as Sallah did.' Dieter looked up at the savage tone of the Admiral's voice. 'Sorry. C'mon. You've the right. And if something goes wrong . . .' Paul left the sentence dangling as he led Dieter down the corridor to the interface room.

Emily had gone with Tarvi to give him what comfort she could so Ezra was manning the room alone. He looked as old as Paul felt after the wringing emotions of the day.

'Any word?'

'None of it for polite company,' Ezra said with a snort. 'She's just discovered the first course correction hasn't occurred.' He turned the dial and the low snarl of vindictive curses was plainly audible.

Paul grinned maliciously at Dieter. 'So you said.' He turned on the speakers.

'Avril, can you hear me?'

'Benden! What the hell did that bitch of yours do? How did she do it? The override is locked. I can't even manoeuvre. I knew I should have sawn her *foot* off.'

Ezra blanched and Dieter looked ill but Paul's smile was vindictive. So, Avril had underestimated Sallah. He took a deep breath of pride in the valiant woman.

'You're going to explore the plutonic planet, Avril darling. Why don't you be a decent thing and give us a running account?'

'Shove it, Benden. You know where! You'll get nothing out of me. Oh, shit! Oh, shit! it's not the . . . oh, shiiiitt.'

The sound of her final expletive was drowned by a sizzling roar that made Ezra grab for the volume dial.

'Shit!' Paul echoed very softly. '"It's not the . . ." the what? Damn you, Avril, to eternity! "It's not the . . ." *what*?'

Emily and Pierre, with Chio-Chio Yoritomo who had been Ika's cabinmate on the *Buenos Aires* and her house mate on Irish Square, took the fast sled to Kenjo's Honshu Stake. While most of Landing knew about Kenjo's death and Ongola's serious illness, there had been no public announcement. Rumour had been busy with the 'unknown' assailant.

When Emily returned that night, she did not bring Ika with her. She brought a sealed message to the Admiral.

'She told us,' Emily said drily 'that she would prefer to stay on at Honshu to work the Stake herself for her four children. She had few needs and would not trouble us.'

'Ika is very ethnic,' Chio-Chio told the Admiral breathlessly. 'She would not show grief for that belittles the dead.' Then she shrugged, eyes down but her hands were clenching and unclenching. She looked up, almost defiant in her anger. 'She was like that. Kenjo married her because she would not question what he did. He asked me first but I had more sense, even if he was a war ace. Oh!' And then she brought her arm up to hide her face. 'But to die like that! Struck behind. An ignominious death for one who had cheated it so often!' Then she turned and fled from the room, her sobbing audible as she ran out into the night.

Emily then gestured for Paul to open the small note, well sealed by wax and stamped with some kind of marking.

He broke it open and unfolded the thick beautiful paper. Then mystified he gave it to Emily and Pierre to see what they could make of it.

'"There were two caves cut to judge by the amount of fuel used and rubble spilled. One cave housed the plane. I do not know where the other was."'

'So he did manage to remove some of the fuel?' Emily asked. 'How much?'

'We'll see if Ezra can figure it out – or Ongola when he recovers. Pierre?' Paul asked him for a pledge of silence.

'Of course. Discretion was bred in my family for generations, Admiral.'

'Paul,' the Admiral corrected him.

'For something like this, old friend, you are the Admiral!' Pierre clicked his heels together and inclined his body slightly from the waist, smiling with a brief reassurance. 'Emily, you are tired. You should rest now. Paul, tell her!'

Paul laid one hand on Pierre de Courci's shoulder and took Emily's arm with the other. 'There is one more duty for the day, Pierre, and you'd best be with us.'

'The bonfire!' Emily pulled back against Paul's arm. 'I'm not sure I . . .'

'Who can?' Paul broke in when she faltered. 'Tarvi has asked it.'

All three walked with reluctant steps, joining the trickle of others going in the same direction, down to the dark Bonfire Square which was dark. Each house had one light left burning. The thinly scattered stars were brilliant and the first moon, Timor, was barely a crescent on the eastern skyline.

By the pyramid of thicket and fern, Tarvi stood, his head down, a man as gaunt as some of the branches that had been cast into the pile. Suddenly, as if he knew that all were there who would come, he lit the brand. It flared up to light a face haggard with grief, with hair that straggled across tear-wet cheeks.

Tarvi raised the brand high, turning slowly as if to place firmly in his memory the faces of all there.

'From now on,' he said, his voice a hoarse shout, 'I am not Tarvi, nor Andiyar. I am Telgar so that her name is spoken every day, so that her name is remembered by everyone for giving *us* her life today. Our children will now bear that name, too. Ram Telgar, Ben Telgar, Dena Telgar and Cara Telgar who will never know her mother.' He took a deep breath, filling his chest. '*What is my name?*'

'Telgar!' Paul replied as loud as he could. 'Telgar!' cried Emily beside him. Pierre's baritone repeating it a breath behind her. *Telgar!*'

'Telgar! Telgar! Telgar *Telgar Telgar!*' Nearly three thousand voices took up the shout in a chant, pumping their arms until Telgar thrust the burning torch into the bonfire. As the flame roared up through the dry wood and fern, the name crescendoed. '*Telgar! Telgar! Telgar!*'

15

●

The shock of Sallah Telgar's death reverberated across the continent. She had been well-known, both as shuttle pilot during Debarkation and as an able manager of the Karachi Camp. Her courage, however, gave an unexpected boost to morale. Almost as if, because Sallah was willing to devote the last moments of her life to benefit the colony, everyone must strive harder to vindicate her sacrifice. Or so it seemed for the next eight days until some disturbing rumours began to circulate.

'Look, Paul,' Joel Lilienkamp began even before he'd closed the door behind him, 'everyone's got a right to access Stores. But that Ted Tubberman's been taking out some unusual stuff for a botanist.'

'Not Tubberman again,' Paul said, leaning back in his chair with a deep sigh of disgust. Tarv ... Telgar, Paul corrected himself ... had phoned the previous day, asking if Tubberman had been authorized to scrounge in the shuttle they were dismantling.

'Yes, if you ask me, he's only accessing half his chips. You've got enough on your plate, Paul, but you gotta know what that fool's doing. I'll bet my last bottle of brandy, he's up to something.'

'At Wind Blossom's request, Pol has denied him further access to the Biology labs,' Paul said wearily. 'Seems he was acting as if *he* was in charge of Bio-engineering. Bay doesn't like him much either.'

'She's not alone,' Joel replied, lowering himself to a chair and scrubbing at his face. 'I want your permission to shut the shop door in his face, too. I caught him in Building G which houses the technically sensitive stuff. I don't want anyone in there without my authorization. And there he was, bald-faced and swaggering like he had every right, he and Bart Lemos . . .'

'Bart Lemos!' Paul sat up again.

'Yeah, he, Bart and Stev Kimmer're doing a good old buddy bit these days. And I don't like the rumours my sources tell me they're spreading.'

'Stev Kimmer's in on it?' Paul was surprised.

Joel shrugged. 'He's mighty thick with 'em.'

Paul rubbed his knuckles thoughtfully. Bart Lemos was a gullible nonentity but Stev Kimmer was a highly skilled technician. Paul had put a discreet monitor on the man's activities after Avril's departure. The man had gone on a three-day bender and been found asleep in the dismantled shuttle. Once he'd recovered from the effects of quikal, he had gone back to work. Fulmar said that other mechanics didn't like pairing with him because he was taciturn if not downright surly. The thought of Tubberman having Kimmer's expertise made Paul uneasy.

'What exactly have you heard, Lili?'

'A load of crap,' the little Storesman said, folding his fingers across his chest. 'I don't think anyone with any sense buys the notion Avril and Kenjo were in league. Or that Ongola killed Kenjo to keep them from taking the *Mariposa* to go for help. But I'll warn you, Paul, if Kitti's bio-engineering program doesn't show positive results, we could be down the tubes, I'll lay odds you and Emily are going to be asked to reconsider sending off that homing capsule.'

The previous evening, Paul had discussed that expedient with Emily, Ezra and Jim. Keroon had been the fiercest opponent of a homing capsule Mayday which he termed an exercise in futility. As Paul remarked, such technological help was, at the earliest, ten years away. And the chance that the FSP would move with any speed to assist them was depressingly slim. To send for help seemed not only a rejection of Sallah's sacrifice but a cowardly admission of failure when they had not exhausted the ingenuity and resourcefulness of their community.

'What sort of material has Ted been requisitioning, Lili?' Paul now asked.

Joel extracted a wad of paper from his thigh pocket and made a show of unfolding and reading from it. 'Grab bag from hydroponics to insulation materials, steel mesh and posts, and some computer chips that Dieter says he couldn't possibly need, use or understand.'

'Did you happen to ask Tubberman what he needed them for?'

'I happened to just do that very thing. A bit arrogant he was, too. Said they were needed for his experiments,' and Joel was clearly dubious about their value, 'to develop a more effective defence against the Thread until help comes.'

Paul made a grimace. He'd heard the botanist's wild claims that *he*, not the biologists and their jumped-up mutated lizards, would protect Pern.

'I don't like that "till help comes" bit,' Paul murmured, gritting his teeth.

'So, tell me to lock him out, Paul. He may be a Charterer but he's overspent his credit and then some.' He waved the sheet. 'I got records to prove that.'

Paul nodded. 'Yes, but next time he presents a list, get him to tell you what he wants, then shut the door. I want to know what he's up to.'

'Restrict him to his Stake,' Joel said, rising to his feet, an expression of genuine concern on his round face, 'and you'll save all of us a lot of aggro. He's a wild card and you can't be sure where he'll bounce up next.'

Paul grinned at the Storesman. 'I'd be glad to, Lili, but the Mandate doesn't permit that kind of action.'

Joel snorted derisively, hesitated a moment longer and then shrugging in his inimitable fashion, left the office.

Paul didn't forget the conversation but the morning brought more pressing concerns. Despite the best efforts of Fulmar and his crews, three more sleds failed airworthiness tests. That meant using more ground crews, the last line of defence and the most enervating for people already worked to the point of exhaustion. Neither Paul nor Emily recognized the significance of three separate reports: one from the Veterinary lab saying that their supply rooms had been rifled overnight; another from Pol Nietro that Ted Tubberman had been seen in Bio-engineering and the third from Fulmar saying that someone had made off with one of the exhaust cylinders from the dismantled shuttle.

When Joel Lilienkamp's angry call came through, Paul had little trouble arriving at a conclusion.

'May his orifices congeal and his extremities fall off!' Joel cried at the top of his voice. 'He's got the homing capsule!'

Shock jolted Paul out of his chair while Emily and Ezra regarded him in astonishment.

'Are you sure?'

'Of course, I'm sure, Paul. I hid the carton in among stove pipes and heating units. It hasn't been misplaced but who the hell could *know* that Carton #45/879 was a homing capsule.'

'Tubberman took it?'

'I'll bet my last bottle of brandy he did.' Joel spoke so fast his words slurred. 'The fucker! The crap-eater, the slime producing maggot!'

'When did you discover it gone?'

'Now! I'm calling from Building G. I check it out at least once a day.'

'Could Tubberman have followed you?'

'What sort of a twat do you think I am?' Joel was as apoplectic at such a suggestion as he was about the theft. 'I check every building every day and I can tell you exactly what was requisitioned yesterday and the day before so I fucking well know when something's missing!'

'I don't doubt you for a moment, Joel.' Paul passed his hand hard over his mouth, thinking rapidly what steps to take. Then he saw the anxious expressions of Emily and Ezra. 'Hold on,' he said into the handset and reported what Joel had said.

'Well,' Ezra replied, a look of intense relief passing over his gaunt features, 'Tubberman couldn't launch a kite. He can barely manoeuvre a sled. I wouldn't worry about him.'

'Not him. But I worry a lot about Stev Kimmer and Bart Lemos being seen in Tubberman's company lately,' Paul said quietly and Ezra seemed to deflate, burying his head in his hands.

'Ted Tubberman has had it,' Emily said, placing the folder she'd been studying on to the table in a precise manner and rising to her feet. 'I don't give a spent chip for his position as a Charterer or the privacy of his Stake. We're searching Calusa.' She gave Ezra a poke in the shoulder. 'C'mon, you'll know what components he'd need . . .'

They all heard the sound of running feet, just as the door burst in and Jake Chernoff erupted into the office.

'Sir, sorry, sir,' the young man cried, his face flushed, his chest heaving from exertions, 'your phone . . .' and he pointed excitedly at the receiver in the Admiral's hand, '. . . too important . . . Scanners at Met . . . something blasted off from Oslo Landing . . . three minutes ago . . . and it wasn't a sled . . . Too small.'

As one, Paul, Emily and Ezra made for the door and ran to the interface chamber. Ezra fumbled at the terminal in his haste to implement the program. An exhaust trail was plainly visible, on a northwestern heading. Cursing under his breath, Ezra switched to the *Yoko*'s monitor which now tracked the blip. For a long moment they watched, rigid with fury and frustration. Then Ezra straightened his long frame, his hands hanging limply.

'Well, what's done's done.'

'Not completely,' said Emily, her voice harsh as she separated each syllable in a curious lilt. She turned to Paul, her eyes very bright, her lips pursed and her expression implacable. 'Oslo Landing, hmmm? That capsule was just launched. Let's go get the buggers.'

Leaving Ezra to monitor the capsule's ascent, Paul and Emily left at a run. The first three big men they encountered on their way to the grid were commandeered to assist. Paul spotted Fulmar and told him to pilot Kenjo's augmented sled.

'Don't ask questions, Fulmar,' Paul said, peremptorily seconding two more burly technicians, 'just head us towards Jordan, and everyone keep their eyes open for sled traffic.' He reached for the comunit as he shrugged into his harness. 'Who's in the tower? Tarrie? I want to know who's in the air above the river, where they're going and where they've been.'

Fulmar took off in such a steep climb that for a moment the noise blanketed any answer Tarrie Chernoff gave.

'Only one sled above the Jordan, sir, apart from that . . . other . . . flight.' She choked on her words and then recovered the impersonal reserve of a comofficer. 'The sled does not acknowledge.'

'They will,' Paul assured her grimly. 'Continue to monitor all traffic in that area.'

Tubberman was just stupid enough to be obvious but somehow Paul didn't think Stev Kimmer was or whoever else Ted had talked into such an arrant abrogation of the democratic decision of the Colony. Tubberman was alone in the sled when Fulmar forced him to land in the riverside desolation of Bavaria, the ill-fated stake of the Radelins.

He was unrepentant as he faced them, folding his arms across his chest and jutting his chin out defiantly.

'I've done what should have been done,' he stated in pompous righteousness. 'The first step in saving this colony from annihilation.'

Paul clenched his fists so tightly to his sides he could almost feel the missing fingers on his left hand. Beside, Emily was vibrating with a fury as intense as his own.

'I want the names of your accomplices, Tubberman,' Paul said through his teeth, 'and I want them now!'

Tubberman inhaled, bracing himself. 'Do your worst, Admiral. I am man enough to take it.'

The mock heroic attitude was so absurd to his auditors that Blackie Nilwan behind Paul let out a short bark of incredulous laughter which he cut off. But the one burst of derision altered Paul's state.

'Tubberman, I wouldn't let anyone touch a hair of your head,' Paul said, grinning in a release of tension. 'There are quite suitable ways to deal with you, plainly set out in the Charter, nothing quite as crude or barbaric as physical abuse.' Then he turned to Blackie. 'Take him back to Landing in his sled. Joe, Feng, go with Blackie. Put him in my office and call Joel Lilienkamp. He'll take charge of the prisoner.' Paul had the satisfaction of seeing the martyred look fade from Tubberman's eyes, replaced by a mixture of anxiety and surprise. Turning on his heel, Paul gestured Emily, Fulmar and the others back into their sled.

Tarrie reported no other vehicles in the area and apologized that traffic records were no longer kept. 'Except for that . . . rocket thing, the pattern was normal, sir. Oh, and Jake's back. Did you want to speak to him?'

'Yes,' Paul answered, wishing that Ongola were back in charge. 'Jake, I want to know where Bart Lemos and Stev Kimmer are. And Nabhi Nabol.' Beside him Emily nodded approval.

By then, Fulmar had covered the short air distance between Bavaria and Oslo Landing. The remains of the launch platform were still smoking. While Paul went with the others to search the area for sled skids, Fulmar carefully prodded through the overheated circle beneath it, sniffing as he went.

'Shuttle fuel by the smell of it, Paul,' he reported. 'A homing capsule wouldn't take much.'

'It would take know-how,' Paul said grimly. 'And expertise, and you and I know just how many people are capable of that sort of technology.' He looked Fulmar square in the eye and the man's shoulders sagged. 'Not your fault, Fulmar. I had your report. I had others. I just didn't put the pieces together.'

'Who'd have thought Ted'd pull such a crazy stunt? No one believes half of what he says!' Fulmar protested.

Emily and the others came back then from an inconclusive search.

'There're a lot of skid marks, Paul,' she said, 'and Ray found rubbish.'

The mechanic held out the collapsed fuel sack in one hand and a handful of connectors and wires in the other. Fulmar's look of desolation deepened.

'We're wasting time here,' Paul said, curbing his irritation with the disastrous morning.

'Let's have Cherry and Cabot waiting in my office,' Emily murmured as they climbed into the sled.

'He's *proud* of what he did,' Joel stormed when Paul and Emily called him into Emily's office on their return. 'Says it was his *duty* to save the colony. Says we'll be surprised at how many people agree with him.'

'He's the one who'll be surprised,' Emily replied. Her jaw was set in a resolute line and her lips curved in a curious smile on her face which her tired eyes did not echo.

'Yeah, Em, but what *can* we do to him?' Joel demanded in impotent indignation.

Emily poured herself a fresh cup of klah and took a sip before she answered.

'He will be shunned.'

'Who will be shunned?' demanded Cherry Duff in her hoarse voice, entering the room at that instant. Cabot Carter was right behind her, having escorted the magistrate from her office in reply to the summons.

'Shunned?' Carter's handsome face was enlivened by a smile that grew broader as he looked expectantly from Paul to Emily and faded slightly as he saw the dour Storesman.

'Shunned!' Paul grinned back.

'Shunned?' Joel exclaimed in a disgusted tone.

Emily had gestured Cherry into the comfortable chair, motioned for the others to be seated and then, at a nod from Paul, gave a terse report on matters which had culminated in Tubberman's illicit use of the homing capsule.

'So we're to order Tubberman shunned, huh?' Cherry looked around at Carter.

'It's legal all right, Cherry,' the legist replied, 'since it is not a corporal punishment, *per se*, which is illegal under the terms of the Charter.'

'Refresh me on such a process,' Cherry said, her tone doubly droll.

'Shunning was a mechanism,' Emily began, 'whereby passive groups could discipline an erring member. Religious communities resorted to it when someone of their sect disobeyed their peculiar tenets. Quite effective really. The rest of the sect pretended the offending member didn't exist. No one spoke to him, no one acknowledged his presence, no one would assist the Shunned in any way or indicate that he . . . or she . . . existed. It doesn't seem cruel but in fact the deprivation is psychologically destructive.'

'It'll do,' Cherry said, nodding in satisfaction. 'An admirable punishment for someone like Tubberman. Admirable!'

'And completely legal!' Cabot concurred. 'Shall I draft the announcement, Emily, or do you prefer to do it, Cherry?'

Cherry flicked her hand at him. 'You do it, Cabot. I'm sure you learned all the right phrases. But do explain exactly what Shunning entails. Not that most of us aren't so fed up with the man's rantings and rumours that they won't be delighted to have an official excuse to . . . ah . . . shun him! Shun him,' and she tipped back her head and gave a hoot of outrageous laughter. 'By all that's holy . . . and legal . . . I like that, Emily. I like that a lot!' In an abrupt switch of mood with no leavening of humour, she added, 'It'll cool a lot of hotheads.' She swept Paul

324

and Emily with a shrewd look. 'Tubberman didn't do it by himself. Who helped?'

'We've no proof,' Paul began in the same minute that Joel said 'Stev Kimmer, Bart Lemos and maybe Nabhi Nabol.'

'Let's shun them, too,' Cherry cried, banging the arm of her chair with her thin old hands. 'Damn it, we don't need dissension. We need support, co-operation, hard work. Or we won't survive. Oh, flaming hells,' and she raised both hands up high, 'what'll we do if that capsule brings those blood-sucking FSP salvagers down on us?'

'I wouldn't bet on that,' Joel answered her, rolling his eyes.

Cherry gave him a hard stare. 'I'm relieved to know there is something you won't make book on, Lilienkamp. All right, so what *do* we do about Tubberman's accomplices?'

Cabot leaned over to touch her arm lightly. 'First we have to prove that they were, Cherry.' He looked expectantly at Paul and Emily. 'The Charter says that a person is judged innocent until proved guilty.'

'We watch 'em,' Paul said. 'We watch 'em. Carter, compose that notice and see that it's posted throughout Landing, and that every stake-holder is apprised of the fact. Cherry, will you impose the sentence on Tubberman?' He held out his arm to assist her to her feet.

'With the greatest of satisfaction. What a superb way to get rid of a bore,' she added under her breath as she marched forward. The unholy joy on her face brightened Joel Lilienkamp's face as he followed them, rubbing his hands together.

The messenger was quite happy to bring a copy of the official notice to Bay and Wind Blossom on duty in the large incubator chamber. The room was separated from the main Bio-Genetic laboratory and insulated against temperature changes and noise. The incubator itself stood on heavy shock absorbers so that, in the precarious early stages, the embryos in their sacs could not be jarred by equipment moved around the main laboratory.

Although eggs within a natural womb, or even in a proper shell, could handle a great deal of trauma, the initial *ex utero* fertilization and alteration had been too delicate to risk the most minute jolt. Development was not yet 'canalized' nor the new genetic structure balanced, and any variation in the embryos' environment would doubtless cause damage. This would not occur in later generations but these first attempts were incredibly fragile. Later, when the eggs were at the stage when naturally they would have been laid in a clutch, they would be transferred to the building where a warmed sand flooring and artificial sun lamps imitated the natural conditions in which dragonet eggs hatched. That point was several weeks ahead, and meanwhile the incubator was their artificial oviduct.

Special low-light viewing panels had been created, so no light filtered into the womblike darkness while observers had a clear view of the incubator's precious contents. A portable magnifier had been devised which could be set at any position on the incubator's four glass sides for very coarse and routine inspections. In the laboratories Bay remembered on First and Earth, each developing embryo could be remotely monitored and it was possible to play back the development at each stage. But, in these relatively primitive conditions, about which Wind Blossom constantly complained these days, the necessity for the avoidance of any toxic substances at all meant that no sensors could be close to the embryos in the culture chambers.

Bay was jotting down Wind Blossom's assessment when the messenger delivered the notice. The lad was quite willing to explain any part of the Shunning but Bay shooed him off on his rounds.

'How extraordinary,' Bay said when she had finished reading it aloud to Blossom. 'Really, Ted has been quite a nuisance lately. Did you hear those rumours he was spreading, Blossom? As if that wretched Bitra had anything but her own plans in mind when she stole the *Mariposa*. Going for help, indeed!' She squinted loyally into the incubator and its forty-two hopes for their future. 'But to send off a homing capsule when we most specifically voted against such an action.'

'I am relieved,' Wind Blossom said, sighing gently.

'Yes, he was beginning to upset you,' Bay remarked kindly. She tried to tell herself that the woman was still grieving for her mother. There were moments recently, though, when Bay wanted to remind Blossom that it wasn't just her family which had suffered a grievous loss. She hadn't because Blossom was rather volatile lately and she might interpret such a comment as an aspersion on her ability to proceed with her mother's brilliant Bio-genetic program. As her mother's primary assistant, she was technically in charge of a program on file in the biology Mark 42 computer. Bay had scanned it to familiarize herself with the procedure. Kitti Ping had left copious notes on how to proceed, what possible minor alignments, balancing or compensations might be needed. She had apparently anticipated everything but her own death.

'You misunderstand me,' Blossom replied, inclining her head in a gesture reminiscent of her mother correcting an erring apprentice, 'I am relieved that the homing capsule has been sent. Now there is no blame to us.'

Bay wasn't certain she'd heard correctly.

'What under the suns do you mean, Blossom?'

Blossom turned and gave Bay a long look, smiling faintly.

'All our eggs are in one basket,' she said with an inscrutable smile and moved the inspection lens to a new position.

When Pol and Phas Radamanth came to relieve them, Bay lingered. She and Pol didn't have much time together these days, and she didn't look forward to another dull supper at the Communal kitchen.

'You got a copy, I see,' Pol said, indicating the Shun notice.

'Extraordinary that.'

'More than time,' Phas said, glancing up from Blossom's notations. 'Let's hope he wasn't as incompetent a launcher as he was a botanist.'

Bay stared in astonishment at the xeno-biologist who had the grace to look embarrassed.

'No one approves of Tubberman's action, my dear,' Pol assured her.

'Yes, but if they come . . .' Bay's gesture took in the incubator and the laboratory, and all that the colonists had managed to do with their new world.

'If it's any consolation,' Phas said, 'Joel Lilienkamp has not opened a book on an ETA.'

'Oh!' Then she asked, 'And what's happened to Ted Tubberman?'

'He was escorted back to his Stake and told to remain there.'

Pol could look quite fierce, she thought, when he wanted to.

'What about Mary? And his young children?'

Pol shrugged. 'She can stay or come. She's not Shunned. Ned Tubberman was looking pretty upset but he never was very close to his father, and Fulmar Stone thinks he's a very promising mechanic.' He shrugged again and then gave his wife an encouraging smile.

Bay had no sooner turned to go than the ground under them shook. She instinctively lunged towards the incubator, and found Phas and Pol beside her. Even without the magnifier they could see that the amniotic fluid in the sacs was not rippling in response to the earthquake. The shock absorbers had proved adequate.

'That's all we need!' Pol cried, outraged. He stomped to the comunit and dialled the Met Tower, slamming down the handset. 'Engaged! Bay, reassure them . . .' He gestured towards the first bunch of technicians heading anxiously to the door of the chamber. He dialled again and got through, just as Kwan Marceau pushed his way into the room. 'Are there going to be more shocks, Jake? Why weren't we warned?'

'It was a small one,' Jake Chernoff replied soothingly. 'Patrice de Broglie called it in but I am obliged to warn Infirmary first in case surgery is in progress and then your line was busy.' That explanation placated Pol. 'Patrice says there's a bit of tectonic-plate action to the east and there may be more jolts in the next few weeks. The incubator's on shocks anyway, isn't it? You don't have anything to worry about.'

'Nothing to worry about?' Pol demanded, jamming the handset back on to its stand.

There was a discreet knock on the door to the Admiral's office and when Paul answered with a non-committal 'Come in', Jim Tillek opened it. Emily smiled with relief. The Master of Monaco Bay was always welcome. Paul leaned back in his swivel chair, ready for a break from the depressing inventory of airworthy sleds and serviceable flamethrowers.

'Hi, there, just up to get my skimmer serviced.'

'Since when have you needed assistance in that job?' Paul asked.

'Since all my spare parts at Monaco got reabsorbed by Joel Lilienkamp,' and Jim's drawl was cheerful.

'And pigs fly,' Paul retorted.

'Oh, is that the next project?' Jim asked with a comic grin. He dropped into the nearest seat and laced his fingers together. 'By the way, Maximilian and Teresa reported on the dolphin search Patrice requested. There are significant lava flows from the Illyrian volcano. It's only a small one so don't be surprised if our easterlies bring in some black dust. It's *not* dead Thread. Just honest-to-Vulcan volcanic dust. I wanted you to know before another rumour started.'

'Thanks,' Paul said drily.

'Logical explanations are always welcome,' Emily added.

'I also dropped in to see our favourite patient,' and Jim pushed himself deeper into the chair and met Paul's eyes squarely. 'He's raring to go and threatens to move into the second storey of the Met Tower and run Communications from there. Sabra threatens to divorce him if he does anything before he gets medical clearance. Myself, I told him he doesn't need to worry as young Jake Chernoff's been doing a proper job of it. He won't even hazard a guess about the weather until he's run the satellite report twice and looked out the window.'

Paul and Emily smiled at his jocular account, both relaxing into their chairs.

'Ongola *needs* to be back at work,' Emily agreed. She glanced at Paul who had been resisting this, considering the severity of Ongola's injury. The extent of any handicap had yet to be discovered.

'He's sure he'll never use his arm again. He'd do better being so busy he doesn't think such negative thoughts.' Jim cocked his head at Paul.

'According to Basil,' Emily said with a grateful smile, 'Ongola will use that arm – even if he refuses to believe it – but the amount of mobility is still in question.'

'Good man, Basil,' Jim said blandly. 'Hey, is there any truth to the rumour that Stev Kimmer was involved with Tubberman?'

Paul pulled a face and Emily shot him a glance. 'I told you that was doing the rounds.'

'Hey,' Jim leaned forward, his expression eager, 'any truth to the one that he skitted out with one of the big pressurized sleds which has been seen near the Great Western Barrier where Kenjo staked his claim? Kimmer's a lot more dangerous than Ted Tubberman ever was.'

Paul ran his thumb over his artificial fingers and stopped when he saw Jim Tillek had caught the nervous habit. 'He is indeed. As the comunit on that stolen sled was in working order when he lifted it, he will also know that he is wanted back here for questioning.'

Jim nodded in solemn approval. 'Has Ezra made any

sense out of the reports of those probes Sallah . . .' he paused and blinked, his eyes suspiciously wet.

'No,' Paul said, clearing his own throat. 'He's still trying to translate them. The printout is unclear.'

'Well, now,' Jim said, 'I've got a few hours to spare while my sled's serviced. I looked at hundreds of EEC survey team reports before I found a planet I liked the look of. Can I help?'

'A fresh eye might be useful,' Paul said. 'Ezra's been at it non-stop.'

'Did I hear correctly,' Jim asked gently, 'that the *Mariposa* plunged directly into the eccentric?'

Paul nodded. 'She made no informative comment.' Avril's cryptic penultimate phrase, *It's not the* . . . still rang with some message Paul felt he must unravel. 'Look, Jim, do stop in and see if you can help Ezra. We need some good news. Morale is still low after the murders and having to Shun Ted Tubberman and explain how he got his hands on that homing capsule have not improved the administration's image.'

'Clever trick, though,' Jim said, chuckling as he rose. 'Keeps you from having to breach stake autonomy and keeps that fool where he can't do more damage. I'll just amble over to Ezra's pod.' He left the room with a backhanded wave at Emily and Paul.

Somehow his visit cheered them immeasurably and they went back to the onerous tasks of scheduling crews for the upcoming Threadfalls, mustering teams to collect edible greenery to be made into silage from places as yet untouched by the ravening organism, and still give people some personal time.

16

●

'Look, Jim, I just can't find any other logical explanation for the destruction of three probes and *these*,' Ezra Keroon waved a handful of probe pics, so blurred that no detail could be seen. 'One, maybe two probes, could malfunction. But I've sent off seven! And Sallah . . .' Ezra paused a moment, his face expressing the sorrow he still felt at her loss, 'told us that there had been no damage report for the probe garage. Then we have the *Mariposa*. It did not hit the surface. Something hit it just about the same time one of the probes went bang!'

'So you prefer to believe that something down on the surface prevents inspection?' Jim Tillek asked wryly and leaned back in his seat, easing shoulder muscles taut from hours of bending and peering through magnifiers. 'I can't credit that explanation, Ez. C'mon, man. How can anything on that planet be functioning? The surface has been frozen. It can't have thawed appreciably in the time it's been swinging in to Rukbat.'

'One does not have such regular formations on any unpopulated surface. I don't say they can't be natural. They just don't look natural. And I certainly won't make any guesses about what sort of creature made them. Then look at the thermal level here, here and here—' Ezra jabbed a finger at the relevant area on the pics he had been studying, 'it's higher than I'd anticipate on a near-frozen surface. That much we got from the one probe that sent data back.'

'Volcanic action under the crust could account for that.'

'But regular *convex*, not concave, formations along the equator?'

'You *want* to believe that plutonic planet could be the *source* of this attack?' Jim Tillek was incredulous.

'I like that better than substantiating the Hoyle–Wickramansingh theory, I really do, Jim.'

'If Avril hadn't taken the Gig, we could find out what that nebulosity is. Then we'd know for sure! Hoyle–Wickramansingh or little frozen blue critters.' Jim's tone was facetious.

'We've the shuttles,' Ezra said tentatively, tapping his pencil.

'No fuel and there isn't a pilot among those left that I'd be willing to trust to do such a difficult retrieval. You'd have to match its orbital speed. I saw the dints on the *Mariposa*'s hull myself where the defence shields failed. Also, we didn't bring down any heavy worksuits that would protect a man out in a meteor storm. And if your theory's correct, he'll get shot down.'

'Only if he gets too close to the planet,' Ezra went on cautiously. 'But he wouldn't have to, to get a sample of the trail. If the trail is nothing but ice, dirt and rock, the usual cometary junk, we'd know then that the real menace is the planet, not the trail. Right?'

Jim eyed him thoughtfully. 'It'd be dangerous either way. And there's no fuel to do it anyhow!' Jim opened his arms in a gesture of exasperation.

'There is fuel.'

'There is?' Jim Tillek sat bolt upright, eyes wide with surprise.

Ezra gave him a wry smile. 'Known only to a chosen few.'

'Well!' Jim made his eyebrows twitch but he grinned to show that he took no offence at having been excluded. 'How much?'

'With a thrifty pilot, enough for our purpose. Or maybe, if we can find Kenjo's main cache, more.'

'More?' Jim gawked at this astounding revelation.

'Kenjo's cache?' Ezra delivered one surprise after another. 'He scrounged fuel?'

'Always was a clever driver. Saved it from his drops, Ongola said.'

Jim continued to stare at Ezra, amazed at Kenjo's sheer impudence. 'So that's why Kimmer's winnowing about the Western Barrier Range. He's out trying to find Kenjo's cache? For his own purposes or ours?'

'Not enough to get anyone's hopes up, mind you,' Ezra went on, holding up a warning hand. 'Maybe it's not too bad a thing that Tubberman sent off the homer. Because if it *is* the planet, we need help and I'm not too proud to ask for it.' Ezra grimaced at this capitulation. 'Not that Kimmer said anything to anyone when he made off with the big sled, enough concentrated food and power packs to stay lost for years. Joel Lilienkamp was livid that anyone would *steal* from his Store. We don't even know how Stev found out about Kenjo's hoard. Except that he knew how much fuel the *Mariposa* had in her tanks eight years ago. So he must have figured out someone had saved fuel back when Kenjo made those reconnaissance flights.' Then, as Jim opened his mouth, he added, 'Don't worry about Kimmer taking off even if he finds fuel. Ongola and Kenjo disabled the shuttles some time back. Kimmer doesn't know where we stash the fuel sacks here. Neither do I.'

'I'm honoured, with your confidence and the cares you have so carefully laid on my bowed shoulders.'

'You walked in here three days ago and volunteered your services,' Ezra reminded him.

'Three days? Feels like three years. I wonder if my skimmer's been serviced.' He rose and stretched again until the bones in spine and joints readjusted with audible clicks. 'So, shall we take this mess,' and he gestured to the mass of photos and flimsies neatly arranged on the work surface, 'to the guys who have to figure out what we do with it?'

*

Paul and Emily listened to the report, saying nothing, until both men had finished expressing their conflicting viewpoints.

'But when the planet is past us in the next eight or nine years, Threadfall will stop,' Paul said, jumping to a conclusion.

'Depends on whose theory you favour,' Jim said, grinning with good-natured malice. 'Or how advanced Ezra's aliens are. Right now, if you buy his theory, they're keeping us at arm's length while the Thread softens us up.'

Paul Benden brushed away that theory. 'I don't credit that, Ezra. Thread was ineffective on the previous try. But the Pluto Planet could be defending itself. I could live with that much of your theory based on the evidence.'

Emily looked squarely at Jim and asked: 'How long will this gunge fall if it's from your cometary tail?'

'Twenty–thirty years. If I knew the length of that tail, I could give a closer estimate.'

'I wonder if that's what Avril meant,' Paul said slowly, 'by "it's not the . . ." Did she mean that it wasn't the planet we had to fear, but the tail it brought from the Oort cloud?'

'If she hadn't taken the *Mariposa*, we'd have a chance of knowing.' Emily's voice had a sharp edge.

'We still do,' Ezra said. 'There's enough fuel to send a shuttle up. Not as economical a vehicle as the *Mariposa* but adequate.'

'Are you sure?' Paul's expression was taut as he reached for a calc pad on which he worked several equations. He leaned back, his face pensive – then passed the pad over to Emily. Jim looked over her shoulder at the result. 'It might just be possible.' He caught and held Emily's gaze. 'We have to know. We have to know the worst we can expect before we can plan ahead.'

Ezra raised a warning hand, his expression wary. 'Mind you, they can't get close to the planet! We've lost seven probes. Could be mines . . . could be missiles . . . but they blow up.'

'Whoever goes will know exactly what and how big the risks are,' Paul said.

'There's risk enough in just going up,' Ezra said gloomily.

'I hate to sound fatuous, but surely there's one pilot who'd take the challenge to save this world,' Paul added.

Drake Bonneau was approached first. He thought the scheme was feasible but he worried about the risk of a shuttle that had certainly deteriorated from eight years' disuse. He then pointed out that he was married with responsibilities and there were other pilots equally as qualified. Paul and Emily did not argue with him.

'Marriage and dependent children will be the excuse of practically everyone,' Paul told their private counsellors, Ezra, Jim and Zi Ongola who was now allowed four hours of 'work' a day by his reluctant medical advisers. 'The only one still unattached is Nabhi Nabol.'

'He's a clever enough pilot,' Ongola said thoughtfully, 'though not exactly the type of man on whom the future of an entire planet should ride. However, exactly the type if the reward could be made attractive enough for him to take the risk.'

'How?' asked Emily sceptically.

Nabhi had already been reprimanded a dozen times, and served Cherry Duff's sentences for social misdemeanours, mainly 'drunk & disorderlys', several work delinquencies and one 'lewd advances'. Lately he had somewhat redeemed himself by being a good squadron leader and was much admired by the young men he led.

'He's a Contractor,' Ongola said. 'If he should be offered, say, a Charterer's stake rights, I think he might well go for it. He's griped about the disparity in land holdings often enough. That could sweeten him. He also fancies himself as a crack pilot.'

'We've got some very good young pilots . . .' Jim began.

'Who have had no experience in space with a shuttle.' Ongola dismissed that notion. 'Though it might be a good idea to choose one to go as co-pilot and give them the eel. But I'd rather trust Nabhi than a complete space novice.'

'If we suggest that he was also our second choice, rather than our last one . . .' Emily remarked.

'We'd better get on with it, whatever we do,' Ezra said, 'I can't keep stalling questions. We need data and we need a sample of the stuff in that trail. Then we'll know for certain what our future is.'

Bargaining with Nabhi began that afternoon. He sneered at the flattery and the appeal to his competence and demanded to know just how much the trip was worth in holding and other rights. When he first demanded the entire province of Cibola, Paul and Emily settled down to their task.

When Nabhi insisted on being granted Charterer status, they agreed with sufficient reluctance to satisfy the man that he had wrung concessions.

Then Emily 'happened' to mention that Big Island was now vacant. Paul managed to suppress their relief when he immediately seized on the notion of occupying Avril's former property.

Nabhi said that he wanted the shuttle he had used during the ferrying operation and he specified the personnel who were under his supervision to handle the *Moth*'s recommissioning. He waved aside the fact that those six people were already heavily involved in crucial projects. He would only make the trip if he was satisfied that the long-disused shuttle checked out technically. But the other inducements were his immediately.

He then demanded Bart Lemos as his co-pilot with the condition that Bart was also to receive Charterer status. Paul and Emily found that particularly unpalatable but agreed reluctantly.

His attitude immediately altered towards both Admiral and Governor, becoming so arrogant and pompous that Emily struggled to contain her dislike of the man. His smile of triumph only one degree less than a full sneer, he

337

left their office with the signed Charterer's Warrant. Then he commandeered one of the speed shuttles, although it was needed for an imminent Threadfall, and went to inspect his new acquisition.

The Admiral and the Governor formally announced the venture, its aims and its personnel. This managed to suppress every other topic of interest and news except for the transfer of the twenty-seven mature eggs to their artificial hatching ground.

The full veterinary contingent assisted the biologists in that manoeuvre. Sorka Hanrahan and Sean Connell, in their capacities as advanced veterinary apprentices, had also done some of the early analysis and tedious documentation for the project, working under Kitti Ping's close supervision. It didn't take long to accomplish the transfer but Sorka noticed that the amount of dithering was aggravating her lover. The project meant more to him than his exasperation with worried biologists and he suppressed his irritation. Finally the eggs were placed to the complete satisfaction of Wind Blossom, Pol Nietro and Bay Harkenon-Nietro in a double circle, seventeen on the inner, twenty on the outer, with the warm sand banked high around them to imitate the natural environment of dragonets.

'The whole thing could have been done in a third of the time,' Sean muttered to Sorka, his eyes dark with controlled anger. 'So much fuss is bad for the eggs.' He scowled at the precise circles.

'They're much bigger than I thought they'd be,' Sorka said after a moment's silence.

'Much bigger than *they* thought they'd be,' Sean said in a scoffing tone. 'I suppose we're lucky that so many survived to this stage: a credit to Kitti Ping considering all that had to be done to create them.'

Sorka knew that it meant as much to Sean to be a part of it as it did to her. They had, after all, been the first to discover one of the wild nests. Eager but tired, she was balancing on one of the edging timbers, keeping her feet off the uncomfortably warm sands of the artificial hatching ground, the heat provided by subterranean coils day and night. The biologists hoped that this would reduce the trauma of hatching.

Although the transfer was complete, the helpers had not yet dispersed. Wind Blossom, Pol and Bay were deep in discussions with Phas and the Admiral and Governor who had taken an official part in the removal. Sorka thought that Emily Boll particularly looked drawn and tired but her smile, when displayed, remained warm and genuine. They, too, seemed reluctant to leave.

Most of the Landing population of dragonets had been in and out of the Hatching Ground, darting up to the rafters and vying to find roosting room. They seemed content to watch. None of them had been bold enough to examine the eggs closely. Sorka interpreted their little chirps as reverent, awed.

'Would they know what these are?' she asked Sean softly.

'Do we?' Sean retorted with an amused snort. He had both arms folded across his chest. Now he unlaced one to point to the nearest egg. 'That's the biggest. I wonder if it's one of the golds. I've lost track of which was put where in that dance we just did. There were more males than females among the ones lost and Lili's opened a book on which of us get what.'

Sorka gave the egg a long speculative look. She thought about whether or not it was a gold, and then decided, somewhat arbitrarily in her own mind, that no, it was not. It was a bronze. She did not tell Sean her conclusion. Sean tended to debate such issues and this moment, surveying the first clutch of 'dragons', was not a moment to spoil. She sighed.

Dragonets had become as important to her as horses – only in a different way. She readily admitted that Sean could make his fair behave better than she could hers. He could and did discipline his for effective use during Threadfall. But she knew she *understood* any of them, hers, his or those impressed by anyone else on Pern better than he did.

Or maybe her sensitivity, developed over the last couple of months along with her pregnancy, tended towards maternal caring. Basil Tomlinson had said she was in excellent health and he found nothing in her physical profile to suggest problems. She could continue riding as long as she felt comfortable in the saddle.

'You'll know when you can't ride any more,' he'd told her with a grin. 'And you'll have to curtail ground crew at five months. That's no time for you to be swinging the weight of a flamethrower about for hours on end.'

Sorka had not yet found the proper moment to inform Sean of his impending fatherhood. She fretted about his reaction. They had enough work credits now to make the Killarney holding a substantial one but not with Thread falling. Sean hadn't even mentioned Killarney since the third Fall but that didn't mean he didn't think about it. She saw the faraway look in his eyes from time to time.

She had thought that he'd mention Killarney when his father returned Cricket from his stud duties. But he hadn't. With everyone working double jobs just to keep essential services going, very few people had time to consider private concerns. Sean and Sorka spent what leisure moments they had keeping their horses fit, riding them out beyond the swathe of destruction for an hour's grazing.

The main door opened to admit one of the Security engineers and there was an instant reaction from the gallery of watchers. Sean chuckled softly.

'They don't need a security system in here,' Sean murmured to Sorka. 'C'mon, love, we've got surgery in five minutes.'

Reluctantly, with backward glances at the circles of mottled eggs, the two apprentices went back to work. As they crossed one of the alleys, they had a clear view of the donks slowly moving the *Moth* shuttle into take-off position.

'D'you think they'll make it?' Sorka asked Sean.

340

'They've been busy enough,' he replied sourly. Neither Nabhi Nabol nor Bart Lemos had made themselves popular since their sudden rise to Charterer rank. 'Still, I wouldn't be in their shoes for anything!'

She giggled. 'Spacer Yvonne. You've never told me, Sean, did that help you on the drop?'

He gave her face a long and searching look, a slight smile tugging his lips. Then he put his arm about her and hauled her into his side. 'All I could think about was proving to you I wasn't scared. But by Jays, I was!' Then his expression changed and he halted, turning her roughly to him, both hands feeling across her stomach, pulling the bulky shipsuit taut across her body. His eyes accused her. 'Why didn't you tell me you're pregnant?'

'Well, it's only just been confirmed,' she said defiantly.

'Does everyone else know but me?' He was furious with her; for the first time in their years together, mad *at* her. His eyes were flashing and his hands rested hard athwart her thickening waistline.

'No one knows except Basil and he doesn't have to ground me for another three months,' and she pulled defensively at one hand to make him release her. 'But there's Killarney and I know you think about it . . .'

'Your mother knows?'

'When do I have a chance to see her? She's minding half of Landing's babies as well as my latest brother. Apart from Basil, you're the only one who knows.'

'Sometimes you baffle me, Sorka,' Sean said, his anger abating. He shook his head. 'Why wait to tell me? Killarney's a long way off in our future now. We're committed here. I thought you understood that.' He put both hands on her shoulders now and gave her a stern shake. 'I've wanted to be the father of your children. I want you to have only mine. I want it to be now, too, Sorka love, but I didn't think I had the right to ask you to bring a child into the world the way it is.'

His voice fell into the special tender tone he always used when they were making love.

'No, it's the best time to have a child. Something for both of us to have,' she said. She did not add 'in case' but he knew what she omitted and tightened his hands. His eyes compelled hers to look at him. The fury had been replaced by resolution.

'Immediately after surgery, we're going before Cherry Duff. This is going to be a two-parent child or my name's not Sean Connell!'

Sorka burst out laughing and didn't stop until they reached the surgery shed.

Ongola ended up as arbiter on the reconditioning of the space shuttle *Moth*. Nabhi Nabol drove the refit crew demented, interrupting them at critical moments of repair, demanding to know if that circuit or this segment of hull had been checked. Despite the fact that he had a good working knowledge of the complexities of a shuttle, and sometimes he was right – that was what irked – he delayed more than he assisted.

Bruce Olivine grumbled that the bloody shuttle would never lift because Nabol would never find it reconditioned to his satisfaction and thus would never have to risk his precious neck. The shuttle *Mayfly*, lying next to the *Moth*, had been one of the animal transport ships and Ongola had it sectioned off with offices for himself, Fulmar, and Nabhi with a half dozen comlines so Ongola could handle other commitments while on hand at the shuttle. His office was festooned with probe pics and survey maps, as well as the various launch windows open to Nabhi. Nabhi would often come in and stand in a brooding posture, staring at the orbits, picking at his lower lip. Ongola ignored him.

Actually, Ongola was surprised that the basic condition was surprisingly good: there had been practically no perishing of interior circuits or lines but they all had to be double-checked. In that he agreed with Nabhi. This put quite a burden on Fulmar's team but that was not where he disagreed with the autocratic Nabhi.

'I wouldn't care what he asked me to do,' Fulmar told Ongola, 'if he'd only ask politely. You'd think he was doing *me* a favour. Are you sure he's as good a driver as he thinks he is?'

'He is good,' Ongola reluctantly admitted.

'I'd've preferred the mission in Bonneau's hands,' Fulmar replied, shaking his head sadly. 'But with that big stake, kids and all, I can't fault his refusal. It's just that . ...' He broke off, raising his big, workstained hands in a helpless gesture.

'The mission has got to succeed, Fulmar,' Ongola said, giving the man an encouraging clout on the shoulder, 'and you're the best man to see that it does.'

As the thirteenth week after Threadfall began, there was a shift in the pattern which caught everyone out. The squadron had reached the projected site, 44° South at longitude 16, mainly unoccupied lands, and only the top of the squadron saw Leading Edge. It was well north of their position but the grey shimmering stain on the horizon was all too easily identified.

'Hell and damnation!' Theo Force cried, ramming a call through to Ongola at Landing. 'The damned stuff's shifted north, Zi. We'll need reinforcements.'

'Give me the co-ordinates,' Ongola said, issuing crisp orders and gesturing to Jake to get in touch with Dieter or Boris. 'Go for it. We'll scramble another squadron or two to help. I'll alert Drake.'

Boris was found and made some quick calculations. 'It's going to hit Calusa and Bordeaux. It seems to have shifted north by five degrees. That doesn't make sense. Why on earth would it shift so suddenly?'

There was no answer to his question. Ongola said smoothly. And rang off. 'Have you the week's rota there, Jake? Check where Kwan is today. I'll call Chuck Havers at Calusa.'

Sue answered the phone and, after her initial shock at the news, rallied. 'We've several hours then, don't we?

And it could just miss us? I hope so. I don't know where Chuck is working today. Thank you, Zi. And,' Sue's voice was less assured, 'are you calling Mary Tubberman or should I warn her?'

'We'll send Ned along.' Ongola rang off.

Shunning was all well and good for the offender but very hard on the relatives. Ned was entitled to assist his mother and his younger brothers and sister in fighting Thread. If he chose also to assist his father in this emergency, there would be only family to witness it. Tubberman had been quick to clad his buildings with metal so his stake was as safe as those precautions could make it.

Ongola then contacted Drake and ordered him to avoid the Tubberman's stake house. To do him credit, Drake at first protested that they couldn't leave any Thread on any ground, Shunned or not.

'Ned can protect that much with his mother's help, Drake, but we cannot assist Ted Tubberman.'

'But it's Thread, man.'

'That's an order, man,' Ongola replied in a steely tone.

'Gotcha!'

Ongola then informed Paul Benden and Emily Boll of the pattern's alteration.

'Ezra will say that proves intelligence directs Fall,' Paul remarked to Emily as they conferred.

'It's heads we lose, tails we lose, as far as I can see,' Emily replied, heaving a sigh.

'It's as well we don't have to wait long to find out.' Paul nodded towards the grid where the *Moth* was now undergoing the final countdown. None of the technicians had been allowed to scramble for additional support squadrons. Their assignments on the shuttle had just become all-important.

Following the courtesy now well established, Drake Bonneau checked in at the Havers' stakehold on his way back from End of Fall which had just tipped Bordeaux across the Jordan River. He landed within sight of the Tubbermans' larger home.

'Ned and Mary were out,' Chuck told the squadron leader, 'with flamethrowers and then, for some insane reason, Ted drove them back into the house. There couldn't have been much damage or we'd have seen results.'

'Well, you're all right here,' Drake said heartily.

'The ground crew arrived well in advance. But does anyone know why the pattern's shifted?' Sue asked. Weary with fighting, she needed some spark of reassurance.

'No,' Drake replied cheerfully, 'but we'll probably be told!'

He accepted the refreshing fruit drink the oldest Havers girl brought him and his crew, then said goodbye. Drake had protested Ongola's order to by-pass the Tubberman stake during Fall but, after what the Havers had said about Ted, Drake was curious. In his opinion, all Thread had to be destroyed, even if it fell on a Shunned homesite. Thread didn't care about human conflicts: it ate. Drake did not want to see a little burrow get started because of man-made restrictions.

Therefore, as he took off, he made a leisurely turn right over the Tubberman property. He saw Ned standing on the green patch surrounding the house. Ned waved and gesticulated rather wildly, at which point Drake felt obliged to follow orders and turn northwest towards Landing.

He was having a quick bit to eat in the dining hall before going to the *Moth* when Ned Tubberman found him.

'You saw it, Drake, I know you did. You have to have seen it,' Ned said, excitedly pulling at Drake's sleeve to raise him to his feet. 'C'mon, you have to tell them what you saw.'

Drake pulled his arm free. 'Tell who what?' He forked up another mouthful of the hot food. Thread fighting gave him an incredible appetite.

345

'Tell Kwan, and Paul, and Emily what you saw.'

'I didn't *see* anything!' Then suddenly Drake had a flash of pure recall. Ned standing on a green square, a green square which was surrounded by sorched earth. 'I don't believe what I saw!' He wiped his mouth, chewing absently as he absorbed that recall. 'But Thread had just been across your place and Chuck and Sue saw your father stop you flaming!'

'Exactly!' Ned grinned hugely and again pulled Drake to his feet. This time he succeeded. And began to lead Drake out of the room. 'I want you to tell them what you saw, to corroborate my statement. I don't *know* what Dad's done,' and the grin faded and some of the buoyancy drained from Ned Tubberman, 'he says Shunning works two ways. Mother told me that he locks himself away in his laboratory and he won't let anyone near it. My brothers and sister go over to Sue's all the time but Mother won't leave Dad even if he isn't in the house much. She keeps the place ticking over.'

'Your father's been experimenting with something?' Drake was confused now.

'Well, he's got botanical training. He did say that until help came, the only defence was the planet itself.' Ned slowed his pace. 'And that patch of grass defended itself – somehow – against today's Fall because it's still there!'

Drake did tell Kwan, Paul, Emily, and the hastily summoned Pol Nietro and Bay Harkenon-Nietro. Ned was insistent that he had seen Thread fall on the ground cover plants, had not seen them wither or ingested, that by the time Drake had overflown the stake, there was no evidence that Thread had ever fallen on that rectangle, 12 metres by 20.

'I couldn't hazard a guess as to how he's done it,' Pol finally said, looking at Bay for agreement. She shook her head. 'Maybe he has been able to adapt Kitti Ping's basic program for use on a less complex life form. Professionally I have to doubt it.'

'But I saw it,' Ned insisted. 'Drake saw it, too.'

There was a long silence which finally Emily broke. 'Ned, we do not doubt *you* or Drake's verification but as your father said, Shunning works both ways.'

'Are you too proud to ask him what he's done?' Ned demanded, his skin blanched under his tan, his nostrils flaring with indignation.

'Pride is not involved,' Emily said gently. 'Safety is. He was Shunned because he defied the will of the Colony. If you can honestly say that he has changed his attitude, then we can discuss reinstatement.'

Ned flushed, his eyes dropping away from Emily's tolerant gaze. He sighed deeply. 'He doesn't want anything to do with Landing or anyone in it.' Then he gripped the edge of the table and leaned across it towards the Governor. 'But he's done something incredible. Drake saw it.'

'I did indeed see ground cover where there shouldn't've been any.' Drake conceded that much.

'Could your mother present evidence on his behalf?' Paul asked, seeking an honourable amend for Ned's sake.

'She says he only talks to Petey, and Petey says he's sworn to secrecy so she hasn't pushed him.' Ned's face twisted with anguish for a long moment and then it cleared. 'I'll ask her. I'll ask Petey, too. I can try.'

'This has not been easy for you either, Ned,' Emily said. 'All of us would like to see the matter happily resolved.' She touched his hand where he still gripped the table edge. 'We need everyone right now.'

Ned looked her steadily in the eyes and gave a slow nod. 'I believe you, Governor.'

'Sometimes the duties to which rank entitles me are more than it's worth,' Emily murmured to Paul as the hatch of the shuttle finally closed on Nabhi Nabol and Bart Lemos. She spoke quietly because every young man in Nabhi's squadron had come to wish their leader good luck. She turned and smiled at them, leading the way off the grid

347

to the safer sidelines. And waited dutifully with the technicians for the take-off.

They waited and waited until both Admiral and Governor were giving the meteorology tower anxious scrutiny. Just when both had decided Nabhi was going to renege – as they'd half suspected he would – they heard the roar of ignition and yellow-white flame poured out of the tubes.

'Firing well,' Paul bellowed at her over the noise and she contented herself with a nod as she plugged her ears with her fingers.

She didn't know that much about the mechanics of shuttles but the young men were grinning and waving their arms triumphantly. The look of relief on Fulmar's face was almost comical. Majestically the shuttle began its run up the grid, its speed increasing at a sensational rate. It became airborne, the engines thrusting it in an abrupt but graceful swoop up. The flame became lost in the blue of the sky as they shaded their eyes against the rising sun. Then the white puffy con trail blossomed, billowing out as a tracer for the shuttle's path. The technicians who had made it possible now cheered. Fulmar Stone and Bruce Olivine were clapping each other on the back.

'Gawssakes, but it's good to get a bird up again,' Bruce shouted. 'Hey, what's wrong with them?' he added, pointing to several fairs of dragonets zipping at low level across the grid out of nowhere, creeling with an odd note in their voice.

'Who's having a baby?' Fulmar demanded.

Emily and Paul exchanged glances. 'We are,' she said and slid into the skimmer. 'See? They're going straight to the Hatching Ground.'

Looking up towards Landing, there was no doubt that fairs of dragonets were streaming in that direction so no one lingered on the grid. The roof of the Hatching Ground was covered with the creeling creatures. The cacophony was exciting rather than irritating. When the Admiral and

Governor arrived, they had to make their way through the crowd to the double doors which had been swung wide.

'Welcome in nine-hundred-part harmony,' Emily muttered to Paul as they made it to the edge of the warm sands. There they halted, awed by the sense of occasion within.

Kitti Ping had left explicit instructions on who was to attend this birth day. Sixty young people between the ages of eighteen and thirty, who had already shown a sympathy for the dragonets, had the privilege of standing around the circle of eggs. Wind Blossom, Pol, Bay, Kwan and Basil stood to one side on a wooden platform, their faces flushed and expectant.

The dragonets' song outside remained softly jubilant while the creeling of those who had found roosting space inside was subdued encouragement, almost reverent.

'They can't know what we expect for today, can they, Paul?'

'Young Sean Connell,' and Paul pointed to where the young man stood beside his wife around the eggs, 'would have you believe that they do. But then, they've always been attracted by birthing! After all, they protect their own young against attack.'

A hush swept around the arena and a distinct crack was heard. One of the eggs rocked slightly and drew excited whispers.

Emily crossed her fingers, hiding them in the folds of her trousers. She noticed, with a slight grin, that others were doing the same. So much depended on this today . . . on this first hatching and on what Nabhi Nabol was now committed to do.

Another egg cracked, a third wobbled, activity on all sides. The chorus became beguilingly insistent, striking an excitable chord in everyone watching.

Then all of a sudden, one of the eggs cracked open and a creature emerged, birth damp, shook stubby wings and stumbled over its shell, squawking in alarm. The dragonets

349

answered soothingly. The young people in the circle stood their ground and Emily marvelled at their courage for this creature was not the graceful being she had been expecting, a beast remembered from old legends and illustrations held in library treasuries. She caught herself holding her breath and exhaled quickly.

The creature extended its wings, they were wider, thinner than she'd expected. It was so spindly, ungainly: its very oddly constructed eyes were flashing with red and yellow. Emily felt a flush of alarm. It gave a desperate cry and was answered reassuringly by the multi-voiced choir above. It lurched forward, its voice pleading and then the cry altered, to one of joy, held on a high, sweet note. It staggered another step, falling at the feet of David Caterel who bent to help it. And looked up with eyes wide with wonder.

'He wants me!'

'Then accept him!' Pol bellowed, gesturing for one of the stewards to come forward with a bowl of food. 'Feed him! No, don't anyone else help you. The bond should be made now!'

Kneeling by his new charge, David offered the little dragon a hunk of meat. It bolted that, urgently creeling for more, pushing at David's leg with an imperious head.

'He says he's very hungry,' David cried. 'He's talking to me. In my head! It's incredible. How did she do it?'

'The mentasynth works then,' Emily murmured to Paul who nodded with the air of someone not at all surprised. Emily was.

'Ye gods, but it's ugly,' Paul said in a very low voice.

'You probably weren't much to look at at birth either,' Emily surprised herself by saying and grinned at his quick glance of astonishment.

David coaxed his new friend out of the circle of people and towards the edge of the Hatching Ground, calling for more food. 'Polenth says he's starving.'

Bay had ordered plenty of red meat to be available, of animals that had adapted well to the improved Pernese

350

grasses. The young dragonets would require plenty of boron for growth in their first months. They would absorb it best from the flesh of cattle.

Another egg cracked and a second bronze male made a straight line dash to Peter Semling. A shrill voluntary came from Peter's fair of dragonets. There was a long wait before any more activity. A worried hum developed among the watchers. Then four more eggs abruptly shattered, two with unexpectedly dainty creatures, one golden and one bronze who partnered themselves with Tarrie Chernoff and Shih Lao: the other two were stolid-looking browns who took to Otto Hegelman and Paul Logorides.

'Do they expect them all to hatch today?' Emily asked Paul.

'Let's go around to Pol and Bay,' Paul said. They inched their way to the right, paused to admire David Caterel's bronze who was bolting down hunks of meat so fast he seemed to be inhaling them. David looked ecstatic.

'Well, they could,' Pol told them. He was masking anxiety well. Wind Blossom was not and barely acknowledged the quiet greetings of Admiral and Governor. 'They were engineered within a 36 hour period. The eight which have hatched were from the first and second groups. We might have to wait. In our observations of wild dragonets, we know that laying the eggs can take several hours. I suspect the greens and golds may be like one of the earth vipers which can keep eggs within her body until she finds an appropriate place, or time, to lay them. We know that naturally clutched eggs do hatch more or less simultaneously. This,' and he pointed to the Hatching Ground, 'is a concession to Kitti Ping's reverence for the ancestral species' habitat. Ah, another one's cracking.' He consulted the flimsy in his hand. 'One of the third group!'

'Six males, but only one female,' Bay said quietly. 'To be frank, I'd rather have more females. What do you think, Blossom?' Almost belatedly Bay included the woman in the conversation.

'One perfect male and one perfect female are all we

351

need,' Wind Blossom said, speaking in a tight, controlled voice. She had her hands hidden in her loose sleeves but there were deep tension lines in her face and her eyes were clouded.

'Peter Semling's bronze looks sturdy,' Emily said encouragingly. Wind Blossom did not respond, her gaze was fixed on the eggs. 'Are they as you anticipated?' she asked, looking at Pol and Bay.

'No,' Bay admitted, 'but then it was Kitti who had the requisite image in her mind. If only . . .' She faltered. 'Ah, another gold female. I believe that Kitti Ping made the choices gender imperative. For Nyassa Clissmann. And such charming creatures!'

Emily failed to see charm in the hatchlings but she was glad to see so many live ones. But what had Kitti Ping had in her mind when she altered the dragonet ova? These weren't ethnic dragons of any kind she knew. And yet, they were ineffably dragons, spindly, small, immature as they were. She had an unexpected vision of a sky full of these creatures, soaring and diving, breathing flame. Had Kitti Ping?

'The shuttle? Did I hear it take off?' Pol asked suddenly.

'Yes, he made it,' Paul replied. 'Ongola will keep us informed. We don't have enough fuel for a direct flight. The shuttle'll have to coast a week before it reaches the trail.'

'Oh, I see.' Then Pol refocused his attention on the eggs.

The crowd shifted, some people going back to complete tasks, and others moved in to take their place. Food was brought to the biologists and the leaders on their wooden dais, and wooden benches to sit on. Wind Blossom remained standing. Food, and small platforms, were also taken to the circle of hopeful dragon riders. The dragonets' encouragement did not abate. Emily wondered how they could keep it up.

It was dark before any other movement and then all at once a brown, and two golden females cracked their eggs. Marco Galliani got the brown and Kathy Duff and Nora

Sejby the two golds. There was a good deal of cheering for the activity.

The crowd at the opening thinned, while the dragonets kept their posts and kept up their encouraging creel. Emily was becoming weary and she could see fatigue catching up with the others. She was half-asleep when Catherine Radelin-Doyle impressed her gold.

'Do they always go female to female?' Emily asked Pol, 'male to male?'

'Since the males will be supposed to be fighters, the females egg-carriers, Kitti made it logical.'

'Logical to her,' Emily said, a trifle bemused. 'There aren't any blues or greens among them,' she suddenly realized.

'Kitti programmed the heavier males but I believe they're to carry sperm for the entire range. The greens will be the smallest, the fighters, the blues sturdier with more staying power, the browns sort of anchor-fighters with even more endurance. They'll have to fight four to six hours remember! The bronzes as leaders and the golds—'

'Waiting at home to be egg-carriers.'

Pol gave Emily a long look, his tired face reflecting astonishment at her sarcasm.

'In the wild, greens don't have good maternal instincts. The golds do,' Bay put in, giving the Governor an odd glance. 'Kitti Ping kept as much natural instinct as possible. Or so her program reads.'

'There!' Nabhi said, leaning back from the console, his swarthy face intense with an inner satisfaction. 'Kenjo wasn't the only one who could save fuel.'

Bart gave him a long look, surprised and confused. 'Save it for what, Nabhi?' He spoke more sharply than he meant to but he'd been wound up with tension which wouldn't ease. It wasn't that he didn't trust Nabhi as a pilot. Nabhi was a good driver or Bart wouldn't have been talked into participating in this insane venture, not for the choicest land on Pern.

353

'To manoeuvre,' Nabhi said and the mocking grin on his face did nothing to ease Bart's disquiet.

'Where? You're not . . . you wouldn't be mad enough to try to land on the farking planet?' Bart clawed at the release straps but Nabhi's indolent gesture aborted the effort.

'No way. I came to get the pods or whatever.' His smile then broadened and Bart was amazed at the humour in it. 'Our course is basically the same one Avril took.' He turned his head and looked directly at his co-pilot.

'So?'

'They said the gig blew up.' Nabhi's smile was pure malice. 'Turn on the screens. There might be some interesting flotsam. Diamonds and gold nuggets and whatever else Avril took with her. No one needs to know what else we scooped up out of space.'

By midnight Pol and Bay decided to examine the remaining eggs and slowly did the rounds. Wooden platforms had been brought out for the candidates to rest on, for the heat in the sand was enervating. None of the chosen was willing to forego their chance at impressing a hatchling by leaving the Ground.

When the two biologists returned, Pol was shaking his head and Bay looked drawn. She went immediately to Wind Blossom and touched her arm.

'The rest of the first group show no signs of life. But, already the outcome is better than projected. We detected viable signs in the others. We can but wait. They were not all conceived at the same time.'

Wind Blossom remained an unmoving statue.

Sean nudged Sorka in the ribs to wake her up. She had fallen asleep leaning against him, her cheek against his upper arm. She was instantly alert and aware of her surroundings. Sean pointed to the biggest of the eggs, almost directly in front of them. He had taken this position at the outset. The egg was now rocking slightly.

'What time is it?' she asked.

'Nearly dawn. There's been no other movement. But listen to the dragonets. Listen to Blaze. She'll have no throat left!'

They had noted their own dragonets early during that long day and Sorka had taken heart from their constant choral encouragements.

'That egg over there has been moving spasmodically for the last two hours,' he said in a quiet tone. 'The one beyond it rocked for a while but it's stopped completely.'

Sorka tried to contain a yawn and then gave in to the compulsion, feeling better for it. She wanted to stretch but Betsy Patrick was draped over her legs, fast asleep. Beyond Betsy, Sasha de Poer stirred and sat up, nudging Aliana Zulueta. And so others roused all around the circle.

At some point while Sorka dozed, the Admiral and the Governor had left. Pol and Bay were leaning into each other and Kwan's head was on his chest, arms limp in his lap. Wind Blossom had apparently not moved since she had taken up her watch.

'She's uncanny,' Sorka said, and turned away from the Bio-geneticist.

A single great crack startled everyone and the egg before them parted into two ragged halves. The bronze hatchling walked out imperiously and, lifting his head, made a sound like a stuttering trumpet. Everyone came to attention. Sean was on his feet and Sorka pushed at his legs to make him move forward to attract the beast's attention. She needn't have worried. He and the hatchling locked eyes and Sean groaned in a low incredulous sound, moving forward to meet him halfway. Their fair were bugling with triumph.

'Meat, quickly,' Sorka called, beckoning urgently to a sleepy steward. She hoped the heat in the building had not soured the meat. She ran to meet the man who was not moving fast enough and grabbed the bowl, returning to thrust it into Sean's hands. She had never seen that look in his eyes before, utterly rapt.

'He says his name is Carenath, Sorka. He knows his own name!' Sean transferred food from the bowl into

Carenath's mouth as fast as he could shovel it. 'More meat. Hurry, I need more meat.'

Everyone in the Hatching Ground was wakened by his vibrant voice. Then the other egg broke open and a creeling golden female sauntered forth, looking about her urgently. Sorka was too busy passing bowls of meat to Sean for Carenath to notice until Betsy tugged at her arm.

'She's looking for you, Sorka. Look at her!'

Sorka turned her head and she, too, felt the indescribable impact of a mind on hers, a mind that rejoiced in finding its equal, its lifelong partner. Sorka was filled with an exultation that was almost painful as a soothing presence flowed in.

'My name is Faranth, Sorka!'

17

'We have actually learned a great deal from eggs that didn't hatch,' Pol told Emily and Paul when he, Wind Blossom and Bay made their report two evenings after the first Glorious Hatching Day. Everyone ignored the fact that the last egg had hatched 27 hours after the first.

'So far, so good?' Paul asked hopefully.

'Oh, very good,' Bay said enthusiastically, grinning and nodding her head vigorously. Wind Blossom managed a prim set smile. The air of impenetrable gloom that had surrounded her on the Hatching Day had been exchanged for an aloof superiority. Her insecurities were as forgotten as if her relationship to Kitti Ping now gave her special priorities over all matters draconic – except their physical care.

'Then you do believe that the eighteen hatchlings will all become viable adults?' Paul asked Wind Blossom.

She inclined her head but not in agreement. 'We must await their maturity with patience.'

'But they *will* be able to produce flame from phosphine-bearing rocks, and go *between* as the dragonets do?' Paul asked her.

'I am, myself, much encouraged,' Pol said, when Wind Blossom said nothing. 'Bay is, too, by the way in which mentasynth has provided a strong empathic bond and telepathic communication.'

'A genuine mind-to-mind contact,' Bay added with a

357

smile of satisfaction. 'Especially strong for Sorka and Sean.'

'The dragons were *designed*,' Wind Blossom added pompously, 'to make Impression with other than their own ancestral species. In that much,' and she apparently did not consider this the achievement everyone else did, 'the program has succeeded.' She held up her hand. 'We must contain impatience and strive to achieve the perfect specimen.'

'The stabilization of Impression to another species was the most important aspect,' Pol said, his brows creasing slightly at Wind Blossom's statement. 'After all, the dragonets have teleported as naturally as they breathe.'

'The *dragonets* have,' Wind Blossom laid the emphasis coolly. 'We have yet to see if the dragons can.'

'Kitti Ping did not alter those capabilities, you know. They will, of course, have to be refined and controlled,' Pol went on. Wind Blossom's attitude had an abrasive quality: she refused to concede the triumphs already achieved. 'I must say, I am very glad that the young Connells both Impressed. With their veterinary training, their general competence, not to mention their proven ability to discipline their dragonet fairs, we couldn't ask for better mates.'

Wind Blossom made a slight noise which the listeners took as disapproval.

'They're qualified,' Bay said with unexpected heat. 'Someone must make the beginning.'

'Their progress must be strictly monitored,' Wind Blossom went on, 'so that we will know what mistakes must be avoided the next time.'

'Next time?' Emily blinked in surprise and noticed that Bay and Pol had the same reaction.

'I do not yet know if these creatures will perform on the other design levels, either natural or imposed.' Her sepulchral tone indicated that she had grave doubts.

'How can you not be encouraged . . .' Pol began with some heat.

A decisive gesture of dismissal cut him off and he stared at Wind Blossom.

'I will begin anew,' Wind Blossom informed them in a tone that verged on martyrdom. Pol and Bay regarded her in astonishment. 'With what we learned from the post-mortem examinations, I cannot be sure that any of the living will be fertile or reproduce. More importantly, reproduce themselves! I must try again, and again, until success is assured. This experiment is only begun.'

'But, Wind Blossom . . .' Pol began, astounded by her sudden announcement.

'Come, you shall assist me.' With an imperious gesture, she swept from the room.

Neither Red Hanrahan and Caesar Galliani as veterinarians, nor AC Soper or Phas Radamanth as xenobiologists had any criteria on which to judge the health of eighteen representatives of a new species. But their hearty appetites, the vibrant colour of their suedelike hides and the ease of their physical exertions – mainly eating and exercising their wings – was taken as a measure of well-being. In the first week of life, they grew at least a handspan taller, had filled out; they looked considerably more substantial. And as their transparent wings became more and more evident, those who had worried about their fragility were relieved.

Fascinated, the official medical support group watched now as the two Connells were bathing and oiling their ten-day-old dragons. Large shallow bathing pools of siliplas had been erected near the homes of all the dragon mates. Faranth was being oiled and was coyly aware of the admiring glances.

'She's preening, Dad,' Sorka said, amused as she poured oil on a scaly patch between the dorsal ridges. 'Is that the itchy spot, Farrie?'

My name is Faranth and that is that *itchy spot,* Faranth said in tones that went from reproof to relief. Sorka thought that her voice was oddly familiar, as if heard down a long tunnel or enclosed space. *Another is starting on my hind leg.*

'She doesn't like to be called by a nickname,' Sorka said tolerantly, grinning at her father. 'But Jay, she takes scrubbing.' A bristle brush had also been made, firm enough to rub in oil but not harsh enough to mar the tender, smooth hide.

Suddenly everyone was drenched as Carenath, sweeping his glistening wings forward in the low bath, showered them with water.

'Carenath, behave yourself!' Sorka and Sean spoke in the same sharp tone.

I am already clean, you polka-dotted idiot, Faranth said in an excellent mimicry of one of Sorka's favourite admonitions. *I was nearly dry, and now my oiling has to be done again.*

Sean and Sorka laughed and then hurriedly explained to the drenched men that they were amused by what Faranth had said, not Carenath's playfulness. Sean gestured to the dragonets on the roof-tree where they were obviously watching everything below them. Instantly, the soaked observers had towels dropped about them.

'Handy critters, Sean,' Red Hanrahan said, drying his face and hands and mopping his clothing.

'Very useful with young dragons, too, Red,' Sean replied. 'They fish constantly for these walking appetites.'

Am I that much trouble to you? Carenath sounded aggrieved.

'Not at all, pet,' Sean quickly assured him, lovingly caressing the head tilted wistfully. 'Don't be silly. You're young, you have a good appetite, and it's our job to keep you fed.'

Red was beginning to get accustomed to these sudden *non-sequiturs* from his daughter and son-in-law but the others were startled. Faranth butted at Sorka for reassurance and received it, her eyes settling to the blue of contentment.

360

'Can't they be ridden yet? And hunt for themselves?' AC Sopers asked.

'You don't attempt to ride a foal, even a good big one,' Sean replied, brushing oil on the rough patch on Carentha's broad back. 'Kitti Ping's program suggests a full calendar year before we attempt it.'

'Can we wait long enough for them to mature?'

Threadfall and the need to fight it was never far from anyone's mind.

'I've never rushed a horse,' Sean said, 'and I'm not about to start with my dragon. However, at the rate they're growing, and if we can be sure that their skeletal structure – it's boron-silicate, you know, which is tougher than our calcareous material – I think they'll be capable of . . .' and Sean grinned wryly, 'manned flight as scheduled. Jays, what times we'll have then, old fella, won't we?'

The tenderness, the concern, the deep affection in Sean's voice was almost embarrassing to hear. Red looked at his son-in-law with surprise. So Impression had had an effect on young Connell as well. He didn't perceive much in his daughter but she'd always been caring and capable. She appeared somehow strengthened, and exuded a radiance that couldn't all be attributed to her pregnancy.

Young David Caterel had altered in the most spectacular way. Badly scarred physically as well as mentally by Lucy Tubberman's tragic death in First Fall, the young man had retreated into a wallow of self-disgust and needless guilt. Not even intensive therapy by Tom Patrick could break through the stubborn façade. David fought Thread with a vindictive intensity that was frightening to watch. Until he had seen how useful dragonets were in ground crewing, Dave had only tolerated their wistful affection.

The renaissance of his personality began the moment Polenth nudged his knee. An openly smiling, ecstatic David Caterel had left the hatching sands, solicitously and deftly assisting the staggering little dragon. Red had noticed other felicitous changes, though Catherine Radelin-

Doyle's tendency to giggle at some unheard comment from her golden mate could be disconcerting. Shih Lao who had Impressed bronze Firth also went about with smiles on his once pensive face, Tarrie Chernoff had stopped apologizing for any minor accident or inconsistency, and Otto Hegelman's stutter had completely disappeared.

'They're credits to you both,' Caesar said to Sean and Sorka, 'though Marco's Duluth, if I say so myself, looks equally as well.'

Sean grinned at the Roma Stakeholder. 'He does, indeed. As long as they're eating, sleeping . . .'

'Being bathed, cosseted, oiled and scratched, they have *nothing* to complain of,' Sorka finished, giving Faranth's nose a final swipe. 'There now, love, why don't you curl up and go to sleep?'

Carenath's not finished, Faranth complained even as she was moving to the sunwarmed plascrete she preferred as her couch. *I like him to lean against. I'm a little hungry.*

Sorka put her fingers between her front teeth and gave a piercing whistle. The dragonets instantly disappeared.

All clean, Carenath cried, hopping out of the bath. Warned by Sean, he did not shake himself all over his audience. Carefully he extended his wet glistening wings, holding them aloft in the slight breeze while Sean, and Sorka, mopped his underparts dry.

'D'you need anything, Sean, while we're here?' Red asked.

'Nope,' Sean half-grunted as he bent to dry the claw sheaths. That was one of the few physical modifications that Kitti Ping had made from dragonet to dragon. More useful, she had thought, for grabbing running animals than the dragonets' pincer type arrangement. 'As soon as they've had their snack, we'll have one, too.'

'Amazing couple,' Phas Radamanth said, smiling up at Red. 'Now if that bronze is fertile, and the gold willing, we'll have our next generation.'

'Let's not rush too far ahead in our hopes,' AC Sopers

said, looking back over his shoulder at the scene. 'Wind Blossom strongly advocates caution about this first batch.'

'Her *mother* bio-engineered them.' Phas spoke firmly, stopping in his tracks.

'Well, she also produced imperfect ones that didn't hatch.'

'Eighteen was a very good result, and we learned a great deal from dissecting the aborts,' Phas said.

They were just turning away when the air was full of dragonets, each carrying a fair-sized packtail in its claws. The dragons merely lifted their heads, opened their mouths, and took the offerings as rightful homage. The three men grinned and continued their morning round.

Once Faranth and Carenath had their snack, they were quite willing to curl up together, Carenath with his triangular head neatly placed on his outstretched forelegs. Faranth draped herself head and neck over his forequarters, her tail twitching occasionally just in front of his muzzle, her wings sagging slightly from their folded position on her back. Both freshly oiled hides gleamed in the sun.

'I will be glad when they *can* hunt for themselves,' Sean murmured to Sorka as they wearily settled on the ground in the shade of the east wall of their home.

'Meanwhile,' Sorka said, reaching for a water jar, 'we couldn't manage it without the fair.' She sent strong feelings of gratitude to Duke, Emmett, Blazer and the others. Their response, muted in deference to the somnolent dragons, was clearly 'You're welcome.'

'The requirements of dragons were never once considered by Landing's architects,' Sean remarked as he took the water jar in turn. Washing dragons was thirsty business. 'When they get bigger, something will have to be done. There aren't enough places to house people in Landing any more, much less dragons.'

'D'you think they'd be comfortable in some of Catherine's caves? She mentioned it again yesterday.'

'Yes, so she did. Then she giggled.'

363

The two Connells exchanged amused and tolerant grins. The human dragonmates had abruptly found themselves a group set apart, by occupation and dedication, as well as the subtler changes within each person. Though they had the unqualified support and help of every member of the medical, veterinary, and biological teams, they found that talking minor problems over among themselves brought better results. One had to *be* a dragonmate to appreciate the problems – and joys!

Sorka noted with quiet pride that it was Sean's opinion which seemed to be sought most frequently by the others. And she agreed. He had always been sensible about . . . she couldn't call 'dragons' animals. They were too . . . human. Carenath's voice was actually a tunnel-like version of Sean's light baritone. She suspected that Faranth sounded a lot like her.

From the moment they had brought the two hatchlings to Irish Square, Sorka realized that she heard both Faranth and Carenath, an unenviable gift. Sean, however, did not hear Faranth. That Sorka could did not distress either dragon. They were amenable to everything in life as long as they had full bellies and oiled hides. Fortunately, as Sean's bond with the bronze developed, Sorka heard fewer private exchanges. She had also learned, as she suspected each dragonmate had, to 'think' on a private band.

'I'd say they'll be ready to hunt in another week or two – if we can use a small corral to pen the beasts.' Sean found her hand and squeezed it, then laid his hand over her belly. 'All this won't harm our child, will it?'

Sorka felt guilty. Lately, she hadn't had time to think about her condition: there was always something to be done for Faranth, or one of the other young dragons. And they were still on duty at the dragonet clinic.

'Basil said I was healthy and could ride . . .' Sorka groaned. 'Will *we* be able to teach them – to fly *between*, Sean?' Her voice was low, and she clutched his hand apprehensively.

'Now, dear heart, we'll be able for what we have to

do.' The unknown clearly did not faze Sean these days.

'But, Sean—'

'If *we* know where we're going, *they* will. They'll see it in our minds. They see everything else. What makes you think directions will be difficult?'

'But we don't even know how the dragonets do it?'

Sean shrugged, grinning down at her. 'No, we don't. But if the fire-lizards are capable of the teleportation, the dragons will be, too. Kitti Ping did not tamper with that area of the cortex. Let's not fret ourselves. We won't fret them.'

She eyed him sourly, then shook her finger at him. 'Then *you* stop worrying about it!'

Laughing, his blue eyes sparkling at her shrewd hit, he took her hand and pulled her into his embrace. She nestled there, taking strength from him, and returning it. Although Sorka had never before felt so in charge of herself, so dynamic, there were moments when she was assailed with the fear that she might fail Faranth in some small but essential way.

'No, you won't,' Sean said, smoothing her sweat-damp hair back from her face. 'No more will I Carenath. They're ours and we belong to them.' He turned her face up to his, his eyes so intense with love and assurance that her breath caught. Sean embraced her again tightly. 'Ever since we dropped to this planet, Sorka, this has been our destiny. Or why else were we the first to find the fire-lizards? Out of all the people exploring the world, why did the fire-lizards come to us? Why did the last of Kitti Ping's creation search *us* out of the crowd? No, believe in yourself, in us and our dragons.' He held her a moment longer and then released her. 'I think we have to give Cricket and Doove to your father. Brian gets along with Cricket very well.'

Sorka had known that some decision had to be made about their horses. Doove, and even the brave stallion, had been terrified of the wobbling dragons. Red and Brian had taken the horses up to the main veterinary barn. Sorka thought of all the grand moments she'd had on the bay mare's back, most of them shared with Sean and Cricket.

'Yes,' she heard herself saying with no further twinge of regret, 'I never thought there'd come a day when I wouldn't have time for horses.' She looked lovingly at the sleeping figure of Faranth and grinned at the bulge in the golden belly which would all too quickly disappear. 'I'll fix us something to eat.'

He kissed her on the forehead. His willingness to display affection now was one of the fringe benefits from Carenath. Sean's alteration was so subtle she was sure that she alone was aware of it. She loved him even more now. She leaned against him, inhaling a manly smell mixed with the herbal dragon oil.

'Make sandwiches, love,' Sean advised. 'Here comes Dave Caterel at the trot. If Polenth's asleep, the others will be along, too.'

'They've got it,' Ongola informed Paul when he answered the comunit in Emily's quarters. He was in anticipation of one of Pierre's excellent dinners. Emily had taken pity on him as Ju had gone back to check on their Boca holding the previous day. And that was another matter that would have to be faced soon. Ban Larr and Mahmoud were doing as much as they could at Boca but, in just three months, the jungle was already encroaching on what they had tediously cleared. 'Nabhi just called in. Bart Lemos got a scoop full. Although . . .'

'Although what?' Paul asked, exchanging glances with Emily.

'Although it took them a long time,' Ongola finished on a troubled sigh. 'They should have been well up in the trail before now.' Ongola sounded puzzled. 'They have what we need, that's the important thing: the pods. The fax are being relayed to the interface right now. Ezra and Jim should have an analysis some time tomorrow.'

'Are you still at the *Moth*?' Paul asked, frowning. Ongola was not completely recovered from his injuries and Paul was proprietary in his concern for him. Ongola would be a key man in the coming struggle of autonomy and survival.

'Yes, but Sabra's brought me dinner.' Ongola was indulging in one of his rare chuckles as he signed off.

'They've got what we need,' Paul told Emily as he reseated himself. 'Now I can enjoy this dinner.'

The first rumblings occurred the next morning, early enough to rattle many people in their beds. Only the young dragons were unperturbed, sleeping through the commotion made by excited, frightened humans.

'Will this planet never let up on us?' Ongola demanded as he untangled himself from his bedsack and fumbled for the comunit set.

'Was that an earthquake?' Sabra asked sleepily. She'd left the children with Theo so she and Ongola could have a few hours together. Sabra felt she needed that comfort almost as much as Ongola must. And she'd signed on a Charter promising order and tranquillity!

'Go back to sleep,' Ongola told her as he dialled. 'What does Patrice say, Jake?' he asked his efficient assistant, certain of receiving a succinct answer.

'He says the gravity meters have all been registering a disturbance in lava chambers along the Island ring. He doesn't know what's going to blow, but the display suggests that something has to. He's trying to guess the most likely escape point.'

Ongola grunted and, putting that direct link to the Met Tower down, picked up the handset that connected him with Paul's home.

'No rest for the weary, huh?' Paul asked in a resigned tone.

'Volcanic disturbance all along the chain.'

'Chain, my foot! That rumble was right under my ear, Ongola, and we do have three volcanoes looming over us.'

Ongola was so accustomed to the great peaks that he

had forgotten that they, also, could pose a threat though experts had all agreed that the last eruption of Mount Garben had occurred a millenium ago.

By mid morning Patrice relieved the worst fears by his announcement that a new volcano was erupting out of the sea beyond the eastern tip of Jordan Province. Young Mountain which had been monitored for the past eight years was throwing up a cloud of smoke, gas and some ash but magma pressure did not seem to be building there.

A second underground churning startled people mid-afternoon. When Patrice arrived, parking his sled in the Administration Square, an anxious crowd quickly gathered to hear the result of that meeting. Finally Paul and Emily appeared on the porch with Patrice who was smiling and waving fax in both hands.

'A new volcano to be named. Like Aphrodite rising from the sea, but I don't necessarily insist on that name,' he shouted.

'Where?'

'Beyond the easternmost tip of Jordan, safely away from us, my friends.' Now he held up the largest photo so that the roiled seas and the protruding tip of the smoking peak could be seen by all.

'Yeah, but that's still the same little tectonic plate we're on, isn't it?' Blackie Nilwan shouted, pushing through. He pointed back, over his shoulder at the lofty peak of Mount Garben. 'That one could go again. Couldn't it?'

'Of course it could,' Patrice answered swiftly, shrugging his shoulders. 'But it is very unlikely in my opinion. It shot its head off thousands of years ago. There has been no evidence of activity here. It's an old one, that volcano. The young ones have more to say, and are saying it. Do not panic. We are safe at Landing.'

All through the day there were sporadic growlings, as Telgar called them. Wandering at random through Landing, he had made himself available to anyone who wished to be reassured. It was the first time since Sallah's death that Telgar had circulated socially. That night, a large proportion of Landing's population gathered in Bonfire Square and the blaze was built up to an unusual, almost defiant size.

'Our beautiful Pern has popped a pimple on her face,' Telgar said with a hint of his former joviality, talking to a group of young people. 'She's not so old that her digestion is perfect. And we have been disturbing her with our borings and diggings.'

When he moved off, young Fritz Fremlich followed him.

'Look, Tar-Telgar,' he began in his earnest fashion, 'we're not on basement rock here in Landing.'

'That is very true,' Telgar replied with just a slight smile for the impudence of an apprentice geologist. 'Which is why we are rocking a little. But I am not concerned.'

Fritz flushed but he could be as dogged as his father. 'Well, there's a wide, long strip of basement rock in the northern continent, along the western mountain range.'

'Ah, how well you have studied your lessons, Fritz,' Telgar agreed. He nodded his head equably as Cobber Alhinwa and Ossie Munson joined him. 'Ah, have a glass with us.'

Embarrassed now by having stated the obvious, Fritz hastily excused himself.

'So people are talking of basement rock,' Cobber said, and beside him Ossie smirked.

'I know, you know, and he knows but we have had enough of insecurity today. The basement rock will not shift. As you know, I have given my opinion to Paul, Emily and Patrice.' Telgar looked beyond the big miner, to a distance only his eyes saw but Cobber and Ossie exchanged meaningful glances. The set, pained look on Telgar's face meant he was remembering something about Sallah who was never far from his thoughts at any time.

Cobber nudged Ossie and propped his elbows on the table, leaning conspiratorially towards Telgar.

'Are we all to go look at some basement rock now, Telgar?'

*

The next morning a rumble of a different kind finally roused Paul as Ju reached across him for the handset which Paul had cunningly stuffed in his bedside drawer.

'For you,' she mumbled sleepily, dropping it on the bedsack and rolling over again.

Paul fumbled for it, got it to his ear. 'Benden.' He cleared his throat.

'Admiral,' Ongola said, urgently, 'they've begun re-entry and Nabhi's on a bad re-entry course.'

Paul pulled loose the fasteners of the bedsack and sat bolt upright on the bed.

'How could he be?'

'He says he's green, Admiral.'

'I'm coming.' Paul had an irrational desire to slam the handset down and go back to sleep beside his wife. Instead he dialled Emily who said she would join him at the Met Tower. Then he alerted Ezra Keroon and Jim Tillek.

'Paul?' Ju asked sleepily, roused by his terse requests.

'Sleep on, honey. Nothing to worry you.' He had tried to keep his voice low.

In the second semester of a new pregnancy, Ju needed more sleep. They had talked late the previous night, regretfully aware that they must set the example and close down their Stake. The constant drain of Threadfall was having a devastating effect on supplies and resources. Joel particularly fretted over the dwindling efficiency of the power packs. The psychological profile of Landing's population in Tom Patrick's report was, in the main, encouraging, although therapy and medication were increasingly required to keep distressed people functioning. Somehow Paul could not bring himself to hope that Nabhi Nabol and Bart Lemos had brought back something as vital as encouragement.

Yesterday Ezra and Jim had produced the latest analysis of the eccentric's orbit. It was as wayward, in Jim Tillek's phrasing, as a drunken whore on a Saturday night at a space facility in the Asteroid Belt. What had looked to be a reasonable, predictable elliptical orbit through Rukbat's system proved to be even more bizarre, at an angle to the ecliptic. The planet would wobble into the vicinity of Pern every 250 years, though Ezra had made extrapolations that provided some variations of its course, due to the effect of other planets in the system. During some of its orbits, it, and its cloud of junk, would 'miss' Pern.

'The most singular planet I've ever tried to track,' Ezra had said, scratching his head, his manner apologetic, as he summed up his report.

'Natural orbit?' Jim had asked, with a sly grin at the astronomer.

Ezra gave him a long scornful look. 'There's nothing natural about that planet.'

Although Thread had shifted 5° to the north in this third round of falls, the Admiral no longer held much hope for Ezra's theory that the falls were deliberate, a softening up procedure by some sentient agency. If that had been the case, he argued, the falls ought to have accelerated in frequency and density after the wild planet swung to its nearest spatial point to Pern. But Thread had continued to drop in mindless patterns, each now consistent with the northern shift. Mathematical calculations, checked and double-checked by Boris Pahlevi and Dieter Clissmann, concurred with Ezra's depressing conclusion. The eccentric would swing away from Pern and the inner system, only to swing back again in 250 years.

The fax Bart had flashed back to Pern had shown the trail of debris to be endless.

'All the way to the edge of the system,' Ezra declared in total capitulation. 'The planet pierces the Oort cloud and drags the stuff down with it. Hoyle and Wickramansingh's theory has been vindicated in the Rukbat system.'

'Aren't we lucky?' Jim added. 'The junk could still be just ice and rock. We won't know for sure until we see what Bart Lemos scooped up out there.' Jim was not at all happy that his theory was right. He would almost prefer a sentient intelligence somehow surviving on the eccentric planet. You could usually deal with intelligence. His theory made it tough on Pern.

In the cold light of a new morning, Paul dressed quickly, toeing his feet into his boots and closing the front of his shipsuit. He combed his hair neatly back and then stumbled into the pre-dawn light. He used the skimmer – it would be quieter than him puffing and jogging down to the Tower. He tried to practise what he preached in matters of conservation but this morning he didn't wish to be heard passing by.

The last few days, with the *Moth* overdue, had been hard on him. Waiting had never been his forte. Decision and implementation were where he shone. Emily had proved once again the staunch, unswerving, resolute Governor of herself and her subordinates. She was the best sort of complement to his strengths and flaws.

He saw lights over in Irish Square and, through the lines of dwellings, he caught a glimpse of fluttering wings and muted creelings as the young Connells gave their dragons the early morning meal. In the next Square, Dave Caterel was up, too, feeding his young bronze.

At the thought of those young people committed to survival on Pern, Paul felt a sudden surge of confidence that he and Emily would bring everyone through. By all that was holy, they would! Hadn't he gone through bleaker days before the Battle at Purple Sector? And Emily had been blockaded for five years, emerging with a healthy functioning population despite shortage of raw materials.

The Tower was still dark as Paul parked his skimmer behind it. The windows were shuttered but the main door was ajar. He went up the stairs as quietly as he could. These days, with dormitories crowded, off-duty communications personnel slept on the ground floor. Crowded with refugees, Paul made himself add. People had even begun to make homes out of some of the Catherine Caves. An atavistic urge but caves *were* Threadproof, and some of them downright spacious. Caves might be

372

a good place to lodge the fast-growing dragons, too.

As Paul reached the top floor, his eyes went immediately to the big screen which showed the *Moth*'s position above Pern, relayed from the moon installation.

'He has not corrected his course once,' Ongola said, swinging his chair towards Paul when he saw him. He motioned for Jake to vacate the second console chair. Young Chernoff's eyes were black holes of fatigue but Paul knew better than suggest that Jake stand down until the shuttle was safely landed. 'He ought to have fired ten minutes ago. *He* says he doesn't need to.'

Paul dropped to the chair and toggled in the comunit. 'Tower to Moth, do you read me? Benden here. Moth, respond.'

'Good morning, Admiral Benden,' was Nabhi's prompt and insolent reply. 'We are on course and re-entering at a good angle.'

'Your instrumentation is giving you false readings. Repeat, you are getting false readings, Nabol. Course correction essential.'

'I disagree, Admiral,' Nabhi replied, his tone jaunty. 'No need to waste fuel! Our descent is on the green.'

'Correction, *Moth*! Your descent is red and orange across our board and on our screen. You have sustained instrument malfunction. I will give you the readings.'

Paul Benden read the numbers off from the calculator pad Ongola gave him. He was sure he heard a startled gasp in the background.

But Nabhi was undisturbed by Paul's information, and he did indeed report readings consonant with a good re-entry.

'I don't believe this,' Ongola said. 'He's coming in from the wrong quadrant, at too steep an angle, and he's going to crash smack in the centre of the Island Ring Sea. Soon.'

'Repeat, *Moth*, your angle is wrong. Abort re-entry. Nabol, take another orbit. Sort yourself out. Your instruments are malfunctioning.' Fardles, if Nabol couldn't feel the wrongness of that entry, he was nowhere near the driver he thought himself to be.

'I'm captain of this ship, Admiral,' Nabol snapped back. 'It's your screen that's malfunctioning . . . Whaddya say, Bart? I don't believe it. You've got to be wrong. Give it a bang! *Kick it!*'

'Yank your nose up and fire a three-second blast, Nabol!' Paul cried, his eyes on the screen and the speed of the incoming shuttle.

'I'm trying. Can't fire. No fuel!' Sudden fear made Nabol's voice shrill.

Paul and Ongola heard Bart's inarticulate cries in the background.

'I told you it felt wrong. I told you! We shouldn't've . . . I'll jettison. They'll have that much,' Bart shouted. 'If the farking relay'll work.'

'Use the manual jettison lever, Bart,' Ongola yelled over Paul's shoulder.

'I'm trying, I'm trying . . . She's heating up too fast, Nabhi. She's heatin . . .'

Horrified, Paul, Ongola and Jake watched the dissolution of the shuttle. One stubby wing sheered off and the shuttle began to spin. The tail section broke off and spun off on a different route, burning up in the atmosphere as the second wing did.

'It'll hit the sea?' Paul asked in a bare whisper, trying to calculate the impact of that projectile on land. Ongola nodded imperceptibly.

Like an obituary, the relay screen lit up with a glorious sunlit spread of many bits and one larger object, disappearing into many faint pricks of glitter.

Dolphineer Ben Byrne sent a team out to the Ring Sea to find the wreck. Maxmillian and Teresa reported back a week later, tired and not too happy to tell humans that they had seen the twisted hulk wedged into a reef in waters too deep for them to examine closely. All the dolphins were still searching the Ring Sea for the jettisoned scoop.

'Tell them not to bother,' Jim Tillek muttered dourly. 'There's unlikely to be anything left to analyse. We know that the junk goes back in a years' long tail. We're stuck with it. Hail Hoyle and Wickramansingh!'

'Ezra?' Emily asked the solemn astronomer. Keroon's butterscotch-coloured skin seemed tinged with grey and he looked bowed by his responsibilities. He heaved a heavy, weary sigh and scratched at the back of his head. 'I have to concede that Jim's theory is correct. The contents of the pod would have been the final proof but I, too, doubt the scoop survived and the energies of our dolphin friends are needed elsewhere. It could take years to find it in such a vast area. Years also apply to that trail, I fear.' Ezra's expression mirrored his words. 'We won't be able to judge until the end of that tail comes in sight.'

'And where does that leave us?' Paul asked rhetorically.

'Coping, Admiral, coping!' was Jim Tillek's proud reply. With a twitch of his sturdy shoulders, he had thrown off his doomsday expression and now challenged them all. 'And we've Thread falling in two hours so we'd better stop worrying about the future and attend to the present. Right?'

Governor Emily Boll looked at Admiral Paul Benden and managed a tentative smile which she also turned on Zi Ongola who was watching them impassively.

'Right! We'll cope.' She spoke in a firm, resolute voice. Surely we can hold out for ten years, she thought to herself, if we're very careful. She wondered no one else mentioned the dratted homing capsule. Perhaps because no one had much faith in Ted Tubberman. 'We've got to.'

'Until those dragons start earning their keep,' Paul said, 'but this settlement must be restructured.' Emily and he had been discussing redispositions for days. They'd been waiting for the right moment to broach the subject to the others of the informal Landing Council.

'No,' Ongola said, surprising everyone, 'we must re-settle completely. Landing is no longer viable. It used to be sort of a link with our origins. With the ships that

375

brought us here. We no longer require that sense of continuity.'

'And most especially,' Jim picked up the thoughts, 'not with volcanoes popping up and spouting off in this vicinity.' Jim shifted in his chair, settling in to discuss basics. 'I've been listening to what people are saying. So has Ezra. Telgar's notion about moving to that cave system on basement rock in the north is gaining strength. The cave complex is big enough to house Landing's population, plus dragons! We're not out of raw materials to make plastic and metal for housing. But making it takes time away from the essential task of fighting Thread and keeping us alive. Why not use a natural structure? Use our technology to make the cave system comfortable, tenable and totally safe from Thread?'

Emily didn't so much as hesitate to take breath. 'Just what Paul and I have been discussing. There's enough fuel, I believe, to transport some of the heavier equipment by shuttle. Then we can use the metal *in situ*. Jim, the Pern Navy is about to be commissioned.'

Paul grinned at Emily. It was much easier when people made up their own minds to do what their leaders had decided was best for them.

PART III

●

Crossing

18

'Holiest of holies,' was Telgar's respectful murmur as he held high his torch and still could not illuminate the ceiling. His voice started echoes in the vast chamber that repeated and repeated down side corridors until finally the noise was absorbed by the sheer distance from its source.

'Oh, I say, mate, this is one big bonzo cave,' Ozzie Munson said, keeping his voice to a whisper. His eyes were white and wide in his tanned, wind-seared face.

Cobber Alhina who was rarely impressed by anything was equally awed. 'A bleeding beauty!' His whisper matched Ozzie's.

'There are hundreds of ready-made chambers in this complex alone,' Telgar said. He was unfolding the plas-sheet on which he, and his beloved Sallah, had recorded their investigations of eight years ago. 'There are at least four openings to the cliff top which could be used for air circulation. Channel down to water level and install pumps and pipe – I came across big reservoirs of artesian water. Core down to the thermal layer and, big as it is, this whole complex could be warmed in the winter months.' He turned back to the opening. 'Block that up with native stone and this would be an impregnable fort. No safer place on this world during Threadfall. Further along the valley, there are surface-level caves near that pasture land. Of course, it would have to be seeded but we still have the alfalfa-grass propagators that were brought for the first year.

'At the time there was no need to investigate thoroughly but the facilities exist. As I recall when we overflew the range above us, we discovered a medium-sized caldera, well pocked with small caves, about a half-hour's flight from here. We didn't think to mark whether it was accessible at ground-level. It might be ideal for dragon quarters, so accessibility isn't a problem, provided they do fly as well as dragonets.'

'We seen a couple old craters like that,' Ozzie said, consulting a battered notebook which habitually lived in his top pocket. 'One on the east coast and one in the mountains above the three drop lakes when we was prospecting for metal ores.'

'So,' Cobber began, having recovered from his awe, 'the first thing is cut steps to this here level.' He walked to the edge of the cave and looked down critically at the stone face. 'Maybe a ramp, like, to move stuff up here easy like. That incline over there's near a staircase already,' he pointed to the left-hand side. 'Steps neat as you please up to the next level.'

Ozzie dismissed his notions. 'Naw, those Landingers will want their smartass engineers and arki-tects to fancify it with the proper mod cons.'

Alhinwa settled a helmet on his head, switching on its light. 'Yeah, else some poor buggers get all closet-phobic—'

'Claustrophic, you iggerant digger,' Ozzie corrected him.

'Whatever. Inside's safest with that farking stuff dropping on ya alla time. C'mon, Oz, let's go walkabout. The Admiral and the Governor are counting on our expertise, y'know.'

He gave an involuntary grunt as he settled the heavy cutter on his shoulder and strode purposefully towards the first tunnel. Ozzie put on his own helmet, picked up a coil of rope, pitons, and rock hammer, gear that hadn't altered much in centuries, except for the indestructible material it was made of. He already had thermal and ultra-violet recorders, comunit and other mining handunits attached to hooks on his belts. Lastly, he slung one of the smaller rock-cutters over his shoulder.

'Let's go test some claustrophia. We'll start left, right? I'll give ya a holler in a bit, Telgar.'

Cobber had already disappeared in the first of the left-hand openings as Ozzie followed him. Alone, Telgar stood for a long moment, eyes closed, head back, arms slightly away from his body, his palms turned outward in supplication. He could hear the slight noises of disturbed creatures, the distorted murmur of low conversations from Ozzie and Cobber as they made their way past the first bend in the tunnel.

There was nothing of Sallah here. Even the place where they had built a tiny campfire had been swept bare to the fire-darkened stone. Yet here she had offered herself to him and he had not *known* what a gift he had received that night!

The sudden high-pitched keening of the stone-cutter shattered all thought and sent Telgar about the urgent business of making this natural fort into a human habitation.

The hum roused Sorka, and she tried to find a more comfortable position for her cumbersome body. Shards, but she'd be everwhelmingly grateful when she could finally sleep on her stomach again. The humming persisted, a subliminal sound that made a return to sleep impossible. She resented the noise because she wasn't sleeping at all well these last few weeks and needed all she could get. Irritably, she stretched out and twitched aside the curtain. It couldn't be day already. Startled, she clutched the edge of the curtain because there was light outside her house – the light of many dragon-eyes, sparkling in the pre-dawn gloom.

Her exclamation disturbed Sean who stirred beside her, one hand reaching for her. She evaded it, shaking his shoulder urgently.

'Wake up, Sean. Look!' Whatever way she turned, she received a sudden stab of pain in her groin so unexpected she hissed.

Sean was bolt upright beside her, arms about her. 'What is it, love? The baby?'

'It can't be anything else,' she said, laughter bubbling out of her as she pointed out the window. 'I've been warned!' And she could not stop giggling. 'Go look, Sean. Tell me if the fire-dragonets are roosting! I wouldn't want them to miss this, any of them.'

Grinding sleep out of his eyes, Sean struggled to alertness. He half-glared at her for ill-timed levity which turned abruptly into another hissing intake of breath as a second painful spasm rippled across her distended belly.

'It's time?' He ran one hand caressingly across her stomach, his fingers instinctively settling on the band of contracting muscle. 'Yes, it is. What's so funny?' he added. She couldn't quite see his face in the dim light but he sounded so solemn, almost indignant.

'The welcoming committee, of course! All of them. Faranth, love, are all present and accounted for?'

We are here, Faranth said. [*Where we should be. You are amused.*]

'I am very amused,' Sorka started to say but another contraction caught her and she clutched at Sean. 'But that was not at all amusing. You'd better call Greta.'

'Shards, we don't need her. I'm as good a midwife as she is,' he muttered, shoving feet into the shoes under their bed.

'For horses, cows and nanny goats, yes, Sean, but it is expected for humans to assist humans . . . oooooh, Sean, these are very close together.'

He rose to his feet, pausing to throw the top blanket across his bare shoulders against the early morning's chill, when there was a discreet knock at the door. He cursed.

'Who is it?' he roared, not at all pleased if someone was going to call him out on a veterinary emergency right then.

'Greta!'

Sorka started to laugh again, which became very difficult to do all of a sudden and she switched to the breathing she'd been taught, clutching at her great belly.

'How under the suns did you know, Greta?' she heard Sean ask, his voice reflecting his astonishment.

'I was summoned,' Greta said with great dignity, gently pushing him to one side.

'By whom? Sorka only just woke up,' Sean replied, following Greta back to their room. 'She's the one who's having the baby.'

'Not always the first to know when labour commences,' Greta was saying in the very calm, almost detached manner she had learned from Dr Basil. 'Not in Landing. And certainly not with a queen dragon listening in on your mind.' She flicked on the lights as she entered the room and deposited her midwifery bag on the dresser. She had been a gangly girl who had turned into a rangy woman, with hair and skin the same coffee colour and a dusting of freckles across the bridge of her nose. Her eyes were very brown in her kindly face, missing few details.

'Faranth told you?' Sorka was astonished. A dragon speaking to someone outside of their group was unheard of.

'Not exactly,' Greta replied with a chuckle. 'A fair of fire-dragonets flew in my window and made it remarkably plain that I was needed. Once I got outside, it wasn't hard to figure out whose baby was coming. Now, let me see what's going on here.'

I told them to get her, Faranth told Sorka in a smugly complacent tone of voice. *You like her.*

As Sorka lay back for Greta's examination, she tried to figure that out. She liked Basil, too, and had no qualms about him attending her delivery. How had Faranth sensed that she really had wanted Greta in attendance? Could Faranth possibly have sensed that she had always been friendly with Greta? Or was it some connection the golden dragon had made because Sorka had assisted Greta in Mairi Hanrahan's latest, Sorka's newest baby brother? But for Faranth to recognize an unconscious preference . . .

Sean slid cautiously on to the other side of the bed and reached for her hand. Sorka gave him a squeeze, laughter still bubbling up in her. She had so hated the last few weeks, when her body had not seemed hers with all controls assumed by the bouncing, kicking, impertinent restless foetus that gave her no rest at all. Her laughter was sheer elation that all *that* was nearly over.

'Now, let me have a look . . . another contraction?'

Sorka concentrated on her breathing but the spasm was far more painful than she had anticipated. Then it was gone, pain and all. She felt sweat on her forehead. Sean blotted it gently.

You are hurting? Faranth's voice became shrill.

'No, no, Faranth. I'm fine. Don't worry!' Sorka cried, though shouting was difficult with the mass sitting on her diaphragm.

'Faranth's upset?' Keeping her hand tight in his, Sean crouched to see out the window to the dragons waiting there. 'Yes, she is! Her eyes are gaining speed and orange.'

'I was afraid of that!' Mutely Sorka appealed to Sean. Expressions fleeted across his face. If she read them correctly, he was annoyed with Faranth, indecisive – for once – about what to do to solve this draconic problem, and anxious for her. Tender concern now dominated his face as he looked down at her. She had never loved him more than at this moment.

'A pity we can't have your dragon heat a kettle of water to keep her out of mischief,' Greta remarked, her strong capable hands finishing the examination. She gave Sorka's distended belly a gentle pat. 'We'll take care of her fussing you right now. Can you turn on one side? Sean, help her.'

'I feel like an immense flounder,' Sorka complained as she struggled to turn. Then Sean, deftly and with hands gentler than she had ever known, helped her complete the manoeuvre. She just reached the new position when another mighty spasm caught her and she exhaled in astonishment. Outside Faranth trumpeted a challenge.

384

'Don't you dare wake everyone up, Faranth. I'm only having a baby!'

You hurt! You are in distress! Faranth was indignant.

Sorka felt a slight push against the base of her spine, the coolness of the air gun and then a blessed numbness spread rapidly over her nether region.

'Oh, blessed Greta, how marvellous!'

You don't hurt. That is better. Faranth's alarm subsided back into that curious thrumming and Sorka could identify her voice in the hum as clearly as she heard the noise intensify. Oddly enough, the humming was soothing or was it simply that she no longer had to anticipate that painful clutching of uterine muscles?

'Now, let's get you to your feet for a little walking, Sorka,' Greta said. 'You're already fairly well dilated. I don't think you're going to be any time delivering this baby, even if you are a primipara.'

'I'm numb,' Sorka said by way of apology as Greta got her to her feet. Then Sean was on her other side.

He had got dressed but Sorka, trying to watch where her nerveless feet were going, noticed that he didn't have his socks on. She thought that endearing of him. Odd the difference between his hands and Greta's – both caring, both gentle, but Sean's loving and worried.

'That's a girl,' Greta said encouragingly. 'Basil's out on another call but I don't think we'll need to bother him. You're doing just fine, three fingers dilated already. No wonder the fairs were alerted.' Greta chuckled as they began to retrace their steps across the lounge, up the short hall and into the bedroom. 'It's the walking that's important . . . ah, another contraction. Very good. Your breathing's fine.'

'Who else is delivering?' Sorka asked because it helped to concentrate on things other than what her muscles were doing to her.

'Fortunately, Elizabeth Jepson. A new baby will help her get over the loss of the twins.'

Sorka felt a pang of grief. She remembered the two boys

385

as mischievous youngsters on the *Yoko*, and how she had envied her brother, Brian, for having friends his own age.

'It's funny that, isn't it?' Sorka said, speaking quickly, 'people having two complete families, almost two separate generations. I mean, this baby will have an uncle only six months older. And be part of an entirely different generation . . . really.'

'One reason why we have to keep very careful birth records,' Greta said.

Sean grunted. 'We're all Pernese, that's what matters!'

Sorka's waters burst then, and outside the humming went up a few notes and deepened in intensity.

'I think I'd better check you, Sorka,' Greta said.

Sean stared at her. 'Do you deliver to dragonsong?'

Greta gave a low chuckle. 'They've an instinct for birth, Sean, and I know you vets have been aware of it, too. Let's get her back to bed.'

Sorka, involved in the second phase of childbirth, found the dragonsong both comforting and soothing: it was like a blanket of sound shimmering about her, enfolding and uplifting, and comforting because the sound suddenly increased in tempo, rising to a climax. Sean's hands grasped hers, giving her his strength and encouragement. Every time she felt the contractions, painless because of the drug, he helped her push down. The spasms were becoming more rapid, almost constant, as if matters had been taken entirely out of her control. She let the instinctive movements take over, relaxing when she could, assisting because she had no other option.

Then Sorka felt her body writhe in a massive effort and when it had been expended, she felt a tremendous relief of all pressures and pullings. For one moment, there was complete silence outside, then she heard a new sound. Sean's cry of triumph was lost in the trumpeting of eighteen dragons and who knew how many fire-dragonets! Oh dear, they'd wake up the whole of Landing!

'You have a fine son, my dears,' Greta said, her voice ringing with satisfaction, 'with a crop of thick red hair.'

'A son?' Sean asked, sounding immensely surprised.

'Now, don't tell me, after all my hard work, Sean Connell, that you wanted a daughter?' Sorka demanded.

Pern date 17.03.09

'Sometimes I feel as if they've forgotten all about us,' Dave Caterel said to Sean as they watched their two bronzes hunting.

Although all the dragons were now well able to fly short distances and had proved capable of hunting down wild wherries, their human partners were anxious if they flew out of sight. Nor was it always possible to use a sled or a skimmer to accompany them. Sorka and Sean occasionally borrowed their horses back to go further afield with Faranth and Carenath but it was an awkward way to go about the exercise.

As a compromise, Sean had talked Red into giving them the culls or injured animals from the main herds. He and the others had rigged a Threadfall shelter for the mixed herd in one of the caves and each took turns on the succession trays that supplied their fodder.

The young dragons were strong, and even the smallest of the golden females, larger than their bronze or brown brothers.

But, erring on the side of caution, the veterinary experts had been decided not to attempt to ride them until the full year had passed. Sean had railed privately to Sorka about such timidity but she had talked him out of defiance, reminding him how much they stood to lose in forcing the young dragons. Fortunately Red, AC Sopers and Phas had reached this decision without discussing it with Wind Blossom, a point which made it easier for Sean to accept what he called 'sheer procrastination'. He didn't like Blossom's proprietary attitude towards 'their' dragons.

She continued to exercise Kitti Ping's program, though without the same success. Her first four batches had not produced any viable eggs but there were seven sacs in the incubator that now promised to mature.

The odds in Joel Lilienkamp's book favoured the success of the first Hatching, but only marginally. Sean was privately determined to upset such odds but he also wouldn't risk official censor or jeopardize young dragons.

'I really cannot repose the same confidence in Wind Blossom as I did in Kitti Ping,' Paul had told Sean and Sorka in a private conference, 'but we would all breathe more easily if we could see some progress. Your dragons eat, grow, even fly to hunt. Will they also chew rock,' and Paul ticked off the points on his left hand, 'carry a rider and preserve their valuable hides during Threadfall? The power-pack situation is getting tight, Sean, very tight indeed.'

'I know, Admiral,' Sean replied, feeling grim and defensive, 'and eighteen fully functional dragons are not going to make fighting Thread all that much easier.'

'But self-reproducing, self-sustaining Thread fighters will make one helluva lot of difference in the long run. And it's the long run, frankly, Sean, Sorka, that worries me.'

Sean kept his opinion about Wind Blossom to himself. Part of it was loyalty to Carenath, Faranth and the others of the first Hatching: a good deal stemmed from his lack of confidence in Wind Blossom where he had every faith in the mother. After all, Kitti Ping had had the training at the source, with the Eridani.

Now as he watched the grace of Carenath, swooping to snatch a fat wether from the stampeding flock, his faith in these amazing creatures was reinforced.

'He really got some altitude there,' David said with ungrudging praise. 'Look, Polenth's dropped his wing now. He's going for that one!'

'Got it, too,' Sean replied in a return of compliment.

Maybe they were all being too cautious, afraid of push

ing down the throttle and seeing the result. Carenath flew strong and well. The bronze was nearly the same height in the shoulder as Cricket, though the confirmation was entirely different, Carenath being much longer in the body, deeper in the barrel, and stronger in the hind-quarters. In fact, one couldn't compare horse size with dragon size for the dragon already was much stronger than a similar equine. The basic structure was much more durable, utilizing carborundum for strength and resilience. Pol and Bay had gone on about the design features of dragons, as if they'd been new sleds, which indeed, Sean thought wrily, was what they were intended to replace. According to the program, dragonkind would gradually increase in size over many generations to the optimum size. But, in his eyes, Carenath was just right.

'At least, they eat neatly,' Dave said, averting his eyes from the two dragons who were rending flesh from the carcases of their kills. 'Though I wish they didn't look like they enjoyed it so much.'

Sean laughed. 'City-bred were you?'

Dave nodded and smiled weakly. 'Not that I wouldn't do anything for Polenth. It's just that it's one thing on 3-D, another to watch it live and *know* that your best friend prefers to hunt live animals. What did you say, Polenth?' And Dave's eyes took on that curious unfocused look that people had when being addressed by their dragons. Dave gave a rueful laugh.

'Well?' Sean prompted him.

'He says anything's better than fish. He's meant to fly, not swim.'

'Good thing he has two bellies,' Sean remarked, seeing Polenth devouring the sheep, horns, hooves, fleece and all. 'The way he's squaffing down the wool, he could start a premature blaze when he starts chewing firestone.'

'He will, won't he, Sean?' Dave's earnest plea for re-assurance worried Sean. The dragonpeople couldn't doubt their beasts for a moment, not on any score.

'Of course he will,' Sean said, standing up. 'That's

enough, Carenath. Two fills your belly. Don't get greedy. There are more to be fed here today.'

The bronze had been about to launch himself into the air again, aiming towards the rise into the next valley where the terrified flock had stampeded.

I would really like another one. So tasty. So much better than fish. I like to hunt.

Carenath sounded a trifle petulant.

'The queens hunt next, Carenath.'

With a petulant swing of his head, Carenath began to amble back down to Sean, spreading his wings to balance himself. A dragon's walk looked odd since he had to crouch to the shorter forelegs. Some of them fell more easily into a hop-skip gait, dropping to the forequarters every few steps or using their wings to provide frontal lift. Sean disliked the dragons looking so ungainly and unbalanced.

'See you later," he said to David as he and Carenath turned to walk back to the cave they now inhabited.

The dragons had quickly outgrown the backyard shelters, and in many cases the patience of neighbours, some of whom worked night shifts and slept during daylight hours. Dragons were a vocal lot for a species that could not speak aloud.

So dragons and partners had explored the Catherine caves for less public accommodations. Sorka had at first worried living underground with their baby son, Michael, but the cavesite Sean had chosen was spacious, with several large chambers so that they actually had far more space than the house in Irish Square. Faranth and Carenath were delighted. There was even a shelf of bare earth above the cave entrance where dragons could sunbathe, the leisure activity they enjoyed even above swimming.

'We are all much better suited here,' Sorka had exclaimed in capitulation and had set about making their living quarters bright with lamps, her handwoven rugs, fabrics and pictures which she had cadged out of Joel.

The new quarters had proved to be more than just a

physical separation, Sean realized as he and Carenath trudged along. Dave Caterel had put his finger on it in his wistful comment about being forgotten.

This walk is long. I would rather fly on ahead, Carenath said, doing his little hop-skip beside Sean. Once again Sean thought that his brave and lovely Carenath looked like a bad cross between a rabbit and kangaroo.

'You were designed to fly. I'll be happy when we both fly.'

Why do you not fly on me, then? I would be easier to ride than that scared creature. Carenath did not think much of Cricket as a mount for his partner.

Scared creature, thought Sean with a chuckle. Poor Cricket. How easy it would be to swing up to Carenath's back and just take off! The notion made the breath catch in his throat. To fly *on* Carenath, instead of shuffling along on the dusty track. The adolescent year for the dragons was nearly over. Sean looked about him in deep speculation. Let Carenath drop off the highest point and he'd have enough space to make that first all-important downsweep of his wings . . .

Sean had spent as much time watching how fire-lizards and dragons handled themselves in the air as he once had patiently observed horses. Yes, a drop off a height would be the trick.

'C'mon, Carenath. I'm glad I didn't let you fill your belly. C'mon, right up to the top.'

The top? The ridge? Sean heard comprehension colour the dragon's mind and Carenath scrambled to the height in a burst of speed that left Sean coughing in the dust. *Quickly! The wind is right.*

Rubbing dust particles out of his eyes, Sean laughed aloud to express the elation he felt, the elation and racing pulse of apprehension. This was the sort of thing you did *now*, at the right time, in the right place. And it was right, *now*, for him to ride Carenath. There was no time like the present!

There was no saddle to vault to, no stirrup to assist

Sean to the high shoulder. Carenath dipped politely, and Sean, lightly stepping on the proffered forearm, caught the two neck ridges firmly and swung up and over, fitting his body between them.

'Jays, you were designed for me,' he said with a triumphant laugh and slapped Carenath's neck in an excess of affection! Then grabbed at the ridge in front of him.

Carenath was perched on the very edge of the ridge and Sean had an awesome view of the bottom of the rockstrewn gorge. He swallowed hastily. This was not the same thing at all as riding Cricket. Sean took a deep breath. Now was also not the time for second thoughts. He took a compulsive hold with legs made strong from years of riding and shoved his buttocks as deeply into the natural saddle as he could.

'Let's fly, Carenath. Let's do it now!'

We will fly, Carenath said with ineffable calm and tilted forward, off the ridge.

Despite years of staying astride bucking horses, sliding horses, jumping horses, the sensation that Sean Connell experienced in that seemingly endless moment was totally different and completely new. A brief memory of a girl's voice urging him to think of Spacer Ives flitted through his mind. He was falling through space again. A very short space. What sort of a nerd-brain was he to have attempted this?

Faranth wants to know what we are doing, Carenath said calmly.

Before Sean's staggered mind registered the query, Carenath's wings had finished their downstroke and they were rising. Sean felt the sudden return of gravity, felt Carenath's neck under him, felt the weight and a return of the confidence totally in abeyance in that endless-seeming initial drop. The power in those wing sweeps drove his seat deeper between the neck ridges as Carenath continued to beat upward. They were level with the next ridge, the floor of the gorge no longer an imminent crash area.

'Tell Faranth that we're flying, of course,' Sean replied.

He would never admit it to Sorka, he could barely admit it to himself, but for one moment he had been totally and utterly terrified.

I will not let you fall, Carenath's tone chided him.

'I never thought you would.' Sean forced his body to relax, forced his long legs down and around Carenath's smooth neck, but he took a firmer grip on the neck ridge. 'I just didn't think I'd stay aboard you for a minute there.'

They'd have to do something about this, he thought and opened his eyes again. Carenath's wings swept up and down, just behind his peripheral vision. He felt them, knew the result of their strong and steady beat even if he didn't see it. Sean could feel the air pressure against his face and his chest. There was nothing around him but air, open, empty, and absolutely marvellous.

Yes, once you got the hang of it, flying your dragon was the most marvellous sensation he'd ever had.

I like it, too. I like flying you. You fit on me. This goes well. Where shall we go? The sky is ours.

'Look, we better not do much of this right now, Carenath. You just ate, and we're going to have to think this thing through. It's not enough to fall off a ridge. Oooooooh,' and Sean's cry was inadvertent because Carenath now banked and there was the wide open dusty thread-barren ground far, far beneath him. 'Straighten up!'

I wouldn't let you fall! Carenath sounded nearly indignant and Sean freed one hand to give him a reassuring slap, much as he would an obedient mount. But he quickly replaced his hand on the ridge. Shards, a rider couldn't fly Thread hanging on for dear life.

'You wouldn't let me, my friend, but *I* might let me!'

Trying to quell the rising sense of panic, Sean hazarded a glance at the ground. They were nearly to the rank of caves that had become their home. Sean could see Faranth on the height where she must have been sunning herself. She was sitting on her haunches now, her wings half-spread. In a few sweeps of Carenath's powerful wings, they had covered a distance that took a half hour of uphill-downdale slogging.

Faranth says that Sorka says that we had better come down right away. Right away! Carenath's tone was defiant, begging Sean to contradict the golden dragon, and anything that shortened this experience. *We are flying together. It is the right thing to do for dragons and riders.*

'It's a fantastic thing to do, Carenath, but as we are now home, can you land us, say by Faranth? Then you can tell her just how we did it!'

It didn't matter to Sean if Sorka had hysterics over this spontaneous and totally unplanned flight. He had done it, they had succeeded and all was well that ended well. The dragons of Pern now had riders! That would change the odds in Joel's book!

The other seventeen riders, including Sorka once Faranth had also reassured her about Carenath's prowess, were delighted at this tremendous advance. Dave wanted to know why Sean had been so precipitous.

'Couldn't you have waited for me? Polenth and I were just behind you. You scared the living wits out of me for a moment, you know.'

Sean clasped Dave's arm in tacit apology. 'It was what you'd said about being forgotten, Dave. I just had to try but I didn't want to endanger anyone else in case I was wrong.' Sean caught Sorka frowning at him and pretended to flinch from such a reproving look. 'I was all right, love. You *know* that! But,' and now he glared warningly at the others, seated on the rugs around him. 'We've got to go about this in a logical and sensible way, folks. Flying a dragon's not like riding a horse.'

His glance held Nora Sejby's. She certainly wasn't the sort of person he'd've said would Impress a dragon but Tenneth had chosen her and they'd have to make the best of it. Nora was accident-prone and Tenneth had already hauled her partner out of the lake, prevented her from falling into the crevices and holes that pitted the hills around the Catherine caves. On the other hand, Nora had been sailing across Monaco bay since she was strong enough to manage a tiller and she had checked out on both sleds and skimmers.

'For one thing, there's all this open air around you. Falling is down on to a hard and injurious surface.' Sean made appropriate gestures, smacking one hand into the palm of the other, a noise which startled Nora.

'So,' Peter Semling said. 'We use a saddle.'

'A dragon's back is full of wing,' Sorka replied drily.

'You ride forward, sitting your butt in the hollow between the last two ridges,' Sean went on, grabbing for a sheet of opaque film and a marker. He made a quick sketch of a dragon's neck and shoulders, and the disposition of two straps. 'The rider wears a stout belt, wide like a tool belt, only you've got buckles. You strap yourself in on either side, and the safety harness goes over your thigh for added security. And we're going to need special flying gear, and protective glasses because the wind made my eyes water and I wasn't aloft all that long.'

'What did it really feel like, Sean?' Catherine Radelin asked, her eyes shining in anticipation.

Sean smiled at her, a smile that included everyone of his seventeen eager listeners. 'The most incredible sensation I've ever had. Beats flying a mechanical all hallow. I mean,' and he raised his fists, tensing his arms into his chest, giving his hands an upward thrusting turn of indescribable experience, 'it's . . . it's between you and your dragon and . . .' he swung his arms out, 'and the whole damned wide world.'

He made a less dramatic presentation at the impromptu meeting where he was asked to account for such risk-taking. He would rather have given it privately, to maybe Admiral Benden or Pol or Red, but he found himself facing the entire Council.

'Look, sir, the risk was justified,' he said, looking quickly from the Admiral to Red Hanrahan. His father-in-law had been both furious and hurt by what he considered a betrayal. Sean hadn't anticipated that. 'We were almost to the ridge when I suddenly knew I had to prove that dragons could fly us. Sir, all the planning in the world sometimes doesn't get you to the right point at the right time.'

Admiral Benden nodded wisely but the startled expression on Jim Tillek's blunt face and Ongola's sudden attention told Sean that he had said something wrong.

'I could risk my own neck, sir, but no one else's,' Sean went on, 'so we've got to take our time getting some of the other riders ready to fly. I've done a lot of riding, and sled-driving, but flying a dragon's not the same thing and I'm not about to go out again until Carenath's got some safety harness on him. And me.'

Joel Lilienkamp leaned forward across the table. 'And what will that require, Connell?'

Sean grinned, more out of relief than amusement. 'Don't worry, Lili, what I need is what Pern's got plenty of – hide. I found a use for all that tanned wherry skin you've got in Stores. It's plenty tough enough and it'll be easier on dragons' necks than that synthetic webbing used in sled harnesses. I've made some sketches . . .' and he unfolded the diagrams, much improved on by that evening's discussions with the other partners, 'for the arrangement of straps and the belts we'll need, the flying suits, and we can use some of those work-goggles Plastic turns out . . .'

'Flying suits and plastic goggles . . .' Joel repeated, reaching for the drawings which he examined with a gradually less jaundiced attitude.

'As soon as I can rig the flying harness for Carenath, Admiral, Governor, sirs,' and Sean politely included the assembled, adding a tentative grin at Cherry Duff's deep scowl, 'you can see just how well my dragon flies me.'

'You were informed, weren't you,' Paul Benden said, and Sean saw him rubbing the knuckles of his left hand, 'that there're new eggs on the Hatching Sands?'

Sean nodded. 'Like I told you, Admiral, eighteen are not enough to take up much slack. And it'll be generations before there're enough.'

'Generations?' Cherry Duff exclaimed in her raspy voice, swinging in accusation on the veterinary team. 'Why weren't we told it'd take generations?'

'Dragon generations,' Pol answered, smiling slightly at her misinterpretation. 'Not human.'

'Well, how long's a dragon generation?' she demanded, still affronted and she shot a disgusted scowl at Sean.

'The females should produce their first independent clutches at three. Sean has proved that a male dragon can fly at just under a year . . .'

Cherry brought both hands down on the table, making a sharp loud noise. 'Give me facts, damn it, Pol.'

'Then, four to five years?'

Cherry pursed her lips in annoyance, a habit which made her look even more like a dried prune, Sean thought idly.

'Humph, then I'm not likely to see squadrons of dragons in the sky, am I? Four to five years. And when will they start flaming Thread? That was their design function, wasn't it? When will they start being useful?'

Sean stood up. He'd had enough of this meeting. 'Sooner than you think, Cherry Duff. Open a book on it, Joel.' With that he strode from the office. It galled him to the bone to have to take a skimmer back to Sorka and the others who waited to hear what had happened.

Ten days later, when Joel Lilienkamp himself brought them the requisitioned belts, straps, flying kit and goggles, flight training on the Dragons of Pern began in earnest.

Pern date 02.04.09

Landing had grown accustomed over the past year and a half to the grumblings and rumblings underfoot. On the morning of the second day of the fourth month of their ninth spring on Pern, early risers sleepily noted the curl of smoke, and the significance did not register.

Sean and Sorka, emerging from their cave with Carenath and Faranth, also noticed it.

Why does the mountain smoke? Faranth wanted to know.

'The mountain what?' Sorka demanded, waking up enough to absorb her dragon's words. 'Jays, Sean, look!'

Sean gave a long hard look. 'It's not Garben. It's Picchu Peak. Patrice de Broglie was wrong! Or was he?'

'What on earth do you mean, Sean?' Sorka stared at him in amazement.

'I mean, there's been all this talk of basement rock, and shifting Landing to a more practical base, with a special accommodation for dragons and us . . .' Sean kept his eyes on the plume curling languidly up from the peak, dwarfed beside the mightier Garben, but certainly as ominous right now. He shrugged. 'Not even Paul Benden can make a volcano erupt on cue. Come, we can get breakfast at your mother's. Let's stuff Mick in his flying suit and go. Maybe your dad will have received some official word.'

He scowled. 'We're always the last people to get news. I've got to convince Joel to release at least one comunit for us.'

Sorka got their wriggling son into the fleece-lined carrying sack before she shrugged into her jacket and crammed helmet and goggles on to her head. Sean carried Mick out to Faranth. With practised ease now, Sorka ran the two steps to her dragon's politely positioned foreleg and she vaulted astride. Sean handed a protesting bundle to sling over her back and then turned to mount the obliging Carenath.

The dragons leapt upward from the ledge before the cave, giving themselves enough airway to take the first full sweep. Over the last few weeks, dragon backs had strengthened and muscled up. They had managed flights of several hours' duration. Riders, even Nora Sejby – Sean had contrived a special harness that made her feel securely fastened to Tenneth – were improving. Long discussions with Drake Bonneau, Theo Force and some of the other pilots who had both fighter experience in the old Nathi War and plenty of fighting Thread had improved the dragonriders' basic understanding of the skills needed. And practice had encouraged them.

Three weeks before, Wind Blossom's latest attempt had hatched. The four creatures who had survived had not been Impressed by the candidates awaiting them although the creatures ate the food presented but certainly made no link as the First dragons had. Indeed, the poor beasts turned out to be photophobic but Blossom, much to the disgust of Pol and Bay, and against their advice, had insisted on special darkened quarters for the beasts to continue examinations of this variant.

Even the fire-lizards were more useful, Sean thought, as the two fairs erupted into the air about them, bugling a morning welcome in their high sweet voices. Now, if the dragons could only prove capable of *that*, Sean thought enviously. But how do you teach a dragon to do something you do not yourself understand? The dragons got smarter every day, they learned quickly, but it was impossible to explain telekinesis to them or ask them to teleport the way the fire-lizards did. Kitti Ping called it an instinctive action. Nowhere in the program which he had memorized did he find any words of wisdom on how to instruct a dragon to use his innate instinct.

And it wasn't the sort of exercise one did on a spontaneous basis. First, they would try to chew firestone and make flame. They knew where the fire-lizards got the phosphine-bearing rock – this area was littered with the stuff. Sean had even watched the browns and Sorka's Duke selecting the pieces to chew and the careful way they concentrated while they chewed. The fire-lizards would produce flame now on demand so Sean felt easy about teaching the dragons that. But going *between* one place and another . . . that was scarey.

Flame of a different kind obsessed Landing's counsellors three days later.

'What people want to know, Paul, Emily,' and Cherry Duff turned her penetrating stare from Admiral to Governor, 'is how much warning you had of Picchu's activity.'

'None,' Paul said firmly and Emily nodded. 'Patrice de Broglie's reports have not been altered. There's been a lot of volcanic activity all along the ring, as well as that new volcano. You've felt the same shakes I have. Landing and all Stakeholders have been apprised of every technical detail. This is as much of an unpleasant surprise to us as it is to you!' Then Paul's stern expression altered. 'By all that's holy, Cherry, all that black ash gave me as much a fright yesterday as it did everyone else.'

'So?' Cherry demanded, her attitude unsoftened.

'Picchu is officially an active volcano!' Paul spread his hands, looking past Cherry to Cabot Francis Carter and Rudi Shwartz who constituted this settlers' delegation. 'And officially, it's likely to continue to spout smoke and ash. Patrice and his crew are up at the crater now. He'll give a full public report this evening at Bonfire Square.'

Cherry gave him a long hard stare, her black eyes piercing, her face expressionless. Now she gave a snort.

'I believe him, but that doesn't mean I like it. Or the obvious prognosis. Landing moves, doesn't it?'

Emily Boll nodded solemnly.

'And your next statement,' Cherry went on in her hard voice, 'is that you have prepared a place for us!'

Paul burst into guffaws, though Emily muffled her laughter when she saw how such levity affronted Rudi Shwartz.

'You had no right,' Paul said, controlling his laughter, 'to steal that line from Emily, Cherry Duff! Damn it, we were working on the official announcement when you barged in. And you fardling well know we've been rushing to complete the northern fort. Landing couldn't continue much longer as a viable settlement even if Picchu hadn't started showering us with ash. That doesn't, of course, mean,' and he held up his hand to forestall Cabot's ex-

losion, 'that stakeholders will be asked to leave their
ands. But the administration of this planet will have to
be in the most protected situation we can contrive. Plainly
Landing has outlived its usefulness. It was never intended
as a permanent installation.'

Emily took up the discussion then, passing to each of
he delegation copies of the directive she and Paul had
been drafting.

'The transfer is being organized much as our space
journey here. We have the technicians and the equipment
to make a northern crossing as easy as possible. We have
enough fuel to power two of the shuttles to transport
equipment too bulky to fit on any of Jim's ships. It'll be
a one-way trip for the shuttles: they'll be dismantled
for parts. Joel Lilienkamp has been working on priority
shipments for the big sleds, taking as few as possible from
he fighting strength.'

'Speaking of fighting strength, has that young upstart
taught them any new tricks?' Cherry demanded, imper-
ously looking down her long nose at Paul.

'Speaking of eruptions, as we were, how are those beasts
of Kitti Ping's progressing? I see them flitting around all
the time. Mighty pretty they look in formation, but are
they any good in battle?'

'So far,' Paul began cautiously, 'they've matured well
beyond the projections. The young Connells have proved
splendid leaders . . .'

'They were the best ground-crew leaders I had,' Cabot
Carter said disgruntled.

'They'll be superior as aerial fighters,' Paul went on,
overriding the legist's unspoken criticism. 'Self-
perpetuating, too, unlike sleds and skimmers.'

'D'you know that for sure?' Cherry demanded in her
raspy voice. 'Blossom's experiments aren't all that successful.'

'Her mother's are,' Paul replied with a firm confidence
he hoped would reassure Cherry. 'According to Pol and
Bay, the males are producing their equivalent to sperm.

401

Genetic analyses have started but will take months. We might have direct proof of fertility by then as the gold females mature later.' Paul tried not to sound defensive but he wanted to counter the very bad publicity surrounding Wind Blossom's brutes. Especially when the young dragonriders were trying very hard to perfect themselves for combat against Thread. Though it wasn't public knowledge, Sean and his group had already served as messengers and transported light loads efficiently.

Paul had a report on his desk from Telgar and his group. They'd done a survey of the old crater above the fort hold, with its myriad bubble caves and twisting passages. They'd pronounced it a suitable accommodation for the dragons and their riders. Telgar had a team working to make the place habitable, while they still had power in the heavy equipment. A stream was being dammed up for a dragon-sized bathing lake, water piped into the largest of the ground-level caverns for kitchen use and a chimney hole had been bored for a large hearth complex.

Obviously, this would be the pattern for future human habitation on Pern, and for some, accustomed to sprawling living space, it would take some getting used to. But it was the best way to survive!

19

'Pol?'

It took a moment for the biologist to identify the anxious voice.

'Mary?' His response was equally tentative but he pulled at Bay's sleeve to attract her attention away from the monitor she was frowning at. 'Mary Tubberman?'

'Please don't turn an old friend away unheard.'

'Mary,' Pol said kindly for fear was the dominant emotion in her voice. He now shared the earpiece with Bay who nodded vigorous approval. '*You* weren't Shunned.'

'I might as well have been,' and the woman's tone was bitter, then her voice broke on a tremulous note and both Bay and Pol could hear her weeping. 'Look, Pol, something's happened to Ted. Those creatures of his are *loose*. I've pulled down the Thread shutters but they're still prowling about and making awful noises.'

'Creatures? What creatures?' Pol locked glances with Bay. Beyond them, their dragonets roused from a doze and chirped in empathic anxiety.

'The beasts he's been rearing.' Mary sounded as if she thought Pol knew what she was talking about and was being deliberately obtuse. 'He . . . he stole some frozen in vitros from Veterinary and he used Kitti's program on them to make them obey him but they're still . . . things. His masterpiece does nothing to stop them.' Again her bitterness was trenchant.

'What makes you think something has happened to

403

Ted?' Pol asked, picking up on the words Bay mouthed to him, accompanied by rather urgent gestures.

'He would never let those animals *loose*, Pol! They might harm Petey!'

'Now, Mary, calm down. Stay in the house. We'll come.'

'Ned's not in Landing!' Her tone was accusatory now. 'I tried his number. He'd believe me!'

'It's not a question of belief, Mary,' Bay pulled the mouthpiece around to speak directly into it. 'And anyone can come assist *you*.'

'Sue and Chuck won't answer.'

'Sue and Chuck moved north, Mary, after that first bad rock shower from Picchu.' Bay was patient with her. The woman had a right to sound paranoid, living in seclusion as she had for nine months, with an unbalanced husband and so many earthshocks and volcanic rumblings.

'Pol and I are coming down, Mary,' Bay said firmly. 'And we'll bring help.' She replaced the handset.

'Who?' Pol demanded.

'Sean and Sorka. Dragons have an inhibiting effect on animals. And that way we don't have to go through official channels.'

Pol looked at his wife with mild surprise. She had never criticized either Emily or Paul, obliquely or bluntly.

'I always felt someone should have investigated the report Drake and Ned Tubberman made. So did they. Sometimes priorities get lost in the shuffle around here.' She wrote a hasty note which then she attached to her gold dragonet's right foot. 'Find the redhead,' she said firmly, holding the triangular head to get Mariah's full attention. 'Find the redhead.' Bay walked with her to the window and opened it, pointing firmly in Sorka's direction. She filled her mind with an image of Sorka, leaning against Faranth. Mariah chirped happily. 'Now, off with you!' Then, as the dragonet obediently flew off, Bay ran a finger over the black grime, once again settling on the windowsill she had swept earlier. 'I'll be glad to move north. I'm so eternally tired of black dust everywhere. Come on, Pol, we'd better get dressed warmly.'

'You volunteered to help Mary because it gives you a chance to ride a dragon again,' Pol said, chuckling.

'Pol Nietro, I have long been concerned about Mary Tubberman!'

Fifteen minutes later, two dragons came swooping over the rise to settle on the road in front of their house.

'They are so graceful,' Bay said, making certain her headscarf was tied, as much against the prevailing dust outside as in hopes of riding. As Bay left the house, Mariah circled down and settled to the plump shoulder with a chirrup of smug satisfaction. 'You're marvellous, Mariah, simply marvellous,' Bay murmured to her little queen as she marched right up between Faranth and Carenath.

However, it was Sorka she addressed. 'Thank you for coming, my dear. Mary Tubberman just contacted us. There's trouble at Calusa. Creatures are loose and Mary thinks something has happened to Ted. Will you take us there?'

'Officially, or unofficially?' Sean asked as Sorka glanced over at her mate.

'It's all right to help Mary,' Bay said, looking for support from Pol who came up to the dragons, his glance admiring as ever. 'And with who knows what sort of beast . . .'

'Dragons are useful,' Sorka replied with a grin, arriving at her own decision. She beckoned to Bay. 'Give the lady your leg, Faranth. Here's my hand.'

With Faranth's assist, Bay was agile enough to settle herself quietly behind Sorka. She would never admit that she was pinched fore and aft between the ridge. Mariah gave her usual squeak of protest.

'Now, Mariah, Faranth's perfectly safe,' Bay said and looked over to see that Pol was settling behind Sean. The young dragonrider's grin was very broad as he winked at Bay. Well, this time it really is an emergency – a woman trapped in her home with small children and unidentifiable menaces prowling outside.

'Hang on tight now,' Sean said, as he usually did and pumped his arm in the signal to launch.

Bay suppressed an 'ouch' as Faranth's upward surge pushed her painfully against the stiff dorsal ridge. Her discomfort lasted only a moment as the golden dragon levelled off and veered leisurely to her right. Bay caught her breath. She would never get accustomed to this: she didn't want to. Riding a dragon was the most exciting thing that had happened to her since . . . since Mariah rose to mate.

Sorka turned her head, checking on her passenger.

Calusa was not a long trip by air, but tremendously exhilarating. The dragons hit one of the many air currents that were the result of Picchu's activity and Bay clutched at Sorka's belt, stuffing her fingers to the knuckle in the belt loops. Flying on a dragon was so much more immediate an activity than going in the closed sled or skimmer. Really, much more exhilarating. Bay turned her head so that Sorka's tall strong body shielded her from the worst of the airstream. And the dust from Picchu that seemed to clog the air even at this altitude.

The journey gave Bay time to ponder what Mary had said about 'beasts'. Red Hanrahan had reported a late-night entry into the veterinary laboratory. A portable bio-scan had been missing but not logged out but the Bio Lab was always borrowing Vet equipment so that the absence was dismissed. Later someone had noticed that the order in which the frozen ova of a variety of Earth-type animals were stored had been disarranged. It *could* have happened during the earthquakes.

Ted Tubberman had been very busy in his discontent, Bay thought grimly. One of the strictest dictums of her profession as a micro-biologist was a rigid limitation of genetic manipulation. She had actually been surprised, but relieved, that Kitti Ping as the most senior person on the Pern Expedition had permitted bio-engineering of the fire-dragonets. Had Kitti Ping any idea of what a marvellous gift she had bestowed on the people of Pern?

But for Ted Tubberman, disgruntled *botanist*, to tinker with ova – and he *hadn't* at all understood the techniques or the process – to make independent alterations was intolerable to her professionally and personally. Bay knew herself to be a tolerant person, friendly and considerate, but if Ted Tubberman was dead, it would be a tremendous relief. And not just to her.

Just thinking about the man produced symptoms of agitation and pure fury which, in their turn, made Bay lose her professional detachment and that annoyed her even more. Here she had a marvellous opportunity for peaceful reflection, with only the noise of the wind in her ears, with all Jordan spread below her, and she was wasting contemplative time on Ted Tubberman. Bay sighed. One had so few moments of total relaxation and privacy. How she envied young Sorka, Sean and the others.

She was astonished to see Calusa in the next valley. It was a sturdy complex which the Tubbermans had built as headquarters for their Stake-acres. The galvanized roofs of the main buildings were now a dull dark-grey from the repeated showers of volcanic ash which Picchu Peak deposited where ever the wind blew it. Bay scarcely had time to notice that when Sorka's cry of astonishment blew back to her.

'Jays, that building's a shambles!' Sorka pointed to her right and abruptly Faranth turned in response to an unspoken request.

The dorsal ridge bit into the soft flesh of Bay's crotch and she gripped Sorka's belt more tightly.

'*Look!*' Sorka was directing her gaze downward.

Seventy-five metres from the main house, there was a roofed compound with separate enclosures along an L-passageway, forming two sides of a fenced-in area. Now one of the outside walls and several of the interior partitions were smashed and a corner of the roofing had burst outward. Bay couldn't recall if there had been any more earth-shocks reported in this area to cause such structural damage.

As the dragon once more changed direction, Bay grabbed at Sorka, felt the girl's reassuring fingers on hers and then they were down.

'I do like riding Faranth. She's so very graceful and strong,' Bay said, tentatively patting the warm hide of the dragon's neck.

'No, don't dismount,' Sorka said. 'Faranth says there's something prowling in there. The dragonets will have a look. Whoops!'

The air was full of chitterings and chatterings of angry dragonets. Bay's Mariah shrieked almost in her ear.

'Now, now, it's all right. Faranth won't let anyone harm you.'

Bay held up her arm for her gold but Mariah joined the investigating fairs. Bay was astounded to realize that the dragon was growling, a sensation she could also feel through her body contacts. Faranth turned her impressive head towards the compound, the many facets of her eyes gleaming with edges of red and orange.

A piercing yowl was clearly audible and then silence. The excited fairs swirled back over the two dragonriders' heads, chittering and clattering with their news. Faranth looked up, her eyes wheeling now as she absorbed the dragonets' images.

'There's some kind of very large spotted beast out there,' Sorka told Sean. 'And something else that is even larger but silent.'

'We'll need trank guns then,' he said. 'Sorka, have Faranth call up some reinforcements. Marco and Duluth, if possible, Dave, Kathy – we may need a medic. Peter's Gilgath is sturdy, Nyassa won't panic and ask for Paul or Jerry. I think we should evacuate Mary and the two children until the beasts can be captured.'

Her ordeal ended, Mary Tubberman wept copiously on Bay's shoulder. Her son, Petey, usually a cheerful seven-year-old, watched poker-faced and taut with anxiety. His two little sisters clung together on a lounger and would not respond to Pol's efforts to comfort them, though he was generally very deft with children. Mary didn't resist the suggestion that she move to a safer location.

'Dad's dead, isn't he?' Petey asked, stepping right up to Sean.

'He could be out trying to recapture the beasts,' kind-hearted Bay suggested. The boy gave her a scornful look and went off down the corridor to his room.

The dragon reinforcements arrived with the trank guns. Sean was pleased to see them landing in the order they had been drilled to use. Sean gave Paul, Jerry and Nyassa the trankers and sent them off on their dragons to see if they could find and disable the escaped animals.

Leaving Sorka to help the Tubbermans assemble their gear, Sean and the others, armed with the pistols, cautiously approached the wrecked compound. Inside the building, the reek of animal was heavy and mounds of recent dung littered the place. They found Ted Tubberman's mauled and gnawed body, pitifully sprawled outside his small laboratory.

'Fardles, nothing we have kills like that!' David Caterel exclaimed, backing out of the corridor.

Kathy knelt by the corpse, her face expressionless. 'Whatever it was had fangs and sharp claws,' she remarked, slowly getting to her feet. 'His back was broken.'

Marco grabbed up an old lab coat and some towelling from a chair and covered the corpse. Then he picked up the remains of a chair, made of one of the local pressed vegetable fibres that were used for interior furnishings.

'This'll burn. Let's see if we can find enough to cremate him here. Save a lot of awkwardness.' He waved in the direction of the main house. Then he shuddered, clearly unwilling to move the mangled body.

'The man was insane,' Sean said, poking a rod into the dung pats in one enclosure, 'developing big predators. We've enough trouble with wherries and snakes!'

'I'll go tell Mary,' Kathy murmured.

Sean caught her arm as she went by. 'Tell her he died quickly.' She nodded and left.

'Hey,' and Peter Semling picked up a covered clipboard from the littered floor of the laboratory, 'looks like notes,' he added, examining the thin sheets of film covered with notations in a cramped hand. 'This is botanical stuff.' He shrugged, held it out to Kathy and picked up another. 'This is . . . biological? Humph.'

'Let's collect any notes,' Sean said, 'anything that would tell us what kind of creature killed him.'

'Hey,' and Peter flipped the cover back on a portable bio-scan, complete with monitor and keyboard, 'this looks like the one that went missing from the vet lab a while back, along with some AI samples.'

Meticulously then, they gathered up every scrap of material, even taking an engraved plate with the cryptic message 'Eureka, Mycorrhiza!' which had been nailed to the splashboard of the sink unit. Dave carried out several sacks to be brought back to Landing. Then Sean and Peter collected enough flammable materials to make a pyre that could be lit once Mary and the children had gone.

'Sean! Peter!' David Caterel called them over to where he was hunkered down by a wide green swath that was the only living thing in the raddled and ash-littered plot, though its colour was dimmed by the pervasive black ash. 'How many Falls has this area had?' he asked, glancing about. He ran his hand over the grass, a tough hybrid that Agro had developed for residence landscaping before Thread fell.

'Enough to clear this!' Sean knelt beside him and pulled up a hefty tuft. The dirt around the roots contained a variety of soil-livers, including several furry-looking grubs.

'Never seen that sort before,' David remarked, catching three deftly as they dropped. He felt in his jacket pocket and extracting a wad of fabric, he carefully wrapped the grubs. 'Ned Tubberman was yakking about a new kind of grass surviving Fall down here. I'll just take these back to the Agro lab.'

410

Just then Sorka, Pol, Bay and Peter, each loaded with bundles, came out of the main house. Sean and Dave began to load the eight dragons.

'We can make another run for you, Mary,' Sorka suggested tactfully when she joined them with two stuffed bedsacks.

'I don't have much besides clothes,' Mary said, her glance flicking to the compound. 'Dave Caterel said it was quick?' Her anxious eyes begged confirmation.

'Kathy's the medic,' Sean assured her smoothly. 'Up you go now. David and Polenth will take you. Mount up. You kids ever ridden a dragon before?'

Sean made a game of it for them and passed quickly over the awkwardness of the moment. He saw them all off before he and Pol ignited the funeral pyre. They took off in yet another shower of the volcanic dust which would eventually bury Landing.

Pern date   03.05.09

'I can't break Ted's personal code!' Pol exclaimed in exasperation, throwing the stylus down to a worktop littered with clipboards and piles of flimsies. 'Wretched, foolish man!'

'Ezra loves codes, Pol,' Bay suggested.

'Judging by the DNA/RNA, he was experimenting with felines but I cannot imagine why. There're already enough running wild here at Landing. Unless—' Pol broke off and pinched his lower lip nervously, grimacing as his thoughts followed uneasy paths. 'We *know*,' and he paused to bang the table in emphasis, 'that felines do not take mentasynth well. *He* knew that, too. *Why* would he repeat mistakes?'

'What about that other batch of notes?' Bay asked, gesturing to the clipboard lying precariously on the edge.

411

'Unfortunately, all I can read of them are quotations from Kitti's Dragon Program.'

'Oh!' and Bay left her mouth in the form of her soft exclamation, cocking her jaw sideways for a moment. 'He had to play Creator as well as Anarchist?'

'Why else would he refer to the Eridani genetic equations?' Pol slapped the worktop with his hand, frustrated and anxious, his expression rebellious. 'And what did he hope to achieve?'

'I think we can be grateful that he hadn't tried to manipulate the fire-dragonets, though I suspect he was practising on the ova he appropriated from the Vet frozen storage.'

Pol rubbed the heels of his hands into his tired eyes. 'We can be grateful for small mercies there. Especially when you consider what Blossom has done. I shouldn't have said that, my dear. Forget it.'

Bay permitted herself a scornful sniff. 'At least Blossom has the good sense to keep those wretched photophobes of hers chained. I cannot think why she persists with them. She's the only one they like.' Bay gave a shudder of revulsion. 'They positively fawn on her.'

Pol snorted. 'That's why,' he said absently, riffling through the notes on the undecipherable clipboard. 'What I don't understand is why he chose the large felines?'

'Well, why don't we ask Petey? He helped his father in the compound, didn't he?'

'You are the essence of rationality, my dear,' Pol said and, pushing himself out of the chair, went over and laid an affectionate kiss on her cheek, ruffling her hair. She was admonishing him when he punched the comcode for Mary Tubberman's quarters. Both he and Bay had visited her daily to help her settle back into the community. 'Mary, is Petey available?'

'Yeah?' Petey's tone was not particularly encouraging.

'Those large cats your father was breeding? Did they have spots or stripes?' Pol asked in a conversational tone.

'Spots.' Petey was surprised by the unexpected question.

'Ah, the cheetah. Is that what he called them?'

'Yeah, cheetahs.'

'Why cheetahs, Petey? I know they're fast but they wouldn't be any good hunting wherries.'

'They were great going after the big tunnel snakes,' and Petey's voice was animated now. 'And they'd come to heel and do everything Dad told them to—' he broke off.

'I expect they did, Petey. Several ancient cultures on Earth bred them to hunt all manner of game. Speediest things on four legs!'

'Did they turn on him?' Petey asked after a moment's silence.

'I don't know, Petey. Are you coming to the Bonfire tonight?' Pol asked brightly, feeling that he couldn't leave the conversation on such a sour note. 'You promised me a rematch. Can't have you winning every chess game.' He received a promise for that evening and disconnected. 'From what Petey said, it would appear that Ted used mentasynth on cheetahs to enhance their obedience. He used them to hunt tunnel snakes.'

'They turned on him?'

'That seems likely. Only why? I wish we knew how many ova he took from Vet. I wish we could decipher these notes and discover if he only used mentasynth or did he implement any part of Kitti's program? Be that as it may,' and Pol exhaled in frustration, 'we have an unknown number of predatory animals loose in Calusa. Loose in Calusa!' Pol let out a derisory snort for his inadvertent rhyming. 'I wonder if Phas Radamanth has had any luck deciphering the notes on those grubs. *They* could be useful.'

Patrice de Broglie burst into Emily's office.

'Garben's getting set to blow. We've got to evacuate. Now!'

'*What!*' Emily rose to her feet, the flimsies she was studying slipping out of her hands to scatter on the floor.

'I've just been to the peaks. There's a change in the sulphur-to-chlorine ratio. It's Garben's that going to blow.' He slapped his hand to his forehead in a self-accusatory blow. 'Right before my eyes and I didn't see it.'

Paul came through from the adjoining office, alerted by Emily's cry.

'Garben?'

'You've got to evacuate immediately,' Patrice cried, turning to him, his expression contorted. 'There've even been significant increases in mercury and radon from the damned crater. And we thought it was leaking from Picchu.'

'But it's Picchu which is smoking!' Stunned Paul reached for the comunit just as Emily did. He jerked his fingers back and let her contact Ongola.

'That Garben is as sly a mountain as the man we named it for. Volcanism still isn't a precise science,' Patrice said, rolling his eyes in frustration as he paced up and down the small office. 'I've sent a skimmer up with the correlation spectrometer to check on the content of the fumarole emissions that just started in the Garben crater,' Patrice went on. 'I brought down samples of the latest ash. But that rising sulphur-to-chlorine ratio means the magma is rising.'

'Ongola,' Emily said, 'sound the klaxon. Volcano alert. Recall all sleds and skimmers immediately. Yes, I know

414

there's Threadfall today but we've got to evacuate Landing *now*, not later. How long do we have, Patrice?'

He shrugged in exasperation. 'I cannot give you the precise moment of catastrophe, my friends, nor which way it will spew but the wind is a strong nor'easterly. Already the ash increases. Had you not noticed?'

Startled, Governor and Admiral glanced out the window and saw that the sky was grey with ash, obscuring sunlight, and Picchu's smoking yellow plume broader than usual. A similar halo was beginning to grow about Garben's peak.

'One can even become accustomed to living beneath a volcano,' Paul remarked with dry humour.

Patrice shrugged again and managed a grin. 'But let's not, my friends. Even if the pyroclastic flow is minimal, Landing will soon be covered with ash at the rate it's now falling. As soon as we've decided possible lava flow paths, I'll inform you so you can clear the most vulnerable areas first.'

'How fortunate we have already planned evacuation,' Emily remarked, selecting a file and bringing it up on the terminal. 'There!' She ran the sequence to all printers, emergency priority. 'That's going to all department heads. Evacuation is officially underway, gentlemen. What a nuisance to have to do it at speed. Something is bound to be forgotten no matter how carefully you plan ahead.'

Trained by repeated drills, the population of Landing reacted promptly to the klaxon alert by going to their department heads for orders. A brief flurry of panic was suppressed and the exercise went into high gear.

The sky continued to darken as thick black clouds of ash rolled up, covering the peaks of the now active volcanoes that had once appeared so benign. White plumes rose from Garben's awakened fumaroles and from crevases down its eastern side. The morning became twilight as the air pollution spread. Handlamps and breathing masks were issued.

In charge of the actual evacuation, Joel Lilienkamp

415

supervised from one of the fast sleds, the canopy open so he could bawl orders and encouragement to the various details, and make on-the-spot decisions. The laboratories and warehouses nearest the simmering volcano were being cleared first as well as the infirmary except emergency first-aid and burn control. The donks trundled everywhere, depositing their burdens at the grid or carrying them on down to temporary shelter in the Catherine Caves.

Patrice's group had already calculated areas of high and low pyroclastic hazard. Warnings had been sent as far east as Cardiff, west to Bordeaux and south to Cambridge. Already favoured with a heavy fall of ash, Monaco was also in range of moderate pyroclastic missile danger. Every boat, ship and barge was mobilized in the Bay to be loaded and sent off to stand beyond the first Kahrain peninsula.

The last sacs of fuel were emptied into the two shuttles' tanks and, fortunately, they were as ready as they ever would be for their last flights. Most of the dragonriders were put to mooching the herds and flocks towards the harbour. For once, no one assembled to fight Thread at Maori Lake: a more deadly fall threatened.

No one had time to cheer as Drake Bonneau and John Aldrin lifted the old *Swallow* with its cargo of children and equipment from Landing just as daylight receded from the plateau. Immediately the hatch was sealed, the technicians moved to the *Parrakeet*.

Ongola and Jake, monitoring in the Tower, took advantage of the respite to eat the hot food that Catering remembered to send them. The communications equipment had been moved to trolleys and could be quickly shifted if the Tower was threatened.

'*Swallow* looks good,' Ezra called in from the interface chamber where he was monitoring the flight. He had spent much of that day erecting a shield of heatproof material around the chamber, not quite ready to accept Patrice's hurried assurance that the room was not threatened by channels of previous lava flows. Unfortunately the interface with the orbiting *Yokohama* could not be disconnected, relying as it did on a fixed beacon to the receiver on the *Yoko*.

That night, the air was choking with sulphur fumes, full of gritty particles and Patrice warned that the build-up was reaching the critical point. White plumes from both Picchu and Garben, ominously rooted in a muted glow from peak and crater, were visible even against the dark sky, casting an eerie light over the settlement.

Drake Bonneau reported that he was safely down after a difficult flight. 'Damn crate nearly shook apart, but nothing was damaged. None of the kids so much as bruised, but I don't think any of them will develop a yen for flying. Hard landing, too, ploughed a furrow when we overshot the mark. We'll need the rest of the day to clear the site for the *Parrakeet*. Tell Fulmar to check the gyros and the stabilizing monitors. I'll swear we had tunnel snakes in the *Swallow*'s.'

There was a constant stream of vehicles down to the harbour, as the bigger ships and barges were loaded with protesting animals prodded into stalls erected on deckspace. Crates of chickens, ducks and geese were strapped wherever they could be attached, to be off-loaded at the Kahrain cove, safely out of the danger zone. With any luck most of the livestock would be evacuated. Skimming over the harbour, Jim Tillek managed to be everywhere, encouraging and berating his crews.

By nightfall, Sean called a halt for dragonriders ferrying people and packages to the Kahrain cove.

'I'm not risking tired dragons and riders,' Sean told Lilienkamp with some heat. 'Too risky, and the dragons are just too young to be under this sort of stress.'

'Time, man, we don't have time for niceties!' Joel replied angrily.

'You handle the exodus, Joel, I'll handle my dragons. The riders will work until they drop but it's bloody stupid to push young dragons! Not while I can prevent it.'

Joel gave him an angry, frustrated glare – the dragons

had been immensely useful – but he also knew better than to put them at risk. He gunned the sled away, perched behind the console like a small ash-covered monument which was what all of Landing was destined to become.

Sean and the other riders did work until they dropped. Each dragon then curled protectively about his rider as they slept. No one had time to notice that there were few dragonets about.

Then all too soon, Joel was there, exhorting them from the air and they joined in the herculean efforts of the people around them.

Suddenly the klaxon sounded a piercing triple blast. All activity ceased for the message that followed.

'She's going to blow!' Patrice's almost triumphant shout echoed throughout Landing.

Every head turned towards Garben, its peak outlined by the eerie luminosity from its crater.

'Launch the *Parrakeet*!' Ongola's stentorian voice followed a minute of the awed, stunned silence.

The engines of the shuttle were drowned by the rumbling earth and an ear-splitting roar of tremendous power as the volcano erupted. The attentive stance of observers broke as people scrambled, not for cover, but to complete tasks at hand, shouting at each other above the noise. Later, those who watched the peak fracture and the appearance of the red-hot molten lava oozing from the break said that everything appeared to happen in slow motion. They saw the fissures in the crater outlined by orange-red, saw the pieces blowing out of the lip, even saw some of the projectiles lifting out of the volcano and could track their dizzying trajectory. Others averred that it all happened too fast to be sure of details.

Bright red tongues of lava rolled ominously up and over the blasted lip of Garben, one flow travelling at an astonishing rate, the westernmost buildings of Landing directly in its path. Evacuation had begun in time to keep catastrophe from turning into tragedy.

In that dawn hour, the wind had dropped, saving much

of the eastern section of Landing from the worst of the shower of smaller rocks and hot ash. The larger, devastating projectiles Patrice had feared did not occur. The lava was sufficiently frightening a menace.

The *Parrakeet*, laden with irreplaceable equipment, pierced the western gloom, her engine blasts visible, if not audible, as she drove northwest and out of danger.

At the sound of the klaxon, the dolphins began to tow laden small boats out of Monaco Bay, a flotilla of vessels not ordinarily suitable for any prolonged sea travel. The dolphins had assured humans that they would get their charges safely to the sheltered harbour beyond the first Kahrain peninsula. *Maid* and *Mayflower* which were not fully loaded left the harbour to wait outside the estimated fall-out zone until they could return for the last of their cargoes. Bernard Shattuck took command of the convoy later that morning while Jim, finally on board the *Southern Star*, shepherded barges and luggers along the coast on their long journey to Seminole where they would make the final run north.

Sleds and skimmers streamed between Landing and Paradise River Hold as the nearest safe assembly-point. Emily and Desi Arthied tried to cope with the traffic there, keeping vital supplies available and shunting loads to appropriate areas on the beach. Landing had to be cleared of all that could be re-used in the new northern hold.

Thick sulphur-smelling ash began to cover Landing's buildings. Some of the lighter roofs collapsed under the load and one could hear the plastic groaning and shifting. The air was almost unbreathable with traces of chlorine. Everyone used the breathing masks without complaint in the sultry, close air.

By mid-afternoon, a haggard Joel Lilienkamp dropped his battered sled in the lea side of the Tower beside Ongola's. He waited a moment to gather enough strength to thumb open the comunit.

'We've cleared all we can,' he said in gasps, his voice raspy from the acrid airborne fumes. 'The donks are parked in the Catherine Caves until we can strip 'em down for shipment. You can leave now, too.'

'We're coming,' Ongola replied.

Moments later he appeared, slowly angling a heavy com package on a grav-unit past the door. Jake came next, similarly encumbered. Paul followed, guiding two more components.

'Need a hand?' Joel asked automatically, though the way he slumped at the console made it difficult to know how the little man would summon any energy.

'One more trip,' Ongola said when they had positioned the equipment in his sled. 'Is your power-pack up to a load?' he asked Joel.

'Yup. My last fresh unit.'

As Ongola and Jake went back into the Tower, Paul went to the flagstaff and, with a bleak expression on his face, solemnly lowered the singed tatters of the Colony's flag. He made a ball of it which he stuffed underneath the seat he took on the sled. He gave the Supply Master one long look.

'Want me to drive, Joel?'

'I got you here, I'll take you out!'

Paul dared not look back at the ruins of Landing but as Joel veered east and then north in a wide sweep, the Admiral saw that he was not the only one with tears coursing down his cheeks.

20

●

A stiff nor'easterly wind kept the Kahrain cove clear of
ash and the acrid taint of Garben's eruption. The grey pall
spread over the eastern horizon as the volcano continued
to spew lava and quantities of ash. Patrice and a skeleton
team remained to monitor the event after Landing was
abandoned.

'We hunt this morning,' Sean said to the other riders.

They had found a quiet cove up the beach from the
main evacuation camp. None of the dragons sprawled in
the warm sun had a very good colour and privately Sean
worried that their maturing strengths had been overtaxed.
He decided stoutly that there was nothing wrong that
a good meal wouldn't restore. He looked around for
fire-lizards and swore under his breath. 'Damn them! We
need all we've got. Four queens and ten bronzes can't
possibly catch enough packtail to feed eighteen dragons!
Surely they've seen volcanoes erupt before.'

'Not on top of them,' Alianne Zulueta replied. 'I
couldn't reassure mine. They just left!'

'Red meat would be better than fish: more iron,' David
Caterel suggested, his eyes on his pale bronze Polenth.
'There's sheep here.'

'Hold it,' Marco Galliani said firmly, raising both hands
in restraint. 'My father's shipping them on to Roma as
soon as sleds are free. Prime breeding stock.'

'So are dragons.' Sean rose, an odd grin on his face.
'Peter, Dave, Jerry, come with me. Sorka, you run interference – if there is any.'

'Hey, wait a minute, Sean,' Marco began, dual loyalties in conflict.

Sean grinned slyly, laying a finger along his nose. 'What the eye doesn't see, Marco, the heart won't grieve.'

'It's for your dragon, man,' Dave muttered as he passed him.

An hour later, several dragons disappeared in a westerly direction, skimming the treetops. The other riders were so conspicuous in their efforts to help Desi and the crew who were struggling to organize the chaos on the beach that no one would have noticed that the riders were not all present at the one time. By noon, seventeen brightly hued sated dragons lolled on the strand. One sat patiently on the headland while fire-dragonets dove into the sea, fishing for packtail.

Caesar and Stefano Galliani, taking a poll count as their sheep were loaded, discovered the tally was short by some thirty-six animals, including one of the best rams. Caesar called on the dragonriders to search the area and herd the missing sheep back to the shore.

'Useless things, always wandering off,' Sean agreed, nodding sympathetically at the frustrated and puzzled Gallianis. 'We'll give a look.'

When Sean reported back an hour later, he suggested to Caesar that the sheep must have dropped into some of the many potholes in the area. Reluctantly the Gallianis took off with the depleted flock. The big transport sleds had schedules to keep and shipment could not be postponed.

As the last of them departed, Emily came over to Sean. 'Are your dragons fit for duty yet?'

'Anything you say!' Sean agreed so amiably that Emily shot him a long look. 'The fire-lizards worked hard all morning to feed the dragons.' He gestured towards the cove where Duluth was accepting packtail from a bronze.

'Fire-lizards?' Emily was momentarily baffled by 'lizards'. 'Oh, yes, then your fairs have returned?'

'Not all of them,' Sean said ruefully, and then added

quickly, 'but enough of the queens and bronzes to be useful.'

'The eruption scared them all, didn't it?'

Sean gave a snort. 'The eruption scared all of us.'

'Not out of our wits, it would seem,' Emily said with a crooked smile. 'At least nobody acted as foolish as sheep, did they?' Sean pretended neither innocence nor understanding; he returned her look until she broke eye contact. 'If your dragons have lost the taste for fish, hunt wherries. That eruption whittled down our herds quite enough, thank you.' Sean inclined his head, still non-committal. 'There's so much to be done, and done quickly.' Consulting the thick sheets on her clipboard, she paused to rub her forehead. 'If only your dragons were fully functional . . .' Then she shot him a penitent smile. 'Sorry, Sean, that's an egregious comment.'

'I, too, wish we were, Governor,' Sean replied without prejudice. 'But we're not sure *how* it's done. Not even what to tell them to do.' He blotted the sweat from his forehead and neck, a sweat not entirely provoked by the hot sun.

'A point well made and a matter we must look into, but not here and now. Look, Sean, Joel Lilienkamp's worried about the supplies still at Landing. We're shifting loads out of here as fast as Desi's crew can move it,' and she swept her arm over the mounds of colour-coded crates and foam covered pallettes. 'The orange stuff has to be protected from Threadfall so it has to go north as fast as possible to be stored in the fort hold. We still have to try and save what's left at Landing before the ash covers it.'

'That ash burns, Governor, burns as easily through dragon wings as—' Sean broke off, staring fixedly towards the western beach, one hand coming up in a futile gesture of warning. Emily twisted around to see what prompted his concern.

The dragon's trumpet of alarm was faint, thin on the hot air but the driver of the sled on collision course with him seemed unaware that he was descending on to another

423

flyer. Just before the sled would have landed on top of dragon and rider, they both disappeared.

'Instinct is marvellous!' Emily exclaimed, her face lit with both relief at the last-minute evasion and joy that a dragon had displayed that innate ability. She looked back to Sean and her expression changed. 'What's the matter, Sean?' She glanced quickly up at the sky, a sky empty now of both dragonpair and the sled which was lost in the many coming and going on the Kahrain cove. 'Oh no!' Her hand went to her throat which seemed to close as she felt the wrenching of fear in her guts. 'No. Oh no! Shouldn't they be visible again now? Shouldn't they, Sean? Isn't it supposed to be an instantaneous displacement?'

Distressed, she reached out to clasp his arm, giving him a little shake to attract his attention. He looked down at her and the anguished expression in his eyes gave her an answer that altered fear to grief. She turned her head slowly from side to side, trying to deny the truth to herself.

Just as Desi came striding up to her, a sheaf of plasfilm in his hand, an urgent expression on his face, the most appalling keen rose into the air. The noise was dissonant and caught piercingly in the earbones so that half the people on the beach stopped to cover their ears. In the same moment as the unbearable sound mounted steadily, the air was full of fire-dragonets, each adding its own shrill voice to swell the sound of lament.

The other dragons rose, riderless, to fly past the point where one of their number had lost his life, and that of his human partner. In a complex pattern that would have thrilled watchers on any other occasion, the fire-dragonets flew round and about their larger cousins, emitting their weird counterpoint to the deeper, throbbingly mournful cry of the dragons.

'I'll find out how that could have happened. The driver of that sled . . .' Emily began and then stopped as she saw the terrible expression on Sean's face.

'That won't bring back Marco Galliani and Duluth, will it?' He whipped his hand sidewise in a sharp dismissive cut. 'Tomorrow we will fly wherever you need us for whatever we can save for you.'

For a long, long moment Emily stood looking after him until the image of the sorrowing young man was indelibly imprinted in her mind. In the sky, as if escorting him back to the dragonriders' camp, the graceful beasts wheeled, dipped, and glided westward to their beach.

Whatever pain Emily felt, it could be nothing to the sense of loss that would be experienced by the dragonriders. She scrubbed at her face, at a chin which trembled, determinedly swallowed the lump in her throat and irritably gestured for Desi to approach her.

'Find out who drove that sled and bring him or her to my tent at noon. Now, what's on your mind?'

'Marco and Duluth disappeared, just the way the fire-lizards do,' Sean said, his voice oddly gentle.

'But they *didn't* come back,' Nora cried out in protest and started to weep afresh, burying her face in Peter Semling's shoulder.

The shock of the unexpected deaths of two of their number had been as traumatic for the riders as the dragons. Their lament had subsided over the afternoon. By evening, their partners had coaxed them to curl up in the sand and sleep. Now the young people hunched about a small fire, dispirited and apathetic.

'We have to find out what went wrong,' Sean continued, 'so that it can never happen again.'

'Sean, we don't even know what Marco and Duluth were doing . . .' Dave Caterel cried.

'Duluth was exhibiting an instinctive reaction to danger,' a new voice said, and Pol Nietro, Bay beside him, paused in the light thrown by the fire. 'An instinct he was bred to exercise. May we offer condolences from all those connected with the Dragon Program. We . . . Bay and I . . . why, all of you are like family to us.' Pol awkwardly dabbed at his eyes and sniffed.

'Please join us,' Sorka said with quiet dignity. She rose

425

and drew Bay and Pol into the firelight. Two more packing crates were hauled into the circle.

'We,' Pol continued after he and Bay had settled wearily, 'have tried to figure out what went wrong.'

'Neither looked where he was going,' Sean said with a heavy sigh. 'I was watching. Marco and Duluth took off from the beach and were rising just as the sled driver made an approach turn. He wouldn't have seen Marco and Duluth coming up under him. Dragons aren't fitted with proximity warning devices.' Sean raised both hands in a gesture of helplessness. 'I have it from very good authority that the sled driver had turned his alarm off because the constant noise in so much traffic was getting on his nerves.'

Pol leaned towards him, his body inclining in a movement of renewed sympathy and understanding. 'Then it is more important than ever that you riders teach your dragons discipline.' A ripple of angry denial made him hold up his hands. 'That is not meant to sound censorious, my dear friends. Truly I mean to be constructive. But obviously now is the moment to take the next step in training the dragons ... training them to make proper use of the instinct that ought to have saved both Marco and Duluth today.'

The comment raised murmurs, some angry, some alarmed. Sean held up his hand for silence, his tired face lit by the jumping tongues of flame. Next to him, Sorka was keenly aware of the muscles tightening along his jawline and the stricken look in his eyes.

'I believe we've been thinking along the same lines, Pol,' he said in a taut voice which told the biologist just how much strain Sean Connell was under. 'I think that Marco and Duluth panicked. If only they'd just come back to the place they'd left, the farking sled was gone!' His anguish was palpable, then he took a deep breath and continued in a level, almost emotionless tone. 'All of us have fire-lizards. That's one of the reasons Kitti Ping chose us as candidates. We've all sent them with messages, telling them where to go, what to do or who to look for. We should be able to instruct the dragons to do the same thing. We know now, the hard way, that they can teleport, just as the firelizards do. We have to guide that instinct. We have to discipline it, as Pol suggested, so panic doesn't get us the way it got Marco.'

'Why did Marco panic?' Tarrie Chernoff asked plaintively.

'I'd give anything to know,' Sean said, the edge of anguish returning to his voice. 'One thing I do know, from now on, no rider takes off without checking what's in his immediate airspace. We must fly defensively, trying to spot possible dangers. "Caution" . . .' he emphasized that word by stabbing his index finger into his temple, 'should be engraved on our eyeballs.' He spoke rapidly now, his tone crisp. 'We know that the fire-lizards do go wherever it is they go, *between* one place and another, so let's stop taking that talent of theirs for granted and *watch* exactly what they do. Let's scrutinize their comings and goings. Let's send them to specific places, places they haven't been before, to see if they can follow our mental directions. Our dragons hear us telepathically. They understand exactly what we're saying – not like the fire-lizards – so if we get used to giving precise messages to the fire-lizards, the dragons ought to be able to operate on the same sort of mental directions. When we understand as much of fire-lizard behaviour as we can, *then* we will attempt to direct our dragons.'

The other riders murmured among themselves, Sean watching them with narrowed darting glances.

'Wouldn't that risk our dragonets?' Tarrie asked, stroking the little gold that had nestled in the crook of her arm.

'Better the dragonets than the dragons!' Peter Semling said firmly.

Sean gave a derisive snort. 'The fire-lizards're very good at taking care of themselves. Don't misunderstand me,' and he held up a hand against Tarrie's immediate protest, 'I appreciate them. They've been great little fighters.

Shards, we'd never have fed the hatchlings without their help, but . . .' he paused, looking around the circle, 'they have got a well-developed survival mechanism or they wouldn't have lasted through the first pass of that Oort cloud. Whenever that was. As Peter said, it's a lot safer to experiment with the fire-lizards than another dragonpair.'

'You've made some very good points there, Sean,' Pol said, beginning to take heart himself, 'though I trust you mean to use the gold and bronze fire-dragonets. They have always seemed more reliable to Bay and myself.'

'I had. Especially since the blues and greens all scarpered off after the eruption.'

'I'm game to try,' Dave Caterel said, throwing his shoulders back and straightening up, sending a challenging look at the others. 'We've got to try something. Cautiously!' He shot Sean a quick glance.

A slow smile broke across Sean's face as he reached across the fire to grasp Dave's hand.

'I'm willing, too,' Peter Semling said, and Nora tentatively agreed.

'It sounds eminently sensible to me,' Otto said, nodding vigorously, and looking about him. 'It is, after all, what the dragons were bred to do, escape from the danger of Threadfall as the mechanical sleds cannot.'

'Thanks, Otto,' Sean said. 'We all need to think positively.'

'And cautiously,' Otto amended, raising one finger in warning.

Stirred from their apathy, the riders began murmuring to each other.

'Do you remember, Sorka,' Bay said, leaning towards her urgently, 'when I sent Mariah to you the day we were called to Calusa?'

'She brought me your message.'

'She did indeed, but all I told her was to find the redhead by the caves.' Bay paused significantly. 'Of course, Mariah has known you all her life and there aren't that many redheads in Landing, or on the planet.' Bay knew she was

428

babbling, which is something she rarely did but then she also rarely broke down in tears either, and when she'd heard the dreadful news, she had cried for nearly an hour, despite Pol's comforting. As Pol had said, it had been like losing family. Without a terminal to consult for possible solutions, they had spent two frantic hours searching for the crate in which they had packed all their written notes of the Dragon Program, wanting to have some positive suggestion to comfort the young people. 'But Mariah did find you with no trouble that day, and you were at our house in minutes. So it can't have taken her very long to do it.'

'No, it didn't,' Sorka said thoughtfully. She looked around the circle of firelit faces. 'Think of how many times we told the dragonets to get us fish for the hatchlings.'

'Fish are fish,' Peter Semling remarked, absently prodding the sand with a branch.

'Yes, but the dragonets knew which ones the dragons like best,' Kathy Duff said. 'And it takes them no time at all from the moment we issue the command. They just wink out and a couple of breaths later they're back with a packtail.'

'A couple of breaths,' Sean repeated, looking out to the darkness, his stare fixed. 'It took more than a couple of breaths for any of our dragons to realize that . . . Marco and Duluth were not coming back. Can we infer from that that it also only takes a couple of breaths for dragons to teleport?'

'Cautiously . . .' Otto held up his finger again.

'Right,' Sean went on briskly, 'this is what we do tomorrow morning at first light.' He reached over and took Peter's stick, and drew a ragged coastline in the sand. 'The Governor wants us to ferry stuff out of Landing. Dave, Kathy, Tarrie, you've all got gold fire-lizards. You make the first run. When you get to the Tower, send your fire-lizards back here to me and Sorka. Bay, do you and Pol have to be anywhere else tomorrow?'

Bay gave a derisory sniff. 'The pair of us are useless

until we get our systems going again at Fort Hold. And we have to wait for transport. We'd be delighted to help you, any way we can!'

'We'll time the fire-lizards. Only, we've got to have handsets to do it on the mark . . .'

'Let me scrounge those,' Pol said, raising his hand.

Sean grinned with real humour. 'I was hoping you'd volunteer. Lilienkamp wouldn't deny you, would he?'

Pol shook his head emphatically, feeling much better than he had that afternoon, vainly searching for mislaid documentation during the nadir of his grieving.

'Well then, Bay and I will leave you now,' Pol said, rising to his feet and giving her a helpful hand to her feet. 'To scrounge handsets. How many? Ten? We'll meet you here at dawn, then, with handsets.' He made a bow to the others, noting that only Bay understood his whimsy. 'Yes, at dawn, we'll begin our scientific observations.'

'Let's all get some sleep, riders,' Sean said, rising and scooping sand over the dying flames.

With a handset to his ear, Pol dropped his finger as Bay, Sean and Sorka set the mark on their wrist timers. Keeping index fingers hovering over the stop pin, they all looked up towards the eastern sky, Bay squinting against the sunglare from the smooth sea.

'Now!' Four voices spoke, four fingers moved as a firedragonet erupted into the air over their heads, chirping ecstatically.

'Eight seconds again,' Pol exclaimed happily.

'Come, Kundi,' Sorka said, holding up her arm as a landing spot. Dave Caterel's bronze cheeped, cocking his head as if considering her invitation but he veered away as Duke, Sorka's bronze, warned him off. 'Don't be ugly, Duke.'

'Eight seconds,' Sean said admiringly. 'That's all it takes them to travel fifty-odd klicks.'

'I wonder,' Pol mused, tapping his stylus on the clip-board with its encouraging column of figures. 'The figure doesn't vary no matter who we send which direction. How long would it take them to go to say, Seminole or the fort hold in the north?' He looked with bright inquiry at the others.

Sean began to shake his head dubiously but Sorka was more enthusiastic.

'My brother, Brian, is working at the fort. Duke knows him as well as he knows me. And I've seen plenty of fax of the place. He'd go to Brian.' As if understanding that he was being discussed, Duke circled in to land on Sorka's shoulder. She laughed. 'See, he's game!'

'He may come when he's called,' Sean said, 'but will he go where he's sent? Landing's one thing: they all know it well.'

'We can only try and see,' Pol remarked firmly. 'And this is a good hour to reach Brian at the fort hold.' He punched the comunit. 'What a boon that the Tower's functional. Ah, yes, Pol Nietro speaking. I need an urgent word with Brian Hanrahan . . . I said urgent! This is Pol Nietro. Get him for me! . . . Idiots,' he murmured in an aside. '"Is this call important?"'

Brian was found and was surprised to hear from his sister. 'Look, what's this all about? You don't just scream priority around here. I can assure you that Mother's taking good care of Mick. She dotes on him.'

His slightly aggrieved voice was clear to the others and Sorka was taken aback by his unco-operative response. Sean took the handset from her.

'Brian, Sean here. Marco Galliani and his dragon Duluth died yesterday in an unfortunate accident. We're trying to prevent a recurrence. We're only asking for a few minutes of your time. And this is a priority.'

'Marco and Duluth?' Brian's tone was chastened. 'Shards, we hadn't heard anything. I'm sorry. What can I do?'

'Are you outside? Some place where you can be easily spotted from the air?'

'Yes, I am. Why?'

'Then tell Sorka exactly where you are. I'm handing you over to her.'

'Hell and damnation, Sorka, I'm sorry I dumped on you. So I'm outside. Have you seen the recent fax? Well, I'm approximately twenty metres from the new ramp. At the vet caves. They finally carved us some more headroom and there's a huge pile of rock about a metre from me and nearly as high. What do I do now?'

'Just stand there. I'm sending Duke to you. When I say "mark", set your timer.'

'Come on, now, Sis,' he began in patent disbelief, 'you're in the Kahrain Cove, aren't you?'

'Brian! For once in your life, don't argue with me.'

'All right. I'm ready to mark the time.' He still sounded aggrieved.

Sorka held her arm high, ready to pitch Duke into the air. 'Go to Brian, Duke. He's at the new place! Here!' She screwed her eyes shut and concentrated on an image of Brian standing in the site he had described. 'Go, Duke.'

With a startled squawk, Duke launched himself into the air and vanished.

'Mark!'

'Hey, I can hear you loud and clear, sister. You don't need to roar. I don't know what good this is going to do. You can't imagine for one minute that a fire-dragonet could possibly . . . Shards!' Brian's voice in her ear faded into astonishment. 'I don't bloody believe it. Shit. I forgot to mark time.'

'That's all right,' Sorka said, nodding her head with delight, 'we used your "shards" to mark!'

Pol was jumping up and down, holding his wrist chrono and shouting 'Eight seconds! *Eight seconds!*'

Then he grabbed Bay by the waist and danced around her. Sean lifted Sorka from her feet and kissed her soundly while Mariah and Blazer led an augmented fair of fluting fire-dragonets in a dizzy aerial display.

'Eight seconds to the fort, only eight seconds,' Pol gasped, reeling to a standstill, Bay clinging to him.

'That doesn't make much sense, does it.' Bay said, panting, one hand on her heaving chest. 'The same time to go fifty klicks or nearly three thousand.'

'Hey, Sorka,' came Brian's plaintive voice. She put the handset to her ear again, mopping the sweat off her forehead against her sleeve. 'I really gotta go, only what am I supposed to do with Duke now you've got him here?'

'Tell him to come back to me. And give us the mark when he disappears.'

'Sure, right. On the mark, now . . . Duke, find Sorka! Sorka! Find . . . he's gone. Shit! Mark!'

On the beach at Kahrain cove, four fingers pressed sweep hands, four pairs of eyes turned westward to the hot afternoon skies, and four voices counted the seconds.

'Six . . . seven . . . eight . . . He did it!'

Their elation had new confidence as Duke, cheeping happily, settled back to Sorka's shoulder and rubbed a cold muzzle against her cheek.

'Well, this has been most satisfying and productive,' Bay said, beaming so broadly her eyes were nearly hidden by her cheeks.

'Report it to Emily, will you, Bay?' Sean said, tucking his hand under Sorka's elbow. 'We'd better go do our share of the donk work today.'

'So the Galliani boy's death proved to be a catalyst?' Paul Benden said to Emily as they conferred that evening by comunit.

'Pol and Bay are much encouraged,' Emily replied, still unaccountably saddened by the tragedy. She was tired, she knew, and while she spoke to Paul, hoping for any sort of good news from the northern continent, her mind was half on things that *had* to be organized.

'Telgar's group has made a tremendous effort, Em. The quarters are magnificent. You wouldn't know you were 20–30 feet in solid rock. Cobber and Ozzie have penetrated several hundred feet down on seven tunnels. There's even an eyrie for Ongola's communications equipment, cut high up in the cliff face. This place is big enough to house the entire population of Landing.'

'Not everyone wants to live in a hole in the ground, Paul.'

Emily spoke for herself.

'There are quite a few ground-level caverns, immediate access,' was the soothing reply. 'You wait. You'll see. And when are you coming over? I've got to put in an appearance at the next Fall or they'll fire me.'

'Don't you wish it!'

'Emily,' and Paul's flippant tone turned serious, 'let Ezra take over from you. He and Jim can liaise on shipments. Desi can handle transportation. That assistant of Fulmar's can see to sled and skimmer maintenance. Pierre should be here to supervise the catering arrangements. He's got the biggest kitchen unit on Pern.'

'That would be a welcome change from the largest single barbecue pit! It's the dragons that I worry about, Paul.'

'I think they have to sort it out themselves, Emily. From what you reported, I believe they will.'

'Thank you, Paul,' she replied fervently, heartened by the absolute confidence in his voice. 'I'll reserve a seat on the evening sled tomorrow.'

After the excitement of sending Duke north, directing fire-dragonets back and forth between Kahrain and Landing was anti-climactic but it helped pass the tedium of the long journey. On the way back, Sean had them practise flying in both close and loose formations and more importantly, learn how to identify and benefit from the helpful airstreams.

Their campfire that night was bigger and Pol and Bay slipped into its light to discuss observations about the fire-dragonets and how to apply them to the dragons. Sean had had no real need to promote caution as a byword; Marco and Duluth were very much in everyone's mind. To counter any morbidity, Sean suggested that they get

434

more formation practice the next day, practice that would stand them in good stead during Threadfall.

'If you know where you are in relation to other wing riders, you'll always know where to come back to,' he said, stressing the last word.

'Your dragons are so young,' Pol went on, seeing the favourable reaction, 'in terms of their species . . . the fire-dragonets do not appear to suffer from degeneration. In other words, they don't age as we do physiologically.'

'You mean, they could go on living after we die?' Tarrie asked amazed. She glanced around towards Porth, a darker bulk against the shadowy vegetation.

'From what we've discerned, yes, Tarrie,' Pol replied.

'Our major organs degenerate,' Bay went on, 'although modern technology can effect either repair or replacement, permitting us long, and useful, life-spans.'

'So they're not likely to get sick or ailing?' Tarrie brightened at this prospect.

'That's what we *think*,' Pol answered but held up a warning finger. 'But then we haven't *seen* any elderly dragonets . . .' Sean gave a snort which Sorka softened with a laugh.

'We've really only *our* generation to judge by,' she said. 'At that we only get to treat our own who trust us, and that's usually for scoring or scorching. An occasional hide lesion. I find it comforting to know that dragons are long lived.'

'So long as *we* don't make mistakes,' Otto Hegelman said in a gloomy voice.

'So, we *don't* make mistakes!' Sean's tone was decisive. 'And so that we don't make mistakes, tomorrow let's split up into three sections. Six, six . . . and five. We need three leaders.'

Although Sean had left choice open, he was nominated at once, Dave and Sorka were selected after a minimum of discussion.

Later, when Sean and Sorka had made themselves

comfortable on the sand between Faranth and Carenath she gave him a long hug and a kiss to his cheek.

'What's that for?'

'Giving us all hope. But Sean, I'm worried.'

'Oh?' and Sean stroked her hair away from his mouth and inched his left shoulder into a new hollow.

'I think we oughtn't to wait too long before we try to teleport.'

'My thoughts entirely, and I'm grateful to Pol and Bay for their comments on dragon longevity. Cheered me up too.'

'So, as long as *we* keep our wits, we'll keep our dragons.' She snuggled against him.

'I wish you'd kept your hair long, Sorka,' he muttered pushing another curl out of his mouth. 'I didn't eat so much of it then.'

'Short hair's easier under a riding helmet,' she replied in a sleepy sort of mumble and they both slept.

Although they could see the diminution of the parcels and plastic-cocooned equipment at Landing, cargo did not move out of the Kahrain cove as quickly. That second evening, when Sean was helping his wing riders unload he caught sight of Desi, seated at a makeshift test peering at the small screen of a portable unit.

'Desi, we'll finish off transferring from Landing by tomorrow,' Sean said.

'That's great, Sean, great,' Desi said with such a dismissive wave that Sean had to curb the resentment he felt.

'What the hell's the matter, Desi?' Sean asked and the edge in his voice caused Desi to look up in surprise.

'What's the matter? I've got a beachful of stuff to shift and no transport.' Desi's face was so contorted with anxiety that Sean's rancour dissolved. Arthied nervously scrubbed his face with a sweat-grimed rag.

'I thought the big sleds were coming back.'

'Only when they're recharged and serviced. I wish they'd mentioned that earlier,' and Desi's voice rose in a quaver of frustration. 'All my schedules . . . gone. What'm I to do, Sean?' Desi's voice rose in a quaver of frustration. We'll be under Threadfall again here soon and all that stuff,' he flourished his rag at the bulk of orange cartons, is irreplaceable. If only—' He broke off but not before Sean had a good idea what he was going to say. 'You've done great, Sean, great. I really appreciate it. How much did you say is still to be shipped forward?'

'We'll have cleared it tomorrow.'

'Look, then, the day after,' and Desi rubbed at his face again, trying to hide his flush of embarrassment, 'well, I heard from Paul. He wants you riders to start making your way to Seminole, and cross to the north from there. And . . .' Desi screwed up his face again.

'You'd like us to take some of the orange out of danger?' Sean felt resentment welling up again. 'Well, I suppose that's better than being good for nothing at all.' Sean strode off before his temper got the better of him.

Faranth and Sorka come, Carenath said in a subdued tone. Sean altered his course to their point of arrival. He didn't fool Sorka but he did work off some of his fury during the unloading.

'All right, what happened?' Sorka said, pulling him to the seaward side of the golden queen and shielding them from the other riders, still sorting packages into the colour-coded areas.

Sean set his fist violently into the palm of his other hand several times before he could put words to the humiliation.

'We're considered nothing but bloody pack animals, donks with wings!' he said. He did remember to keep his voice down though he was seething.

Faranth turned her head around her shoulder, regarding the two riders, hints of red beginning to gleam through the blue of her eyes. Carenath shoved his head over her back. Beyond them, Sean heard the other dragons muttering and the next thing he knew, he and Sorka were surrounded by dragons and their riders were weaving into the central point.

437

'Now, see what you've done,' Sorka said with a sigh.

'What's the matter, Sean?' Dave asked, squeezing pas
Polenth.

Sean took a deep breath, burying anger and resentmen
If he couldn't control himself, he couldn't control other
There were flares of the yellow of alarm in the dragon
who looked down at him. He had to quiet them, himse
and the other riders. Sorka was right. He had done some
thing he had better quickly undo.

'We seem to be the only available aerial transportatio
unit,' he said, managing a sort of a smile. 'Desi says a
the big sleds are grounded until they've been serviced.'

'Hey, Sean,' Peter Semling protested, jerking his thum
over his shoulder at the masses of material on the beach
'we can't shift all that!'

'No way,' and Sean made a decisive cut with his hand
'That's not been laid on us. When we've cleared Landing
Paul wants us to fly across to Seminole, and make th
final crossing north from there. Okay,' and now he adde
a genuinely rueful smile, 'but Desi would like us to tak
some of the irreplaceable stuff with us.'

'So long as everyone understands we're not in the freigh
business,' Peter said in an aggrieved tone of voice tha
echoed Sean's sentiments.

'That's not at issue, Peter,' Sean said firmly. 'We'r
improving as dragonriders, coming along fine. But Desi
caught between a rock and a hard place and he needs us

'I just wish we were needed for what we're supposed t
do,' Tarrie remarked.

'Once we've fulfilled our commitment here,' Sean sai
'we concentrate on that, and that alone. I mean to see u
all teleporting by the time we reach Seminole.'

'To places we've never seen?' asked the practical Otto

'No, to the places we've just been. Look on our fligh
to Seminole as a chance to see the most important Stake
in the south,' Sean replied in a bracing tone. He wa
surprised to find himself believing it. 'We'll need suc
reference points to teleport when we're fighting Thread

438

Sorka's face was glowing with pride as he managed to turn round not only his own anger but restate the dignity of their future. And above their heads, the yellow was fading from dragon eyes. 'I can smell food. I'm hungry. Let's go eat. We've earned it.'

'We're going to have to hunt for the dragons before we go skiting across the continent,' Peter said and he jerked his head towards the animal enclosures.

Sean shook his head, smiling as he remembered Emily's oblique warning. 'Can't go to that well twice, Pete. Tomorrow, we'll hunt the critters that got through the roundup in the Landing area,' Sean promised as he pushed through the ring of dragons. 'Food tomorrow, Carenath,' he said, affectionately clouting the bronze as he passed him.

Fish? Carenath queried in a tone that carried dismay.

'Meat. Red meat,' Sean said when some of the dragons bugled gratefully. Laughing, he added, 'But this time we won't kidnap it for you.' Then he put an arm around Sorka and started up the beach to the cooking fires.

The next day, as the three wings of dragonriders crossed the Jordan River, they spread out in three different directions, bypassing the ash-covered settlement, and heading south and east at low levels.

Faranth says, Carenath reported to his rider, *that she has found running meat. Have we?*

Sean had his binoculars trained on a little valley. They were now north of the path of the two Threadfalls that had dropped on this area so there was vegetation to attract grazers.

'Tell her we've hit pay dirt, too.'

Not meat? Carenath asked wistfully.

Sean grinned and slapped his dragon's shoulder. 'Yes, meat, by another name. And all you can eat this time,' he added as the small mixed herd of sheep and cattle stampeded to escape the danger above them. He signalled to the rest of his wing in the exaggerated arm gestures that

439

they had been rehearsing as flight instructions. Handsets were not strictly needed when dragons could communicate with each other though Sean had retained those Pol had scrounged. Too useful to have surrendered but too valuable to risk dropping from a height. 'Land me on that ridge, Carenath. There's enough room for the others.'

Porth says they've enough for all of us, Carenath reported as he touched down gracefully and dipped his shoulder for Sean to dismount.

'Tell Porth we're grateful but you'd better hurry to catch that lot,' Sean advised for the herd was making all possible speed down the valley. He had to shield his face from the gravel and omnipresent ash thrown up by Carenath's abrupt departure. Bright streaks followed the bronze. 'Welcome back,' Sean said derisively as he distinguished blues and greens among the colourful bodies following Blazer as she led the way.

The rest of his wing soon joined him, Nora Sejby managing a creditable landing on Tenneth. She was improving all the time but he had kept her in his wing. He didn't worry half as much about Catherine Radelin-Doyle: she hadn't giggled with Singlath since the tragedy. Nyassa, Otto and Jerry Mercer completed his wing. Once their dragons followed the hunt, Sean turned his glasses on Carenath, saw him swoop and grab a steer neatly without slowing his forward motion.

'Nice catch, Carenath!' Sean passed the binoculars to Nyassa to check on Milath.

'Seemed to me there were quite a lot of cattle in that bunch,' Jerry said, pulling off his helmet and ruffling his sweat-damp hair. 'What'll happen to them?'

Sean shrugged. 'The best stock went north. These survive or they won't.'

'Sean, look who's come to dinner?' Nyassa said, pointing northwards at the unmistakable outline of five wherries. 'Go to it!' she added as she caught a glimpse of fire-dragonets launching an attack on the intruders. 'Wait your turn!'

'I brought some lunch,' Catherine said, twisting out of er backpack. 'We might as well take a meal break, too.'

Sean called a halt to the hunt when each dragon had nsumed two animals. Carenath complained that he'd ad only one big one, so he needed two of the smaller nd. Sean replied that Carenath's belly would be so full e'd be unable to fly and they still had work to do. The agons grumbled, Carenath ingenuously remarking that aranth wanted another meal, too, but Sean was adamant d the dragons proved obedient.

Sean reformed the wing once they were aloft.

'All right, Carenath,' Sean said, thinking ahead with lief to the last loads at Landing, 'let's get back to the ower as fast as we can and get this over with!'

He raised his arm and dropped it.

The next instant he and Carenath were enveloped in a ackness that was so absolute Sean was certain his heart ad stopped.

I will not panic! he said fiercely, pushing the memory f Marco and Duluth to the back of his mind. His heart ced now and he was aware of the stunning cold of this ack nothingness.

I am here!

Where are we, Carenath? But Sean already knew. They ere *between*. He focused intense thoughts on their desti- ation, remembering the curious ash-filtered light around anding, the shape of the Meteorology Tower, the flatness f the grid beyond it, the bundles awaiting them there.

We are at the Tower, Carenath said, somewhat sur- ised and in that instant, they were. Several hundred rds above it and Sean cried aloud with relief.

'Shards! What have I done?' he shrieked, wide-eyed ith a sudden terror. 'Where are the others, Carenath? eak to them!'

They're coming, Carenath replied with the utmost calm d confidence.

Before Sean's unbelieving eyes, his wing suddenly mater- lized behind him, still in formation.

441

'Land, Carenath, please, before I fall off you,' Sean said in a whisper made weak by the unutterable relief he felt.

As the others circled in to land, Sean remained seated on Carenath, reviewing everything, half in wonder, half in remembered terror at the unthinkable risk that had just been unaccountably survived.

'Keeeeyoooo!' Nyassa's yodel of triumph brought him up short. She was swinging her riding helmet above her head as Milath landed beside Carenath. Catherine and Singlath came in on the other side, Jerry Mercer and Manooth beyond them, Otto and Shoth beside Tennet and Nora.

'Hip, hip, hooray!' Jerry led the cheer while Sean stared at them, not knowing what to say.

It was easy, you know. You thought me where to go and I went. You did tell me to go as fast as possible. Carenath's tone was mildly reproving.

'If that is all there is to it, what took us so long?' Otto wanted to know.

'Anyone got a spare pair of pants?' Nora ask plaintively. 'I was so scared I wet myself. But we did it!'

Catherine giggled. The sound brought Sean to his senses and he allowed himself to smile.

'We were ready to try!' he said, shrugging nonchalantly as he unbuckled his riding straps. Then he realized that he, too, would need to find a clean pair of pants.

21

●

I said, we'll maintain silence about Emily's condition,'
Paul said sternly, glaring at Ongola, Ezra Keroon, and the
scowling Joel Lilienkamp. He did *not* want Lilienkamp
taking book on whether or not Emily Boll survived her
concussion. That would be unacceptable as well as
macabre. He moderated his expression as his eyes rested
on the bent head of Fulmar Stone who kept pulling with
agitated fingers at a wad of grease-stained rag. 'As far as
Fort Hold is concerned, she's resting comfortably. That is
the truth, according to Basil and all the support systems
monitoring her condition. For outside inquiries, she's
busy, shunt the call to Ezra.'

Abruptly Paul pushed himself to his feet and began to
pace his new office, the first apartment on the level above
the Great Hall. Its windows gave an unimpeded view of
that end of the valley. Eventually, the ordered rows of
cargo and supplies would be stored in the vast subter-
anean caverns of Fort. So much had to be done; he sorely
missed Emily's supportive presence.

Paul caught himself fingering the prosthetic fingers and
jammed both hands into his pockets. His position had
required him to contain his distress, in order to avoid
alarming people already under considerable tension. But,
before these close and trusted friends, he could give vent
to anxieties which they all shared.

The disastrous failure of the big sled's gyros and its
crash had been visible to the inhabitants of Fort Hold but
few had known that the Governor had been a passenger

that night. They could be honest about the severity of Theo Force's injuries for the pilot would recover from two broken arms and the lacerations. None of the other passengers had been severely hurt and those who rescued the injured hadn't recognized Emily, her face bloodied by the head wound. At least until she was, Paul would not allow the facts to be common knowledge. Following so closely after the exodus from Landing, that crash, with the loss of some irreplaceable medical supplies as well as the sled, had to be minimized to sustain morale.

'Pierre agrees,' Paul went on. He could feel the resistance from the others, the unspoken opinion that suppression would undermine his credibility. 'Even insists on it. It's what Emily would want. He's with her constantly, talking to her, reading aloud.'

In his pacing, Paul inadvertently glanced out the deepest window and averted his eyes from the view of the deep scar which the sled had gouged two days ago. 'Ezra, get someone to smooth that over, will you? I see it every time I look out the window.'

Ezra murmured a response and made a note.

'How long can we expect Emily's state to be kept a secret?' Ongola wanted to know, his face graven with new worry lines and his disapproval of this expedient. His people were famous for their discretion but you could almost count on bad news leaking: the worse the news the quicker it disseminated.

'As long as we have to, dammit, Ongola! We can at least spare people one more worry, especially when we haven't got a positive prognosis.' Paul drew in a deep breath. 'The head wound wasn't serious – no skull fracture, but it was a while before she was removed from the sled. The trauma wasn't treated quickly enough, and we don't have the sophisticated equipment to relieve the shock of multiple fractures. Monitor indicates no cerebral dysfunction. Basil says we just have to wait. Fulmar,' and now Paul swung to the engineer, 'there will be a transport

444

sled ready to go south today, won't there? I can't keep stalling Desi.'

'All that orange coded stuff is irreplaceable,' Joel added, rearranging himself in the chair. 'Not that we've got half the stuff moved inside here yet, but it'd be a sight more protectable in our front yard than on some frigging beach half a world away. Otherwise,' and Joel addressed Paul, 'you're going to have to send Keroon back for it. And I'll figure out a new schedule of priorities. You couldn't make that two sleds to go, could you, Fulmar?'

Fulmar looked up at him with eyes so reddened by strain and grief that even the doughty Storesman recoiled in dismay. He knew that Stone's crews had been working impossible hours to service the big transport sleds. Joel would admit only to himself that more of the blame of that crash could be attributed to Stores than to Maintenance. But what could you do with one emergency after another dumping on you?

'Whenever you can, Fulmar,' Joel said in a gentler tone, 'whenever they're ready.' He walked out of the room without a backward glance.

'We're doing our best, Admiral,' Fulmar said wearily, struggling to his feet. He looked at the rag in his hands, perplexed to see it in tatters and then jammed it into his hip pocket.

'I know, man, I know.' Placing his arm across Fulmar's hunched shoulders, Paul guided the man to the door, giving him a final appreciative squeeze. 'In all that spare time you have, Fulmar, run up a list of servicing dates on the smaller craft. I've got to know how many I'll have for this Fall.'

'The accident was no one's fault,' Paul said, returning to his desk and slumping down into his chair. 'There's Fulmar, blaming himself for not insisting on servicing earlier. For that matter, I shouldn't have urged Emily to come north. The cargo was inadequately secured in the cabin. However, gentlemen, it is folly to read more into such an accident than bad timing and a lousy concat-

445

enation of circumstances. We evacuated Landing in reasonable order. A place had been prepared for us,' and Paul managed a thin smile at a reference to happier moments, 'and we've got to mobilize enough personnel and machines to fight Thread.' He no longer hoped for support from either dragonets or dragons.

'You did *what*?' Sorka cried, her skin blanching and the next instant flushing brightly, as only a redhead's can, in fury. Faranth, her eyes whirling orange in sympathy with her rider, lowered her head. Carenath bugled alarm.

Sean grabbed Sorka by the arms, obscurely irritated by such reactions. He had managed to get the others to wait until Sorka's wing had landed before broadcasting their feat.

'Look, it wasn't something I planned, Sorka! Jays, it was the last thing in my head. I just told Carenath to get back to Landing as fast as possible. He did.'

It was really very simple, Carenath was saying modestly. *I've told Faranth. She believes me.* And he swivelled his head to cast a reproachful look on Sorka.

'How . . . how . . . did the others know?' Fear returned to shadow her eyes. She ignored the general carry-on about her as Sean's wing cavorted with her riders, babbling the good news and going into specific detail at the top of their lungs.

He told them, Faranth replied, an edge on her tone.

'We've spent two hours figuring that out,' Sean said, smiling to coax one from Sorka. Putting his arm about her shoulders, he drew her back to the others. 'I think . . .' and he chose his words carefully, 'we were all scared shitless by Marco and Duluth dying like that. Now we know, firsthand, why Marco panicked. Sorka, it's like nothing you've ever seen, and you can't feel anything, even your dragon between your legs. Otto called it total sensory deprivation.'

It is between, Carenath said in an almost didactic tone. He and Faranth followed their riders back to the mass of

446

netted bundles which would be their final load. The dragons of Sean's wing were sitting on their haunches in a loose circle, occasionally shaking themselves to dislodge windblown ash. Faranth made a noise low in her throat which made Sean grin. The golden queen was as sceptical as her rider.

'Can Faranth tell me how far away Dave's wing is?' he asked her.

They are in sight now, Carenath said just as Sorka replied, 'Faranth says they're in sight now,' and she pointed northeast. 'Polenth says that they hunted well. Meat!' Sorka gave a brief smile and Sean decided that she was halfway to forgiving him.

There was of course renewed astonishment and rueful congratulations when Dave and his wingriders heard the news.

'Okay then,' Sean said, mounting a carton to address them all, 'this is what we do, riders. We teleport to Kahrain Cove. We know its aerial aspect as well as we know Landing's. So it's the perfect test. Carenath insists that he told the other dragons where they were going, but I'd prefer that you riders tell your own dragon where to go. I think that has to be as much part of our preflight drill,' and he grinned at them, 'as strapping on and checking the immediate airspace.'

'What're we going to tell *them*?' Dave asked, jerking a thumb in a northerly direction.

'Emily's gone to join the Admiral. Pol and Bay were supposed to get the first sled back.' Sean paused, looking around again, and then gave Sorka a long look. She gave him a slow nod of approval. 'I think we keep this to ourselves for the time being. We'll spring the finished product on them, fighting ready dragons! It's one thing to send a fire-lizard north on the strength of fax, but I sure wouldn't want to risk Carenath going someplace *I've* never been.' Sean took another deep breath, having gauged the favourable reaction. 'Desi said we're to make our way along the coast to Seminole. That'll give us time to practise teleporting between where we are and where we've been. That way we'll know exactly how to get back to any of the major Stakes when we need to fight Thread over them.'

'Yeah, but the dragons don't flame yet,' Peter Semling pointed out.

'There's phosphine-bearing rock all along the coast. We've all watched the fire-lizards chew rock. That's the easiest part of this whole thing,' Sean replied dismissively.

'It's one thing to go from one place to another,' Jerry began slowly, 'we've *done* it now. We go from here—' and he stabbed his left index finger, 'to there' and he held up his right finger, 'and the dragons do the work. But dodging Thread . . . or a sled—' and he broke off.

'Duluth caught Marco off-balance, he panicked,' Sean spoke quickly and confidently. 'Frankly, Jerry, that place between scared me and I'll lay book the rest of us were. But now we know, we adapt. We'll plan emergency evasive tactics.' Sean pulled the knife out of his boot-cuff and hunkered down. 'Most of us have flown sleds or skimmers in Threadfall so we've seen *how* the junk drops . . . most of the time . . .' and he drew a series of long diagonal stripes in the ash. 'A rider sees he's on a collision course with Thread . . . here . . .' he dug his point in, 'and *thinks* a beat forward . . .' he jumped the point ahead. 'We'll have to practise skipping like that. It's going to take quick reflexes. We see fire-lizards using such tactics all the time . . . wink in, wink out . . . when they're fighting Thread with ground crews. If they can, dragons can!'

The dragons bugled in answer to the challenge and Sean grinned broadly.

'Right?' Sean's question dared the riders now.

'Right!' was the enthusiastic reply and fists were brandished to show staunch determination.

'Well, then,' and Sean stood up, bringing his hands together with an audible smack. Ash shifted off his shoulders. 'Let's load up and teleport ourselves back to Kahrain.'

'What if someone sees us, Sean?' Tarrie asked anxiously.

'What? The flying donks doing what they were designed to do?' he asked sarcastically.

'Obviously,' Paul told the worried pilots, 'we're not going to be able to protect as much land with such a depleted aerial coverage.'

'Dammit, Admiral,' Drake Bonneau said, twisting his face into a worried frown, 'we were supposed to have enough power packs to last fifty years!'

'We did,' Joel Lilienkamp jumped to his feet once again, 'under normal usage. They have *not* had what anyone could possibly term normal usage, or even normal maintenance. And don't blame Fulmar Stone and his crew. I don't think they've had a full night's sleep in months. The best mechanics in the world can't make sleds operate on half-charged or badly charged packs.' Glaring belligerently around him, he sat down hard and the chair rocked on the stone floor.

'So it really is a case of taking the greatest care of the sleds and skimmers we have left, or have no aerial vehicle at all in a year?' Drake asked plaintively.

No one answered him immediately.

'That's it, Drake,' Paul finally replied. 'Burn a swathe around your homes and what vegetable crops you've managed to save, keep the home Stake clear . . . and thank whatever agency you will that hydroponics are available.'

'Where're those dragons? There were eighteen of them . . .' Chaila wanted to know.

'Seventeen,' Ongola corrected her. 'Marco Galliani died at Kahrain, with the brown Duluth.'

'Sorry, forgot that,' Chaila murmured but continued. 'Where are the others? I thought they were to take up when vehicles failed.'

'They're en route from Kahrain,' Paul replied.

'Well?' Chaila prompted pointedly.

'The dragons are not yet a year old,' Paul said. 'According to Wind Blossom—' and he noted the subtle disapproving reaction to her name, '—Pol and Bay, the dragons

will not be mature enough to be fully . . . operational . .
for another two or three months.'

'In two or three months,' someone called out bitterly
'there'll have been between eighteen and twenty more
uncontained Falls . . .'

Fulmar rose, turning to the back of the chamber. 'We
will have three completely reconditioned sleds back on
line in three weeks.'

'I heard there were more creatures hatched,' Drake said
'Is that true, Admiral?'

'Yes, that's true.'

'Are *they* any good?'

'Six more dragons,' Paul said, more heartily than he
felt.

'Removing six more young people from our defensive
strength!'

'Giving us six more potential self-maintaining, self-
propagating fighters!' Paul rose to his feet. 'Consider the
project in the right perspective. We have got to have an
aerial defence against Thread. We have bio-engineered an
indigenous life form to supply that critical need. They
will!' He laced his voice with conviction. 'In a few generations—'

'Generations?' The cry elicited angry murmurs from an
audience already unnerved by an unpalatable briefing.

'Dragon generations,' Paul said, raising his voice over
the reactions. 'The fertile females are mature enough to
reproduce when they're two and a half or three years. A
dragon generation is three years. The queens will lay
between ten to twenty eggs. We've ten golds from the first
Hatching, three from this second one. In five, ten years,
we'll have an invincible aerial defence system to combat
the intruder.'

'Yeah, Admiral, and in a hundred years there won't be
any space for humans left on the planet!' The suggestion
was met with a ripple of nervous laughter and Paul smiled,
grateful to the anonymous wit.

'It won't come to that,' he said, 'but we will have

450

a unique defence system, bio-engineered to our needs. And useful in other ways. Desi tells me the dragon-riders've been delivering supplies to the Stakes as they make their way here to Fort. Meanwhile, you have your orders.'

Paul Benden rose and left quickly, Ongola right behind him.

'Dammit, Ongola, where the hell are they?'

'They check in every morning. Their progress is good. We can't ask more of an immature species. I heard Bay tell you that she and Pol both worried that the dragons had been dangerously extended during the evacuation.'

Paul sighed. 'Not that there is any other way for them to get here with the transport situation.' He started down the winding iron stairs that went from the executive level to the underground laboratory complex. 'Wind Blossom's staff has to be reassigned. We don't have time, personnel or resources for further experimentation no matter what she says.'

'She's going to want to appeal to Emily!' Ongola replied.

'Let's devoutly hope that she can! Any news from Jim this morning?' Paul had reached the state of mind where he was so saturated with bad news he didn't feel additional blows so keenly. Yesterday's news that Jim Keroon's convoy, a day's sailing past Boca, had been caught in a sudden tropical storm which capsized nine craft had seemed almost inconsequential.

'He reports no loss of life,' Ongola said reassuringly, 'and all but two of the boats have been refloated and can be repaired. The dolphins are recovering cargo. There is some heavy stuff, though, that divers will have to locate. Fortunately, they were in shallow water and the storm didn't last long.' Ongola hesitated.

'Well, let me have it,' Paul said, pausing on a landing.

'There were no manifests so there's no way of checking that they've recovered everything.'

Paul regarded Ongola stolidly. 'Does he have any idea how long that's going to hold him up?' When Ongola shook his head, 'All the more reason, then, to reassign Wind Blossom's personnel. When that's done, I'll have a word with Jim. It's incredible that he's got such an ill-assorted flotilla as far as he has! Through fog, Fall, and storm!'

Ongola agreed fervently.

While Carenath concentrated very carefully on chewing, Sean stood slightly to one side of him, trying not to be anxious. Fire-dragonets flitted around the dragons, chirping what was obviously encouragement. Duke and some of the other bronzes had found pebbles which they were masticating in demonstration.

The dragons and their riders had located the necessary phosphine-bearing rock on an upland plateau halfway between the Malay River and Sadrid. Over the past few days, the confidence of the riders had improved as time and again they were able to teleport to and from given landmarks. Otto Hegelman had suggested that each rider keep a log, noting down reference points for later identification. The notion had been enthusiastically adopted although it was immediately necessary for them to request writing materials at the Malay River Stake. They'd been surprised to find only children there with Phas Radamanth's sixteen-year-old daughter in charge.

'Everyone's out fighting Thread, you know,' she said, cocking her head at them in what Tarrie later said was pure insolence.

'Desi gave us supplies for you,' Sean replied, stifling his resentment of her implied criticism and the present menial status of dragonriders. He gestured for Jerry and Otto to bring the cargo net into the house. 'Would you have any notebooks we could have?'

'What for?'

'We're doing a coastline survey,' Otto said at his most pompous.

The girl blinked, surprised, and her face relaxed into a less antagonistic expression. 'I guess so. There's all that sort of stuff in the schoolroom over there. Who has time for lessons these days?'

'You're most kind,' Jerry said, giving her a quick bow and a broader grin as they withdrew.

The incident had reinforced the riders' determination to accomplish their purpose during their westward journey and this was the first 'firestone' they had found. Actually, it was the fire-dragonets who located it and were doing their best to instruct their larger cousins in its use.

'It isn't as if you can chew for him, Sean,' Sorka said, holding out another piece to Faranth. 'How much do they need to eat?'

'Who knows how much stoking it takes to start a dragon's fires?' Tarrie sang out cheerfully. 'I'd say this,' and she hefted the stone in her hand, 'is comparable to the pebble-size I used to feed my gold dragonet. Isn't it, Porth?'

The queen obediently lowered her head and took the offering.

'The dragonets chew at least a handful before they can flame,' Dave Caterel said but he was watching Polenth dubiously as the bronze worked his jaws with the same solemn contemplative look the others had. 'Look, Sorka, your fair's setting the example!'

Indeed Duke let go a fine long plume of fire while Blazer took to the air, scolding him.

Just then Porth let out a squawk, her mouth opening and a green-stained rock fell to the ground, just missing Tarrie's foot. Porth snapped her mouth shut and moaned.

'What did she do?' Dave asked.

'She says she bit her tongue,' Tarrie replied and patted Porth's shoulder sympathetically. 'She did, too. Look!' The green ichor on the rock glistened in the sunlight. 'Should I look, Sorka? She might have done herself damage.'

'What does Porth say?' Sorka asked with professional detachment. She couldn't recall ever having had to deal with self-inflicted dragonet bites.

'It hurts and she'll wait until it doesn't before she chews any more rock.' Tarrie retrieved the offending piece and put it back in the pile they had gathered.

Another draconic exclamation of pain and Nora's Tenneth followed Porth's bad example. Sean and Sorka exchanged worried glances and continued to offer the firestone to their dragons.

Suddenly Polenth burped and a tiny flame leapt beyond his nose, startling the bronze backward.

'Hey, he did it!' Dave cried proudly. 'Phew!' he added, waving the air from his face. 'Stand down wind, folks. That stinks.'

'Watch it!' Sean leapt sideways as Carenath belched, surprising everyone with a respectable tongue of flame that just missed searing his rider. Overhead the fire-lizards flew in congratulatory circles, alternately chirping or expelling flame, their eyes whirling bright-blue with approval.

'Downwind and to one side, riders!' Sean amended. 'Try it again, Carenath!' Sean offered a larger chunk.

'Shards, that's awful!' Tarrie said as the wind blew the overpowering stench of the fire-making stone straight into her face. Choking, she ducked around Porth to escape it.

'Where there's fire, there's smell,' quipped Jerry. 'No, Manooth, turn your head that way!'

Just as the brown dragon obeyed, a blast of flame erupted from his mouth and seared into charcoal one of the scrawny bushes that dotted the plateau. Jerry pounded his dragon's shoulder in exultation.

'You did it! Manooth! Master blaster!'

The others returned to stoking their dragons with renewed enthusiasm. An hour later, all the males had produced flame but none of the females, though the golds had chewed and chewed until one after the other, they had regurgitated an awful grey pastelike substance.

'As I recall the program,' Sean said as the gold riders stood disconsolately about, 'the queens aren't mature until

454

they're nearly three. The males are . . . well . . .' Sean cast about for a diplomatic phrase.

'Functional now . . .' Tarrie finished for him, none too pleased.

'Even seven recruits are going to be well received at Fort,' Otto said, for once not trying to sound pompous.

Sorka was frowning though, an unusual enough expression on her face to cause Tarrie to inquire.

'I was just thinking. Kitti Ping was such a traditionalist . . .' Sorka regarded her husband for a long moment and then he ducked his head, unable to maintain the eye contact. 'All right, Sean, you know every symbol in that program. Did Kitti Ping introduce a gender discrimination?'

'A what?' Tarrie asked. The other queen riders now gathered close and the young men took discreet backward steps.

'A gender inhibition . . . meaning the queens lay eggs and the other colours fight!' Sorka was disgusted.

'It may just be that the queens aren't mature enough yet,' Sean said, temporizing. 'I haven't been able to figure out some of Kitti Ping's equations. Maybe the flame production is a mature ability. I don't know why the queens all barfed. We'll have to ask Pol and Bay when we get to Fort. But I tell you what, there's no reason you girls can't use flamethrowers. With wands a bit longer, you wouldn't singe your dragon by mistake.'

His suggestion did much to mollify the queen riders then but Sean did hope, fervently, that Pol and Bay could give a more acceptable verdict. Seventeen dragons made a more impressive display than seven. And he was determined to impress when the dragonriders flew into Fort Hold. The only burdens dragons should ever carry again would be their riders and firestone!

'Actually, Paul,' Telgar said, glancing at Ozzie and Cobber, 'those photophobes of Wind Blossom's have proved to be extremely useful in subterranean explorations. Their

455

instinct for hidden dangers ... pitfalls, in fact ...' and the geologist gave one of his humourless smiles, '... blind tunnels is infallible. I'd like to keep them now that Wind Blossom has abandoned them, so to speak.' Telgar turned to Pol and Bay.

'It's a relief to know they've some use,' Pol said, sighing heavily. Both he and his wife had tried to reason with the indignant Wind Blossom when the dragon program had to be suspended. Though she maintained that the emergency transfer from Landing to Fort had damaged many of the eggs in the clutch she had manipulated, Pol and Bay had seen the autopsy reports and knew that claim to be spurious. They'd been lucky to hatch six live creatures.

'Once they get to trust you, they're quite harmless,' Telgar went on. 'Cara adores the latest hatchling and it won't let her out of its sight ...' again that mirthless smile, 'unless she leaves the Hold. Keeps watch at her door by night.'

'We can't have uncontrolled breeding of those creatures,' Paul said quickly.

'We'll see to that, Admiral,' Ozzie said solemnly, 'but they're right useful little buggers.'

'Strong, too, carry more'n they weigh themselves out of the mines,' Cobber added.

'All right, all right. Just limit the breeding.'

'Eat anything,' Ozzie added for good measure. 'Anything so they keep a place clean.'

Paul continued to nod agreement. 'I just want any further propagation cleared with Pol and Bay for the biology department.'

'We're delighted, I assure you,' Bay said. 'I didn't approve of them but I also cannot approve summary termination of any living creature which can be useful.'

Telgar rose abruptly and Bay, wondering if her words had reminded him of Sallah's death, mentally chastised herself for not thinking before she spoke. Had her mention of summary termination reminded him of Sallah's death. Ozzie and Cobber sprang to their feet as well.

'Now that you've finally finished mapping the Fort Hold complex,' Paul said, deftly filling the awkward moment, 'what are your plans, Telgar?'

A flash of enthusiasm briefly lightened the geologist's face. 'The probe reports indicated ore deposits in the Western Range that should be assayed as an alternative to power-costly haulage from Karachi Camp. Best to have resources close to hand.' Telgar inclined his head in an abrupt farewell and then strode from the room, Ozzie and Cobber mumbling something suitable as they followed him.

'How that man has changed!' Bay said softly, her round face sad.

Paul observed a respectful silence. 'I think we all have, Bay. Now, is anything to be done about Wind Blossom's intransigence?'

'Nothing until she has an interview with Emily herself,' Pol said, his expression neutral. Of necessity, the two micro-biologists had been informed of the Governor's true condition which, twelve days after the accident, remained virtually unchanged.

'I don't know why she won't accept your decision, Paul,' Bay said, showing some agitation.

'Tom Patrick says Wind Blossom chooses to distrust the male half of this leadership,' and Paul grinned. Actually he did find the situation ludicrous but, now that Wind Blossom had immured herself in her quarters until she 'had had a fair hearing', he had grasped the opportunity to transfer personnel to more productive employment. Most of them had been grateful. 'You will, of course, continue to monitor the new dragon hatchlings.'

'Of course. What's the latest word from Sean and the others?' Pol asked, a trifle anxious. He and Bay had discussed their continued absence and begun to wonder if it was deliberate. They both knew that Sean harboured a certain amount of resentment for their messenger status. But what else could he expect? Everyone had to do what they could. He and Bay were not exactly inspired by Kwan

457

Marceau's project to monitor the grubs from the grass plot at Calusa, but that was where they could perform a useful service.

'They should be here soon,' Paul's voice and expression were neutral and he changed the subject immediately. 'When does Kwan anticipate a northern trial on those worms of his?'

'More grub than worm,' Pol said didactically. 'Sufficient have been propagated for a ground test.'

'That's good news indeed,' Paul said heartily, rising to his feet. 'Remember, tomorrow won't be a good day for any kind of test!'

Pol and Bay exchanged looks. 'Is it true, Admiral,' Pol asked, 'that you're not going to fly the full Fall across the mountains?'

'That's right, Pol. We have neither the personnel, the power nor sleds enough to do more than protect the immediate area. So, if those grubs are of any assistance, we will all be grateful to you.'

When they had left, Paul sank back down in his chair, swivelling to look out the window at the starlit night. It was cold up here in the north but the crisp air made these now familiar star patterns crystal clear. Sometimes, he could almost imagine that he was back in space again. He sighed heavily and picked up the terminal. He had to find some vestige of hope in that depressing inventory Joel had submitted.

If they were extremely careful, used sleds and skimmers on only the most critical errands, they might just last out this pass through the Oort cloud matter. When it came around again, what would they do? Paul winced as he remembered the arrogance of Ted Tubberman in pre-empting the dispatch of the homing device. Had the man known how to activate it properly? Ironic, that! Would it be received? Acted upon? With the help of the technological society they had foresworn, his descendants could survive. Did he want them to? Had they any other choice? With adequate technology, the problem of Thread could

458

ossibly be solved. So far ingenuity and natural resources ad failed miserably.

Fire-breathing dragons, indeed! A ridiculous concept, traight out of folk tales. And yet . . .

Resolutely Paul began to scroll out the stark facts and igures of the colony's dwindling supplies.

Tarrie!' Peter Chernoff came rushing to greet his sister rom the cavernous barn set on the east edge of the eminole Stake headquarters. He was much like his older ister in feature but topped her by inches, able to look lown at all the other riders who now surrounded him. Say, you guys, where have you all been?'

'We've been reporting in to Fort every day,' Sean said, urprised.

'I made yesterday's report and even spoke to brother ake,' Tarrie cried, alarmed, her expression anxious. What's the matter, Petey?'

Peter Chernoff was reluctant to explain, stamping his eet as he hedged and hawed.

'Things are getting tougher. We're not to fly anything nywhere that isn't priority number-one top emergency.'

'So that's why we saw so much Thread damage,' Otto aid, shocked.

Peter nodded solemnly. 'And there's Fall at Fort Hold oday and they'll have to sit it out.'

'Without any attempt . . .' Dave Caterel was appalled.

'Transporting Landing to the north put too big a strain n sled and power packs.' Peter peered down at them, udging their reaction. 'And the Governor was injured, ou know. No one's seen her in weeks.'

'Oh, no,' Sorka said, leaning into Sean for comfort. Nora Sejby began to weep softly.

Peter gave another of his solemn nods. 'It's pretty bad. Pretty bad.'

Suddenly everyone was demanding news of their own in and Peter did his best to answer when he could. 'Look, guys, I don't sit on the comunit all the time. The word is

out to sit tight and keep the home stake as clear as possible
with ground crews. There's plenty of HNO-3, and it's
easy to maintain tanks and wands.'

'But not the land,' Sean said, raising his voice authoritat-
ively. The babble around died abruptly and his riders
looked to him. 'There's Thread at Fort today, you said.
When?'

Peter stammered, 'Right now! Well, it starts out over
the Bay—'

'And you have throwers here? Ten of 'em that we could
use?' Sean asked eagerly.

'Use? Well, you'd have to ask Cos and he's not here
right now . . . And what do you need ten throwers for?'

Grinning his head off, Sean turned with a flourish
of his hand to indicate the gold riders. 'The girls need
them to fight Thread! And we've got to work fast to be
ready—'

'Whaddya mean?' Peter was dumbfounded. 'The Fall's
started. You wouldn't even make it out across the sea
before it's over. And you're supposed to get in touch with
Fort the moment you get here!'

'Peter, be a good lad, don't argue. Show the girls where
the throwers are kept and let me see the latest fax of Fort
Hold. Or better, the Fort harbour I heard they built.
Dragons are a lot faster than that fleet Jim Keroon's
shepherding. They haven't passed the Delta West Head
yet.'

Sean gave Peter no time to think or protest. He sent
Otto to make use of Cos Melvinah's office and ran off
copies of the installation at the mouth of the Fort Hold
river. Tarrie chivvied her brother into showing them where
the flamethrowers were kept and helping the girls check
out the tanks. In a flurry of golden wings, the queens
landed at that storehouse and permitted Sean, Dave and
Shih to secure additional tanks to their backs. Sean
shouted directions to Jerry and Peter Semling to check the
cargo nets of firestone on the browns and bronzes. Peter
Chernoff went from one rider to another, pleading with

hem to stop. What was he to do? How was he to explain
ll this to Cos? When would they bring all this equipment
ack? They couldn't leave Seminole defenceless.

Then all the frenzied preparations were completed and
he bronze and brown dragons had chewed as much
restone as they could swallow.

'Check straps!' Sean roared. He was developing quite a
owerful bellow. He didn't need to shout, all the dragons
vere listening to Carenath, but it served to release adrena-
ne into his system and it was what a leader should do to
ncourage those who followed him into danger.

'*Checked!*' was the prompt response.

'*Do we know where we're going?*' Setting the example
imself, he spread out the fluttering fax for one last long
)ok at the seafront installation, the wharf, the metal
nloading crane looking like an awkward alien species
unched high over the metal beams that had once been
art of a spaceship.

'*We know!*'

'*Check your airspace?*' He turned his head to the left and
he right of Carenath who was vibrating in his eagerness to
ımp off.

'*Checked!*'

'*Remember to skip! Let's go!*'

Rising up from Carenath's neck as far as his riding
traps would permit, Sean raised his arm high, rotated his
and and then dropped it as the signal to spring.

Seventeen dragons launched themselves skyward,
rrowing upwards in the bright tropical sky in two V
ormations. Then, as a bewildered and incredulous Peter
Chernoff watched, the Vs disappeared.

Chin dropped, Peter stared for one more long moment
nd then, turning on his heels, raced to the office and
aunched himself at the comunit.

'Fort, this is Seminole. Fort, do you copy? Only you
von't.'

'Peter, is that you?' asked his brother Jake.

'Tarrie was here, but she left, with a flamethrower.'

461

'Get a hold of yourself, Pete. You're not making an sense.'

'They all came. They took our flamethrowers and ha the tanks and left. All of them. All at once.'

'Peter, calm down and make sense.'

'How can I make sense when I don't believe what I sav anyhow!'

'Who was there? Tarrie and who else?'

'Them. The ones who ride dragons. They've gone t Fort. To fight Thread!'

Paul picked up the comunit. Any occupation was prefer able to sitting like a barnacle on a hull in a shuttered roor while a voracious organism rained down outside.

'Admiral?' Excitement tingled through Ongola's singl word. 'We've had word that the dragonriders are on the way here.'

'Sean and his group?' Paul wondered why that woul excite Ongola. 'When did they start?'

'Whenever they started, sir, they're already here.' Pav wondered if disappointment had got the better of Z Ongola, his imperturbable second-in-command, for h could swear the man was laughing. 'The seaport ask should they join the aerial defence of the harbour? And Admiral, sir, I've got it on visuals! Our dragons are fightin Thread! I'll patch it in to your screen.'

Paul watched as the picture cleared, focus lengthened t show him the unbelievable vision of tiny flying creature: undeniably spouting flame from their mouths at the silve rain that fell in a dreadful curtain over the harbour. H had that one view before the picture was interrupted b a sheet of Thread. He waited no longer.

Afterwards Paul wondered that he hadn't broken h neck, going down stone steps three at a time. He ran fu pelt across the Great Hall and down the metal stairwa leading to the garage where the sleds and skimmers wer stored. Fulmar and one mechanic were bent over a gyr and stared in surprise at him.

'You there, get the doors open. Fulmar, you'd better come with me. They may need help.' He all but fell into the nearest sled, fumbling with the comunit. 'Ongola, tell Emily and Pol and Bay that their protégés have made it. Record this, by all that's holy, get as much of this on film as you can.'

Paul had the sled motor turning over before Fulmar had shut the canopy. He slipped the sled under the door before it was fully open, a manoeuvre he would have reamed anyone else for attempting and then, turning on the power, he made an arrow ascent straight up out of the valley. Emerging from the shelter of the cliffs of Fort, he could see the ominous line of Thread.

'Admiral, have you gone mad?'

'Use the screen, high magnification. Hell, you don't need it, Fulmar, you can see it with your bare eyeballs!' Paul pointed wildly. 'See. Flame. See the bursts. I count fourteen, fifteen emissions. The dragons are fighting Thread!'

It was frightening, Sean thought. It was wonderful! It was the finest moment in his life, and he was scared stiff. They had all emerged right on target, just above the harbour, dragon lengths ahead of the Fall.

Carenath started flaming instantly, and then skipped as they were about to plough through a second tangle of the stuff.

Are the others all right? he anxiously asked Carenath as they slipped back into real space.

Flaming well and skipping properly, Carenath assured him with calm dignity, veering slightly to flame again, turning his head from side to side, searing his way through Thread.

Sean glanced around, saw the rest of his wing following in the step formation they had adopted from Kenjo's sled tactics. That gave them the widest possible range of destruction. Even as Sean looked, he saw Jerry and Manooth wink out and back in again, neatly escaping. Then he and Carenath skipped.

A thousand feet below them, he caught a glimpse of Sorka's wing of five and following that formation, Tarrie leading the remaining queens.

More! Carenath said imperiously, arrowing upward in a trough between Thread. He turned his head backward, mouth wide open. Sean fumbled for a lump of firestone but managed the exchange.

That will have to be practised, he thought, and Carenath skipped them out.

Shoth has a wing-score, Carenath announced. *He will continue to fly!*

He'll learn to fly the better for it!

Then the straps strained at the belt as Carenath seemed to stand on his tail to avoid a stream of Thread which he then followed with flame.

Back in formation! The last thing they needed was to sear each other. Sean saw that the others had held their positions as Carenath resumed his.

After that first exhilarating cross of the Thread fall, they all got down to business until flame and evasion became instinctive. Carenath went *between* several times to lose Thread that wrapped about his wings. Sean locked his jaw against his dragon's pain each time Carenath sustained a score. By then all the bronzes and browns had received minor injuries. Still they had fought on. Faranth and the other queens constantly encouraged. And Faranth reported the arrival of a sled, reported again that ground crews were out in the harbour area, destroying the shells that had made it to the surface. Then she said that they had used up the tanks they'd taken from Seminole. Sorka was going to get more from the harbour hold.

Faranth asks how long will we fight? Carenath asked.

As long as we have firestone to fight with! was Sean's grim and determined response. He'd just taken a faceful of char and his cheeks stung. They really needed full masks for this sort of action.

Manooth says they have no more firestone! Carenath said suddenly, after a nearly mindless length of time

464

of action. *Shall they see if there is more at Fort Hold?*

Sean had not realized how far inland their battle had taken them. They were indeed over the imposing ramparts of Fort Hold. He stared in a moment of bewilderment. He was suddenly very much aware of how he ached from cold and strain: that his body felt bruised from the riding straps, his face smarted and his fingers, toes and knees were numb.

Tell them to land at Fort! Thread has moved up into the mountains. We can do no more today!

Good! Carenath replied with such enthusiasm that Sean forgot his sore cheeks and grinned. He slapped affectionately at his dragon's shoulder as the formation executed a right-handed turn, spiralling down to land.

'Emily!' Pierre burst into his wife's room. 'You'll never believe it!'

'Believe what?' she said in the tired voice that seemed all she could muster since the accident. She turned her head on the cushioned back of the support chair and smiled wanly at him.

'They've come! I heard, but I had to see it to believe it myself. The dragons and their riders have all reached Fort. They reached it in triumph! They've actually fought Thread, just as you dreamed they would, as Kitti Ping designed them to do. All seventeen brave fine young people. And they cut a real swath in the Fall, Paul says. He watched. They didn't do the entire Fall, of course, part of it was over the sea anyhow, and the rest will fall in the mountains where it can't do much harm.

'Paul said it was the most magnificent thing he's ever seen. Better than the relief at Cygnus. They have a record of it, too, so you can see it when you want.' Pierre bent to kiss her hand. He had tears in his eyes for Emily, for the valiant young people who had ridden against so terrible a menace in the skies of their wondrous and terrible new world. 'Paul's gone down to greet them. A triumphant arrival. My word, but it puts heart in all of us. Everyone

465

is yelling and cheering and Pol and Bay were weeping which is something quite unscientific for that pair. I suppose they feel that the dragonriders are their creations. I suppose they're right, don't you agree?'

Emily struggled in the support chair, her fingers clutching at him. 'Help me to the window, Pierre? I must see them. I must see them for myself!'

Most of the inhabitants of Fort Hold turned out to greet them, waving impromptu banners of bright cloth, shouting tumultuously as the dragons backwinged to land on the open field, where here and there groundcrews had got rid of what Thread had escaped the dragon fire. The crowd surged forward, mobbing the individual riders, everyone eager to touch a dragon, ignoring at first the riders' strident appeals for something to ease Thread-pierced wings and scored hide.

Gratefully Sean saw a skimmer hovering, with loud-spoken orders to give the dragons room, let the medics in.

The hubbub subsided a decibel or two. The crowds parted, allowing the medical teams access, giving the dragonriders space to dismount, whispering sympathetically when the cheering had died down enough so that the dragons could be heard whimpering in pain. Some of those around Carenath eagerly helped Sean doctor him.

Is everyone here to see us? Carenath asked shyly. The bronze turned his left wing so that Sean could reach a particularly wide score and sighed in audible relief as anesthestic cream was slathered on.

'I don't know how we got so lucky,' Sean muttered to himself when he was certain that all Carenath's injuries had been attended. He looked around him, checking to see that all the other dragons had been treated. Sorka gave him a thumbs-up signal and grinned at him, her face smeared with blood and soot. He returned her sign with both fists. 'Sheer fluke we got out of that with just sears and scores. We didn't even know what we were doing. Blind luck!' His mind roiled with ways to avoid any sort of scoring and ideas for drills to improve how much Thread a single breath could char. Their fight had been, after all, only the first, brief skirmish in a long, long war.

'Hey, Sean, you need some, too,' Sue O'Hara said, pulling off his helmet to anoint his cheeks. 'Got to get you looking spruce. The Admiral's waiting!'

As if her words were a cue, a murmurous silence fell over the plain. The riders converged together, gold and bronze and brown, and moved forward to the foot of the ramp where Paul Benden in the full uniform of a Fleet Admiral, with Ongola and Ezra Keroon similarly attired standing on either side of him, awaited the seventeen young heroes.

In step, the dragonriders walked forward, past people grinning foolishly in their pride. Sean recognized many faces, and more ranged nearer the Admiral: Pol and Bay looking about to burst with pride; Telgar tears streaming down his cheeks, Ozzie and Cobber on either side of him, Cherry Duff upheld by two sons, her black eyes snapping with joy. No sign of Governor Emily Boll and Sean felt his heart contract. What Peter Chernoff had said was true, then. This moment wouldn't be the same without her.

They reached the ramp and somehow the queen riders had dropped a step behind the others and Sean stood in the centre. When they halted, he took a step forward and saluted. It seemed the correct thing to do. Admiral Benden, with tears in his eyes, proudly returned the salute.

'Admiral Benden, sir,' said Sean, rider of bronze Carenath, 'may I present the Dragonriders of Pern?'

THE END

PROVINCES, PLACES, STAKENAMES, ETC.

JORDAN PROVINCE

1	*Landing*	Administration
		Supply Depots
		Tuition
		Laboratories
		Main Animal Breeding
2	*Monaco Bay*	Tubberman
3	*Calusa*	Harbourmaster James Tillek
		main dolphineer site
		main fishery/cannery
		main mariner training
		a) base for *Perseus*
		b) *Southern Star* Jim Tillek
		c) *Maid of the Sea* Per Bagnesjo
		d) *Mayflower* Bernard Shattuck
4	*Cambridge-on-Jordan*	Cabot Francis Carter
5	*Cardiff*	Bar Hamil-Jessup

KAHRAIN

6	*Oslo Harbour*	Gus Gustavson
		Grant-van Toorns
7	*Amsterdam*	Du Vieux
		Holstroms
8	*Bavaria*	Radelins
9	*Milan*	Ciottis
10	*Bordeaux*	Kwan Marceau, Hempenstahls
11	*Vienna*	Langsams
14	*Killarney site*	Sean Connell/Sorka Hanrahan

469

ARABY

12	*Tuareg land*	Andriadus, Byrnes, Duff, Kaarven
13	*Sea of Azov*	a) base for *Pernese Venturer*
		Captain Kaarvan
13a	*Paradise River*	Lake Caspian (courtesy of the
	(on coast)	Ostrovskis)

CATHAY

15	*Malay River*	Phas Radamanth, Chuck Kimmage
16	*Xanadu*	Sopers, Xi Chi Yuen
17	*Mexico* on the Maori	Cooney, Duff, Jepson
	Lake	

MACEDONIA

18	*Sadrid*	on the coast
19	*Thessaly*	Logorides, Trury
20	*Roma*	Gallianis
21	*Honshu*	in Eastern Barrier Range
		Kenjo + Ika Fusaiyuki

DELTA

22	*Boca*	above Delta on the Boca River
23	*Suweto/Drake's Lake*	Drake + Svenda Bonneau
24	*Drake's Lake*	Valli Lieb
25	*Yukon/Drake's Lake*	Bart Lemos, Saki Tiffin, Blackie
		Nilwan

DORADO

26	*Karachi Camp*	main maining centre – Tarvi Andiyar
27	*Seminole*	Cos Melvinah, Brooks, Chernoff
28	*Key Largo*	(coastal tip)

IERNE ISLAND

four different counties in this province (Longwood, Uppsala, Orkney, Lockahatchee)

Tom Partrick, Bill Duff, Andrew and Jennifer Kiersey Fremlich, Joe Tobin, Pei Pei Ting

CIBOLA as yet unoccupied, leads into desert lands further west

THREADFALLS –
TERRITORY COVERED

FIRST *dangerous* Fall: 4

Starts over Jordan Province
TZ14-TZ11
22S-48S

HITS	*Monaco Bay*
	Landing
	Oslo Landing
	Amsterdam
	Bavaria
	Milan
	Tuareg Camp Site

SECOND FALL: Double Hit 5   TZ11-TZ8
Macedonia   2N-30S
Oversea until end
Hits *Sadrid*
(*Thessaly & Roma* warned)
Second wave falls over unoccupied
Bordeaux – unexpectedly

THIRD FALL: Cathay Province: 6   TZ11-TZ8
     19A-49S

Clips edge of *Malay River*
Mexico on *Maori Lake* – stops
mid-lake

FIFTH FALL: A Baddie: 8   TZ8-5
     20S-48S

Macedonia – Dorado
Drake's Lake
Yukon
narrowly misses *Suweto*
Smack on *Karachi* Camp

SIXTH FALL:	Double Hit: 9. Ends just on edge of Kahrain TZ13 at sea – observed Hits Cathay, *Maori Lake* again TZ8-d.o.
SEVENTH FALL:	Double Hit: 10 Jordan – hits TZ14-13. 30S- river hits *Cardiff*, southern edge of Landing *Calusa & Bordeaux* TZ5-2, 20S-48S Dorado – hits *Seminole* & just misses *Ierne*
EIGHTH FALL.	Double hit – 11, just tip of Kahrain unoccupied end of *Karachi* Camp – mountains Longwood area of *Ierne*
NINTH FALL:	Kahrain-Cathay – 12 TZ13-10/ 15S-44S *Paradise River* right in the centre
TENTH FALL:	Double Hit – 13 TZ13-11.50 TZ10-7 Kahrain & Delta *Killarney* (unoccupied) *Boca River*
ELEVENTH FALL:	14 – Sea and *Cathay* TZ10-7 just misses *Malay River* tips southeast edge of *Thessaly*
TWELFTH FALL:	15 – Double TZ10-7 *Araby/Cathay* Just misses *Maori Lake* Clips into *Seminole* East

DRAGONFLIGHT
by Anne McCaffrey

Set in a medieval world of the future, *Dragonflight* tells of Holds and Castles and Keeps, and of a great flight of dragons, led by a golden Queen and ridden by men sworn to the defence of their fantastic and incredible planet . . .

The men who rode the dragons were a breed apart. Chosen when the dragons were first hatched, they became soul-mates for life with the huge, magnificent beasts they controlled – the green, blue, brown and bronzes – beautiful – terrible – the only creatures who could defend the planet Pern from the blood-red star. But without the Queen, the dragons would become extinct – only the gigantic, golden Queen could breed the new flights. And the Queen was fading . . . dying . . . leaving behind one last, huge, golden egg . . .

0 552 08453 0

DRAGONQUEST
by Anne McCaffrey

Another Turn, and the deadly silver Threads began falling again. So the bold dragonriders took to the air once more and their magnificent flying dragons swirled and swooped, belching flames that destroyed the shimmering strands before they reached the ground.

But F'lar knew he had to find a better way to protect his beloved Pern, and he had to find it before the rebellious Old-timers could breed any more dissent . . . before his brother F'nor would be foolhardy enough to launch another suicide mission . . . and before those mercurial fire lizards could stir up any more trouble . . .

0 552 11635 1

DRAGONSONG
by Anne McCaffrey

Menolly – Mistress of Music, Ward of Fire Lizards.

Every two hundred years or so, shimmering Threads fall, raining black ruin on Pern. The great dragons of Pern hurl themselves through the beleaguered skies, flaming tongues of fire to destroy deadly Thread and save the planet. It was not Threadfall that made Menolly unhappy. It was her father who betrayed her ambition to be a Harper, who thwarted her love of music. Menolly had no choice but to run away. She came upon a group of fire lizards, wild relatives of the fire-breathing dragons. Her music swirled about them; she taught nine to sing . . . Suddenly Menolly was no longer alone.

0 552 10661 5

DRAGONSINGER: HARPER OF PERN
by Anne McCaffrey

When Menolly, daughter of Yanas Sea Holder, arrived at the Harper Craft Hall, she came in style, aboard a bronze dragon followed by her nine fire lizards. The Masterharper of Pern, aware of her unique skills, had chosen her as his only girl apprentice. But the holdless girl had first to overcome many heartaches in this strange new life. Two things sustained her; her devoted lizards – a subject on which she was fitted to instruct her Masters – and the music . . . music of transcendent beauty, music-making where at last she was accepted. In the great Hall, Menolly could fulfil her destiny.

0 552 10881 2

THE WHITE DRAGON
by Anne McCaffrey

Never had there been as close a bonding as the one that existed between the young Lord Jaxom and his extraordinary white dragon, Ruth. Pure white and incredibly agile, Ruth possessed remarkable qualities. Not only could he communicate with the iridescent, fluttering fire lizards, but he could fly back in time to any WHEN with unfailing accuracy.

Nearly everyone else on Pern thought Ruth was a runt who would never amount to anything, but Jaxom knew his dragon was special. In secret they trained to fight against the burning Threads from the Red Planet, to fly Back in time as well as Between, and finally their close and special union was to result in the most startling and breathtaking discovery of all. . . .

0 552 11313 1

DRAGONDRUMS
by Anne McCaffrey

Piemur, a boy soprano, had been chosen out of all the singers at the Harperhall of Pern for the leading role in the dramatic choral work to be presented at Lord Groghe's Gather. But during practice one day his voice broke – and suddenly his whole future at the Harperhall seemed uncertain.

But Masterharper Robinton, Menolly, and Sebell had other plans for Piemur – they were sure that his quick wits and discretion could be used to keep a check on the troublesome Old-timers and their strange traffic in fire lizards.

So whilst serving as a messenger-drum apprentice, Piemur carried out special errands for the three. And it was on one such errand that he realized his wildest dream – and got into deeper trouble than ever before . . .

0 552 11804 4

MORETA: DRAGONLADY OF PERN
by Anne McCaffrey

Some fourteen hundred turns after men first came to Pern rode Moreta, on her great golden dragon, Orlith.

It was towards the end of the Pass of the Red Star – a time when every living creature on Pern was threatened by Threadfall – when the courage and daring of dragons and riders was all that kept the planet from extinction.

And then, at the height of the battle against Thread, came a new and terrible evil. Moreta, in one last super-human endeavour, was to save her people, and become the greatest legend of dragonlore until the end of time.

This is the story of Moreta's ride.

0 552 12499 0

NERILKA'S STORY & THE COELURA
by Anne McCaffrey

It was in Moreta's time – a time of legend, of heroic valour, of terrible Threadfall, and the Great Plague that devastated both Holders and Dragonfolk.

For Lady Nerilka of Fort Hold the tragedy was twofold for, with the death of her mother and sister, her father's mistress took possession of the Hold. Angry and betrayed, Nerilka decided to escape and, as Pern seethed in turmoil, she began her perilous journey to Ruatha, Lord Alessan, and an unknown destiny.

Nerilka's Story & The Coelura, two spellbinding novellas from Anne McCaffrey, creator of *The Dragons of Pern*.

0 552 12817 1

THE RENEGADES OF PERN
by Anne McCaffrey

They were the misfits, the outcasts, the murderers without Hold or Crafthall. Some were resentful, some sought vengeance, but it was not until Thella, Lady Holder of Telgar, began to weld them together into a terrifying and brilliant clan that they became the Renegades of Pern.

It was a time of great turmoil on the planet. The pass of the Red Star had brought a new terrible reign of Threadfall, and in the southern Hold, Toric was carving out an enormous empire for himself from lands that had not yet been properly charted. And as the times of trouble grew, so did the ravages of Thella and her band, turning from theft to murder to vicious and insane revenge.

Jayge Lilcamp, the young and roving trader, was one of the first to fall foul of the renegades, and as he saw what Thella had done to his family and his line of beasts and wagons he began to seek his own revenge, a revenge which grew into a determination to destroy the most evil woman on Pern.

The Renegades of Pern is a new chronicle which runs concurrently with the events told in *The White Dragon*.

0 552 13099 0

ALL THE WEYRS OF PERN
by Anne McCaffrey

When AIVAS – the Artificial Intelligence Voice Address System – was first discovered at Landing, the entire planet of Pern was awed at the knowledge it divulged. All the history of the people of Pern was there.

Dragonholders, Lord Holders and Craftmasters crowded into the tiny inner room to learn the secrets of their beginnings. And AIVAS had other gifts to offer – stored information of old crafts that had been forgotten, of medicine, music and technology.

But the greatest promise AIVAS offered was the chance to rid Pern of Thread forever. Jaxon, F'lar, Lessa, Piemur, and all the great ones of Pern, began the long and arduous task of learning just how to operate the incredible plan – a plan of such daring and epic proportions that both dragons and riders would be put at risk.

All the Weyrs of Pern is a new chronicle which follows the discoveries made at the end of *The Renegades of Pern*.

0 552 13729 4

A LIST OF OTHER ANNE McCAFFREY TITLES AVAILABLE FROM CORGI BOOKS

THE PRICES SHOWN BELOW WERE CORRECT AT THE TIME OF GOING TO PRESS. HOWEVER TRANSWORLD PUBLISHERS RESERVE THE RIGHT TO SHOW NEW PRICES ON COVERS WHICH MAY DIFFER FROM THOSE PREVIOUSLY ADVERTISED IN THE TEXT OR ELSEWHERE.

☐ 08453 0	DRAGONFLIGHT	£5.99
☐ 11635 1	DRAGONQUEST	£5.99
☐ 10661 5	DRAGONSONG	£5.99
☐ 10881 2	DRAGONSINGER: HARPER OF PERN	£5.99
☐ 11313 1	THE WHITE DRAGON	£5.99
☐ 11804 4	DRAGONDRUMS	£5.99
☐ 12499 0	MORETA: DRAGONLADY OF PERN	£5.99
☐ 12817 1	NERILKA'S STORY & THE COELURA	£5.99
☐ 13099 0	THE RENEGADES OF PERN	£5.99
☐ 13729 4	ALL THE WEYRS OF PERN	£5.99
☐ 13913 0	THE CHRONICLES OF PERN: FIRST FALL	£5.99
☐ 14270 0	THE DOLPHINS OF PERN	£5.99
☐ 14272 7	RED STAR RISING: THE SECOND CHRONICLES OF PERN	£5.99
☐ 14274 3	THE MASTERHARPER OF PERN	£5.99
☐ 14762 1	THE CRYSTAL SINGER OMNIBUS	£6.99
☐ 14180 1	TO RIDE PEGASUS	£5.99
☐ 13728 6	PEGASUS IN FLIGHT	£5.99
☐ 13763 4	THE ROWAN	£5.99
☐ 13764 2	DAMIA	£5.99
☐ 13912 2	DAMIA'S CHILDREN	£5.99
☐ 13914 9	LYON'S PRIDE	£5.99
☐ 14629 3	THE TOWER AND THE HIVE	£5.99
☐ 09115 4	THE SHIP WHO SANG	£5.99
☐ 08661 4	DECISION AT DOONA	£4.99
☐ 08344 5	RESTOREE	£4.99
☐ 10965 7	GET OFF THE UNICORN	£5.99
☐ 14436 3	THE GIRL WHO HEARD DRAGONS	£5.99
☐ 14628 5	NIMISHA'S SHIP	£5.99
☐ 14271 9	FREEDOM'S LANDING	£5.99
☐ 14273 5	FREEDOM'S CHOICE	£5.99
☐ 14627 7	FREEDOM'S CHALLENGE	£5.99
☐ 14098 8	POWERS THAT BE (with Elizabeth Ann Scarborough)	£5.99
☐ 14099 6	POWER LINES (with Elizabeth Ann Scarborough)	£5.99
☐ 14100 3	POWER PLAY (with Elizabeth Ann Scarborough)	£5.99
☐ 14621 8	ACORNA (with Margaret Ball)	£5.99
☐ 14271 9	ACORNA'S QUEST (with Margaret Ball)	£5.99
☐ 14273 5	ACORNA'S PEOPLE (with Elizabeth Ann Scarborough)	£5.99

All Transworld titles are available by post from:

Bookpost, P.O. Box 29, Douglas, Isle of Man IM99 1BQ

Credit cards accepted. Please telephone 01624 836000, fax 01624 837033, Internet http://www.bookpost.co.uk or e-mail: bookshop@enterprise.net for details.

Free postage and packing in the UK. Overseas customers allow £1 per book (paperbacks) and £3 per book (hardbacks).